SAVING THE SINGLE DAD

MOUNT MACON BOOK 3

ASHLEY MUÑOZ

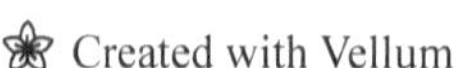 Created with Vellum

SAVING the Single Dad

PROLOGUE

Haley
Age 13

I STARED at the silver flecks clinging to my fingers.

Mom warned me that the glitter would get everywhere, and as I clung to the edge of the kitchen table, I realized she was right. It was everywhere—all over the shimmery tablecloth, gleaming on the edges of the wooden chairs, and yep, there was even a little on the carpet. Mom was going to kill me. That was, of course, if she didn't first disown me for being a total loser.

My party started at two. It was already half past and not a single friend had shown up. I knew Pricilla James was having a party this weekend too, but hers was supposed to be tomorrow. Mine wasn't even going to be a big event...we were going to play in the pool, watch a scary movie in the theater room, and stuff our faces with junk food.

Tillie helped me plan out everything and was the brains behind the glitter covering the table. She said glitter was in...that it would be cute and make my party pop.

The three-tier cake had edible glitter frosting, with thirteen tall candles already placed strategically along the surface, so as not to interrupt the large *Happy Birthday* wax piece that was covered in glitzy paint.

My mother hardly approved, and I knew the only reason she wasn't saying anything now was because she was expecting an audience. I didn't want her to come in here and see me sitting alone, but there was nowhere to go. I was frozen to my seat, staring at the clock, hoping my friends were all just running late.

The sound of my mother's expensive shoes echoed along the hardwood. She sauntered in with her hair in a low twist, her lips painted red, and a tight black blouse. Her lips thinned as she walked closer, and all I could ever remember of her in this house was that expression. She hated this house, always had, probably because it belonged to my dad's first wife, who was my half brother's mother. Dad had once fought with my mother over moving, saying he needed a familiar place for his sons. He never mentioned what I might need. He never really looked at me much, unless it was to discuss a trip, lessons, or something business related. Once in a while I could get him to hug me, but it was just never for very long. Never too many hugs, no compliments of any kind, and never too much attention.

Especially if one of my brothers were around.

"Haley, where are your guests?" mother trilled from the arch of the hallway.

My palms were sweaty, and my stomach tied itself into knots as I glanced at the clock once more. Thirty after…and not a single friend had shown.

"Let me text Tillie and see," I mumbled, but my mother clicked her tongue loud enough to stop me.

"Tillie's mother already called and said she was going out of town this weekend."

My stomach dropped.

No, she wouldn't do that. Furrowing my brows, I dug my cell out of my back pocket and pulled up Snapchat, about ready to message her when her most recent story caught my attention.

Pressing my thumb onto the image, I waited as a video played of her dancing with Tia and Rachel, my other two best friends. There in the background was Pricilla, surrounded by other kids from our school. She'd moved her party, and no one told me.

A sickening feeling began to expand in my stomach as tears rushed to my eyes. I didn't like to cry in front of my mother; she would always chide me and tell me to grow a backbone. It always hurt, but I knew it would devastate me if she said it right now.

Pressing my fingers to the screen, I pulled up my group text with the girls and saw there were no new messages. Then went to my private messages with Tillie.

Nothing.

No warning, no apology…absolutely no explanation as to why my three best friends had blown me off.

"What about the other kids in your school?" Mother asked, impatiently.

She assumed because I was a Hanes that I was popular.

I wasn't.

I had three friends, and every single one of them had just bailed on me without saying a word, which meant I never really had them at all.

I wasn't even sure what to say to get her off my back, or how to fix this. No one was coming, but if I told her, she'd throw a fit. She'd cry, go find a drink, and mix it with happy pills, all because her daughter isn't the popular girl in school. It would be one more thing she could blame me for. It wasn't enough that I ruined her life by existing, or that I ruined my brother's lives by moving in.

My oldest brother, Colson, hated me more than the others. Brock, Nathan, and Trevor treated me more like a houseplant that could occasionally pop in Bagel Bites if they were hungry. But not Colson. He wouldn't even acknowledge my existence after my dad broke the news that I wasn't just his secretary's daughter, but also *his* daughter…his dirty secret.

I was an unwanted reality that haunted them by walking these hallways and breathing the same air as them. No one in the family tried to hide it. My mother used me as a weapon to hurt my father or brothers.

My father ignored me, mostly, and my brothers…their hatred was as tangible as the waves crashing below our house.

I looked up to say something to my mom, but she was already gone, striding back into the kitchen.

Now was my chance to bail before she caught me. I was about to scoot back and dismiss myself from the table, in hopes of sneaking back to my room and forgetting all about turning thirteen, when there was a soft commotion coming from the back patio. Colson was coming in. His golden hair was all shoved to the side and wet, so he had probably been out surfing. He was eight years older than me and was attending college. He was rarely ever home. But when he was, I always tried to get his attention, even if it did hurt to have it. It was like wanting the sun even knowing it would cause a burn.

I sat as still as a stone as my heart pinged in my chest. He had a friend with him, and they were muttering and laughing as they walked through the house.

I knew if he was ever going to see me, now would be it. I was finally a teenager; he'd realize I wasn't just a baby anymore. I was a person. *I was his sister.*

My party decor was all over the dining room; there wasn't a chance he'd miss it.

But as he walked past the gaping arch that led into the dining area, I heard his friend ask, "Who's that?"

Colson lifted his head and stared right at me, no emotion…*nothing.*

"No one."

The words echoed in my head as loud as thunder, sharper than the sting of lightning.

A single tear slid down my face as he jogged up the stairs and left me behind.

For some stupid reason, my heart had lifted the smallest bit when I saw him, thinking maybe my brother would take pity on me and call in our other siblings, and we'd all sit and eat cake. We'd say forget them to everyone who bailed, and we'd have our own fun. Part of me *hoped,* and that's where I went wrong.

Hope was the gleam of sunlight, which most people thought was good, but caught in a magnifying glass it would catch shit on fire, and that's exactly what it did to me on a regular basis.

A sob caught in my throat as loneliness tore my heart open with sharp talons then curled into a tight little ball, right there in my chest.

Mom was always talking about how I needed a backbone; maybe she was right. Maybe I needed to harden, shove all the pain out. Get away from it.

Right as I thought it, Blaire, our house manager, hustled out of the kitchen.

"You're still here?"

I hiccuped as the sob finally let loose.

"Oh, child. Come on." She grabbed my hand and hurried me out of house, grabbing the top tier of the cake on her way.

Tears streamed so thick I couldn't see where she was leading me. It wasn't until I smelled the lilac bushes that I realized we were in the garden. I wasn't allowed in here. I didn't know why, I just knew I wasn't permitted to step foot in it, according to Colson and Dad.

"Hush now. It's your birthday. You will make a wish and you will smile."

Blaire dug in her apron and pulled a small box of matches free.

My knees pressed into the dirt as stalks of corn towered behind me on one side and purple flowers surrounded me on every other side. I could hear the waves crashing against the cliff below. The sky was crystal clear, a blue so bright that it made my eyes hurt.

"Here. Wish."

Blaire gently cradled my jaw and directed my gaze down toward the candles now flickering against the sea breeze.

I shook my head as more tears rushed forward.

"It's ruined."

She hushed me. "No such thing."

"Everyone forgot." I hiccuped again.

She sat back, her knees bent like mine, both of us just resting in the soft dirt of this sacred garden.

"Did I?"

No, Blaire hadn't. None of the staff had forgotten. A few of them had even slipped me a few gifts and smiles.

"Make a wish, my girl, and if I were you, I'd wish for patience."

"Why?" I shifted in the dirt, running my finger up the stalk of a lilac bush.

Blaire smiled sweetly, her southern accent still heavy on her tongue as she clicked it.

"Because you're a *knife*, my girl. Born to shape, divide, and prune. You're a gift to this family, and while you can't see it, one day they'll need you. *He* will need you." She shifted her gaze around the garden, her face softening. This was Colson's special place, so I assumed she was talking about him.

"How do I wait?" I swiped at my eyes, slicking away the mascara that had run from my lashes.

"Make a list, every single day, of all the good things you can think of. You make those lists until you feel your heart grow strong enough to love in the midst of pain. One day you'll have your own family, and you'll show them how powerful your love can be. Some of them will need your love, and others will need your honesty. You keep your eyes open, Haley Hanes. Watch and see. You'll hold all the power soon enough, and never forget—in all this wealth, the most powerful asset you will ever have is the power to forgive."

I closed my eyes, letting her words sink in, and blew out my candles.

CHAPTER ONE

haley

THE CHIPPED MUG really should have been the first sign that this place wouldn't have espresso or anything other than drip coffee on the menu. I didn't know why, but damaged mugs just said something about a place. As did the booths pockmarked with tiny rips. The carpet was in desperate need of replacement—in my opinion they should swap it for hardwood—but the location wasn't bad. I could see the entire street from my seat in the diner.

Today marked one week since I arrived in Macon, Oregon, and I was still trying to figure out exactly what I was doing here. Malibu had been my home for all twenty years of my life, and as much as I didn't fit there, this leap I decided to take didn't make much sense either.

It wasn't like I just drove up here on a whim. My brother sort of deserted his girlfriend at our parents' house, and when I offered to drive her back, she took me up on it. So, after taking a fifteen-hour road trip with Nora, I plopped myself here in my brother's town. I just happened to pack everything I own in the back of my SUV when I left.

So, here I was, being a dutiful sister to the one brother who never saw me as one.

"How are you doing? Can I refill your coffee?" a waitress offered with a beaming smile and a pop to her hip. Her coral lips stretched, causing a few wrinkles to appear near the edges of her mouth. I hated that my first thought was how she seemed to fit into this entire small-town-diner aesthetic.

Returning her smile, I covered my mug. "No, thank you, I'm okay."

"Well, look at those nails and that hair! I haven't seen hair that shiny since I took a trip down to L.A. I saw Hillary Duff. She was just out there walking her dog like it wasn't a thing at all, can you believe that? A lot of people around here think I'm lying, but I saw her, and I remember her hair being so shiny that it looked like liquid gold."

I caught sight of her name tag, pressed against a pink shirt.

"Thank you, Tammy, that's sweet of you to say. And I believe you about Hillary Duff; she's a national treasure and has been seen a lot around Los Angeles."

Tammy took a seat, sliding in across from me, her pot of coffee going right in front of her.

"Isn't she? I just loved her in that modern Cinderella movie. She did such a good job, and my nephew showed me that she's on that Clock app too. I think it's so fun to be able to see these stars on those videos. So what part of California are you from?"

Feeling a little apprehensive about being locked into this conversation, I spun the mug around in slow circles.

"Uh…well …"

"Tammy, leave that poor girl alone and get back here with that pot of coffee," a woman with a soft gray cardigan yelled, only her head showing through the door that led to the kitchen.

"Sorry, Millie!" Tammy said as she winced and began to slide out of the booth.

"That's the boss lady; she owns this place. Usually she's real nice, but I'm new and I have been testing her patience. At least that's what some of the staff tell me."

Tammy rolled her eyes with a bit of a laugh.

"Anyway, sorry, I have the tendency of being too nosy. I just assumed with your tan and overall look—like you just stepped out of one of those fancy spas—that you were from California. You haven't had to endure a Macon winter yet, have you?"

Giving her a soft smile, I shook my head. "I haven't...this is my first."

Tammy grabbed her pot of coffee and smiled.

"Well, welcome to Macon, honey. Hope you enjoy your visit."

Tammy gave me a wink before walking away, but her words wrapped around me as tight as a fist.

Visit.

That's what this *should* be...just let this be a vacation. Get to know Colson. There was no reason at all I should be toying with the idea of staying.

Staring a hole into the seat that Tammy had just vacated, I was lost in my thoughts when a little girl suddenly slid into the seat across from me.

I blinked and glanced around.

She had big blue eyes and round face with cute, chubby cheeks. She was somewhat familiar, maybe, but it was hard to tell under all her winter gear.

"Hey…" I said hesitantly. Had she really just sat down at a stranger's table?

"Hi," she replied sweetly.

"Uh, I think your mom or dad might not wanting you to sit with strangers." I glanced around again for someone who might have lost a kid.

The girl nodded and grabbed the sugar shaker. "My dad says we can't sit with strangers, but you're not a stranger."

I'm not?

Another little girl walked up, slipping into the booth with ease.

Where had she even come from?

"Hey, it's the makeup lady." This one had the same blue eyes but long, dark hair, tucked behind her in a low ponytail.

Oh. The makeup.

It finally clicked as the third member of their group found us and slid in next to her sisters. After I had arrived in Macon and thrust myself into my brother's life, his best friend had come over with his three little girls. Wanting a chance to spend the evening with my brother, I did the little girls' makeup and fed them marshmallows.

I smiled at the newcomer. She wore a black beanie over her hair, but it did nothing to hide the eyes that I was now learning was a family trait.

"Hi, guys, I remember you."

The oldest tucked a little strand of hair behind her ear. "You're Uncle Colson's sister, right?"

My heart warmed at her use the word "sister." It made me think of Blaire. She had moved back to be near her grandbabies in Alabama, but we still talked on the phone from time to time. She had a lot of thoughts regarding me being here.

"You're right where you should be. Cuttin' and sharpening out all the hard edges in that family. Don't give up on him."

He'd rejected me my entire existence, but here I was, inserting myself into his life like a weed. Forcing him to talk to me and, for once, see me as his sister.

"Yep, that's me," I answered the girls who had all started toying with the jams and Splenda packets in the little carousel at the edge of the table.

"We were supposed to be going to Uncle Cole's house, but our dad started talking on the phone with someone important," the youngest said while getting to her knees to reach for my silverware. She slid it toward her while giving me a sly smile, almost like she was daring me to tell her no.

I covered the bundle with my hand and moved it away from my side so she could have it free and clear.

"Remind me of your names again?" I asked, starting with the girl in the black beanie on the end.

"I'm Seraphina, but I like to be called Seraph…I'm seven." Her face was less round, and I couldn't see her hair at all under her hat.

"I'm Mila, and I'm five!" the youngest interrupted, completely oblivious to taking turns or how loud she was being.

The oldest gave her younger sister a scathing look and straightened her shoulders. "I'm Maddy, I'm ten."

"Well, it's nice to meet you guys again. I'm Haley."

"And how old are you, Haley?" Mila asked, propping her hand under her jaw.

Biting back a laugh, I brought my hands together, all business, and said, "I'm twenty years old."

Right as I finished, a man I recognized approached the table. Ah, here was their dad. Leo, or Logan. Something like that.

"Hey…" His eyes bounced around on his daughters' faces then on mine, a dark brow lifted as if he wasn't sure why I was talking to his kids. He had the air of a man who was wary, protective and dangerous if he needed to be, which was only driven home by his tall stature and lean muscle. Dark hair that looked overdue for a haircut brushed against his brow, and matching thick lashes framed a pair of unusually gray eyes. They were the one thing I did remember about this man, because they reminded me of liquid mercury.

I tried to give a reassuring smile.

"They just sat down. Sorry if I overstepped by letting them."

His lips quirked in the corners, lifting the tiniest bit, but his eyes stayed glacier like he was waiting for me to move away from his little family. Except I was here first, so…

I stared at him, raising a brow of my own in challenge, until finally he broke.

"No, it's fine. Millie usually takes them in the back when I come in or if I have to take a phone call."

Their dad's eyes assessed me slowly, moving from my hair down my temple to my eyes, then my lips and all the way down to my folded hands.

I felt squirmy as he inspected me, so I word vomited. "We met the other night at my brother's house; I don't know if you remember? It's okay if you don't. My memory is horrible when it comes to remembering people's names. Numbers, I have down…but names? Not so much." I let out a nervous laugh. Why was I rambling?

Because he's watching you like a wolf watches his prey.

"Haley." His deep voice was an unexpected mixture of tenderness and violence. His hand was soft when he offered it to me. "Liam Croft…"

"Now tell her how old you are, that's how it goes," Mila sassed, sitting up on her knees again.

My face flushed for some reason. I didn't want him to think I was trying to coax his kids into conversations about their ages.

Liam smiled at his daughter and sassed right back. "Thirty-two, Nancy Drew."

"Whoa, you're way older than Haley." Seraph laughed then smothered her smile with her hand.

"Who's Nancy Drew? My name in MILA." Liam's youngest pronounced her name slow and loud like her dad couldn't hear her.

I laughed, but Liam just gave them a smirk that made his eyes crinkle.

"Girls, we were only stopping in to get out of the cold while I took the call. Let's get going."

"I'm actually on my way out, too." I slid out of the booth and left a ten on the table, as Liam's girls all exited the row.

"You can walk with us; that way you feel safe," Mila instructed, pushing through the diner's glass door first.

I shoved my hands into my pockets as a gust of wind blew down Main Street. The sun was shining, and most of the snow had melted, but damn, with that wind, it didn't seem to make any difference.

Liam slowed his steps, his brown boots scuffing the white sidewalk. I realized maybe he was waiting to find out if I would be joining them.

"Uh, sure, thank you," I muttered then ducked my neck so my mouth would be covered by my coat.

"Are you going to Uncle Colson's right now too?" Maddy asked, turning her head slightly to the left to catch my eye.

Liam glanced over once then focused on the street ahead.

"Nope, I actually have to call in about my work and then I'm going next door to Nora's house. That's where I'm staying."

"What do you work at?" Mila asked. I smirked at the wrong use of words, but it was cute so I didn't correct her.

"I work from wherever my laptop is."

Seraph twisted her head my way, her face scrunching in confusion. "Why don't you stay at Uncle Cole's house?"

The question slammed into me harder than the wind. It was such an innocent question, but a reminder just the same. How was I supposed to explain that my brother was slowly warming up to me but wouldn't be offering me his spare room any time soon? Maybe if I used Harry Potter references? I was like Harry, living under the stairs, but I didn't have any powers or owls and I wasn't the cousin…I was the little half sister everyone hated.

"Uh…" I started, but Liam covered for me.

"Nora is out of town right now and asked if Haley would house sit for her."

All three girls murmured in understanding.

I turned my face to catch Liam's gaze and mouthed the words, "Thank you."

He didn't respond, just kept walking.

Okay…

We advanced down Main Street a little further, but Liam still hadn't said anything. It bugged me on a weird level. He was Colson's best friend, so it only made sense that we had some kind of familiarity, but I didn't want to feel like I had to push for it this hard. If he didn't like me, or want anything to do with me, it was honestly fine, but I knew his girls would be around Colson a lot, and I had every intention of being around my brother just as often. We were going to have to get used to one another. I wanted to say as much to him, but now his face was drawn tight as he stared at his cell phone, so I kept my mouth shut.

Finally, we were in front of my SUV.

"Well, thanks for making sure I got to my car nice and safe," I said, mostly to Mila.

She waved, and sweetly said, "You're welcome."

Liam added, "Macon isn't really dangerous though, just so you know."

"But she's a girl all alone, you always tell us to never be alone in the town," Maddy countered, furrowing her dark brows.

I laughed, loving how complicated this had gotten and how fast. Kids were funny.

Opening my door—and hopefully helping end the questions—I politely said. "Bye, guys, I'll see you around."

Then I shut myself inside and waved through the window, letting out a sigh as I watched the back of Liam's wool sweater disappear around the corner.

I felt so out of place here in this town, and Liam's standoffish attitude only hammered that home. The reminder that it had taken Colson three days to finally speak to me after I arrived in Macon resurfaced, making me blush with shame. I should have left by day two, but I had nowhere to go.

I burned a bridge with my parents by following Cole to Oregon. My dad had tried to undercut Cole in the purchase of a company. I ratted him out then bought the company myself. Now I was here because I felt guilty about how royally not only our dad but my mother too had screwed him over. Don't even get me started on what my mother did to Cole's poor garden. They were written out of my life for good, and I wasn't going back.

While the seats and steering wheel warmed, and I worked to shake off my thoughts, my phone connected to the car's Bluetooth, and began playing my voice messages.

A nasally voice filled the car as the message played.

"Hello, Ms. Hanes, this is Daniel from Hush Shoes. I work with Clyde in the San Francisco Office…anyway, sorry to bother you, but

Clyde is out sick, and his assistant seemed unsure of who is next in the chain of command aside from you. Clyde was working on getting a management team set up, but I believe he's still in the interview process. Anyway, can you give me a call at your earliest convenience?"

Shit.

I hit call on Daniel's contact while I began navigating out of the parking space and headed toward Nora's.

"Ms. Hanes, thank you for calling me back so quickly," Daniel answered on the first ring.

I had met the man last fall and he was nice enough, but I was focused. "Daniel, what happened to Bryant James?"

There was a pause and the rustling of a few papers being shuffled around. "He's no longer a part of Hush Shoes."

I signaled at a four way stop, letting out a heavy sigh.

"How long has Clyde been out?"

More shuffling echoed along with a few muttered whispers. I could imagine a frantic search going on around Daniel's desk as the junior associates tried to piece together the leadership of this new company. I had purchased Hush Shoes only six months ago, but Clyde and Bryant were already set in place to run it. As far as I knew, things were going well. We'd just checked in on a conference call two weeks ago. I had no idea how so much had gone this wrong so fast.

"He's been out for five days."

Double shit.

I didn't understand why they were suddenly flaking out when Hush Shoes was *their* company. I merely backed them as an investor. Maybe Clyde was just having cold feet, but our projections were up, the new shoe was set to launch within a few months and from the early responses we had in a few focus groups, the product was a hit. We already had three different celebrities on board with trying the product, and at least five thousand fashion influencers. For a low-level startup, we were doing great.

"I'll call Clyde. For now you're acting manager, Daniel. Do you know what needs to be done?"

"Yes, ma'am. I just need approval for a few expenditures that exceed five thousand."

I nodded, turning into Nora's driveway. "Send everything to me. I'll approve whatever you need, just keep things on track."

"Yes, ma'am."

Shoving the gear into park, I let out another sigh.

"And Daniel, stop calling me ma'am. I'm Haley or Ms. Hanes."

"You got it, Ms. Hanes."

Our call disconnected, and I sunk against my headrest.

While the timing was terrible, there was something soothing about work. The ease and finesse of knowing exactly what to say and what to do next. I knew when I graduated that I would walk in my father's foot-steps; it came so naturally to me. It was why I began shadowing his associates and tagging along in board meetings and hopping onto all of his business calls. Why I put up with as much as I have over the years, being as young as I am in an industry full of sharks and monsters.

I learned that Blaire was right, I was a tool…and a sharp one, at that. I trained and studied. I hustled and obtained my BBA in record time, kept my head down, and helped Dad as he needed me. Then I discovered something about my father, and everything changed.

He had been opening shell companies in his children's names for years, straining lines of credit and setting us as the CEOs without our knowledge, all to pad his ventures and expand the purse strings of his own wallet. I learned how to take control of those companies, and how to cut away the fat, just like Blaire taught me.

I controlled everything, took the money in them and created an empire, all under my father's nose. My father's associates learned what had happened, and since I had started running things at eighteen, most of them became *my* associates. Gunther, one of my father's oldest friends, was my mentor, and he had been helping me smooth out the areas I wasn't familiar with. And since I was only twenty years old, I leaned on him a lot.

My age didn't prevent me for reaching for every single thing on the table in business meetings, but at home, in my own life? I felt insecure, tiny. Unsure of what the future would hold and how I'd look in five years. Did I want a family? A husband…kids? My chest felt cold as the familiar numb feeling swept through me. I had no clue.

No plans.

No aspirations.

I just wanted to matter and make a difference somewhere, and for now that would have to be enough. Maybe I could carve a life out here… maybe I'd be that sharp knife Blaire talked about, but instead of cutting or helping my family, I'd be able to create a space where I could matter.

I had to stop overthinking things and get busy. Exiting the car, I made my way along the shoveled path to Nora's house and eyed the one next door.

My brother Colson was home, and while he'd started warming up to me, I was still hesitant to head over unless I had something to offer him. So, I trudged inside Nora's freezing cold house and decided to start baking.

Right as I set my purse down on the counter, my phone rang.

Nora.

"Hey!" I answered.

Nora sounded like she usually did—sad.

"Hey, I just wanted to check in."

Nora was not only my brother Colson's girlfriend but also the owner of the house I was currently staying in. She had a spare room and told me to stay as long as I wanted.

She was one of the good ones. I knew because I was practically a pro at picking out the bad ones.

"Things are good. I haven't burned anything down," I joked, eyeing the oven. The first time I burned a dish of food, I had called her because it did sort of catch on fire. She assured me it was fine, and that I hadn't ruined anything, but I had to keep the windows open for a long time. She doesn't know this, but I checked into a hotel that night because it was too damn cold to stay here.

She laughed softly.

"Good. Well I just wanted to tell you that I'm still unsure of my plans. I feel like it might be time to come back, but I don't know. It's so peaceful up here…"

We were going on seven days since she'd left. Colson was a mess, but I didn't know either of them well enough to get involved.

"Well, do whatever you feel is right. Things are good here. I'm fine. The house is good." I stopped, not wanting to mention my brother.

"Well, I'll text you again in a few days. I should know by then when I'll be coming back."

"Okay, sounds good. And Nora?"

I slammed my eyes shut, digging my fingers into the counter.

"Yeah?"

"Colson misses you, but he's all right. Take the time you need."

She waited a second, sniffed, and with a wobbly voice, replied, "Okay. Thanks, Haley."

I set the phone back down on the counter and looked around. Now, how the heck do I get the house to feel a little warmer?

2

LIAM

THE BEEPING from downstairs woke me.

It was echoing through the house, which meant the kitchen fire alarm was blaring. Warm sunlight fought with my wooden shades to illuminate the white carpet in my room as I lifted my head to see into the hall through my open door. Maddy wasn't running and neither was Seraphina, which meant it wasn't a fire. But just to be sure, I tugged my phone off the charger next to my bed, then opened one eye and navigated my home screen.

Pulling up the app to check the camera set up in the kitchen, I ensured there were no flames or any smoke before letting out a groan.

I set the phone down, turned to my back and yelled. "Mila!"

She wouldn't hear me, but it was early, and I didn't want to get up. The incessant noise continued, and my five-year-old wasn't materializing in front of me.

Closing my eyes, I tried again. "Maddy! Mila!"

Seraph would still be sleeping, even with the noise, she'd learned how to sleep through it.

Finally, the beeping stopped, and I heard the sound of little feet thumping up the stairs.

"Sorry, Daddy," Mila said in that extra sugar-sweet tone she knew made it impossible to stay mad at her.

I turned over and hung my arm over my eyes. "What did you make?"

Her silence had me popping open one eye to watch her tiny fingers come together and twist.

"Mila."

She deliberated for another moment before giving in with a sigh. "Pop-Tarts."

I sat up and swung my legs over the bed, running my hands through my hair.

"We don't have any Pop-Tarts."

Mila's little chin dipped to her chest, making her hair fall forward. It was impossibly tangled, but hell if I knew how to brush it without making her scream.

"Well, I *made* the Pop-Tart."

Oh shit.

"And how did you make the Pop-Tart?"

Her little nose twitched as she launched into the recipe. "I took two graham crackers," she held up two fingers, "and then I put jam in between them and then…"

Her head tilted like she couldn't remember.

"You put it in the toaster?"

She clapped her hands. "Yes! I forgot for a second." Her laugh untied the small knot that had tangled inside my gut. Undoubtedly there was a huge mess in my toaster now, might even be ruined, but at least she didn't try and microwave anything this time. I had installed it above the stove just so she couldn't reach it, but she still climbed shit.

"What did we talk about, Mila Jane?"

Her blue eyes narrowed on me, and this was when I had to bite back a laugh. My feisty five-year-old should sniffle and act contrite, as though she's scared of punishment, but no, she'll fight me on this.

"I don't know."

Yes, she did.

I let out a sigh. "Mila you can't use the microwave, toaster or oven unless I'm in the room."

Her head tilted again, "Are you sure it's not in the house? Because I thought you just had to be in the house."

This girl.

"Mila. Stop using the toaster. You could start a fire."

"The fire alarm works, though. You'd wake up and save us." She lifted her shoulder like it was as easy as that.

I needed coffee. "Just listen to me, okay, honey?"

"About what?"

"You know what Mila."

I stood and stretched.

"Daddy, I think you should try to erase all your pictures off your arm and chest and see if you can make someone love you. When we clean up Seraph's Barbies and shoes, they always look better when they're clean. Maybe it's like that with you."

She was at my waist, her head tilted all the way back.

I laughed and ruffled her hair. "You're probably right."

"Maddy!" I called for her older sister, knowing the only reason the alarms stopped were because she'd climbed up on the stool and hit the button like she usually did.

"Yes, Dad?"

Maddy, being the oldest, was the one who made me feel like I had my life together. She was a huge help with keeping her sisters in line.

"Can you go turn on my coffee maker?"

She nodded and ran off as I dipped down and pulled Mila up into my arms, running down the stairs, roaring like a troll.

She giggled in my arms as I caged her in and acted like she was my prisoner.

"Daddy, can we go to Uncle Cole's house and see if the makeup lady is there?"

I dumped Mila on the couch and then tossed a pillow on top of her. She laughed again as I moved toward the kitchen. Maddy had popped a coffee pod into the machine for me and already had my favorite mug propped under the spout, filling.

Once it was done, I took it by the handle and started sipping it. There was a pile of unopened bills neatly stacked on the edge of the counter, ready for me to dig into. Maddy liked to organize them for me so I wouldn't forget to pay them. I never have, but after everything her mother put her through, I understood her quirks. Stability was a big deal to her.

"Daddy, pleassssseee can we go see the makeup lady today?" Mila pushed her hair out of her face and then plopped down on the chair.

I took a sip from my mug and headed toward the fridge.

"Why are you suddenly so interested in seeing the makeup lady?" Giving her a little glare, I added, "Whose name is Haley, by the way."

Mila straightened, looking all business. "She's nice, and she let us play with all her makeup for as long as we wanted. She even let us eat extra marshmallows when Uncle Cole said we couldn't."

We were out of eggs. Fuck.

I turned toward Maddy, who had entered the kitchen. "Do we have any bread?"

"In the freezer."

I ruffled her hair as I slid open the freezer and tugged the extra bag out.

"Daddy, why aren't you paying attention to me?" Mila whined.

After the fire alarm and the stack of bills, realizing we were out of eggs and I had just gone shopping the day before, I was agitated. I had to get to the gym and prepare for the investor meeting, but Cole was meeting me there, which meant no makeup lady for her. She'd throw a fit until I gave in, and I just didn't have it in me this morning to argue.

"Mila, we have to go to the gym today."

"Not again. We always have to go with you, and it stinks. Bad!" My five-year-old's voice picked up an octave as her little arms crossed over her chest.

Maddy kept her face down, focused on making toast. She was growing up too fast. It was something I noticed often, but today I could actually feel it. She was only ten but had the maturity of a girl much older, and yet every now and then she'd break down and cry for a mother she didn't have and a life she had to give up. I saw so much of myself in her. My mom passed away when I was eleven, and my dad raised me on his own, dragging me with him to each new base he was stationed at. I learned how to be efficient, organized and quiet.

My dad now lived over in England with his new wife, and we didn't talk much. He wasn't much support during all the shit that went on with my ex, and he never really called to ask about the girls.

"I know, but I don't have anyone else to watch you, kiddo, and Uncle Cole will be at the gym too." Pretty soon Maddy could watch her sisters, but that was burden I didn't want to put on her shoulders.

"What about Cassie? I thought she was our babysitter." Seraphina asked, walking in while rubbing the sleep out of her eyes.

"Cassie, quit." I faced the cupboard as my jaw clenched tight.

The girls were getting old enough now to remember shit, and the situation with Cassie was a hot fucking mess.

"Why did she quit? Were we bad?" Mila asked, her voice tipping with raw emotion. Two of our other babysitters had been mean to the girls, and when I confronted them on it, they'd quit but blamed the kids. Fucking cowards. They quit because they didn't want to be held accountable for their behavior. Now, it was a sore spot for the girls.

"Cassie needed a different job that gave her more hours. She needed more money."

She also needed to learn how to take rejection. She'd tried to kiss me one night when I got home from a date. It was awkward as fuck because I had been training her boyfriend at the gym earlier that morning. She was young, in college. Too young for me, but even without that, she was my kids' babysitter, and that shit was so unprofessional. So, I fired her and asked her not to call or text anymore. Last I heard, she'd moved back to Portland to be near her parents because I told her boyfriend what she did. Everyone deserved to know if their person was being unfaithful to them. It was bullshit to keep people's secrets when they were so willing to hurt them.

"So, we don't even have a babysitter now?" Mila's voice rose higher with each word, like I'd told her we were homeless.

Maddy took a seat, handing out three pieces of toast with jam to her sisters.

"We can watch that one princess movie in dad's office when we get to the gym, and if you want to bring your Barbies, I'll play with you."

My heart softened at Maddy's offer to her little sister. She knew the right thing to say all the time, and it was another punch in my chest. She shouldn't have to worry about it.

"Let's eat, get our stuff, and head out. Maybe we can ask Uncle Cole to bring us donuts."

I had no shame in asking my best friend to spoil my kids; he loved it as much as they did.

All three girls squealed in excitement as they grabbed their toast.

MY BOXING GYM was located about a mile outside of town in the old lumber mill off exit five. A man named Kent Capson had owned this mill and had attended every single one of my fights. When I announced that I was retiring from boxing, he asked if I would ever consider opening a gym. Since I wasn't fighting, and I was still so young, I decided it couldn't hurt. Capson cut me a deal, and I sunk nearly sixty thousand dollars into the gym to get it renovated.

Pulling into the front spot, I jumped out of the truck and rounded it to help Mila unbuckle. She was still in her little booster seat, so she could do it herself, but the truck was tall and I wanted to be sure she didn't get bold enough to try to open the door on her own and jump down.

"Uncle Cole is already here!" Mila yelled excitedly as I pulled her into my arms. My best friend's silver truck was indeed parked two spots down and he was exiting the vehicle, his expensive sunglasses making him look like an extra in *Top Gun*.

"Did you bring donuts?" Seraphina ran up to him, trying to peek into the white carryout box. He tugged her to his side as he walked toward the door. Maddy trailed us, carrying her backpack and pulling her head-phones on.

The sounds of fists slamming into heavy bags and loud music greeted us as we pulled open the door and strolled in. I had one guy who helped me open up shop on the weekends so I could sleep in and spend time with the kids, but since they were still on winter break, he was handling things for a bit.

"Here." Colson handed the box over to Maddy and ruffled Seraphina's hair. I walked to the office and set Mila on the couch, where she snuggled under blanket and waited to be served a donut.

Once I set them up with their show, I walked back out and met Colson behind the counter.

"So are you ready for the meeting tomorrow?" Colson asked, leaning back while he sipped his coffee. Now that his sunglasses were gone I could see the bags under his eyes and how exhausted he looked.

"Nora still gone?" The woman he'd been pining over for nearly a year had finally started dating him, but because of some mix up, they came back from their trip to California in separate cars, and then Nora took off to the mountain and didn't have a return date. I guess they were technically broken up right now, but like hell was I going to use that term in front of my friend. He was hurting, and it felt like shit watching him go through losing her. I was married at one point of my life…happy, in love. Still, the way Cole looked when he checked to see if his girl had called or texted? Honestly, I had never felt that before.

He looked like he'd lost a piece of himself. When I lost Lacey, it felt like I had finally gotten a piece of myself back. Maybe it was because of what she put us through. What she did to the girls. Maybe I just slowly fell out of love with her, but either way, every now and then I selfishly wondered what it would be like to feel that way about someone.

"Yeah…" he finally answered, clenching his jaw tight, "Haley keeps me updated when she calls and texts. Says she's doing okay. I guess she's healing, doing a lot of meditating up in some cabin."

I nodded my head, unsure of exactly what to say. I figured moving away from the topic of Nora would be safest.

"So having Haley around…how's that going?"

Colson had opened up to me over the years about his family. He hadn't mentioned Haley much—just that she had ruined his life by being born, which was a little dramatic, but then again, his history and what happened to his mother *was* dramatic, so I kind of understood.

Colson sipped more of his coffee, shifting around, until he was perched on a stool.

"It's actually been really nice. I really fucked up with her for so many years. I owe her a lot. Plus she's always cooking and baking…I haven't had much of an appetite, but it's nice to hear her talk while she eats."

That was different, but I was thankful he had his little sister during this time.

"The meeting… You never told me how you were feeling about it." Colson lifted his cup in my direction, as if he wanted to change the subject and put it back on me.

I chose that moment to move around the small space, so I could organize all the forms and binders. "I feel ready. I made sure the locker rooms were clean and looked presentable. All the gear has been organized, mended, and replaced. I did what I could so when they do their walk through it doesn't look like a total shithole."

Cole clicked his tongue. "It's not a shithole; you're just behind a bit on payments and need a backer. It's completely normal for businesses to ask for investors."

I tried not let his comment burn, but Colson didn't really understand because he was born into money. The kind of money that could buy an entire construction company from his boss. He had a trust fund—and the Hanes name that opened doors most people didn't even know existed.

He was a good friend, though, and I knew he'd help me prep for this meeting better than anyone else.

"You looked over the numbers? Are they going to bring anything up that I missed?"

Colson shook his head. "It all looked good, you didn't miss anything. Just walk them through the gym and tell them how good of an investment this place is."

Right.

My face felt warm. I wasn't behind on gym payments yet, but I wasn't going to be able to pay on time next month if I didn't get some help.

Talking about it was humbling. Especially with someone as wealthy as Colson. Not that he acted like he had money or cared about that shit but still…there was only so much pride I could sacrifice without feeling it. The stress was getting to me on a level I hadn't experienced since the divorce.

I had to change the subject.

"The girls keep asking about your sister…it's something about makeup, I guess?"

The timer went off for one of the guys training. Mila and Seraphina were arguing in the office, I could hear them from here, but I was still waiting to see if they could work it out before I stepped in. Colson's head turned in that direction, likely wondering the same thing. He had probably broken up just as many arguments as I had, given how much time he'd spent with them. I would never know why he decided to stick to us like glue after he'd moved here from California, but I never stopped being grateful for him. This shit was lonely, and having him in my corner —in my kids' corner—meant everything to me.

"She's actually bringing over dinner tonight. Why don't you guys come by? She always makes enough to feed ten people anyway."

I nodded, grabbing a rag and dusting off the computer monitors. Dinner would be nice; it would save me from having to make something tonight.

"You sure?"

He waved me off. "Of course. Bring the girls, I know Haley would like to see them too. She's bored. I can tell."

"She staying?"

His sister had literally just showed up out of nowhere after his trip to California. Her entire car was packed full of all her belongings and she was rooming with Nora, Colson's girlfriend…or staying in her house while Nora was gone. Either way, it was weird. Who just picked up and left their entire life to move to a small, nothing town in the middle of nowhere? It made no sense to me, unless she was hiding from someone or had a secret of some kind. Maybe she was in some trouble. She seemed young. Maybe she met the wrong guy and was laying low because of it.

But yesterday when I saw her, she seemed happy. Not like she was worried or in fear. She seemed a little aimless, but happy just the same.

"I'm not sure yet. I think I want her to. We have some shit to clear up…" He looked off to the side, his jaw clenching tight. "Time to make up for. I haven't treated her well, so if she is looking for a place to start over, then I wouldn't mind."

I wasn't really paying attention to where I was wiping as I considered his words. Colson having family was good. I knew he didn't get along well with his dad or stepmom and didn't see his brothers often. Haley, as far as I knew, wasn't even considered family, but I guess things can change.

"That's good, man, I'm happy for you."

I could see the pain etched into his face as his head hung, likely reflecting on the fact that Nora was still gone. I still wasn't sure how to help him through that. I had lost my wife. Rehab couldn't keep her with me and didn't keep her connected to our kids, either. That shit hurt.

He let out a sigh and leaned off the counter. "Can I take them off your hands today? I'll take them to the farm store, they like picking out the eggs and Mrs. Pruitt lets them walk around out back to see the goats."

The girls loved going to the farm store with Colson. I don't know what he said to charm the owner—she didn't let anyone wander around her farm that was attached to the store—but when Cole showed up with my girls, she melted on the spot. She hated me, but I had no reason to go there, so it didn't really matter. I couldn't afford eight dollars for a dozen eggs.

"Yeah, go ahead, I still have some work to do. I'll see you tonight for dinner."

My best friend slapped my back on his way out, and I tried to get my mind back on the meeting that would make or break my livelihood.

CHAPTER THREE

haley

Wool Socks
Stars
4 Wheel Drive
Background noise
Resilience
My Fake ID
McGrady's

BLACK INK HAD GOTTEN all over my hands from writing down the ingredients for tonight's dinner. I was at the sink, scrubbing my hands as I tried to soak in the warmth. The sun was out, shining down on a white world and the way it spilled in through the skylight above the kitchen had me smiling.

It was a new day, with new things to be happy about.

Nora hadn't returned yet, but that was okay. I was taking care of her home, cleaning every day and making sure her firewood box remained full. She had a huge supply of chopped wood on the side of her house, so thankfully I didn't have to cut anything. I liked having fresh flowers to put around the house, so I added that to my list and headed out.

The small market in town was bustling with people. I gripped my list as I navigated the different aisles looking for the ingredients I'd need for tonight's dinner. I knew Colson didn't really care if I made another casserole or not, but it kept me busy and I really liked cooking, so for now I was thankful he was accepting it.

At the checkout, I smiled happily, but the more I smiled at people the more wary they seemed to become.

"You have ID for the wine?" the checker asked, her tight curls held in place with a glittering headband that might have been a gift from someone much younger.

Tugging my wallet free and navigating to the fake ID I kept behind my billfold, I handed it over and tried to make polite conversation.

"I love your hair band."

No response. Her brows came together as she viewed my fake driver's license that had my photo but showed I was born a year earlier than I actually was. It was ridiculous that I even needed this, considering I had just closed on a hard seltzer beverage company not even three months ago.

"You're from California?" The woman at the register made a scoffing sound then shook her head handing my ID back.

"Guess it's startin'." The woman aggressively moved the rest of my groceries over the scanner.

"What's starting?" I swallowed around a lump in my throat. I didn't like confrontation unless it was in a board room and I had on my favorite stilettos and was dressed for the occasion. Currently I was in gym clothes, yoga pants, and a loose T-shirt.

"You fancy Californians are going to start moving up here permanently, not just skiing and dropping cash at those fancy resorts. You're messing with our economy. Some of us had to sell, close up shops. But I guess if you're rich enough, you can have any view you want. Beach, mountain, desert. Doesn't matter."

My face heated as her voice rose and people began to gather in line behind me, their eyes darting up and around as they noticed the scene she was making.

"I'm not—"

She cut me off, her mouth drawn down and her watery blue eyes stern. "Sixty-two fifty."

I slid my card over the top of the machine for the tap-to-pay option, and bit my lip. There was nothing I could say to make her feel better about my presence here in town. There were obviously a few things I was missing, maybe a hardship this town had endured that I didn't know about.

I set my bags in my cart and noticed the bagger walk off without asking if I needed help out, like the other customers had been offered. It didn't matter.

I pushed my cart to my car, saw a few more people sneer in my direction as I opened the back gate, and began unpacking my things. The California plates likely didn't do me any favors with the way the town saw me. I wondered if Colson dealt with this sort of welcome when he arrived here. I mean, he'd gone to high school here for a while, so maybe they considered him a local? I never did come here, not even for vacations. It was something they had done with their mother, and it wasn't repeated when their father married my mom.

My nerves were raw as I got into the car, and I decided now was a good time to look into that gym that I'd heard about. I had wanted to search it out a few times before, but there was always something that got in the way. Today I had an energy thrumming under my skin that could only be expelled with a good run on the treadmill or some time spent on the rower.

Once I returned home to put away the groceries, I headed back out.

My GPS guided me north out of town, on a road lined with tall trees. Taking the exit indicated, I saw a solitary gas station and a fly-fishing shop, then a massive grade leading up to what looked like an old lumber yard.

"Weird…" The gyms in California didn't look like this. They were usually in the downtown area, within walking distance, with lots of bright colors and big signs for curb appeal.

This place was in the middle of nowhere and still pretty much looked like a warehouse.

The parking lot was covered with snow, so it took me a minute to figure out how to park without being able to see the marked spaces. Out here, it was like the sun hadn't hit at all, leaving piles of white powder. Shit, my shoes were going to be soaked. Why hadn't I thought to wear my boots today? They were basically a permanent fixture on my feet ever since arriving. Yet today, I left the house without them.

I paused at the door before pushing inside, stomping to shake off the excess snow on my shoes. *Croft Gym* was etched into the glass door with a picture of boxing gloves dangling underneath it. A boxing gym? A tiny flutter of excitement shot through me.

Tugging the door, my eyes rounded as I took in the sight before me.

At least four different elevated boxing rings were spread out throughout the large space, and rows of heavy and speed training bags hung in a line. Along the other side of the gym was an open space with mats where two people trained doing a series of kicks and punches. I took a few steps and inspected the wall to my right. There were plaques and pictures of some famous boxer who apparently worked out in this gym.

My heart fluttered happily in my ribs.

I was hoping for a treadmill, but boxing—or even better, self-defense —would be perfect.

"Can I help you?" a deep voice called from my left, right as a series of loud beeps echoed around the gym. It was then that I noticed the tall registration counter I had bypassed when entering.

Pivoting, I blushed the smallest bit and tucked some hair behind my ear.

"Yes, I am trying to…" My eyes moved up and landed on a familiar pair of gray eyes.

I pointed at him, slowly smirking.

"Liam? Hey! What are you doing here?"

He did a double-take, his expression going from polite to confused within a blink.

"Haley…hey. I own this place. What about you, why are you here?" he asked, setting the gear aside.

"Wow, that explains the name on the door I guess. That's crazy." I approached the counter, setting my hands down on the smooth surface.

"So, what brings you in?"

Liam's firm jaw flexed as he reached for another padded head piece.

He seemed stressed or agitated. Wasn't sure why, but I hadn't done anything but breathe, so I knew it wasn't because of me.

"Well, I wanted to ask about a membership or just see what you offered."

Liam paused his movements, his eyes bouncing back up to meet mine. His dark hair was unruly, like a tidal wave of raven feathers, deliciously soft and silky. It reminded me of the photos I had seen on my way in of the famous guy. The guy in the photo had a busted lip and black eye, but that hair…

"Membership?" His dark brows arched high on his forehead while his eyes remained focused on his task wiping down the padded gear.

I nodded as a squirmy feeling invaded my stomach. I wished he'd stop what he was doing and just talk to me. I mean, I was a potential customer.

"So does that mean you're staying in Macon then?" He shifted something under the counter, making his rounded shoulders flex. Good lord, I hadn't seen muscle like that on a man in—well, ever. It wasn't bulky, though; he was all lean and toned, like sculpture.

Suddenly his eyes were on me, and mine were on his shoulders.

Fuck.

"Sorry, what?" I blinked.

His gaze narrowed the slightest bit, and the smallest inkling of a smile curled the outer edges of his lips.

"Macon. You staying?"

"I—I think so…at least for now. I haven't decided yet."

Giving me a slight nod with zero emotion whatsoever, he tugged out an application and a pen.

"My gym is open from nine to ten every day. Most guys come in and have their own gear, but we do have gloves and headgear here you can use. It's cleaned after each use."

I watched the application, curious if he was going to hand it over at any point.

"What about training with someone? For like self-defense?"

My hands felt heavy as they lay limp on the counter.

Leaning forward on his elbows, his face came impossibly closer.

"I offer sessions to guys training for fights. I have a few guys who offer beginner courses on how to use the equipment and how to punch so you don't break your wrist. We can get you set up on a few bags and drills so when you come in, you're getting a good workout. If you're wanting some kickboxing or basic boxing drills…"

Eyeing his scrap of paper on the counter, I repeated my question.

"What about self-defense? Is there anyone here who teaches that?"

There was a flicker of annoyance that flashed in his eyes, but it was gone just as quickly.

"I don't offer self-defense classes at the moment, but basic boxing drills should suffice."

I took a step back and mumbled, "Umm, that's okay…"

I had already trained in basic drills. I wanted to learn how to defend myself. Not really for any other reason than it was on my list of things to make happen now that I was branching out on my own.

Watching my retreat from the counter, Liam pressed his lips together then said, "Maybe you should stick to town…there's a yoga studio that opened down there. Might be a better fit."

I stopped mid step, my eyes narrowing.

"Why would it be a better fit?"

Liam crumpled the application into a ball and tossed it into the garbage and grabbed the headgear he'd been wiping down before I walked up. It was a blatant display of being done with me; there wasn't even anything written on the paper. He could have saved it.

"You don't seem like the type that would be able to handle the instruction. You seem like you're used to being catered to and waited on. *Rich.*"

He added that last part with a bit of a sneer.

My heart swiveled and turned in my chest as yet another male in my life decided my worth without a second thought.

I shouldn't care what he thinks. It didn't matter what his opinion was of me—most guys underestimated me. Even more assumed I wasn't worth their effort. I was always shuffled out of the way, or moved around like a chess piece; always a pawn, but never a queen.

Clenching my jaw, I bit down on the retort I had on my tongue and the defense I had of myself and how I wasn't that girl. Not the spoiled, rich girl who thought hard work was for the working class.

He judged me, knowing nothing at all about me.

Instead, I laughed and shrugged my shoulder. "I may be rich, but as a businessman, shouldn't that, I don't know, be your ideal clientele?" I made a point of looking around and lifting my lip in disgust. "Looks to me like you might need to revamp your business plan if you want to keep your doors open."

Asshole.

I spun on my heel and pushed through the door until the cool air calmed my heated face.

THE OBNOXIOUS BEEPING from the oven reverberated through the empty house, making me jump from the couch.

My feet, were covered in warm wool socks, had me slipping a little as I crossed the hardwood floor. I stopped myself in front of the oven, jamming my thumb into the timer button to make it stop. Once the sound quieted, I inhaled and smiled. The smell of butter, sage, and onion permeated the air, which meant there was a good chance my casserole hadn't burned.

"Please, please, please…" I chanted, popping the oven door open.

I had practically scorched the last four casseroles I had made, but Colson ate them anyway. Tonight, I was hoping for less cringe and more smiles from him as we met for dinner. I stared into the heated oven and smiled. The tips of biscuit showing were perfectly browned and matched the recipe I had found on Pinterest.

Finally, one of my creations had gone right.

Shoving my hands into two large oven mitts that had images of plants all over them, I bent over and tugged the glass baking dish out. Gently setting it on the burner, I shut the oven door and tilted my hands until the potholders slid off.

Nora's house was cute. A little outdated, but cute just the same. But it was big for one person and freaking cold.

A chill running down my arms set me in motion.

Pushing my feet into a pair of snow boots, I pulled on my coat then shoved my hands back into the oven mitts before leaving Nora's and walking next door with the casserole.

Crossing the yard and walking up Colson's steps, I rang the doorbell by pushing my glove against the small button. The snow had finally stopped falling, which made it seem almost warm, assuming I ignored how my breath clouded in front of my face.

The door swung open, and my older brother greeted me with a smile.

"Haley, hey!"

I shoved past him and kicked my boots free all while holding the casserole. I'd gotten really good at using my snow boots like flip flops. It was easy if you never tied them.

"Cole, I didn't burn it this time, you're gonna lo—"

My words fell flat, dying on my tongue as I took in the person lounging at Cole's table with his leg kicked out, lifting a beer to his lips.

Colson walked up behind me, guiding me forward so I could set the casserole dish down.

"Sorry, I should have texted you…Liam and the girls are going to be here for dinner tonight."

My eyes narrowed on the long legs that stretched out as if he owned this place. His jeans were messily shoved into a pair of brown boots that were untied. He had on a plain black T-shirt that revealed a full sleeve of tattoos down one arm, he had a few days' worth of growth covering a firm, wide jaw…and a professional glare. Narrowed eyes of mercury focused on me while he sipped from the neck of his bottle. The anger from earlier fizzled and crystalized in my veins, popping like tiny sparks.

The corner of his lip quirked as he lifted the neck of his glass bottle in a silent hello.

Turning on my heel, I faced Cole. "You know what? I totally forgot that I have a zoom call."

"Right now? It's like six at night, who are you talking to?"

My hands were still shoved into the oven mitts as I tried to think up a lie.

"London."

My brother's lips quirked. "It's two in the morning in London."

I settled my hands at my hips, oven mitts still in place. Liam chuckled behind his glass bottle, and it made me want to scream.

"I'll just leave this here for you guys. I will see you tomorrow."

"Makeup lady!" a tiny voice squealed, interrupting my exit.

Mila ran into the kitchen and wrapped her little arms around my waist like she'd known me my entire life.

I settled my hand on her back, hugging her to me as I battled a smile.

"I'm so glad you're here, can you come play with us?" She took my wrist and led me out of the kitchen, but Liam stirred behind us.

"Mila, Haley has to leave."

I turned my head so quick, my hair lifted off my back. "No, I'm fine. You guys eat, we'll be in the room."

Liam narrowed his eyes but nodded, giving me his silent permission.

The girls all stopped what they were doing and watched as I closed in on their little group.

"I found makeup lady!" Mila yelled excitedly. She had dark brown hair that matched her father's and about a thousand different tangles in each strand. It didn't look like she'd brushed it in months.

Pushing my knees into the soft carpet, I smiled at Mila and then looked over at the other two. "Haley, remember?"

Mila waved me off, settling back near her toys. "We just like calling you Makeup Lady."

"You guys are playing Barbies? I used to love playing with these as a kid. Can I play with you?"

Mila moved forward, handing me a big pink RV. It clumsily dropped into my arms, opening one of the side hatches.

"You can be in charge of our camping trip. Maddy is the mom but she's too busy for us, so it's just me and my cousin Sally, the tattoo artist, who are going."

I gently held the RV like it was made of gold and set it to the side.

"How come the mom is too busy?" I flicked my gaze to Maddy and then Seraphina.

Mila didn't look up as she brushed out her little dog's hair, "She just owns all the places in the whole world."

Maddy rolled her eyes and set the doll down. "No, she doesn't. This is stupid…I don't even want to play."

Mila looked up then, her blue eyes suddenly watering out of nowhere.

"You promised you would play!"

Seraphina moved next, tossing her doll to the ground. "It's lame, Mila. Let's just watch TV or go sneak into Uncle Cole's garage again."

Mila was full-on crying now, and my heart ached for her. I knew what it felt like to be the rejected one in the family, the sibling no one wanted to be around.

"Hey, what if we build a fort?"

All three girls paused and slowly turned toward me.

"A fort?"

I nodded, standing up and walking toward the bed.

"We could use some chairs, and toss blankets over them…put pillows inside…then maybe I can do your hair or your nails?"

Why was I volunteering to brush out Mila's hair? That was going to take a lot of arm strength and the girl was going to cry for sure. I didn't want to make her cry.

"Sorry, girls." Liam suddenly stepped inside the room, and it seemed like all the air left it.

He had ink on his chest, too, from the sneak peek he was offering at his throat.

I swallowed and looked down. Unsure why, but I felt like an intruder in here while he knelt down to get at eye level with his kids.

"It's time to go. Uncle Cole isn't feeling well and wants to go to bed early."

That meant Colson was thinking about Nora and likely going to drink.

"Here, let's clean up," Liam said, reaching for the dolls.

"But Dad, Haley was going to build a fort with us," Mila whined, swiping at her eyes again. Was it weird that I counted it a victory that she finally stopped calling me Makeup Lady?

"Yeah and do our hair…" Seraphina added, while putting the doll she had played with away.

"And nails," Maddy tagged on at the end as they shuffled the basket of dolls back into the closet.

"Well maybe some other time." Liam glanced up at me briefly before looking back down at his girls.

What was that look? Did he want me to bail him out of this somehow? I wasn't really used to being around kids; I wasn't sure what parental looks were or how to decode them.

"But when?" Mila pressed, and Liam glanced up at me again. This time his eyes seemed to narrow. Shit, he wanted me to do something… but what?

Fuck it.

"Tomorrow! You guys can come see me if you want, if your dad is okay with it. Nora has a beautiful tea set I'm sure she'll let us use and maybe we can wear some of my fun sun hats and pretend we're in London."

"Yes!" all three girls screamed in unison.

Liam hung his head as if I had done something wrong.

"You guys have school tomorrow, did you forget?"

"It's still school break, we have until after this weekend…" Maddy argued, crossing her arms.

Liam's face grew tight, but he ducked it to hide any emotion.

"Let's go. Shoes, coats…come on."

The girls listened, filing out of the room.

"Can we please go see Haley tomorrow? I've never had a tea party before, and she looks fancy, like she knows how to have them," Mila whined, tugging on a coat that looked like it was too small for her. Something probably from last winter.

I eyed the other girls and sure enough each of them seemed to have older coats, worn, faded…torn and ripped in a few places. My gaze traveled to their boots next. They were in even worse shape. The rubber around one sole was split on Maddy's shoe. Seraphina had colored flowers and hearts all over hers, but the laces had been removed.

Liam glanced up and noticed me looking, which made his jawline clench tight. Fuck I didn't want to embarrass him. The comment I had delivered in his gym burned like acid in my stomach. But he shouldn't feel ashamed; he had three kids, girls at that who needed all sorts of things.

"No, I'll see if Millie can watch you at the diner for a bit. You guys' love helping her with the sugar shakers."

All the girls whined in unison, all complaining about different aspects of the small-town diner.

"Look, I know you don't know me well, but Cole will be right next doo—"

"Let's go," Liam interrupted, cutting a sharp look my way and walking outside.

He was being ridiculous. Grabbing my coat and sliding my feet back into my boots, I ran after Liam.

I noted the black truck he drove so I would know to look for it next time I traipsed over to my brother's house. As quick as I could, I plucked one of my business cards I kept inside my cell phone case and once Liam shut the back passenger door, I shoved it at him.

"Here."

It seemed to catch him off guard, although he didn't miss a step or even move backward. Probably because he was nothing but muscle. Still, his brows jumped, and his mouth gaped.

The tiny cardstock ridges indented his shirt under his unzipped jacket. It was dark enough now that the streetlights had come on and the shadows of his face were highlighted.

"If for some reason the diner lady can't watch them, call me. I'm happy to help."

Before he could respond, I started toward Nora's porch.

In Malibu, the sway of my hips in my six-inch stilettos would have kept a man's eye on me and likely have him pull up his phone and call me before I even got inside my house. Here, in Macon? My snow boots were too loose. There was no swaying of hips…just awkwardly navigating chunks of ice and bits of snow while trying not to face plant.

4

LIAM

YOU'D THINK after being a parent for ten years I would learn not to let my kids have ice cream before bed, but no, I just had to let Millie give them a scoop of her famous marionberry. That was only an hour ago, and now Mila was standing in the tub, crying, while Maddy was arguing with her over it being her turn to take a shower. Seraphina was trying to brush her teeth at the sink, and I was standing in the hall with my head hanging in defeat.

They had two speeds when they had too much sugar; they either became incredibly cranky, or hyper. It seemed tonight was going to be a full-on meltdown.

"It's my turn, did you take all the hot water?" Maddy yelled, which made Mila cry harder. I just needed Mila to wash the ice cream out of her hair before her tangles got any worse. She could usually do this on her own, but when she felt like her sisters were mad at her, she had the tendency to overreact.

"Stop yelling at me!"

"Girls, that's enough!" I bellowed from my place in the hall.

Maddy turned toward me with a red face and her arms tucked into her chest.

"Maddy, go take a shower in my bathroom. Mila has to wash her hair before the ice cream dries."

With a roll of her eyes, Maddy agreed and took off upstairs.

With Mila turning five, we were past the point where I helped her in the bath anymore unless she wore a bathing suit. I was her dad and I'd never hurt her, she knew that, but I wanted to drill into her head that she was growing up, and there were ways to be safe as she grew up, no matter who it was. We kept a suit hanging on the towel rack for situations like this.

"Seraph, toss Mila her swimsuit, will ya?" I asked and waited for my five-year-old to yell at me that she was ready.

When she finally gave me the green light, Seraphina headed out, and I knelt next to the tub to wash Mila's hair.

"Daddy, I'm sorry I got it in my hair."

I used the plastic cup to scoop up warm water.

"Close your eyes, baby."

Pouring it over her head, I grabbed the shampoo and began lathering it into her hair.

"It's okay, sweetheart, I probably should figure out how to comb your hair better and keep it out of your face."

She let out a little sigh. "Yeah, my teacher says I look like I just got out of the jungle."

I dipped my sudsy hands into the water and scooped up more water with the cup.

"Close your eyes again."

I didn't like that my girls looked like a single dad was raising them. I just didn't know how to brush hair the way maybe I should. Lacey never really had patience for it either, she was always tugging on Maddy's hair roughly and yelling when she cried. I never liked it, which was why I didn't like doing it now. But it was getting bad; they definitely needed help.

My mind went back to earlier tonight when Haley had shoved her contact info at me. I could admit that I was a prideful man, but I didn't need some rich girl here on vacation babysitting my kids as some hobby while she got her fill of mountain living, just to have her leave and head back to her rich boyfriend in Malibu again. My girls liked her, and they didn't like women easily. I guess that wasn't entirely true. They had warmed up to Nora quickly, but they never liked Cassie or really any of their other babysitters.

Lathering the conditioner in Mila's hair I let out a sigh.

"You want to play with your Barbies for a little while, while this sits in your hair? Maybe it will help us brush it out."

"Okay." She shrugged her little shoulder as I handed her the little basket of Barbies we kept on the back of the tub.

Once she was playing, I turned my back and rested against the tub and pulled up my contacts. What did it say about me that I had already added Haley in? I had been sitting in the diner listening to Millie talk about how she couldn't help me watch the girls tomorrow because she would be going to Portland to look at something wedding related for her daughter, Rae.

I already knew I had no one else to ask. Colson wasn't in the right state of mind to watch the girls. He was stressed out over Nora and drinking more than he normally did, and I had no idea if he was still working or what the situation was.

Fuck, my kids deserved to have fun for once. They were always in my gym, waiting for me, and by the time I got off work it was too dark to take them to the park, and we didn't have the money to do anything fun, like bowling or heading to a big city for one of those party places with all the arcade games.

The girls had asked for Haley and wanted to spend time with her. Would it be so terrible to let them have a little fun until she decided to head back home to California?

Hanging my head, I tried to discern what was really holding me back. I had no idea why I was being so weird about this; she was just Cole's little sister. I was a prick to her at the gym because she'd so quickly dismissed wanting to train just because we didn't offer what she wanted. It was such a typical rich girl response. She didn't even want to hear me out or see if we could eventually work her into something like that. She just dismissed me and shut down the idea. Suddenly my temper had flared, and I was pissed. Then she went and spoke out loud my biggest fears regarding my gym, and fuck did it hurt.

I hadn't really reacted to anyone like that in a long time. There was no reason behind it, just that I was so tired of it being so easy for everyone else. I was tired of stretching myself so fucking thin that there was nothing left at the end of the day. I had gone on a date a few days ago, and it was such a clusterfuck because she kept asking me what I did for fun and all I wanted to tell her was that I occasionally woke up before my kids and got to drink a cup of coffee without having to be a dad for just a few minutes. Otherwise, I didn't do things for fun. I worked, I got to see my best friend if he came to the gym, or he watched my girls.

Otherwise, that was it.

Pathetic.

"Is it ready, Daddy? I'm getting wrinkled."

I turned around and used the cup to scoop up the warm water and rinsed her hair.

Once Mila was waddling up the stairs, tugging her towel around her shoulders, I pulled up Haley's contact and instead of texting her, I pushed call.

It rang a few times while I gripped the back of my neck.

Then her soft voice hit my ears, and the weirdest sensation hit my sternum. It felt like a bird had got caught in my chest and was beating its wings like crazy to get free.

"Haley? Hi…"

She paused, and I realized I hadn't said who I was…and she didn't have my number.

"It's Liam."

"Oh, hey…" She trailed off, sounding guarded.

I walked into the living room, nearly tripping over one of Mila's Barbie cars.

"Umm, sorry, I know it's late."

She gave a little laugh. "It's only eight-thirty."

Right, not late to a twenty-year-old. She probably partied back in California.

"Well, I would like to talk to you about your offer."

"Okay."

The living room was a disaster. I needed to have the girls pick up their toys before bed.

"Uh, well, is the offer for watching them tomorrow still open?"

She paused for a moment, and the girls started yelling upstairs. I pinched the bridge of my nose.

"It is…"

Mila ran down the stairs shrieking at the top of her lungs. "Daddy, she put stickers all over my favorite Barbie!"

"So what? It's just a dumb Barbie. You're such a baby, Mila." Seraph trailed after her sister, yelling just as loud.

Fucking hell.

"Girls, I'm on the phone." I covered the receiver, but it was no use, they were already in a full-blown argument.

I heard Haley lightly laughing in my ear.

"Want to just call me back, or text me?"

"Uh…" I maneuvered around the kids and toys until I was in the kitchen, but the girls followed me. This was a bit more serious than a text, but also, I needed to be able to talk to her without being interrupted every five seconds. If she were here in person, the girls wouldn't behave like this. They'd want her to be their babysitter, so they'd want her to be able to sit and talk with me without being interrupted.

"Would you be willing to come over? I know that seems weird, but it's strictly professional, and the girls are here, so…"

There, that clearly established I was just asking her to come to my house at nearly nine at night because we had business to discuss.

"Sure, can you text me your address? I'm in sweats, so I'll have to get dressed really quick."

"We're all in sweats too. Just come over, it's not a big deal."

Besides, maybe it would help to see her undone a bit. She was usually so perfect: no hair out of place, her skin looking like something from an app filter, and her lashes were the longest I had ever seen on a real person. She was young, but she intimidated the hell out of me, and I didn't intimidate easily.

"Uh, okay. Sure, I'll be there in a few minutes then."

"Okay, thanks, I'll text you the address."

I hung up and sagged back into the chair, realizing I had tuned out the girl's argument. They were starting to tire out, which meant I needed to finish up their bedtime routine.

THIS WAS A DUMB IDEA.

My gut was screaming at me to just leave her at the door, let her knock and realize I'd changed my mind. She would get back in her car and leave. The end.

She'd already insulted me once. This whole plan of asking her to help with the girls was stupid. So fucking stupid.

Yet, my feet carried me to the door faster than necessary. The camera showed her breath clouding in front of her, which meant she was cold, and that didn't sit right with me. I unlocked and swung the door open, feeling the cold hit my face…and something else.

Sweats my fucking ass. She looked…

Too pretty. Too fuckable. Too much.

"Where are the girls?" Haley asked, her dark brows drawing in together as she hustled inside and shed her coat. Tan skin met me as I caught sight of where her sweater cut off right below her breasts. I could see the bottom of her black sports bra, and those sweats were molded perfectly to her body. The waist sinched around her narrow hips but was tight enough that it showed off her high, rounded ass.

Jesus.

Clearing my throat, I looked down and tried to gather myself.

"They actually just went to bed. Knowing them, they'll hear you and sneak down for water or something else they don't need."

She chuckled, slipping out of her boots and then looking up and around as if she were surprised.

Shit, she probably was. My gym did look like it was falling apart, and

I noticed her catch sight of my girl's snow boots and clothes. She was probably curious why I lived in such a nice house.

"I bought it back when I was fighting." I said curtly, moving down the hall.

She trailed me. "Oh…it's nice. I wasn't—" She trailed off, quietly saying, "Never mind."

"Can I get you some water or coffee?"

I opened the cupboard, seeing her take a seat at the table out of the corner of my eye.

"Water is fine, thanks."

Hopefully she didn't have a problem with tap. The filter on the fridge had gone out, and I had yet to replace it. Oregon water wasn't like California water, though, so drinking from the tap wasn't that big of a deal for us.

I set it in front of her and moved around to the other side.

"Thank you." She smiled up at me, taking a sip.

I hated how I mentally noted that she didn't seem to be too good for tap water. I hated even more that it made that weird fluttering sensation in my chest act up again.

Clearing my throat, I ignored how natural she seemed to look sitting at my table.

"I thought over your offer and wanted to explain why I hadn't outright accepted. It's not that I don't trust you or want you near my kids. They seem to really like you, and I trust Cole like he's my own brother, but beyond that, he cares for my girls like they're his own. He'd never let you watch them alone if he didn't think you were capable."

She seemed to visibly relax at that, which made me feel better. I didn't like the notion that she thought I didn't trust her. I hadn't known her long, but she was Cole's little sister and she seemed genuine. Even if I had been a prick and she'd said something that insulted me, it didn't change that deep down, I knew she was safe for my kids.

"What was the issue then?" her small voice seemed to echo loudly in the kitchen.

I realized the sink was full of dishes, and the counter still had remnants of dinner on it.

Heaving a sigh, I considered how honest I wanted to be with her. I didn't love looking destitute in front anyone, let alone her. Not with her glossy lips, or those big green eyes. Fuck, were those dark lashes natural? The way her body moved…it was wrong that I liked it. She was too young for me. Twelve years was too much, *wasn't it?*

"Honestly, I've run into some financial strains recently. So, keeping a consistent babysitter and paying them twenty bucks an hour to watch my kids just isn't feasible at the moment. Usually, I just have the girls tag along with me to the gym but I have to meet with some pretty important people tomorrow so I can't have the girls there, and well, I—"

"I'm not interested in money," Haley muttered softly, dipping her chin to her chest.

I appreciated that she didn't make it seem like it was nothing or wave me off like she was pitying me. It seemed genuine.

Pausing to take a sip, I watched her shift in her seat until the silence stretched long enough.

I asked, "Then what do you want?"

Haley's long hair was falling out of the elastic she had used, and pieces framed her face as she pushed a few strands away. It left a clear view of how the tops of her cheeks flushed. It made me wonder if the tops of her breasts would flush as well, or if they had any freckles. She had four dark freckles on her face, and each one made me curious.

"Well, I'm self-employed and have no need for another job, so to speak, but I like your girls and would love to hang out with them."

Leaning forward, I set her with a firm stare.

"But see, that's just it, you wouldn't be *hanging* out. You would be taking care of my children. Feeding them, driving them around, helping them if they needed something…this isn't some fun hobby. My kids aren't a trendy thing you can start and stop whenever you want to."

Her beautiful face flushed an even prettier color of pink. "I know…I didn't mean"—that flush deepened—"I just meant, I like being around them."

The girl's mom liked being around them too, until she didn't.

Haley must have read my expression, which was essentially telling her to do fucking better. My daughters would not be left with someone who would just pawn them off or leave them somewhere.

"I'm—well, you don't know anything about me really, so I understand your hesitancy. I'm from Malibu…I've lived there my whole life. I have taken several CPR classes and am well versed in what to do with allergic reactions. I'm a decent but not perfect driver—no accidents but a few tickets. I have insurance on my car, a license. I carry pepper spray on my key chain and would never take them anywhere unsafe."

"You don't know what places are unsafe in Macon. You just got here."

Her head dipped, making more of her hair fall out. Damn. It looked silky, and my fingers twitched, practically begging to touch it.

I sunk back into the chair, kicking my leg out. I was being too hard on her, I knew that I was, but a part of me also wanted to know how hard she'd come back swinging. She had fight in her. I saw it earlier in the gym, and even tonight at Cole's. I liked it. But her face was so pink, and those beautiful green eyes looked almost like they were watering, so I knew I had to back off a bit.

"How about we just try things out tomorrow…keep it casual. The girls can come over for a few hours, and Cole will take them off your hands around three, so…ten to three, if you're okay with that?"

"Yeah, sounds good." Her voice trailed off, her eyes fixed on the floor, and I knew I'd offended her by bringing Cole into this, but this was new. What if she wasn't as great at taking care of kids as she thought she was? What if she couldn't do this? Thankfully, Cole was right next door, and better to not overwhelm her with an entire day of stuff. No, this was better.

"Well, okay then, I'll see you tomorrow."

Nodding again, she gave me a flat smile while she stood from the table.

Her perfectly manicured nails were curled into her palms as she walked toward the entry way. It was a quick conversation, much faster than I had anticipated, and for some reason, it felt like she needed to be here longer. I needed to know more about her and why there were parts of me that seemed to crave pieces of her.

"One more thing…"

Green eyes with flecks of gold looked up at me, waiting.

Swallowing around the thickness in my throat, I cleared it.

"Are you involved with someone?"

I didn't need to know—it wasn't my business—but if she was going to be around my kids, I had a right to the information. Especially if he was some rich asshole from California who decided to surprise Haley on a whim.

She shook her head. "I haven't dated anyone in a while."

Why did I suddenly need to know how long a while was, and if she did casual hookups, or if she was pining for someone from her past?

"Okay." I finally said, stepping away from her.

"See you tomorrow?"

I gave her a nod, "See you tomorrow."

Maybe by then I'd finally be over whatever it was that kept making me want to kiss her.

CHAPTER FIVE

haley

Fresh Snow
Fur-lined gloves
Face Masks
Mount Macon
Happy Giggles
Comforts from Home

I WATCHED through the blinds as the black truck came to a slow stop along the curb in front of the house. Butterflies shot off like rockets in my chest, flittering down to my stomach. I hadn't been able to stomach a single thing this morning because of how nervous I was. Like hell was I about to confess this to Liam last night, but I hadn't ever actually babysat anyone before. I hadn't lied about the CPR training, but that was to become a surfing instructor. We did cover kids, even babies in the coursework…but entertaining children? I didn't know the first thing about it.

But I wouldn't admit it.

Deep down there was a loneliness that clawed at my soul and gnawed at my hope, always taunting that no one loved me. That no one wanted me. Some days I gave in, and other days I chose to believe that I just hadn't found the people who needed my love yet. Obviously, my family didn't need it, but someone out there might.

Today was one of those days. I was fighting on the inside, but on the outside, I was wearing a floral halter dress, open toed heels, and my hair was in bouncy ringlets down my back. Oh, and on top of my head was the largest sun hat I owned.

The girls clomped up the stairs with their heavy snow boots and then knocked on my door. I couldn't help but smiling as I swung it open and took in their expressions.

Each one gaped as they took in my appearance.

"You look like a princess!" Mila gasped as she was being carried by her father.

I watched, smiling down as the girls took off their coats and boots. I finally let my eyes drift to Liam's. Standing tall and outrageously handsome in a black suit, his gaze was unreadable, his brow furrowed. His lips slightly parted as if he had gasped along with the girls, and that jaw of his was clenched as if he'd just chewed on glass.

I felt like I did the first time he'd inspected me in the diner, like I wanted to squirm right out of my skin.

Finally, Liam walked past me while muttering a curse under his breath.

"Um…" I brought my fingers together, suddenly unsure if he was okay with this arrangement. "If you'd prefer Cole be here, I'm sure he can come over."

Liam's face snapped up.

"No. Why?"

I tried to hide my blush. "Never mind."

His lips tugged down into a frown before turning back to the kids.

"Be good. Listen. No fighting. Eat the lunch she prepares." He looked at each girl sternly. Each one nodded as if they'd heard this a million times.

"I love you." His voice cracked the slightest bit as he leaned in to kiss the tops of each of their heads. They all waved to him and then Maddy had the remote for the television in her hand and was navigating Nora's Netflix account.

Walking back over to the foyer with Liam, I waited for him to give me a few more instructions.

"Okay, you have my cell number?" He patted his pockets as if to make sure he had his phone.

I nodded. "Yes."

"None of them have allergies. Mila will tell you she can't eat salad, or peas, but she can."

That was cute but wouldn't be a problem today.

"Can I drive them anywhere or would you prefer I didn't?" I wasn't sure I'd take them anywhere, but just in case, I wanted to be sure I had his blessing.

Liam considered it for a second, tugging out his cell to inspect a message or email.

"Yeah, just get the extra booster from Colson. He has one in his truck."

Shit, that must be for Mila…right?

"Do they all need one, or just Mila?" Seraphina was pretty light and short…what are the weight requirements?

Liam chuckled at that, giving me a smile. "Just Mila."

My face flushed the slightest bit, assuming everyone must know that.

"Look, if there's any issues, just ask Colson…he's with them almost as much as I am." Gray eyes looked me up and down as he finished and then moved to the porch. Before he was off the first step, he turned toward me once more.

"You smell like some kind of flower. Don't know which one, but it smells good."

I followed him to the banister, curling my fingers around it as my brows dipped.

"What?"

He was a little further down the path when he turned again.

"You heard me cursing. Wasn't mad at you, just really liked how you smelled."

His strong jaw clenched once before turning again, heading to his truck.

The smile cresting my lips couldn't be rivaled. A compliment? I didn't even think he was capable of—

"Rich people can afford the best shit. Must be nice not to have to worry about real life problems like rent or the cost of gas," he called as he rounded his rig and tugged on the door.

My mouth parted as shock settled in my core, and he drove away.

Holy shit, that was so… He was so—there was a burning behind my eyes that was common when my brothers would say something like that to me. When they'd say I didn't do anything all day but spend Daddy's money, even though I was out there working my ass off, doubling his money because I was smart and good with hustling the shit out of wealthy businessmen.

Returning inside, I saw the girls and realized that Liam never explained Mila's appearance or why she looked like she'd just rolled out of bed. Her hair was a rat's nest, the worst I had ever seen. Seraphina's wasn't much better. Maddy had hers brushed but pulled back into a low ponytail with a lot of fluff and frizz.

"When are we going to do our tea party?" Mila asked, yawning.

Checking my watch, I realized what had to be done first.

"Ladies!" I popped my hip and placed my hand there as all eyes went to me. "Have you ever been to a salon?"

"A what?" Seraphina asked, her blue eyes narrowing in the cutest freaking way.

Maddy's face flushed. "Our dad can't really afford that stuff for us."

Waving her off, I grabbed their coats. "Don't worry about that…this all comes with the babysitter package."

"It does?" Mila lit up then looked over at her sisters. "Just like with Uncle Cole."

"No…he buys us stuff because he's friends with dad…" Maddy corrected, then swung her gaze to me, "Haley is just babysitting us because…"

I tugged on Mila's hand and pulled her up while responding to the moody ten-year-old. "Because I like you guys. Also, going to the salon is a fun thing you can do with your friends, and I want to be your friend, so we should go."

"I don't know if we can get our hair cut," Maddy whispered, tugging at her sleeve.

I tugged on my pea coat. "I'm not cutting your hair or anything, I just thought it would be fun to get our hair washed and blow dried and then styled fancy for our tea party."

Mila squealed in joy, Seraphina smiled brightly at me, and Maddy gave me a tiny, baby smile of appreciation that I would still accept.

"So, it's settled. First, we find Mila's shoes then we go get beautified!"

THE GIRLS WERE all relaxing in their white robes with towels twisting their hair on top of their head and cucumbers over their eyes. Soft music played overhead while each of us lounged back in our chairs, being completely pampered. It felt so good to have the comforts from home here in Macon—although technically we weren't in Macon. We were about twenty minutes outside of it at some fancy resort that has a five-star spa.

I asked my brother Colson what he thought of me taking them here, and he thought the girls would love it. And they did.

The squeals and gasps from the girls as they got their hair washed, and then their faces were done up with clay masks, it was too cute. The stylist was so sweet, helping with Mila's hair. She'd lathered extra detangling product and gently combed it while letting her watch cartoons, so it was a tearless event. I decided to do our tea date here at the lavish restaurant and see what the girls thought of the large fountain inside. I had spotted it on the way in and knew we had to eat lunch there.

"Haley, is this how you lived in Cawifornia?" Mila asked with her darling lisp.

I smirked and took off the towel that had been warming my hair.

"Sometimes, yes."

Maddy let out a sigh and plucked off the cucumbers. "This is nice… probably nicer than anything we'll ever get to do with our dad."

"Hey, don't think like that. We should always believe the best about our people."

Maddy crinkled her brows together. "Our people?"

"You know…the ones in our corner. The ones who are happy when we succeed and sad when we're hurt…the ones who would do anything for us. You three have your dad and you're a unit…you'd do anything for each other, right?"

Mila grabbed her cucumbers next and tossed them on the floor. "Yes, but also Uncle Cole too…he's our people."

"Yeah, he's definitely our people," Seraphina added in, keeping her cucumbers over her eyes.

"Anyone else in there? It's good to have a picture of them, that way when they do something big in your life, or their life, you can be happy for them."

All three girls seemed to think it over then Maddy added, "Nora…I think she's going to be in there…"

"And you, if you want to be nice to us some more," Mila added.

I smiled. If they only knew what I would do for them if they wanted me in that circle.

"I think Nora and Cole are going to be together for a very long time, so I like the idea of having her there, and I'd be honored to be there too."

My next question came out hesitant and slow, nervous that I might be stepping on a landmine.

"And what about your mother…should she be in this circle?"

Mila and Seraphina turned to Maddy as if she would answer for them. Maddy's eyes watered, and it was like a record scratch. *Oh my God.*

Inside I was begging for a time machine.

The sniffling came next, and I felt like the shittiest human alive. Fuck. Fuck. *Fuckkkkk.*

"I'm so sorry, I shouldn't have asked. Can we pretend that I didn't? I'm so sorry." I got up and rounded Maddy's chair, pulling her into my arms. A steady stream of tears trailed her cheeks, and I felt like a knife was lodged in my chest.

"How about lunch? Are you guys ready for some tea, and maybe some cake? There's a fountain." I cradled Maddy's face to the terrycloth robe of my chest and rocked her as she silently sobbed. With a loud sniffle and a swipe of tears from Seraphina and Mila, they all broke out of it and finally started smiling.

"A real fountain with water and everything?"

Smiling at them and relieved the blunder was behind me, I nodded.

"You can throw in pennies!"

I knew the girls were in, so we dressed, and while each of them stared at their silky, tangle-free hair in the mirror, I made a mental note to buy them some hair accessories to help them at home.

Lunch was a breeze as the girls ate and stared in wonder at the large room with ceilings at least sixty feet tall, and the sight of the mountain left me speechless. Snowcapped, and standing tall against a blush-colored sky, the outline of the moon was already up, tucked behind the tip of Mount Macon. Little dots of black splattered the mountain where pieces of snow had melted from the trees. It was the most gorgeous view I had ever seen. Even the girls chewed in peaceful silence as we all stared in wonder.

Once we were done with our sandwiches, each girl took a handful of coins from my purse and unloaded them into the fountain, each one with a wish.

We were laughing all the way back to Macon as a call came through my Bluetooth car speaker. Seeing that it was Liam, I pressed answer without thinking twice.

"Hey, Liam."

"Where are you?" he snapped.

Maddy's face swung my direction quick as lightning, realizing I was in trouble.

I hastily disconnected and swapped to my cell phone.

"I texted you the address of where we were going."

I had. Before we even left the city, I had texted him…

"I haven't had a chance to check it all day. Haley, do you have any idea what it was like to pick up my phone and see that you'd decided to drive my kids out of the city? It's still snowing at that resort and the roads are slick. What the fuck were you thinking?"

I wasn't a fan of his tone, or the fact that he seemed to be panicked when there was no need for it.

"I'm on my way back to Nora's house…"

He just got confirmation that his kids were safe and on their way home. Hopefully he'd relax a little.

"Fuck. Do you have any idea how fucking terrified I was, not knowing where they were?"

A splintering feeling compressed in my lungs as I listened to him yell. Why was he so upset?

I finally cut into his tirade with my business voice. "I'm literally five minutes away. Surely this rant can wait until I get there. I don't want to be unsafe with the girls in the car." It was the sort of tone I used in board meetings and when men tried to make me feel less than just for being a woman. Fuck this guy if he honestly thought just because I babysat for him—for free— he had the right to talk to me like I was dirt beneath his feet.

The car was silent as we drove through the city limits and past Main Street and finally pulled into the driveway. Liam stood outside the house, his arms crossed and the breath clouding in front of his face.

"Okay, girls let's get out. I am assuming your daddy will be taking you home, so I will see you next time, okay?" I said, injecting enthusiasm in my tone.

They had done nothing wrong, so there was no reason whatsoever to make them feel like they had.

Liam was at their door, helping them down.

"Let's go. Get in the car," he said sternly.

I noticed how his fingers trailed through Mila's hair, and he inspected it as if he wasn't sure it was real. He inspected Maddy's and Seraphina's next.

Slowly, I made my way around the car and tucked my purse into my side. I wasn't in a hurry to explain myself, because it didn't really seem like he'd even be interested in what I had to say. What was the point?

Finally, once the girls were safe inside his running vehicle, Liam turned toward me.

His eyes flashed, and my chest tightened. I hadn't intentionally done anything wrong, but the look on his face undid me. He was genuinely afraid for his girls, and it was just plain shitty that I had made him feel that. I decided right there I'd just take whatever he said. I wouldn't defend my actions or explain, I'd just take all of his words and emotions like a dart board and let his words stick wherever they landed.

Right as he was about to lay into me, my brother's door opened, and Colson stepped out. He looked like hell, but his face was set hard, like stone, his eyes glued to Liam.

"Whatever you're about to say, you better be damn certain of every fucking word, because I might just break your jaw afterward."

Chills spread out along my arms and down my fingers as a tiny flicker of warmth invaded my chest.

No one had ever stood up for me before…no one from my family, especially.

Liam's jaw tensed while he stared up at Colson, then ever so slowly he lowered his eyes until he met my gaze.

"I honestly can't even begin to fathom what must have gone through your brain for you to think it would be okay to take someone else's children out of town to—."

"You had no reason to worry; I told you where they went," Colson said with exasperation.

Liam scoffed, shaking his head while muttering a few curses.

"You know more than anyone why I freaked out, Cole…you know—"

Suddenly Colson was stomping down the steps and getting in Liam's face.

"I *do* know, and I know my sister wouldn't put them in harm's way. She even double-checked with me before she left. She would never do anything to hurt them."

Liam pushed Colson out of his space. "Oh, suddenly she's your sister now? That's rich…"

"Fuck you!" Colson seethed, standing in between Liam and me.

"No, fuck you, Colson. How could you agree to letting her take my girls outside of the city? Why the fuck would you think I would be okay with that?"

Liam's eyes were watery, his face red, but it was more than that… something was off. I had done something irrevocably wrong by taking them. This was a trauma response.

"Liam, look, I shouldn't have taken them out of town." I raised my hands. "I was out of line for doing it."

"You don't need to apologize," Colson snapped at me, pulling my hand so I wasn't moving closer to Liam. I hadn't actually apologized once, all I did was own up to what I did do wrong, but I wasn't sorry about it.

"I get that you're pissed, but when I asked if I could drive them around that was your opportunity to tell me no." I stepped closer, gaining steam.

"I may not be a parent, but if I was *that* nervous about them being out of town, I would make damn sure the person caring for my child knew about my reservations." I was practically toe to toe with Liam at this point.

His chest heaved up and down as his eyes burned into mine. He didn't seem worried now, he looked like he wanted to fight. He was all hard lines, and under his suit was a myriad of dark tattoos and a broken heart and a pacing lion, desperate to protect what was his.

I stared at Liam. He stared back.

He stepped closer, towering over me.

Our fingers brushed. His pointer fingers barely twitched, and then it stroked down the length of mine. It was so small, so minuscule, I thought I had imagined it, but his eyes were on mine, and that's when I saw it. This need to be touched. To be settled and calmed. So, I stepped closer, then very awkwardly lifted my arms, feeling so uneasy until I slammed my eyes shut and just wrapped my arms around his neck.

The breath I was holding came out jagged and rough when I told him, "They're safe. They had a good day."

He didn't return my hug, which was fine. I stood still as stone, and Colson muttered "Prick" at my back.

The wind blew snow off the top of Nora's house, swirling around us as we stood in the yard.

Right when I was about to pull away, Liam's arms came around me, crushing me to his chest. He held me there, not saying anything. It was an odd, silent truce, unlike anything I had ever felt or encountered before. Time seemed to slow, the darkening sky blinked as fresh snow fell, and I felt his fingers tangle through the ends of my hair.

Just then I remembered his earlier comment and how rude he'd been about me having money, *again*. That, paired with how he treated me tonight, and suddenly I was less than enthused about making him feel better. I pulled away and kept my face down.

"Haley—" He swallowed around what sounded like a lump in his throat.

I kept my eyes low as I stepped away.

I triggered the dude. I could own that. It was shitty. But I wasn't a doormat. I was here in Macon, trying to create a new life for myself, and the last thing I wanted was for people to assume they could treat me anyway they felt was okay. The whole damn town seemed to be perfectly comfortable with treating me that way.

He turned, repeating my name once more, but the day had caught up with me. I had hurt Liam, but he had hurt me first. He was thoughtless and careless first. He had judged me first. I was so tired of becoming small so that others' hurts could fit. I put myself on the back burner time and time again because someone else needed the attention. It was exhausting.

Without looking back, I walked to my door, unlocked it, and shut myself inside.

6

———

LIAM

MY BREATH CLOUDED in front of my face as I watched my best friend glower at me. He was pissed, and I guess he had every right to be, but he didn't get it. He of all people *should,* but he didn't.

"You can't treat her like that," Colson said, taking a step closer.

This was bullshit. I had heard the way he talked about Haley. More than a few nights when he'd drink until he couldn't think straight, he'd go off on the sister he never wanted. The girl who ruined his life. Yet here he was, protecting her.

She didn't need protecting, did she?

She understood my panic, and that was odd for me. Most people didn't get it…not the teachers, when they couldn't place where my kid was if I randomly showed up to pick them up. Not their doctors, who didn't understand why I was so adamant that they not allow Lacey to call and ask about her kids records. No one understood this fear that rattled my chest and tore at my soul on a regular basis. No one got that it was like fighting in the ring: A darkness clouded my vision, and survival kicked in, making it to where no one else but my kids mattered.

Somehow Haley understood.

I glanced back toward Nora's house on instinct, unsure how I would go about fixing this. That hug and the sad way she pulled away from me tugged at my chest. I owed her an apology.

"I know." I swallowed, looking down. "I'm sorry…it won't happen again."

Colson flicked his gaze to my car where my girls were waiting, and he seemed to soften.

"You know I would never let anything happen to them."

I nodded, I did know that, but… "You're busy right now, distracted, and at the end of the day it's not you who has to worry about them. Not completely. You love them, but I'm the one who keeps them safe, I'm the one who makes sure they have food on their table. It's on me if something happens."

I had to get home. I needed to calm down, hug my girls, and get reassurance that they were okay.

Stepping away from my friend, I waved him off. "I'll talk to you tomorrow."

With one last glance at the door that swallowed Haley up, I got into my truck.

"Daddy, why are you so mad?" Mila was the first to ask, always chomping at the bit.

Maddy turned around from her spot in front to scold her little sister, but Seraph beat her to the punch.

"Yeah, what did Haley do wrong? We heard you yelling at her." Seraphina asked, sounding guarded. Seraph was the easiest going out of the group, and it took a lot to get her interested or upset about something.

Shit, I had my work cut out for me. I had fucked up in a big way.

"Nothing. She didn't do anything. Daddy just had a bad day."

The silence stretched as I navigated the streets. We lived just few blocks from Colson, so it didn't take long to pull into our driveaway. I helped the girls out of the car and couldn't help noticing once again that their hair all looked silky and shiny, like Haley's always did. Once we were inside, the girls kicked their boots off and shed their coats.

"So…what did you do today?" I asked, trying to fix what I'd messed up.

Each one of my girls was somber and seemed sad, their faces drawn in tight, heads lowered as they fixated on putting their stuff away. Which they never did…

"Come on, guys, I'm sorry…talk to me," I begged, loosening the tie I'd been wearing all goddammed day.

Maddy finally huffed and looked up me. "She took us to a fancy spa. They washed our hair, gave us fluffy robes—"

"Painted our faces!" Mila joined in, talking over Maddy.

Seraph added, "We got to wear cucumbers on our eyes, it was cool."

Wow…she had to have spent a fortune.

"Then we ate lunch, and it was so cool!" Maddy regained the conversation, eyeing her sisters, daring them to interrupt again.

Seraph ignored Maddy's warning. "There was a fountain, and this view of Mount Macon that was really pretty, and she gave us money to make wishes!"

I tucked my boots under the bench near the door. I had worn nicer shoes in the meetings, but honestly it didn't make a lick of difference with how those men saw me.

Not a safe bet.

Too much of a risk.

"Wow, sounds like you had fun."

"Haley's nice. She doesn't act like she only likes us for your sake… not like those other women you've made us meet."

Those little ball busters. They meant their other babysitters. Unless I found a high schooler looking for some cash, which was rare, I had to find someone older…and usually whoever I found wanted to date me. Honestly, I'd indulge a few dates, and as shameful as it was, I did it because I wanted them to keep babysitting, but my girls always saw through it.

"But Haley doesn't talk about you. She cares about us. She cares that we have nice hair and eat near fountains, she let us throw in all the coins in her purse even though we weren't supposed to throw in any at all. So, all the wishes belong to us." Yeah, of course the one girl who didn't want anything to do with me would treat my kids like they were her own.

Fucking figured.

Mila ran upstairs and emerged a few seconds later with her blanket. I knew she had to be tired. Once she was snuggled on the couch and the other two had set up a movie, I grabbed myself a beer and began hunting for dinner ideas. I had no idea what to make. Nothing was thawed out, and the kids had this big fancy lunch. I didn't want to follow that up with macaroni and cheese, but it didn't look like I had much of anything else.

Just as I was about to set the hot water on the stove, a knock sounded from the front door.

"I'll get it," Maddy yelled, running down the hall until her hand just barely wrapped around the knob. Right as she was about to pull it open, I placed my hand on the frame above her head and stared down at her.

"Remember?"

Rolling her eyes, she released the handle and slid away from the door. "You need to answer it after dark."

"Yes, now go sit down."

Maddy skulked back a few feet, but her gaze was still fixed on the door. It made my stomach clench. I didn't think she even realized she did it, but whenever there was a knock on the door, especially in the evening, she would watch and wring her fingers together. Subconsciously I thought maybe she was expecting her mother to show up. It didn't seem to matter how often I told her I would never let her back in, or that she never had to worry again. She was still afraid.

I swung the door open and froze on the spot.

Wearing a tiny scowl, Haley stood on my porch in a white coat that looked soft and molded to her frame so perfectly, I wondered if it was designed for her. Before I could even invite her in, she shoved past me.

"I just wanted to bring these for the girls. The hairdresser gave them to us, along with this spray stuff to help detangle their hair."

The girls all crowded around her as I secured the door.

"What's in the bag?" I couldn't help but ask. She had four large containers stuffed inside a plastic grocery bag, dangling from her arm.

Haley's gaze swiveled to mine, just as she began pulling each girl in for a quick hug.

"Here, the girls had leftovers." Her blank expression made something pull in my gut.

Pride was a fickle thing, hardening my heart, but I forced it down as I accepted the bag.

Haley wouldn't meet my eye line.

Once my kids took their containers to the table, Haley spun on her heel, facing me. Her green eyes narrowed as she stepped away. I followed suit until we were in the foyer, away from little ears listening in.

Clearing my throat, I decided to just pull the Band-Aid off.

"Look, about earlier—I shouldn't have yelled at you. It was an over-reaction…"

I couldn't really dive into it much deeper because Haley was still a stranger. She didn't need to see everything under the surface. She'd run if she knew how fucking deep and messy all this shit was. Didn't change the fact that I owed her an apology.

Firming up her delicate jaw, she lifted that chin and glared.

"Thank you for the apology, but you owe me one for what you said before you left, too."

What was she talking about?

"I didn't say anythi—"

She took two steps closer, her pouty pink lips curved upward like she was about to enjoy this. "I don't believe in holding on to grudges or staying mad. I think it's a waste of time. I also don't believe in misunder-standings. So let me be clear."

Her hair hit her waist as she tilted her head back.

"I am rich, but I earned every fucking penny. I will not be treated less than because you're too insecure to accept that I have money. It doesn't make me a bad person that I was born into it. Men like you will not make me feel like I'm not worth your time simply because you're a dick."

Jesus. I—

"And I am not too *delicate* for self-defense. I like yoga, but I need someone to train me to defend myself against a man twice my size. If that's not you then fine, just say so, but don't ever try and make me feel like I can't fit into your world simply because mine is made of gold and yours is currently being held together by duct tape."

Her green eyes took on a determined sheen, and there was this swirling happening in my gut. No woman—fuck, no person—has ever put me in my place like she just did. It felt exhilarating… like a spark just landed in a dry forest full of dead trees. Like I've been waiting for the right person who could not only make me burn but withstand the heat.

I was so awestruck, I hadn't even noticed that she'd side stepped me and was nearly out the door. Regaining composure, I quickly walked after her, tugging the door and trailing on her heels in my socks.

"Haley."

Her hair bounced, shifting against her back as she stalked to her SUV.

"Wait!" I finally caught up and tugged her hand until she faced me.

I wasn't even sure what I would say once I caught her, but now that burning…that roaring in my chest created more clarity than I've had in a really long time. I dropped her hand like it was made of that fire.

"Do you want to do this"—I waved between us—"watch the girls, I mean…?"

Out here, in the dark, it was difficult to make out her expression. The streetlight only provided the most basic of features, and the cloud in front of her face hid the rest. I wanted to pull her closer so I could catch the glint in her eye and see if those pouty lips had thinned.

"Like on a regular basis?"

Nodding, I stepped closer because I couldn't stand the space.

"Yeah, whatever you want. You'd help with getting them to school. I mean, there's no pressure…basically just helping me with them. You'd be the first person I call when I need a babysitter. You could pick them up after school. I work every day from eight to six, sometimes later depending on what's going on, but if that's too much for you then I—"

"You can't pay me." She said it almost like she was reminding me, or ensuring it wasn't something I would offer.

The tightening in my stomach was pure fire. I hated this. I fucking loathed it, but she was right. I couldn't treat her like she couldn't be in my world simply because I was insecure.

"I'm offering a trade."

That seemed to pique her interest. Her head tilted the smallest bit, and I quickly made my offer while she seemed in a listening mood.

"I'll teach you self-defense. Once a week."

"Three times a week," she countered with a twitch of her lips.

Her nose was getting red from the cold. My feet were numb, and I didn't have a coat. But fuck if I cared.

I stepped closer, and at this point it wasn't really appropriate. There wasn't any space left between us, but she didn't shy back.

"Two." Why exactly was I trying to get less time with her?

Because she's too young and way too beautiful.

"Deal!" Her hand jutted out and a brilliant smile spread across her face.

I took her hand and closed mine over it, sealing a deal I hoped I wouldn't regret.

CHAPTER SEVEN

haley

Making Friends
Good Coffee
Learning How to Use a Nail Gun
The Community Center
Baking
Tinted Windows

NORA CAME BACK a few days ago, and things have been a bit of a whirlwind since. She and Colson seemed to have worked things out, which was a relief. I didn't know all the details, but Nora had spent every night at Colson's since getting back, so I was assuming they were good.

More importantly, she was fine with me staying in her house. She was planning to move into Colson's sometime but would be leaving all her furniture behind. It would do for now. If I was going to stay in Macon, I would need to find something smaller and more suited to my taste, but it could wait. I was also working on creating friendships, and with Nora back I had the perfect opportunity.

I parked in front of the soon-to-be Community Center a few blocks down from Main Street. Nora and Colson's cars were already against the curb, along with several other work trucks. Nora had been talking about this project nonstop, and now that she was back, she needed all the help she could get. Liam had called to set up a time for me to help with the girls later this afternoon. So, until then, I was filling my time with whatever I could. Incidentally I had also baked three dozen cookies and four different kinds of muffins. Tucked under my arm was a basket full of plastic-wrapped goodies.

"Haley, you're here!" Nora called, smiling as she headed toward me. She had gorgeous curly hair that had two forms: tight spirals or loose spirals. Today they were tight, half tossed up in a bun, while the other half hung down her back. She had big aqua eyes rimmed with dark lashes that looked too long and dark to be natural. I wondered if she'd had them done.

Lifting the basket, I said, "I come bearing gifts!"

"Perfect, you can set those over here. I know all the guys will love them."

We walked over to a large makeshift table where coffee and bagels were set up. The room was spacious, but walls were framed and on the verge of being ready for insulation and dry wall, if my home decor show knowledge was accurate. There were light fixtures and recessed lighting being put in, with ladders set up and men working on threading the wires inside. There were a few saws going off every now and then, and the sound of power tools popping in nails every few seconds or so.

"What can I help with?"

"How do you feel about nail guns?"

I was terrified of them. "I can point and shoot whatever you tell me to."

Nora laughed and then put her arm around my shoulder.

"Let me introduce you to Jeffery. He's one of the foremen, and he'll explain exactly how to use the gun without shooting yourself in the foot or anything."

I laughed softly but inside I was screaming. Shoot myself in the foot? *Ohmyfreakinggosh.*

"Jefferey?" Nora called over to a guy who had on a dark ball cap, a heavy coat, and pair of thick brown work pants. His warm brown eyes lingered a little too long on my chest and curves, but he seemed to shake himself out of it a second later with a slight flush.

"This is Colson's little sister, Haley. She's helping us while she can, so could you put her to work? I figured you guys could work together and she could be your shadow or assistant."

Jefferey's eyes lit up as he smiled. "Yeah, sure."

Nora waved as she left us there in the open room. While several people were milling about, we were the only two in this particular room. He still hadn't said anything, which was making it awkward.

"So…do I just start nailing things, or…?"

His face dipped as he chuckled. "Sorry. Here, I'll show you what we're doing today."

He guided me toward the window. "I'm framing this window, so if you want to hold this"—he picked up a large ruler looking thing that was shaped like an L—"and this." He handed me a drill.

His brown eyes focused on me. "Okay, you tell me when you want to try to drill, or how involved you want to be. I don't want you to be uncomfortable."

I let out a small sigh of relief.

"Thanks. This isn't really within my wheelhouse."

He gave me another warm smile as he began to work. He used the L thing to measure, and made a marking with his thick grease pencil.

"So, what is in your wheelhouse?"

I let out a small nervous laugh. I didn't like talking about what I did for a living. Especially with people I just met. I tried to stick to something a bit easier.

"I like being around kids. I actually just started helping with Liam Croft's kids."

There was a small tingle of pride in my chest at saying it out loud. I had told Colson and Nora that I was going to start working with Liam's kids, but they both seemed more perplexed by it than anything else.

"Wow, Liam Croft?" Jeffery lifted a blond brow.

Under his cap was a shock of golden hair, and a few days' worth of growth covered his square jaw. Objectively he was handsome, but his attitude so far was sort of overshadowing how broad his shoulders looked, or how defined his muscles looked under that jacket.

I nodded, shifting the drill in my palm. It was getting heavy.

"Can I set this down, or—" I looked around for a spot to put it.

Jefferey continued to focus on his project. "Just be careful with Liam…you know he used to be a pretty big deal. He won a ton of titles when he was boxing."

"Why would that mean I'd have to be careful?"

I let the drill hang limp in my hand. Didn't seem safe, but neither did this conversation. Part of me felt protective of Liam. No idea why—the man was a jerk and had been awful to me too many times to count—but it didn't change the fact that I still felt guarded.

"Word just gets around, and according to a few of his past babysitters, he's got a bit of a temper."

I thought back to how he'd yelled at me in the yard. I didn't feel afraid at all, but was it because Colson was there? No, deep down I didn't think he'd hurt me. He wasn't like that.

"Okay, well, thanks for the warning, I guess."

Jefferey peered over his shoulder, and his lips turned down.

"I mean he's a nice guy and all, and I know he gets enough dates and all the women want him, but just be careful."

What the actual fuck was he going on about? I hadn't mentioned how Liam looked or dating or literally anything. He seemed to be drawing a lot of conclusions, and his general know-it-all attitude about a man he didn't seem to have even met was starting to piss me off.

"Hey Jefferey, can you please take this drill? It's getting heavy. And not to be rude, but could you not talk about Liam around me anymore?"

The man in front of me rotated, looking surprised.

"Wait, I didn't mean anything by—"

"I'm sure you didn't, but still. I'm helping him and have to work closely with him, and I just don't love hearing rumors about people before I've had a chance to get to know them."

Jefferey scrutinized me carefully as he took the drill from my hand.

"I'm really sorry, I shouldn't have said all that. I just thought I was doing the right thing if you're going to be working for him, but I wasn't thinking straight. Can I show you how to use the drill? I promise not to be an ass again."

My face warmed. It would be childish to leave just because some idiot said a few things I didn't like.

"Sure." I shifted my feet until I could see how he was lining up.

I flicked my gaze up to Jefferey's face and saw he was already watching me, but he quickly turned away. I caught the smile he tried to hide as he did it. I didn't like how my chest felt, or the way his words had found a way inside there, like an animal burrowing around for food. If I looked carefully at his words, it wasn't so much the insinuation that Liam was dangerous that bugged me. If I had a microscope and stared at this whole conversation closely, it would be the fact that he'd pretty much said that Liam was a player that got to me. I had no frame of reference at all, no reason…other than maybe it was the protective thing.

Maybe I had taken his family and decided they earned my loyalty.

I glanced up at Jefferey again, this time appreciating how his jaw looked against the light filtering in from the window. He'd shed his jacket and now worked in a long thermal shirt, which showed his defined arms and chest.

Fuck.

I couldn't blindly defend the Croft family simply because there was a tiny piece of me that might be attracted to how Liam's eyes seemed to melt when he stared at certain parts of my body. Anyway, it didn't matter. I was just confused by how protective I felt. Surely it would fade.

LIAM DROPPED the girls off at one p.m., and the girls barely said goodbye to their poor dad as they dashed inside my house.

I hated how the feelings from earlier fluttered inside me like a windstorm. I stared at Liam as he stood in the doorway and tried not to notice how he looked in just a simple black hoodie, or how broad his chest was.

These were things I hadn't noticed about Liam until Jefferey warned me away from him. These were things I didn't care about, because Liam was rude.

So why was I looking?

Feeling that flush overwhelm my face, I turned away and ran into the kitchen to quickly grab a muffin from earlier.

"Here, I hope you have a good day," I awkwardly proclaimed, and my hands suddenly shook.

What in the world was wrong with me?

Those silver eyes lowered to my outstretched palm. His strong fingers delicately took the baked good, and while he stood there staring, he scoffed.

"Of course, you bake."

It was like ice cold water doused over my head, taking me right back to the gym when he'd told me I was too delicate to learn self-defense.

Yes, I baked, and it wasn't like I was trying to win any awards. I just liked learning how to do new things, and I had never been given permission to create when I lived with my parents. Now I could do what I wanted.

He turned and left, unwrapping the muffin as he went. I shut the door and tried to shake his comment. It didn't matter.

The girls all finished off their muffins with a glass of milk as I considered what to do with our afternoon. The snow hadn't melted quite yet, but the temperatures had risen, and that, paired with the sunshine… Well, it felt warm outside, but was it safe for the kids to play in? How did parents know if it was safe for their kids to play outside?

Deciding Colson would know, we all bundled up and went on a field trip to his house. Nora was still at the Community Center as far as I knew, but his truck was in his driveway, which meant he was home. I knocked lightly before pushing through the door.

"Uncle Cole!" the girls all shouted in unison.

My brother poked his head around the corner with a carrot stick hanging out of his mouth.

"Girls!" he mouthed around his snack. He hugged each of them but they were gone as soon as he released them.

His thumb jutted over his shoulder, finishing his mouthful. "So, you're serious about this then?"

I shrugged. He and I had become closer over the past week, and with Nora back, it seemed like we'd been together our whole lives and not living in the divide that my parents created.

"You know I think it's cool, right?" he said as he chopped up a few more veggies at a cutting board.

I slid onto one of the stools at the counter, waiting for him to elaborate.

"Liam doesn't have many friends. I mean, I'm basically it. His ex…" He shook his head as he kept his back to me, the sound of chopping filled the space, along with the distant sounds of the girls laughing from the guest room.

"She just did a number on him. He can be rough around the edges, but he's a good guy. Just be careful."

He turned toward me, carrying his trey of veggies. I snuck a green bell pepper strip, giving him the same glare, I had given Jefferey when he'd warned me away from Liam.

"Don't give me that look. I'm just trying to be your big brother and watch out for you. I owe you at least that."

"Then why do I need to be careful? We're just trading services. I help with the girls; he teaches me self-defense. It's a good deal."

Cole's eyes narrowed on the tray in front of us, his jaw flexed as he considered what I said.

"It sounds weird when you say that out loud; try to limit how often you do that."

I rolled my eyes and let out a sigh before grabbing another bell pepper.

"The reason I came over is because I need to know if it's warm enough for the kids to play outside if they wear all their gear?"

He chewed another carrot, narrowing his gaze. His eyes flicked from me to the snack in front of us, like he wanted to say something else, but I really couldn't handle any more warnings about Liam.

"It's just…in California we don't have anything near this cold to compare it to, and I'm just not familiar with what's normal."

Letting out a sigh, he looked up to the ceiling like he was still strug-gling with letting the subject drop. "Yeah…it's safe. They'd probably love it. Twenty and anything lower is usually too cold unless they're geared up real good, but their boots…"

"Yeah, I saw that."

He'd already warned me about Liam, but deep down I knew it had more to do with the fact that Liam looked like he belonged in a thirst trap video versus him just being a jerk.

"Do you think he'd get mad if I…" I trailed off because I wasn't sure if my question would come across as rude.

"Get them new ones?" Colson finished my thought for me.

I nodded. "Yeah...would that piss him off, would I be over stepping?"

My brother turned to grab his water and then faced me again, shrugging.

"I stopped caring what he thought about me spoiling them. I try to stick to foods and comforts or toys, I haven't ever ventured into the needs category. But they need new boots. Plain and simple. If you want them to play outside in the snow, that rubber on the sides can't be split like that."

He was right, and it wasn't my place to judge Liam on providing for his daughters. For all I knew they had new ones but just loved wearing their old ones around. But with me, today, I needed them to have the right gear on or else I'd worry.

"Okay, we're going to head out, go over to the park." I walked toward the guest room and dipped to grab the basket full of toys. "I'm also taking this, but I'll bring it back."

"You better, that shit cost me a small fortune," he yelled after me as I gathered the girls and headed outside. We traipsed back to the house under a blue sky and warm sun.

"Now what?" Maddy asked, glancing around nervously.

"Now we shop."

Mila gasped excitedly. Seraph's eyes got big, and Maddy nodded.

Then we were off.

CHAPTER EIGHT

haley

Blue Skies
Patience
My brother Cole
Fast-acting nail repair
Variety
Tinted Windows
Oversized Sleeping Shirt
Heat
Kindness

WE WERE in some department store that sold chicken coops and troughs on the outside of the building. There were also so many barbeques and so much winter gear, I wasn't sure where to start looking. Men and women who were fitting themselves with thick jackets and fur-lined boots took up the aisles. Camo gear dotted the middle section of the store, tents with green and orange hung from the ceiling, and there were a few dead animals mounted and stuffed on the wall.

None of this was familiar to me, but I was trying to roll with it.

Rolling meant we were tucked away in the kids snow boot aisle with all three girls sliding their feet into shoes.

"Daddy usually takes us to Wal-Mart for boots," Maddy said, wincing as she struggled to pull up the strap of her boot.

There wasn't a Walmart for twelve miles, and I refused to freak Liam out again by taking the girls out of town. But I didn't want to tell Maddy that.

"If you're struggling to put it on then I don't think it's the right one for you. Let's try a different one." I bent down and tugged a different brand and size free.

It was a deep purple color with black rubber along the bottom and white fur inside.

Her eyes widened and lips parted as she gently set it down. I knew she liked it, so I hoped it would fit comfortably.

Sitting on the ground, she pulled her sock up high then gently shoved her foot into the boot with ease. Standing, she walked around and the smile that broke out on her face would be something I tucked away forever.

"They fit!"

I beamed, and then Seraphina jumped up and down in her all-black boots.

"I like these better than the ones Dad got me with the *butterflies* on them."

Seraph didn't seem to like many typical girly things, which was endearing and something I needed to note.

"I want Elsa or Anna on mine," Mila sniffed, standing in a pair that were each on the wrong foot.

"What if we settle for the colors from *Frozen*? These are blue and white."

I handed her the pair I found that had white fur on the inside and light blue coloring on the outside.

With a resigned sigh, she finally accepted them. Once we got the boots, I took the girls to pick out new coats. It was another hour before we finally left.

. . .

"OKAY, girls, where is your favorite park?"

I watched in the rearview mirror for some general directions, or a name. The town wasn't that big; surely there were only a few for them to choose from.

"The one over by the water," Mila yelled from her little car seat in the back.

Maddy was back there, too—begrudgingly. But the visor on my car has all the airbag warnings on it, and it says she should be twelve if she's going to sit in the front. It made me feel better to have her in the back.

"There's one by our school…it's fun in the snow if you have sleds and stuff," Maddy offered, looking out her window.

We didn't have sleds. Did that mean they wouldn't have fun?

"What about you Seraph, do you have one you like?" I inched up to catch her expression in the mirror.

"I like Hayden Park. It has a tower."

Finally, a park with a name that I could locate on my maps. Pulling over for a brief second allowed me the opportunity to pull it up. Thankfully it was just a few blocks away from where we were.

Once we rolled along the curb, I could see why Seraphina liked the park. It sprawled out along the expanse of the large square it was built within. Tall wooden towers and spires mimicked a castle. The girls unbuckled, and I exited to help them get out near the park and away from the road.

"Okay, let's only stay here until you guys get cold."

I was already cold, but they needed fresh air, so I wanted them to have the chance to play.

As we walked toward the center of the park, I noticed a few other cars parked along the opposite end, and near the basketball court were three people talking. Two were smoking. There was a woman who kept laughing while taking a puff in between jokes. It sent a shiver of unease through me, but there were also a few other parents on the playground, their kids laughing and playing in their winter gear.

Maddy held Mila's hand as they crawled up the steps to get to the wiggly bridge. Seraphina had already taken off, running down it at a breakneck speed, and now she was tucked away in one of the towers.

I watched with my arms crossed over my chest. Every move Mila and Maddy made, my gaze tracked and then bounced up to ensure I still had Seraph in my sights. How did parents do this? My brain was in overdrive trying to ensure I didn't lose track of anyone. It was terrifying. After about ten minutes passed, the smoking woman with dirty blonde hair made her way closer to the play equipment. Her eyes bounced around the place like she was looking for someone. That greasy, uneasy feeling intensified.

Taking several steps closer to the stairs, so I was right next to where the girls were, I gauged the woman's movements. When Mila slid down the slide, I relocated around the edge to be there when she finished.

Right as I reached her, I saw that the woman had walked over too.

"Mila, is that you, baby doll?"

My heart suddenly burst into a rapid rhythm in my chest.

Oh my God.

What was I supposed to do? On instinct, I grabbed Mila's hand and guided her back to my side. I had no idea who this woman was, but I'd rather be safe than sorry.

The woman's eyes jumped to me as if it finally registered that I was there.

"Who are you?" she asked, her voice hoarse.

The blue sky that had been overhead all day long was finally starting to fade to a darker color, indicating it might snow again. But the girls' cheeks were rosy, and I felt like we'd had plenty of time here. It was time to go.

Mila tugged on my hand, but I wouldn't let go. I knew the woman had asked me a question, but my brain was still registering the other people in the park and whether she was alone or if someone had traveled behind us.

"Aunt Julie?" Maddy came around the slide, her blue eyes wide in surprise.

"Hey kiddo!" the woman said, pulling Maddy into a side hug.

She had a cigarette dangling from the side of her mouth as she held Maddy there.

Seraph peered over at us from up above in her tower, it was over the slide, so she was looking down. She made eye contact with me, then looked over at the woman, then back at me. When she slowly shook her head back and forth, I knew this wasn't a good idea.

"Hi, I'm Haley, their nanny." I stuck my hand out, but she didn't take it. She held firmly onto Maddy's shoulders.

"Nanny? Damn, that sounds fancy…didn't realize Liam had that sort of money now."

"It's a trade situation…classes for babysitting." I didn't owe this woman anything, but I also didn't want it to seem like Liam had all this money when he was struggling. I didn't know what the situation was with the girl's mother, but my gut told me this woman wasn't Liam's sister.

"Well, your mamma sure misses you girls. You want to go see her? She's just a few blocks away, at my apartment."

Again, my heart hammered against my ribs so quick and hard that spots began to dance in my eyes. I had been afraid before, but this fear… this *terror* over losing someone else's children was unlike anything I had ever experienced.

I stepped forward, pushing Mila behind me and grabbing Maddy's hand. Thankfully she came to me without hesitation.

"We were actually heading out." I glanced up briefly, and Seraph caught my eyes then disappeared. Hopefully that meant she was coming down.

The woman sized me up, her eyes bouncing between my face, my jacket, my gloves.

"You look like you just stepped out of one of them fancy magazines with all your name-brand shit and shiny lips. You must be fucking him. Can't blame you; it's why my sister had such a hard time letting him go."

Oh, fuck.

This was not happening.

I pulled on the girls' tiny hands, towing them away. I wouldn't even deign to answer her because she'd just said all that *in front of Liam's daughters*.

"Hey!" Julie called after us.

Seraph was running toward my car, watching us with apprehension. All I could think was that I wanted her inside, safe and sound. My eyes glanced around for anyone who might be with their aunt, hoping no one else was here. What if their mother showed up? What would I do?

"You can't just walk away from me! That's my family, you bitch!" she screamed, and I started to run.

"Get in the car, quick." I unlocked the doors and fumbled with the handle.

Thankfully Julie wasn't running after us. She was trying to walk quickly but weaving so much she was slow. She might be high or drunk, but she didn't seem to be sure of her footing as she continued to yell and scream obscenities at us. Maddy was shaking, and Mila's face was red as little tears started trailing down her cheeks.

I wanted to throw up. I wanted to scream.

I couldn't do anything but pray that woman didn't try to attack me as I buckled Mila into her car seat.

Once everyone was in the car, I quickly slipped in and locked the doors.

"Are you okay?" I whispered to Maddy, turning to face her in the back. My SUV had heavily tinted windows, so while my car was still there, Julie couldn't see inside.

Maddy nodded but kept her head down.

I looked at Seraph, but she was just staring out the window.

"Can we leave? I'm scared," Mila whined as more tears trailed down her cheeks.

Swallowing the thick lump in my throat, I nodded and turned around.

I drove around for a while, ensuring I wasn't followed by anyone, and then I finally settled in front of Nora's house.

Once we made it inside, I realized Nora was over at my brother's, which was good. The girls were still shaken up. So, I put on a cartoon for them and made some hot cocoa. Once they settled and sipped their drink, and chewed on a few cookies, they seemed to settle down.

It was another fifteen minutes before Liam knocked on the door, and my nerves still felt raw.

Not wanting to upset the girls further, I decided not to get into everything with him right away, but he did need to know what happened. I opened the door with a smile and stepped aside. I had on warm socks and skinny jeans that had cost me upward of one hundred dollars. For some reason the realization made my gut sink. What in the world was I doing watching three little kids? I had no idea what the hell I was doing…this wasn't me.

"Hey, how did it go today?" Liam smiled, walking in toward the girls.

All the fear and terror from the past hour had finally caught up with me and forced my hand out, grabbing onto the back of his shirt. I tugged, not really knowing what I was doing.

He stopped briskly and turned his head. Those gray eyes landed on mine and narrowed in question. I gave him a quick head gesture toward the kitchen. He followed me with his dark brows drawn in close and his eyes full of concern.

Keeping my voice low, I crossed my arms tight.

"We can talk more about this later, but just so you know, there was a woman at the park today. Named Julie…"

Liam's head snapped up. He was on high alert, his body coiled tight and his fists clenched at his sides.

"What happened?" His voice was low and slightly scary.

Shaking my head, I battled the emotions still surging back up. "They're fine."

It was the first thing I could think to tell him because I knew that's where his mind went.

"She started by suggesting they go see their mom a few blocks away, and she hugged Maddy. When I pulled Maddy away from her and started walking away, she got belligerent and started yelling ugly things at us."

He stepped closer, his hand going to my elbow, I wasn't even sure if he knew he was doing it, but his eyes had a warning in them. He didn't like this news. He wasn't happy at all.

"What ugly things?" he asked, deadly quiet.

I blinked back tears, hating how the adrenaline I had felt was like an oil spill inside my chest.

"Just stuff. I said I was their nanny, because I wasn't sure what else to tell her. She said you must have money, and I told her it was a trade for classes. But then—" I trailed off.

I bit down on my bottom lip to hold off the strange emotions clogging my chest.

It was equal parts humiliation and fear swirling around like a tornado.

"What else. What did she say?" His voice softened, his torso brushing my elbows that I had like two bars of steel across my chest.

"She said we must be fucking. Her words."

He blew out a breath, muttering a curse.

"She said that in front of the girls, Liam. All right there. She called me a bitch, which I don't care about, but the poor girls... Mila was crying by the time we got to the car."

"Fuck!" Liam spat, finally turning from me and running a hand through his hair.

I wanted him to explain it to me—tell me what was going on, and why a woman claiming to be family would say such terrible things in front of such small girls—but right as I wished it, Mila ran in with her arms out.

"Daddy! Are we going home?"

He dipped down to pick her up.

"Yeah, baby, we are."

With one last glance in my direction, he headed to his girls and kissed each of them on top of the head. I watched on in awe, wondering what it must feel like to be loved like that. To feel secure and protected, to have someone worry so much over your safety and do anything for you.

Before I knew it, the girls were pulling on their new boots and coats. Liam's jaw tensed as it seemed to dawn on him that I had bought it all for them. He didn't look at me, though, not once.

Even as they left, and the girls all said their goodbyes he didn't say anything to me. I didn't take it personally. Part of me understood this was just how he processed fear...especially fear over his girls. He needed to think, to work out what had happened, then he'd text me or call me and ask follow-up questions if he needed to. Besides, I didn't do anything for him to be angry at me for. We needed to talk about safety and whatever else was going on with his ex, because I didn't ever want a repeat of what happened today.

Once he left, I headed next door. I needed to shed this strange feeling in my heart, like the organ had been shoved into a tin can and someone found a can opener. I wasn't used to feeling like this, terrified over the welfare of these girls, so much so that I would literally do anything to keep them from harm. What the hell sort of bullshit emotions were going on with me today? This wasn't me. I was in control of my life.

Right as I was about to knock on Colson's door, I could hear Nora laughing. It was high- pitched, like Cole was tickling or chasing her or something else equally romantic and ridiculous, but either way, I didn't want to interrupt them. They were still very much in that honeymoon phase I had never once experienced with anyone in my entire life.

I quickly walked back to the house and shut myself into my room.

Working only shoved my thoughts aside for so long. I caught up with Daniel regarding Hush Shoes. Clyde had returned with more vigor than ever, and the product was in the early stages of launching, right on schedule, so there wasn't much more for me to handle on this end.

Baking didn't hold its usual sway or distraction, and no matter what I did, my fingers somehow kept navigating back to Liam's texting thread. Nothing new was ever there, but my mind kept thinking he'd reach out.

Finally, I grabbed my keys, deciding I couldn't stay there any longer.

I wanted a shot of something strong. I wanted to dance, and to let loose, but more than anything, I just didn't want to be alone.

The local bar was likely the last place I should go tonight. The locals didn't like me, and anywhere I went with my car was like waving a red flag in front of a bull. Mix that with alcohol and bad decisions, and it wasn't a great idea.

Still, somehow, I ended up in front of the large warehouse that had faux logs along the outside, creating a cute aesthetic that seemed to fit every other building in town. Iron fire pits blazed, with people gathered around, and long-necked bottles were raised as men and women laughed conversationally.

Women moved their hips, wearing cute denim skirts with tall boots, leather jackets, and fuzzy earmuffs. Music blared from an open garage door, where patrons danced, and a few played pool. I was idling in my SUV against the curb, people watching, when I saw someone waving their hand at me.

Jefferey walked over, wearing a nice button-down shirt under a brown leather jacket. His hat was gone, revealing unruly blond hair that had been swept to the side with product and what seemed like a lot of finger grazing.

I rolled down my window, keeping my heater blasting.

"What are you doin' here?" He smiled wide, revealing straight white teeth.

His palms landed on my door where my window had just slipped under.

"I was thinking about going in." Although with how many people there were, I already knew I wouldn't brave it. I didn't want to be alone, but this wouldn't be a good idea.

Jefferey's smile grew, and a lock of hair fell across his forehead as he dipped his face then focused those brown eyes on me.

"Well, come on then."

My stomach clenched tight. My mind was on Liam and the girls, and no matter how many shots I had tonight, it wouldn't change that. I wanted to know if he was okay.

"I was just checking it out. Maybe another time."

"You sure?" Jefferey's eyes searched my face, silently asking me to change my mind.

Part of me wanted to—the part that wanted not to care about Liam Croft. The part that wanted to heed the warnings about him. The part that didn't want to give in to the strange dips and pricks inside my belly every time those silver eyes landed on me.

But I barely knew Jefferey. We'd spent a few hours together this morning, but that didn't mean I trusted him. Tonight, I needed to feel safe and in control, not anxious and worried about my surroundings.

"Yeah, I'm sure. See you around?"

He shoved off my door and nodded, biting his lip. "Yeah."

I rolled up my window and started to drive. Jefferey watched me the entire time until I was out of sight.

My car headed toward the store almost on its own. I would settle for ice cream and maybe some cheap wine. I was almost there when a text came through over Bluetooth.

Liam:

Can you come over?

I pulled over so fast my tire jumped the curb. I shoved the parking gear up, and then shamelessly grabbed my cell from the console.

Yeah. Now?

He answered immediately.

Yes

I didn't play it cool and wait.
I instantly replied.

On my way…

THERE WAS a set of ropes playing tug of war in my belly as I walked up the few steps to his porch and rapped my knuckles against his door. The entrance looked newer, with fresh pewter paint and a security camera, along with a keypad to access. It was similar to what we had at our house in Malibu.

After a few latches clicked from behind the door, it swung open, and for some reason I wasn't prepared for the gravity of seeing Liam dressed down, barefoot and looking worried. Fear and anger practically vibrated off him in waves as he moved aside to let me in.

I set my things down and shrugged out of my jacket.

"The girls asleep?" I asked quietly, not hearing any sound other than the dishwasher.

"Yeah, they just went down."

I nodded and moved into his living room. It was nice, cozy for such a large space. A sectional took up most of the room, and the couch was so soft it looked like you'd sink right into it. A coffee table rested in the space directly in front of the couch, and a recliner sat on the opposite side of the living room. A large, flat-screen television was mounted on the wall to my right with a tidy little entertainment center below it.

My eyes were up, taking in the stairs that led to the second level and how there was a balcony overlooking the living room. I remembered what he'd said about buying this when he was fighting. It made me curious about that past, and why he stopped.

"Do you, uh...do you want water or anything?" Liam's hand tunneled through that thick, inky black hair. He'd had a shower, from the looks of the wet strands on top of his head, and with the white T-shirt that bunched at his biceps and stretched tightly along his pecs, my mind went back to him being an entire thirst trap. My pulse started racing like crazy, making me feel off kilter, making my voice shake.

"No, I'm okay."

He nodded but his smile fell away as his gaze became distant.

"So, were they okay tonight?" I hedged, pulling at a loose string in the couch.

Liam groaned, stretching. Sculpted muscles that had been trained and harnessed into deliciously thick cords bulged as he pushed his arms out. I thought again about his fights, and how he'd been so good that he'd been called a *legend* in one of those pictures.

"It was a hard night."

Those poor girls. I hated that they were put through that today.

Liam let out a small sigh, resting his elbows on his thighs. He wore a pair of faded, loose jeans, but they molded perfectly to his legs, and just like everything else, made him look hotter than it should.

I wanted to ask more questions, but he was the one who requested me to be here, so there must be something he wanted to discuss. I had to bite my tongue so he wouldn't get derailed.

"Thanks for coming on such short notice," Liam started, his voice raspy and worn.

"Of course," I nodded, bringing my hands together tightly.

Was he going to fire me? I mean, he wasn't even paying me…but he could cancel out on our deal before we even started.

When Liam didn't continue, I decided to ask the question that had been burning in my head since this afternoon.

"Can I ask what the situation is with their mother?"

He seemed to consider my question, his brows caving in and his eyes narrowing on the floor like he wasn't sure how much to share. Normally I'd dismiss my question, knowing it seemed too personal, but after what happened today, I was going to stand my ground.

After a few more tense seconds, he finally relaxed into the couch.

"Their mother is an addict. She wasn't always… We actually had a really good life there for a little while." He shook his head like he was remembering.

"She always had the connection to drugs through her sister and family. Her parents were meth addicts, and her brother and sister fell into that life, but Lacey wanted a different future. At least I thought so. But thinking back on how young we were when we met, I honestly don't know."

His scoff grated along my skin.

I hated it. I wanted to take out his pain, wash his heart clean, stitch it up, and give him something better to have hanging there in his chest.

"I was fighting professionally, making really good money…but I was gone a lot. She started using when I was away for a fight…at least that's what I assume. The first time she'd just passed out on the couch while Seraph and Mila were here. Maddy was in school, but Seraph thought her mom was dead until the fire department got here. Lacey went into a treatment center after that. I paid for the best one. A year later, she was back with us, and things were better. But then I talked about retiring from fighting, and she freaked out. Mila was just a baby, and suddenly she started leaving her with me to go to run random errands that didn't seem to make any sense. She disappeared in the middle of the night from time to time. I was in denial about it. Not after we'd spent so much money on her treatment, and she had worked so hard on herself."

He paused, digging at a loose thread on his jeans.

"She…" He shook his head. "I should have known sooner, we'll just say that. She doesn't have custody, so if she ever tries to take the kids, call the cops. Same goes for her sister or anyone else claiming to be a relative."

His lips thinning the smallest bit told me he was done explaining, and honestly, I was glad for it. This was so far out of my wheelhouse it wasn't even funny, and what happened today had shaken me enough that I just needed a warm bath and a good cry. I knew he didn't want pity, and from the rigid way he held himself on the couch, I knew if I spoke on anything he'd just said, he'd clam up. Being around brothers who didn't really want me around had taught me how to read the "fuck off" vibe when someone gave it.

Lifting off the couch, I gave him a small nod.

"Okay, well, thank you for telling me."

He should have told me before. There should be a sheet or something for all of this. Right? Wasn't that a thing that parents did?

Liam tracked me standing, and those dark brows raised up to his hairline.

"You gotta be somewhere?"

Confused, I just gawked down at him while toying with the hem of my shirt.

"No…it's just you seem to—I just want to respect your boundaries."

Also, I'm so flustered, and entirely confused as to why it feels like you cut my heart open and pulled threading from yours, then started knitting us together.

I wasn't prepared for when his hand shot out and grabbed my wrist, tugging me back down to the couch.

"I wanted to check on you, make sure you were okay after all that went down today."

Our knees were nearly pressed together, and I had to twist my body at an angle to get the smallest amount of distance from him. Whatever soap he decided to use in his shower was noticeable and slightly intoxicating.

"So…you okay?"

Shit, I was spacing out.

"Yeah…" I shrugged my shoulder. "I mean, it scared me. I was worried about the girls. Being in charge of their safety is a new feeling, something I take really seriously. It just…"

My eyes narrowed on his hand, which was still lightly cradling my wrist.

"She can be dangerous…that whole family can. Hell, that whole part of town can be. I'll send you some addresses to a few parks that are safer. But we need to set up our first session. Get you in shape to defend yourself or anyone else."

In shape sounded good. I was fit, but I knew what he meant in regard to defending myself. Fear controlled me in such a way that I practically froze earlier today. I wanted to be able to push through that.

"When is a good time for you to start?"

It was on the tip of my tongue to tell him whatever worked best for him, but something had me forcing out a different reply.

"Tomorrow."

His hand was still on my wrist, and I hated how much I liked it—and not because it was sexual in anyway, but merely because I liked the sense of comfort. I hated how it seemed to settle the jagged nerves in my belly over the whole incident.

"Tomorrow it is. We'll have to meet before the gym opens, you okay with that?"

I nodded, wetting my dry lips. His thumb traced a delicate line down the edge of my thumb.

"Also…" His rough voice trailed up my spine as if he were ghosting the space with his lips. His head turned, his eyes on me…his finger stroked mine and my heart burst into tiny pieces.

"I want you here when you're spending time with the girls. I know Cole is next door at your place, but it will make me feel safer knowing you're here. I have a lot of security measures in place to protect the house."

"Of course." I whispered, my gaze darting to his lips.

Why was my face so hot? My pulse thundered under my skin, and his hand was so warm on mine. I wanted him to stop, but I also wanted him to touch more of me.

"Haley?"

"Hmmm?" Oh shit, had I closed my eyes?

His body shifted, until his fingers gripped my chin and forced my face to lift, making my gaze divert directly to his.

"I think you're bullshitting me about being okay. I think you're rattled and scared, and I think you should stay here on my couch tonight."

My mouth parted with a denial…but I paused. *How did he know?*

But I couldn't stay here. That would be too weird. I blinked and pulled away from his touch. "I can go to Cole's, I'm sure he'll let me stay there."

Liam chuckled and then reached around me, grabbing a pillow.

"Just stay. You're probably going to be here a lot anyway." His gaze dipped to my lips before he added, "You know, for the kids. If I work late, or anything, I would ask you to stay here with them."

"True…"

He adjusted the pillow, his face coming within mere inches of mine.

"So stay. Then when you're feeling ready, head home, grab your workout clothes, and we'll go to the gym."

I should turn him down, but I was so lonely.

Would it really be so terrible to stay the night in a house where other people slept, where I felt safe? He was right; I didn't want to be alone. I hated being alone, and yet so much of my life, it was all I had ever known. I was sick and tired of accepting it, so why should I?

Giving him a tiny smile, I said, "Okay."

"I'll grab you a blanket and a shirt you can sleep in."

I just watched him get up and walk away, as words failed me.

I had no idea what I would even say to him. I knew I should reject his offer, but I didn't want to. I wanted to be selfish. So, when he came back downstairs and handed me a shirt, I walked into the guest bathroom without question and changed. My jeans came off—my wool socks would stay on—but my bra and shirt came off next. My nipples would show through the thin fabric, but if the lights were off, no one would notice. The shirt went to my thighs, with a faded logo of boxing gloves and Croft Gym printed across it.

I flicked the light, grabbed my pile of clothes, and headed back out to the living room. Liam was standing near the side table, his arms crossed over his chest as he stared down at the pile of blankets like he was lost in thought.

There was a tiny lamp on, right next to the couch, offering enough light to see by. The couch had been made up with three pillows, a sheet, and a fluffy down comforter.

"Thank you so much for making this up," I said, setting my clothes at the end of the couch.

Liam's eyes darted up, landing on me. He didn't even try to hide the way he trailed my chest and legs, only to have his eyes bounce back up to my chest. I didn't feel embarrassed or like I should cover up. It was the opposite—and the later it got, the more my inhibitions seemed to loosen. There was a piece of Liam that I wanted, and a part of me was desperate enough to try to grab it.

I wanted his gaze, his touch, his words. I wanted whatever he'd give me, and I knew it was dangerous. It definitely wasn't smart. I knew enough from my therapy sessions that letting my hormones, much less my heart, get attached to someone like Liam wasn't a good idea. He had a fortified fortress around his and his girls' lives. He'd never let me any further, and eventually I'd want my own key to that barbed wire entrance to his heart.

It was a mess in the making.

Still, I was desperate to dabble.

His Adam's apple bobbed as he cleared his throat. I didn't miss how his left hand went to the left side of his crotch, likely to cover the growing bulge there.

"Uh." He cleared his throat. "I'm just upstairs if you need anything."

I nodded, pushing a few loose strands of hair back.

He took a few steps closer, until he was in my space, his breath on my face, and his hands dove under the neck of my shirt, pulling my hair free.

"There, you had some stuck." His voice rumbled nice and low, grating against my skin in the most delicious way. I swallowed thickly and whispered my thanks.

He didn't move right away, and it took all of my strength not to pull him closer.

"Goodnight, Haley."

My eyes were finally on his, my head slightly slanted back.

"Goodnight."

His finger trailed down my arm on his way past me, and then he was jogging up the stairs, leaving me there, flustered and confused.

LIAM

I TAPPED my finger against my leg, watching the stairs.

The sound of the blow dryer was still going as my girls giggled and laughed. Apparently having Haley here when they woke up was the equivalent to Christmas morning. By the time I had come downstairs, she was already dressed in the clothes she'd had on last night. My T-shirt was folded in a nice, neat square, along with all the blankets from the couch last night.

I was exhausted because I didn't get any sleep. Every tiny noise made me jump, thinking it was her—and the fact that I had left my door open meant absolutely nothing. I just wanted to be sure if she needed something she could find me.

I'd be sneaking that shirt into her bag the second she brought one over because it was hers now. The memory of her standing there in my living room, thick socks pulled up to her knees, and that shirt barely hitting her thighs, sliding off her shoulder, would be imprinted on my brain forever. Those perky, full breasts pressing against the fabric had me so fucking hard last night. Around two in the morning, I finally gave in and succumbed to gripping my cock and stroking it as I thought of her.

I sipped my coffee, trying to push those images out of my head. The things I thought last night...the things I wanted to do to her were so wrong. She was so young… And fuck, she'd probably think I was a creep. Although, the way she didn't pull away from me last night made me wonder. *You're twelve years older, asshole. Stop thinking about how soft her skin is, or how her hair would look wrapped around your hand as you fuck her from behind.*

"Girls, you're going to be late for school!" I yelled from my spot at the table. My coffee was cold, and so was the cup I had poured Haley. She had made breakfast—or tried to. The bacon was burned and the eggs undercooked, but the toast was perfect. None of us cared because no one had bothered to cook for us in years. The girls were all dopey smiles and excited giggles. I had explained that Haley might spend the night some nights. For their sake.

"Sorry, they're coming!" Haley called from the top of the stairs, her silky hair swaying as she poked her head over and then ducked back into the bathroom.

My heart did an odd thing, thudding erratically like a wild animal was caught inside, scratching to be freed.

Moments later the blow dryer turned off, and all three of my girls jogged down the steps. Mila had shiny hair that was parted into two symmetrical braids and tied off with pink ribbons. Seraphina had her hair in a perfectly straight ponytail without a single piece of hair out of place, and Maddy had ringlets bouncing against her shoulders as she hustled down the stairs. They didn't look like my girls. They looked like tiny princesses.

"Don't they look amazing?" Haley beamed, walking over to the where I was standing. They slid into their brand-new boots and zipped up those expensive coats, all of which she had purchased for them. It was a mallet to my pride, but somehow seeing Haley smile at them as she helped situate their backpacks and hair eased the sting. She had done this for them. She had made them feel pretty. My girls were beautiful with or without that stuff, but I knew there was something to feeling it—owning that confidence in a way that no one could take it from you.

"Will you be here when we get out of school?" Mila asked Haley.

Haley glanced over at me, the question in her eyes. I nodded, knowing we'd talk about that later. I didn't want her to feel like she *had* to be here, but if she wanted to then she was welcome.

"Yay!" The girls all beamed as we headed outside.

"So, I'll meet you at the gym in like thirty minutes?" Haley asked tentatively, walking toward her SUV.

The girls all piled into my truck as I agreed.

"Yeah, half an hour. Dress in clothes you can move in."

She nodded again and got into her car. I waited for her to pull out, then we took off for school. All the while I hoped I wouldn't make a complete ass out of myself at the first opportunity to be alone with her.

I BEAT Haley to the gym, letting myself in and turning on the overhead lights. It was freezing, so I also turned on the heater, and powered up all the computers. Two of them were on the fritz, same with the scanner I used for membership cards. We pretty much just went with the honor system at this point.

I recalled the conversation I had with Colson after that tense night in the yard where he threatened to break my jaw. Once things had cooled down, he'd come over and we'd talked through the investor meetings I'd had.

"So, you gonna tell me how the meeting went with the investors? Based on how you freaked out on Haley, I'm assuming it didn't go well."

I heaved a sigh and sipped my beer. "They came, they saw the gym, we talked… They don't think I'm a safe bet."

Colson's head popped up.

"What the fuck does that mean?"

I appreciated his incredulous tone, but he was a business major—he knew what it meant.

Still, I shrugged as if to go along with it. "Gym's too far under water. They don't think I could turn it around even with their backing."

"That's bullshit." Cole shook his head, and that look on his face was

why I was so glad to have him. Just to have someone agree with me, even if we both knew it was true, was such a gift. It took me back to all the sore spots in my life, when I felt alone. When I felt like no one else could understand how fucking shitty it was to play out this hand I'd been dealt. Colson may have a silver spoon, but he was always lending it to me and my kids. He was generous and kind. A good man.

"Yeah," I mused, sipping from my water bottle.

"So what then, that's it? They're out and you're back at square one?"

I didn't want to think about closing up my gym, but if I didn't have any financial backers and the bank wouldn't extend or increase my loan, there wasn't going to be another choice.

Colson swiped at his face again, lowering his voice. "So what are you going to do?"

He knew about my past, but he didn't realize how the fear of losing it all really rode me. He wouldn't until he became a father himself. The stress of keeping your family fed, and in clothes that didn't have holes and wouldn't embarrass them in school, it was like a monster on my back all the goddamn time.

"I gotta figure something out... Pathetic, isn't it?" I scoffed, shaking my head.

Colson waited, letting me continue.

"I have all these titles, these pictures of me winning shit. I was someone important at some point in my life, and now I can't even keep my doors open."

Colson let out a heavy sigh next to me. "Shit. That's not pathetic, man, it's just a failed business plan." His eyes swung to me, suddenly alive, like he'd just thought of something. "You know what?"

I waited, leery that he was about to offer a handout. I'd turn it down, and it would strain our friendship. But he knew that. Still, my heart thud wearily in my chest as he seemed to contemplate what he was going to say.

"You should pitch a proposal to Haley."

What?

Even hearing him mention her made those tangled pieces of my heart seem to tug together.

"Why would I pitch to her?" She was my—well, I suppose she was sort of my nanny, and while I knew she was rich, I wasn't about to take her money.

Colson seemed completely energized by this idea, so much so he stood and began pacing.

"Haley just bought Peter's company. Saved my ass, too, so she's now technically my boss, but it's fine. A weird sort of irony if I think about it too hard, but I promised myself I wouldn't. I almost lost Nora because of my pride over it, so I'm just accepting it."

Haley had purchased an entire company?

"She owns several, apparently...she hires people to run them, but if you're looking for a backer, she could be it." Colson finished, all excited like he'd just had the best idea of his life.

My stomach soured.

Even if he was right, and she was in a position to back me financially as an investor, I would never ask her. I couldn't. Not when thoughts of tasting her kept me up at night. Images of how she'd one day spread those beautiful legs for me, and welcome me into that tight—

"So what do you think, you want me to ask her with you?"

God, that made it worse.

I stood, shaking my limbs and getting those images of Haley out of my head.

"I'll think about it."

I WOULDN'T BE STRESSING out over losing my gym if my savings weren't shot to hell because of all the legal fees and the rehab centers. For someone who bailed on her kids as often as she did, Lacey sure made a ton of noise regarding getting any sort of time with them. My lawyer thought it might have something to do with the potential to receive child support if she somehow landed partial or even full-time custody.

After what she did, it should be impossible for her to even have the chance to request it, but according to her lawyer, she's been in rehab and AA meetings. Even got herself a sponsor. I'd be thrilled if I believed it, but I don't. After everything she put us through, I would never underesti-mate her ability to cause chaos again.

I thought back to last night what I had told Haley and felt that souring in my gut. How I hadn't told the entire story of that first time I realized my wife had a problem, and how it was my fault. How I was gone, but I had received a call from the school that Seraph hadn't shown up to daycare. When I tried to call Lacey, she hadn't picked up.

I called the police, asking them to just go check to be sure everything was okay. Apparently, when they got there Seraph was huddled in a corner, crying for God knew how long. She was only three at the time. Mila was one, her diaper soaked, and she had a horrible rash. Her face had been beet red from crying. When I finally pulled them into my arms that night, I broke.

They both were evaluated at the hospital just to be sure there was no lasting damage done.

That was the beginning of the end for us.

I hung in there, doing everything I could to support my wife, help her get better. I was fully signed up for the "in sickness and in health" part of my vows. And then things got worse, a whole hell of a lot worse.

"Hello?"

I blinked, shaking myself of the thoughts.

Haley rounded the front desk wearing a puffy coat and snow boots. Once she shed the layers and stepped out of her boots, her eyes landed on me, and her easy smile nearly floored me.

"Hey," I managed to respond after taking her in.

She wore yoga pants that cut off at her calf, and a cropped T-shirt that showed her sports bra, it left her stomach bare and fuck if it didn't feel like I was in high school again, getting worked up over seeing the smallest patch of smooth skin from the girl I was crushing on.

Was I crushing on her? Fuck, I couldn't be.

"So, did the girls get to school okay? Sorry if I messed with your routine this morning," she said, lowering her duffel bag to the ground. For some strange reason I hoped that bag would be packed full of enough clothes for her to stay at my house again.

I lifted my shoulder, "it was no problem, they enjoyed it and yeah, they got to school fine, got all excited on their way in."

"Oh, good."

I had to get my mind off her and the memory of waking up to her in my house. I had to stop thinking about how perfectly she seemed to fit there.

I grabbed her bag from the floor and then headed in the direction of the floor mats where we'd be working.

The sooner she was out of my gym and away from me, the sooner I could breathe again.

Haley lowered to her haunches and pulled out two pink boxing gloves from her bag and a mouth guard.

"Okay, I came prepared. I even purchased head gear, but I don't want to put it on unless you say I have to because I know I'll look ridiculous."

She was rambling and it was cute as fuck, and the gloves she got seemed tiny. Like her.

"We'll get to those, but we're going to just get the footwork down first."

She stood and gave me a slight nod.

"Come here." I held my hand out and didn't really even mean to, but her hand suddenly landed in mine and it was like all the blood rushing around in my chest quickly shot to my cock.

Her hand was so soft, and me holding it wasn't necessary, but she didn't know that. It was like last night when I grabbed her wrist and trailed my hand over her delicate skin. She never pulled away. It still felt like a firework had exploded in my chest when I thought about it.

It made me wonder what else I might be able to get away with.

"Should I stand here?" She looked down, watching her feet as she positioned them on the mat.

Tugging her hand, I made her shuffle directly in front of me.

"There will be some scenarios in which I'm going to stand behind you and direct some of your movements, so you get the hang of it, okay?"

Her shiny hair was swept up into a ponytail, which made the ends kiss her neck when she dipped her head down.

"So the first thing we need to establish is what you already know?"

I was still standing in front of her, but I'd dropped her hand.

Her green eyes tipped up as she met my stare, then she swiped her tongue across her bottom lip as she seemed to think over my question.

"Um…I picked up a few things on this YouTube video. I know I need to trust my instincts, show confidence, right? I can't remember if that was one of them or not. Um, what else?" Her eyes went to the ceiling.

She snapped her fingers excitedly. "Keep a safe distance…"

"Yeah, those are a great place to start."

She let out small chuckle. "I need to get better at using this stuff. Sometimes I just dive into things headfirst."

I began stretching my arms above my head, curious at her odd statement. "What do you mean?"

"Nothing, it's just last night, before you texted, I was going to go to McGrady's."

I scoffed, not liking the image of her there, drinking…getting hit on.

"You're not old enough."

Her cynicism transitioned into a full-bellied laugh as she began to follow me into a series of stretches.

"Technically not, I suppose, but I have a fake ID and I really needed to be around people last night…or at least not be alone. I didn't go so it doesn't even matter."

I moved my arm in front of me and watched as she did the same. I *had* texted her to come over, but she seemed almost like there was another reason she chose not to go.

"What happened?"

I noticed that her nails had pink on them, hot pink. It was the same color on my girls' nails this morning as they waved goodbye to me.

Her lips tipped down as she focused on the mat.

"There's this guy I met at the Community Center. Jefferey Adkins or Aspen…something like that. Anyway he was nice enough in the center, but he was there last night. He came up to my window, and I rolled it down without thinking and let him get up in my space."

I lifted a brow as a ball of jealousy tightened in my gut.

"What did he want?" I already knew what he wanted.

He wanted what every guy who saw her wanted. *To taste those lips and touch that skin.*

She followed me into a lunge, shoving her foot in front of her. Her little ankle socks were white and looked vibrant against her tanned skin.

"He just wanted me to go in with him. I mean, I insinuated I wanted to go in, and he just offered to go with me. But my point is, regardless that he's totally harmless, I should have considered these self-defense tips I had already looked up and put them to use. I feel like I need a reprogramming session or something."

"How do you know he's harmless?" She was right, Jeffery Akers was harmless.

But I didn't like that he was talking to her outside of a bar at night and was comfortable enough to invite her inside.

"I guess I don't, but while I was home this morning, he swung by with coffee and flowers."

That knot in my gut grew.

I pulled my leg behind me, stretching my quad. "Sounds a little dangerous to me. How did he know where you lived?"

Those beautiful green eyes rolled as she shifted her leg to mirror mine, but her head dipped.

I didn't like that, so I released my leg, and stepped forward. Those eyes were back on me, and she didn't seem to be bothered that I had grabbed her chin, or that we were standing so close.

"Tell me how he knew where you lived."

She searched my face; her fist clutched the hem of my shirt, which made me feel wildly possessive.

"He texted Cole, asking for my number."

There was a roaring in my ears, and it wasn't good.

Why did I care if Jefferey Akers asked for her number or that my best friend gave it to him? Why did it matter that he showed up with coffee and flowers?

I took a few steps back and cleared my throat.

"Okay, well, let's get back to the lesson. You're right, those are all great places to start with self-defense. Your instincts will betray you, so something we're going to work on is sensing tells and when to start getting yourself into a defensible position."

"I think I have pretty good instincts."

She was joking, but I caught the hint of offense underneath her tone.

Remembering that this woman already owned a few companies made me realize it was her professional instincts she was taking offense over. But instead of explaining rationally what I meant, I decided to be an asshole.

"Well, you're dating Jefferey Akers, so…"

I was petty and pissed, and for some shitty reason, I felt like I was in high school again and not thirty-two years old. It was a good thing that she was dating someone else; it would draw a line in the sand between us that I personally needed to be there.

She had been watching her feet again, but when I said that her head snapped up.

Green eyes narrowed on me as her lips thinned into a serious line.

"I'm not dating him. He's a friend. Not even that, he's an acquaintance."

"Coffee and flowers *is* dating, babe." I moved around her until she was following me.

She scoffed, her face flushing all the way down to her neck.

"I'm not. That's not—"

"Can we get on with the lesson?" I gave her a serious look, and I knew she was flustered. So, I decided to take advantage.

She was still fuming when I advanced. It was so quick there was no room for her to do anything. One second, I was across the mat, and the next, my chest was pressed against hers, her wrists cradled between us, and my grip was firm.

Her eyes went wide as her chest heaved.

"Now, your instincts should have told you to stay on the defense. You let down your guard, and I took advantage. Show me how you'd get out of this." My voice was low, and fuck, she was about to feel my hard-on press into her stomach in three seconds, but there was nothing I could do about that now. Her body felt so perfect against mine, and the way she looked up at me, like there wasn't a single chance in the world I would ever hurt her, was addictive.

She twisted her hips, which had her brushing against my shorts.

I couldn't help but groan and lower my face until my forehead pressed into her shoulder.

"That is not going to get you out of someone's hold. It will get you fucked, though, so try something else."

She was breathing harder now. I could feel her tits press against my fingers as I held her hands in place.

She tried to pull away, but by doing so she thrust her hips forward and fuck, I had trained plenty of people without *ever* getting turned on, but I was fully erect now and lacking any self-control.

I let go of one of her wrists and lowered my hands until I was cupping her ass. I pulled her against me, breathing heavily.

"Try again."

She paused, and I thought she'd tell me to stop. I was clearly crossing lines; I was being unprofessional. All she had to do was tell me no and I'd stop, but instead, she rotated her hips again, slow and measured until she was brushing against my cock. This time, I pulled her by the hips and purposely held her there as I ground back.

"Still not free," I growled in her ear, but we both knew this was just a game at this point. She wasn't trying to get free. Fuck, I'd give anything for a wall or a beam to press her against. But I knew if I walked us backward, it would break this spell we were under.

This time she hiked her leg up to wrap around my hip. I instantly caught her thigh and held her there. Then she rubbed herself against me, parting her lips with a gasp.

My fingers tightened, holding her against me so she'd feel every fucking inch of what she was doing to me.

My chest heaved as my hand traveled up into her hair, and the silky strands slipped through. "Haley—" I wasn't even sure what I wanted to say, but I didn't get the chance.

A loud banging came from the front door.

"Yo! Liam!" I could hear Rex yell through the glass.

"Fuck."

I let Haley go, and her eyes closed for a brief second as she seemed to catch her breath.

She walked away toward the bench and took her duffle bag with her. I waited a second until my dick wasn't bulging in my shorts before going to unlock the door. Rex made his way through, complaining about how cold it was outside. The retired Marine was built like a brick wall, all muscle and mass, but he whined worse than my five-year-old. Haley was at one of the heavy bags with her pink gloves fastened to her hands, pounding away in a series of punches.

"How did she make it in before me?" He grabbed a towel, canting his head toward her.

I made a grunting sound, not in the mood to answer him.

"Just get started on your warm-ups."

Rex watched me with a dark brow raised. He glanced again over at Haley once then back at me.

He could draw whatever conclusion he wanted; I didn't have anything to hide. Minus my still slightly erect cock.

"Can you at least play some music?"

"Yes, you miserable fuck. I will put on the music, just give me a second."

I was behind the counter a second later, starting the music on the computer. Van Halen streamed through the overhead speakers.

I returned to the mats, expecting to see Rex warming up, but he was over talking to Haley. She was laughing at something he was saying. He thrust his arm out, showing her how to hit the bag at a more powerful angle. She copied what he showed her, but she didn't hit it with the same velocity, so he stood behind her and gripped her wrist to demonstrate.

There was something about him being near her that I didn't like. I knew he wouldn't hurt her, but it was just that he was standing too close, and he was touching her. It made my skin feel stretched too thin.

"Rex, I'm working with Haley. You head over here and get your warm-ups started."

He turned toward me, lifting that brow again.

Fucker.

"Sorry boss man, just didn't want her to break her wrist."

Haley had enough knowledge about boxing that she wasn't anywhere close to breaking her wrist. His smirk said as much.

"Don't worry about her wrists, or her arms, or anything else attached to her body. Got me?"

He could barely hold back a smile as he passed by me. "Oh, I got you."

He started whistling as he grabbed his jump rope and began warming up.

My gaze swung back to Haley, who was jabbing at the bag with her back to me. She didn't seem to catch what just happened, but if I knew her like I thought I did, she was just letting it go for now. I walked over and hovered near her shoulder, watching as she punched.

After a few combos, she stopped and turned toward me.

"Should we pick up where we left off?"

Her eyes rounded, and I rushed to add, "Self-defense. I thought we could work through a few moves unless you want to keep working the bag."

She watched me suspiciously, likely trying to gauge if I was going to act like nothing happened. I had no intention of doing that, but I made a deal with her to give her lessons, and I was a man of my word.

She nodded and tugged off her gloves, walking back to where we'd been stretching.

This time I led her through a few defensive moves while Rex worked across the gym and others filtered in. I made sure to keep enough distance between us that I didn't get worked up again, and for the last half of the session, I had her working a bag with a few kick combos. Finally, after her timer had gone off and she cooled down with some stretches, she told me she was going to hit the showers.

I gave her a slight nod, keeping my eyes down. The second she was behind the wall that divided the gym from the locker doors, I shifted.

This was a bad idea, but I couldn't seem to stop my feet from moving.

CHAPTER TEN

haley

Fast Dry Nail Polish
Glittering Snow
Heavy Bags
Boxing
Liam's Eyes
Privacy

I SHOULD HAVE JUST SHOWERED at Nora's, but I was in worse physical shape than I had originally thought. That workout had kicked my ass. Sweat dripped down my spine, coated my forehead, and made my neck slick. I needed to rinse off before I did anything else, and since I had brought extra clothes, it didn't seem like a big deal to check out the locker room.

The setup was interesting.

The women's locker room was within view of the main gym just slightly, but there was a small wall you had to walk behind to get to it. Since I hadn't seen a single woman in the two times I had been here, I was fairly confident that I would have the room to myself. Sure enough, the space was empty, the showers dry as if no one had been in. I set my duffel down on the bench and stripped out of my shirt and leggings, pulling off my socks and replacing them with shower shoes.

I was bent over, digging out my small toiletries bag, when I felt two hands skim over the globes of my ass. Then the air whooshed out of me as I was pulled against a firm chest, and hot air hit my ear.

"I shouldn't be in here."

Liam.

Lifting my hand, I wrapped it around his neck so that I was flush against his chest. My eyes fluttered closed as his strong fingers moved over my stomach and down along my hips. He touched the strap along my hip until he dipped under, the pad of his finger rubbing the sensitive skin there.

"Fuck," He whispered harshly against my throat as he spun me and pushed me up against the row of lockers.

Those silver eyes held something in them I had never seen before on another man—at least not on one that had ever looked at me. There were unspoken words, confessions, and the hint of something dangerous. Like he was ready to claim and own things he had no business considering. Like me, or my heart.

But he was holding back, and that was probably good because we weren't thinking clearly. We were worked up. He'd already said he shouldn't be here.

Caging me in, his hands moved from the row of lockers behind me. Searching my face, he waited, his face impossibly close, until he lifted his right hand and cradled my jaw. Indecision stalled his fingers on my jaw and had his eyes flitting over my face, so wary and unsure that I nearly pulled away. But then his lips were on mine, soft and tentative, like he was giving me a chance to stop it. I threaded my fingers through the hair at the base of his neck and tilted my head to the side to force our connection deeper. I wanted more of him, and on the surface, I understood how stupid of an idea it was, but still, I craved him just the same.

He let out a guttural sound that felt rough and tortured, which had him moving closer. A rough palm landed on my ass, sliding over the cheek until he gripped the back of my thigh and lifted. My other leg followed suit until I was completely wrapped around him. Pulling me away from the lockers, he walked with me, marking my neck with open-mouthed kisses, his tongue working along my pulse at my throat and then he was going lower, kissing along my cleavage.

"Liam," I breathed, needing more.

Needing a bigger piece of him to keep inside so no one would ever see.

Pulling back to see me, his chest heaved as he searched my face. His mouth parted, like he was about to say something, when there was a loud shout from the door of the locker room.

"Haley, you in here?"

My eyes went wide as I processed that my brother was calling for me. Liam's mirrored mine, but then his expression shuttered as he muttered a curse. I wanted to tell him to keep me against him, to not let me go. We could hide in here. No one would know. I needed more of his kisses, his touch. I wanted to know what he was about to say. But none of that was going to happen. His arms loosened around me, and I gently slid down his frame until my feet were back on the ground.

Suddenly cold, I crossed my arms and stepped back. Then, remembering Cole, I yelled back.

"Yeah, almost done!"

Liam ran a hand through his hair, skewing it as he paced the floor.

There was another echoing yell from the entrance. "No rush, but Jeffery Akers texted, asking if you were free this afternoon to help down at the Community Center. He said you weren't answering your texts, and I guess he was worried. I remembered Liam saying you would be here…"

My face flushed.

Liam's jaw clenched tight, and I wanted the floor to swallow me up.

"Can we talk about it when I get out?" I yelled back.

Colson replied with something vague and then it was quiet in the locker room again.

I stared at the floor, unsure how to move forward from the awkwardness of what had just happened. I wanted to go back in time, back to when I had Liam's gunmetal eyes on mine. Back to when he touched me.

He wasn't looking at me, but the muscle in his jaw hadn't stopped jumping, whatever that meant. Without any words, the silence stretched and ate up all the space, scorching all the possibilities of might have come out of this.

I didn't want to wait anymore, so I moved. Walking past him, I grabbed my duffel and pulled out my clean clothes—a tank top and shorts. Right, this had been my gym bag that I used in California, where it was warm. It was going to suck walking to the car.

I pulled on the shorts, ignoring the tall giant at my back who was still smoldering, hands on his hips, chest moving up and down in silence. I stood there, watching out of the corner of my eye as he glanced over once, twice…a third time.

I had one foot up on the bench, about to tie my shoe, when he finally sat on the bench next to me and tugged my foot into his lap.

I stood, watching as he took over tying my laces. His chin dipped to his chest as he gently held my ankle, then he set it down and reached for my other foot.

I was being stubborn.

If he wanted my foot then he could give me a few words. I waited; he didn't move.

Finally, his head tipped back, his eyes landed on me, and my heart lurched.

"Give me your foot."

For some stupid reason, my eyes nearly watered. There was something in his gaze that I wanted to hold onto, but it was still so guarded that I knew I wouldn't. I needed something sure. I hated that I was wired this way. I couldn't do casual, not with the way our arrangement had been set up. I hated that I wanted him, that my stupid heart had chosen him, of all people, to be obsessed with. He was my estranged brother's best friend, my trainer, my boss—in a strange way—and twelve years older than me. All the flags waving in my face were red, and yet, I couldn't help but to brush them aside for one more glance at his wide jaw and blazing silver eyes.

I knew deep down that this response was dangerous. It was a silent scream, and echo in an empty room. A yawning opening in my chest, a cavity created for this feeling that had begun to unfurl from the moment Liam touched me this afternoon. Like smelling something sweet then finally tasting it on your tongue, and the realization that your senses hadn't led you astray.

"What are we doing, Liam?"

His hand moved up, along the back of my thigh.

The light from the tall windows above the lockers shone in; the safety lights had turned off from lack of movement and he just sat there in front of me looking like the legend they spoke of, but my stupid heart reached with greedy hands and tugged the expression on his face in and decided it was mine now.

"We're getting your shoe on and then we're going to talk about you walking the girls home from the bus this afternoon. Then, if you want, once the girls go to bed, we can talk about if you want to sleep on the couch again, or in my bed."

The wings fluttering in my chest took a nosedive and swooped into my belly, they must have caught fire first because now it burned. It hurt. I could *feel* that Liam regretted this. I didn't like being around people when my gut told me they didn't want me. Liam might sexually be attracted to me, but this whatever it was—it was too much for him. I knew in the deepest parts of me, I knew. I just needed to leave, to clear my head.

So, I lifted my other foot and watched in silence as Liam gently held my shoe, tying the laces nice and tight. Once he was done, he set it down and looked up at me again. I took the opportunity to step back and cross my arms over my chest. I had no idea why I was acting like this, except that this feeling in my gut that wouldn't go away.

He stood, and then his fingers were gently griping my chin, forcing my eyes on his.

"We'll talk later?"

I nodded, and then he was gone, walking out of the locker room. I had no idea if Colson would see him or not, but my mind played back the way he let me go and turned away when my brother had interrupted us, and how those eyes seemed to find their way back to me as soon as he mentioned Jeffery. I wasn't an idiot; that's what had spurred Liam on earlier too.

I was young, but I was old enough to recognize jealousy when I saw it, and I wasn't going to be playing any games where the guy I was developing feelings for seemed to respond to me only when another guy was in the picture. I made a deal with Liam, and I had every intention of sticking to it, but I would do so with my heart intact. To do that, I'd have to stop whatever this was and make sure it didn't happen again.

I DROVE TO NORA'S, only to find that once again she wasn't home. Honestly, it was a reprieve. It gave me a chance to shower and carefully tuck my emotions away. Once I was done, I caught up on work, and then finally decided to text Jefferey back. I didn't want to lead him on if he liked me, but I wasn't going to not talk to him either. We could be friends, and it was nice to know more than just my brother, Nora, and Liam in this town.

> Me: Sorry, I was busy earlier. Did you still need help at the Center?

He responded about fifteen minutes later.

> Jefferey:
>
> If you have the time, but it's not big deal if you're busy.

I deliberated, still feeling like I was doing something wrong by agreeing to help him, but I had to shake the idea. Jefferey wasn't even really a friend yet, just a nice guy who seemed to care if I was offended by his actions and liked to follow up with flowers and coffee if he messed up.

Me: Yeah, I have some time before I have to
pick up the girls. How about I come by in about
twenty minutes?

Jefferey:

Sounds good

I had dressed for the day, drying my hair then slightly curling the ends. I put on jeans and a hoodie, then slipped my snow boots on before heading out.

Once I pulled up to the Community Center, it looked like there were only a few trucks parked along the curb, including Nora's and her best friend, Rae's. I was just getting to know both Nora and Rae, but from what I gathered, they were just a few years older than me and had been friends since they were little. Rae was the one who'd been put in charge of the Community Center, and Nora was in charge of designing it.

Pushing through the door, I immediately found Nora with her arms full of what looked like samples of some kind. Rae held a clipboard and was pointing at things with a pen in her hand.

"Haley!" Nora said, walking over.

I eyed her full arms. "Hey, do you want any help with that?"

Rae walked over and rolled her eyes. "She's being dramatic and stubborn."

Nora's best friend had long, dark hair that was currently being hidden by a cute, forest green ball cap that had a mountain peak on it, with a circle around it. The words *Mount Macon* were printed within the circle. It was cute.

"Hey, Rae, where did you get that hat?" I asked, walking forward with them, until Nora released her load of samples onto a table.

Rae smiled at me. "This is going to be featured in Davis's new shop. The grand opening is next week, will you be there?"

I had met Davis when I first arrived. He was Rae's fiancé and the town grump from what I had gathered. He'd always been nice to me, but I had learned that not everyone was used to seeing him around so often.

"She will absolutely be there; she's helping us set up," Nora said as she picked through the samples. Rae and I watched her until she noticed us.

"Sorry, I hope you don't mind being a part of our little group. It's sort of out of your control. We like you, so you're with us, whatever we do."

Rae chimed in with a lift of her shoulder. "It's true."

My eyes felt a little watery, but I pushed it back and just smiled.

"I'm in, and I'll absolutely be there to help you set up."

Nora skirted the table. "Maybe we can do a little planning session, first? Haley needs to see your house anyway, Rae."

"Yes, a thousand percent yes!" Rae said, smiling at me, "We need to do margaritas!"

"Awesome, let's plan on this weekend." We were talking about the plans when Jefferey wandered out of one of the classrooms that was being renovated. His golden hair was covered by a backward facing hat and his thick brown coat was replaced by a dark hoodie, but it had white smudges from paint, same with his jeans and boots.

"Hey, you made it," he said warily, eyeing the two women beside me. He was probably wondering why I was over here talking when I had agreed to come and help him.

Nora and Rae both stopped talking and swung their gazes to Jefferey and back to me.

"Yeah, I was just catching up with them, but I'm here to help."

He gave me a warm smile and lifted the hammer in his hand.

"Perfect, I could use your help holding some of these boards in place while I drill, and then I can teach you how to hammer if you want."

Rae bit her lip, watching the two of us. I knew what they were thinking, but for some reason my face still heated like I was a teenager caught flirting. I had to cut this off, so I walked away from their table and followed Jefferey into the room.

We worked side by side in the chilly room. The window was covered in some kind of industrial plastic, but the winter air still made it through the cracks.

"So, you were busy this morning?" Jefferey asked, looking over his shoulder.

I gripped the wood he'd indicated for me to hold in place, keeping my eyes on the line he'd drawn with his pencil.

"Yeah, I was training with Liam at his gym." I would never be that girl who lied to people just to make them feel better. I had no reason to. I owed Jefferey nothing.

His hum and the gruff way he pushed the nail gun against the cut made me wonder if that response hit wrong, but I brushed it off. It wasn't my problem, even if it did.

We stood in silence for a few more minutes while he worked his way down the wood, the sound of the air compressor going off every now and then, in between the sound of the punch of the gun.

Jefferey's long legs ate up the space of the room as he walked down it, and I tried to keep up.

"So, you almost came into McGrady's last night…" He trailed off, giving me a lopsided smile.

I nodded, giving him a small laugh. "People don't really like me around here because of my California plates, but even without those, most people here seem to know where I'm from."

A grunt came from my side as he continued to work.

"Well, only way to get past that is to show that you don't care."

That was true, except I did care.

"Want to come out tomorrow, try it out?" His brown gaze shifted over to catch mine.

My chest did a little panicked squeeze. I didn't want to lead him on, but I also didn't want to ruin it by assuming that's what he wanted. This was just going out with one of my friends…maybe I could see if Nora or Rae wanted to go too.

"What time were you thinking?" I asked, keeping my eyes forward.

Our first row was done, so he twisted and grabbed another board.

"Maybe nine…that's when things get fun over there, but it's really up to you."

Bending at the waist, I dipped to pick up the scraps from the cut he'd made with his table saw, just for something to do.

"How about eight? That way it's not so packed, and I won't be tempted to bail."

He gave me a wide smile and nodded. "Eight, can I pick you up, or…?"

"I'll meet you there. I have to help at Liam's for a bit before I go."

I turned so I didn't have to see his response to that because it didn't matter. I had made a deal with Liam to help him, and I'd honor that regardless of whatever confusing shit had happened between us. In the meantime, I was making my own friends, and I was going to have fun.

CHAPTER ELEVEN

haley

Cute Kids Sized Drinks
Dreaming about the Future
Boy short underwear for platonic reasons
New Friends
Baking
Ignoring Red Flags
Orgasms

I HELD a cardboard drink carrier in my hand when the yellow school bus stopped by the row of mailboxes a block down from Liam's house. I watched as all the little kids hopped off and ran to waiting parents who readily pulled them into hugs. It made something ping in my chest, as if a light suddenly shone on something I had never dared desire. Seeing them all the smiles and cute little faces… Yeah, I could definitely see myself as a mom someday.

It was the first time I had ever really considered it, but for whatever reason, it was imprinted on my mind now. Like a little picture pinned to my dream board.

Maybe I could settle down with a guy like Jefferey. Objectively, he was handsome. Suddenly I imagined what that would be like. Growing to like him…eventually learning to love him. We could have a family and be happy like these other families seemed to be. But that scenario suddenly flipped, to where I'd always know that across town lived Liam, Maddy, Mila, and Seraphina. Suddenly that ping in my chest turned into a tight squeeze.

"Haley!" Maddy called, stepping off the bus. She waited for Mila to come next and held her hand, leading her away from the bus. Seraphina came after, and all three girls walked over to me. I knelt and pulled them each into a snug hug.

"Here, I got us mochas." They were more like milkshakes, made with chocolate instead of any coffee, but the cute, kid-sized cups made it look like they were drinking coffee.

"Yay!" Mila squealed, reaching for hers.

I plucked each drink out of the holder and handed it to each girl.

We walked in easy conversation while the sun shone brightly down on us. The weather had started to warm up, which was such a nice reprieve. It was still the first part of January, but the sun felt nice, and seeing all the melting snow made me think spring might be on the way.

"Are you going to pick us up every day?" Maddy asked as we crossed the street and headed into their driveway.

I focused on entering the code Liam had given me and then opened the door.

"I'm not sure yet. This is still something we're trying out, but I would like to," I said, shutting and locking the door.

The girls all dropped their things in the entryway, jackets on the ground, boots all tossed chaotically, and backpacks dropped randomly. We'd done this yesterday too, where I walked them home from the bus and then came inside, only to have them drop everything.

"Ladies," I called, staying in the entryway.

They all turned toward me. I tucked my boots under the bench, and hung up my coat on the wall hook, all while raising my brow, hoping they would catch on. Maddy moved first. She picked up her backpack and hung it, then her coat, and put away her boots.

I smiled, watching as the other two fell into line next, copying their older sister.

"Can we have a snack?" Mila asked, tipping those big blue eyes up to me. Her hair had come loose from this morning, but it was still so adorably perfect.

"Yes, I went and picked up a few things from the store."

I realized yesterday that they had only a few things to snack on, and since I finally had a reason to splurge on kids' snacks, I went a little crazy. Yesterday was a great test to see how things would go. I chickened out on making dinner and instead chose to leave the second Liam came home, but today he'd already texted, asking if I would stay to talk to him. I think he knew I was trying to dodge him. I kept our text conversations professional and short, and all the while my stomach flipped when his name popped up on my phone. I knew I would have to see him when he came home, but I had a plan. I would stay to talk, but I would let him out of this strange dilemma we'd found ourselves in, where we'd kissed and now he felt obligated to act interested in me.

I put out the apple sauce packets and string cheese, along with three tiny water bottles, while each girl grabbed a seat and began to fill me on their days. Each girl had so much to say— and so much to tell me—it was a little overwhelming trying to keep up.

"Jessa Anderson is just always acting so cool; she took my spot in the game during P.E. today, and I can't believe Mr. Monson allowed it." Maddy was still going on about the girl she didn't like.

Seraph was quiet, looking out the window—slowly eating her cheese, pulling one string at a time.

"How about you Seraph, how was your day?"

Her eyes swung to me, a blank expression on her face.

"Fine, we had free reading time today. I liked that even if I'm not the best reader yet."

"Want me to do any reading with you?" I offered, working on the chicken marinating in the glass pan. I had bought dinner ingredients, too, but I already had it in my head that I wouldn't be staying to eat it.

Seraph gave me a small smile with a flushed face. "Sure."

The rest of the afternoon went by easily as the girls did reading, relaxed, and played Minecraft. Seraph doodled in her journal, and Maddy did math homework. I ventured upstairs and helped Mila clean her room and organize her things, until eventually she brought out a huge plastic tub of Barbies and emptied it the living room. She played while I finished up with dinner. Soon we all heard the garage door opening, and I peeked out the curtains to see a big black truck crawling inside it.

Their dad entered the house through the attached garage door in the laundry room.

"Daddy!" the girls all yelled in unison, jumping up to run to him.

I stepped out of the kitchen with an apron tied around my waist, watching as each girl wrapped their arms around their dad's waist. His head dipped, watching them all as they rattled on and on about their days, and what they had been doing since school ended.

I loved watching them interact with him, and then he stepped forward with Mila's toes on top of his, and those gray eyes were on me. His heated gaze took in my face, my chest, down to the apron at my hips and my sock-covered toes. Fire invaded my chest as I watched him draw closer, and I couldn't help but feel like I needed to fidget or move, so I ducked back into the kitchen, severing the connection.

It was too much.

Especially after the locker room.

A few moments later, Liam entered the kitchen, holding Mila in his arms as she continued to talk about her day.

"Smells good in here," he said, giving me an earnest smile.

I nodded, pulling the glass dish from the oven.

"I found this recipe and thought maybe it would be nice to try."

He let Mila down, and she dashed out of the room, leaving us all alone.

"I made some steamed veggies and rolls too." My eyes stayed on the meal in front of me when I felt him at my back.

His lips came to my ear, whispering.

"You know you don't have to do this, right? I don't expect you to cook and clean. This deal wasn't about that."

His words rushed through me like cold river water.

Deal.

I moved down the length of the counter to get free of him.

"I know, but I like cooking. It's no problem."

I evaded him by opening the fridge. As soon as I tugged out the jam, he pulled on the loop of my jeans until he had me against him.

"You're being weird."

His voice came out like a harsh whisper against my ear. My heart thrashed like a trapped animal in my chest, my pulse jumping against my throat.

I placed my palms on his chest and pushed.

"The girls…" My voice came out in a rushed whisper.

His gray eyes searched my face, his fingers tugging on my jeans so that my waist was trapped against his.

"They're outside right now, in the backyard."

They were? I hadn't even noticed they'd gone out. He stepped forward, his fingers still looped through my jeans, so I moved back until my butt hit the counter.

His forehead pressed against mine as my breathing began to come out slow and labored.

"You're staying tonight."

He didn't ask it, just stated it like it was a fact.

Tipping my head back, I opened my mouth to respond but the back door opened, and Mila started yelling.

"I have to pee, but my boots have mud on them! Daddy, hurry!"

Liam grinned and ran out of the kitchen.

I could finally breathe, and even though my fingers shook, I began to set the table and prepare the food. The rolls were perfectly browned and glistened as I brushed them with melted butter. The veggies smelled incredible, and the chicken made my mouth water.

The kids had all made their way inside. I heard Liam tell them to wash their hands, and then all four of them were in the kitchen pulling out chairs and settling in.

"This smells so good," Mila declared to the room as she stood up on her knees in her seat. Seraph nodded, grabbing a roll. I took my apron off and folded it.

"Okay, I'm going to get going, you guys enjoy dinner."

Liam's gaze snapped up, as did Maddy's, almost at the same time.

"You're not eating with us?" Mila asked, tilting her head to the side.

The chair slid out across from where Liam sat, his foot pushing it from under the table.

"Sure she is."

All their eyes were on me, waiting.

Fuck it.

I took a seat, and Liam stole my plate and began piling chicken and veggies on to it. Maddy handed me a roll, and we all started eating. Mila launched into a story about a cartoon show, and Seraphina jumped in, adding her two cents. Maddy was quiet most the time then opened up about her school day and a field trip that would be coming up.

"Have you heard about the grand opening for Davis Brenton's shop?" I asked the table, but it was obviously mostly for Liam. His jaw clenched as he chewed and then his eyes moved up, meeting mine.

"Can we go?" Mila asked excitedly.

I smiled at her and the other two. "I was going to help Nora and Rae get it ready, and I was going to see if you three would be my helpers."

"Yes, we will!" they all said in unison. Liam smiled and gave a soft laugh.

"Guess we're going then."

The rest of the meal was full of little jokes and laughter. I found myself relaxing into the seat, my face hurting from smiling so much and my stomach aching from laughing. Mila kept counting to one hundred over and over, and Maddy tried to block her out by explaining some playground drama that had taken place a few days ago. Seraph had a black pen in her palm, and while she ate, she doodled on her napkin.

Once the kids were done eating, they all worked together to take plates to the sink, and Maddy found containers for the leftovers.

I stood side by side with her as she packed away the food and I rinsed the dishes. "You're pretty good at keeping all this together, huh?" Liam was at the dishwasher loading them while Seraphina wiped down the table and Mila helped her dad.

"Yeah, we sort of got used to just doing a little extra if we can." Maddy blushed, snapping the lid shut.

"Thank you for dinner, Haley," Seraphina sweetly said, shaking the rag out in the sink.

My heart grew. There was no other explanation for why it felt like someone had pried my chest open and tugged the organ out and squeezed.

"Of course."

Mila walked over and wrapped her arms around my waist. "Will you be here every night to eat with us?"

"Mila," Liam warned her, but I waved him off.

Returning her hug, I softly replied. "For as many nights as I can, but I might miss a few, which is okay. I don't live here. I'm just hanging out and spending time with you guys."

Maddy gave me a little glare, but it went away just as quickly as it brushed across her soft features.

The girls filed out, heading upstairs to play with their toys, and I realized this was when I needed to leave.

Liam chose the moment to tug my hand until I followed him into the small office below the stairs. It was all wide windows, facing the backyard. A nice oak desk sat in the middle of the room, but all along his walls were pictures of him boxing, a large belt with a gold plate in the center was encased in glass, and on the bookshelf were dozens more trophies, pictures of the ref holding his hand up in victory, a large crowd in the arena, surrounding the ring he boxed in. Seeing it made my stomach swoop and my heart swell with pride.

"Wow, this is—"

Liam perched on the edge of the desk, watching me. "My past."

I held my elbows and moved down the wall.

"Would you ever go back?"

Liam's jaw flexed as he looked down. "It would depend on what's going on in my life. Right now, with the girls, that sort of life would be impossible."

"Was it hard on you?"

He seemed to consider the question, tilting his head to the side. He had on a pair of gray sweats, white socks on his feet and a thin, black T-shirt. I loved how comfortable he seemed, and I also hated it because all I wanted to do was pull his hand and have him cuddle me on the little couch tucked against the far wall.

"You get used to the bruising. It's shitty, the feeling after. It takes a few days to get better, and it's dangerous. Getting hit like that is risky. But I was good at it. After I became a dad it wasn't as enjoyable. And it's an impossible schedule to keep as a single parent."

For some reason my chest heated at hearing him say that. Mostly because the idea of him single made my stomach hurt. I knew he dated, and it was only a matter of time before he found a new woman to settle down with. A mother for the girls. Someone to hold at night while they all slept in this house together. Someone else who would cook them dinner and then clean it all up together like a family.

"So, we gonna talk?" Liam must have taken my somber attitude for a desire to change the subject.

"I don't know that we need to," I murmured quietly, my stomach twisted in knots.

He moved, pulled my hand until I was in front of him, standing in between his legs.

"The girls," I softly warned, but he made some sound of frustration.

"Would it be that horrible for them to see?"

My eyes snapped up to his.

"Yes. It would confuse them."

His lips were so close, and he smelled so good. Like heady pine, and whatever the fuck they put in Old Spice to make it so mouthwatering.

"Only if there's something to be confused about."

I pulled away from him, feeling annoyed.

"*I'm* confused, so I know they absolutely would be."

"I like you," he confessed, thinning his lips, silver eyes bright from the recessed lighting above us. The sky was getting dark outside as time slipped by, and the girls thumped around in the room above us.

His finger trailed over the midriff at my waist, and I sucked in a harsh breath.

"I like you too, but we have this arrangement…and we don't know each other that well."

Liam's jaw flexed. "What do you want to know?"

"It's not that simple. I just want to be careful."

His face slipped, lowering so that his eyes were on the floor, and for some reason I wanted to pull his chin up, like he always did with me.

All too soon the kids were running down the stairs and I stepped back a few feet, so we had distance between us.

"Daddy, we're going to build in a new world in *Minecraft*, and you're the fourth controller!" Mila called, running into the room.

Her eyes shifted to me. "Actually, Haley, you can do it, but only if you know how to build good. Daddy makes the best horse stalls for us."

I wanted to stay and just watch all four of them as they worked on whatever world they were talking about. I'd be happy to sit on the couch and observe, just be a part of whatever they were doing. But I had to create some separation, or this would get too complicated.

"That's okay. I have to actually head out." I lowered my head to avoid Liam's gaze.

On my way to the front door, he trailed me. Hands shoved into the pockets of his sweats, he kept his gaze lowered while I pulled on my boots and grabbed my coat.

Then he asked, "You headed home?"

Shit. I didn't want to tell him, but I wasn't about to create drama by lying, and I owed him the decency of being candid.

My chin was to my chest as I zipped my coat and muttered, "Actually, I'm headed to McGrady's."

"What?" Liam's voice came out sharp with a touch of surprise.

"Yeah, um…" I shrugged my shoulder, "Jeffery asked me to go with him, as a friend."

Liam's expression was guarded, but those eyes had flames dancing inside. His jaw tensed, lips turned down, and the rigid way he stood there spoke everything he wasn't saying with words.

"So me telling you that I like you—that doesn't mean anything to you?" he asked quietly.

It meant too much. More than I knew how to handle.

"Of course it does, but I'm not going romantically with Jeffery. We're friends."

Liam scoffed with a clench of his jaw.

"I guarantee you he isn't thinking *friendly* thoughts about you, Haley."

Why did I feel like my chest was on fire? Why did Liam look like someone had just stolen something from him? There was an edge to his gleaming eyes and coiled muscles.

I tried to keep my voice calm as I said, "You can't know that. It's just one night out. I'll see you tomorrow morning at the gym."

I turned toward the door, only to spin back just as quickly.

"I think I'll come by closer to when it opens, that way we don't have a repeat of yesterday."

His brows arched into his hair line as he shook his head with a scoff.

"Fine by me. Being open didn't stop me from nearly fucking you in the shower today."

Oh my gosh.

Heat unfurled in my stomach, low and deep in the same place that was desperate for his touch in that locker room. I spun away so he wouldn't see his effect on me, but I caught his laugh as the door swung shut.

12

LIAM

"HOW COME we're going to Uncle Cole's again?" Maddy asked as I drove out of the neighborhood. Mila and Seraph were holding onto their stuffed animals, wearing their pajamas, all ready for a sleepover.

I looked over at my ten-year-old and then glanced back at the road. "Because I have a late meeting."

"How come you're not wearing your suit?"

I gripped the steering wheel a little tighter, forgetting how observant my kid always was.

"It's a different kind of meeting."

She watched the windshield for a few more silent seconds before she asked, "Does it have to do with Haley?"

My head swung, probably too fast. "Why would you think that?"

She lifted her slender shoulder, keeping her eyes on the road.

"I don't know, I was just wondering. She's been around a lot lately, and you look at her differently."

I flicked the turn signal for Cole's street. "How do I look at her?"

"You smile more, and even when she isn't looking at you, you're watching her. I hoped it meant you liked her."

The irony of this entire fucking conversation.

I tucked away the sigh that sagged heavily in my chest. "Even if I did, wouldn't mean that she liked me back."

Glancing once more over at my kid, I noticed she tucked her body against the door and pushed her fist under her jaw. That was what she did when she was getting frustrated or feeling too much. I didn't want her to get hurt from all this. Maybe Haley was right. We had to be careful with them.

I pulled up in front of Colson's house and put the truck in park. Once we all filed out and were up the stairs, Nora answered the door with a huge smile and eagerly hugged the girls.

"I'm so excited you guys are sleeping over! I set up the whole room for you, and I thought we could play a board game before you go to bed."

She trailed off as the girls followed her into the living room.

I stayed in the entryway, being stared down by my best friend. Colson's arms were crossed over his chest as his gaze tightened on me.

"Where are you going?"

I shrugged. "A date."

"A date that requires your kids to sleep over?" His blond brow raised as if he was trying to catch me in a lie.

"What do you want me to say, Cole? It's been a while. Can't a guy try to get his needs met?" I lied, hoping he didn't notice.

He shifted on his feet, peering over his shoulder before stepping closer.

"And your needs have to be met on a random weeknight?"

If I didn't know better, I'd think he knew about my little plan. I glared, bringing my hand up to rub my jaw.

He took the opportunity to press me further.

"Where is Haley tonight?"

Hearing her name was a quick rush of adrenaline. Why was he asking about her?

"Why would you assume I'd know?"

He stepped nearer, his eyes narrowing in concern.

"I thought she was nannying for you or something? She was over there yesterday, and tonight she wasn't home."

Oh. Right.

"No idea…maybe she's getting out too?" I shrugged like I had no idea.

"Look, we haven't really talked since you two made this deal or whatever it is. Just remember she's twenty years old, Liam."

He stared at me, as if he already knew what I had done to his little sister. Even if it wasn't much, it was enough.

I stared back. Why was he insinuating something was happening?

"Why are you telling me this?"

He stepped back, looking behind him before heaving a sigh.

"Just making sure we're on the same page, that's all. And reminding you she's only ten years older than Maddy."

Shame splintered inside my chest like brittle wood. I hated that he'd just gone there. I knew he was right. The age should deter me; it should be the largest reason I ignore the fact that Haley was out with Jefferey. She pulled away this afternoon. She left.

Why the fuck was I trying to chase this?

Lowering my head, I gave up and sunk to the bench in his entryway.

"We're clear on Haley. There's nothing there to worry about, I promise you. I just need to clear my head over some of the investor stuff. Get my mind off it."

Colson took a seat next to me, leaning forward on his elbows.

"Okay, then try and have fun. Just be here for their school routine in the morning."

I nodded my agreement. After kissing the girls goodnight, I left feeling like my heart had been flooded with something thick and slippery.

My plan originally was to show up and mess with Haley, get her attention, and have her leave with me. But maybe Colson was right… maybe I needed to focus on someone my own age.

Unfortunately, there weren't a lot of places to go to pick up dates, so I'd be going to McGrady's after all, but I'd be there for myself. Maybe I'd find someone, and it would get Haley out of my system.

MCGRADY'S WAS LIVELY for a weeknight. There were couples dancing and a trivia game going on in the corner where Earl served curly fries and chicken tenders. Then there were all the people gathered around the screen, watching football. It was madness. I walked to the counter, squeezing in between a few people and raised my hand to get Tanya's attention.

"Hey! Haven't seen you in a while." She said, swaying her hips on her way over.

I smiled but wasn't in the mood for her to flirt.

"Can I get a beer?"

"Sure, where's those cute babies at?" She dipped to grab the glass bottle and then popped the cap off, handing it to me.

"At home in bed." I took the beer and handed over a ten, not wanting to do small talk or divulge the actual whereabouts of my kids.

Tanya's red nails slid over the cash, and then her eyes were darting around.

"Lacey was in here earlier—not that she'll come back, but I wanted to give you a heads- up." My stomach nearly bottomed out at the mentioned of my ex. It wasn't uncommon to run into people who saw her or even knew her. There were only a handful of times over the past few years we'd ever actually been in the same place at the same time, but every time she saw me, she'd act like I left her, crying and causing a scene.

I didn't want that tonight.

"Thanks, Tanya."

I turned and leaned against the bar, scanning the floor as an unfamiliar feeling began to thrum through me. Colson's words played in my head, tugging at different pieces of my pride. Haley was young, and I had lived nearly a whole life before she'd even graduated from high school. I was married once. Fuck, I had three kids.

But what good did it do me to play by the rules, or do what people said I should? That landed me here, divorced and broke, all alone on a Wednesday night with a bright pink hair tie on my wrist because I forgot that I was holding it for Mila earlier.

Society seemed to have this perfect blueprint of what our lives should look like. What marriage and happiness should imitate. But how long until we all acknowledged that the image they gave us was fucked. The cookie-cutter picture of a perfect house, happy dad and mom with that picket fence, was nothing but a piece of barbed wire wrapped around our society, cutting off all our oxygen and turning us all into judgmental assholes.

Love didn't look like that.

Happiness wasn't the laminated bullshit image they kept perpetuating, demonizing anything and anyone who didn't do it the way they said.

The beer was sour on my tongue as I swallowed and stewed over this idea of Haley. Of what I should do instead of what I wanted.

Why did the two have to look different? I wanted to fuck her, so I should.

I wanted to date her, wake up to her. Shit, it was deeper than just wanting to sink inside her…maybe that's what was giving me pause.

This was more serious than some fling. I *liked* her.

Her smile made something flutter in my chest. When I knew she'd be somewhere my adrenaline would spike. She was funny and bright. Brilliant, in fact, and while I knew she had already conquered the business world, she seemed shy and insecure when she'd bake or learn something new. Not to mention the way my daughters completely adored her; that was enough to have me thinking about her long after she'd left.

I wasn't really looking for Haley, but the song changed and the crowd on the floor parted, then there she was. Her hips caught my attention first, because they were swaying with the music, and there were two hands attached to them, holding her while she danced.

Her hand went up into her hair, shoving half of it off her face, revealing her slender neck and how deep the tank top dipped into her cleavage.

Jefferey fucking Akers stood behind her, moving with her as the music played and the beat dropped into something seductive and sultry.

He pulled her closer to his chest until there wasn't any space left between their bodies.

Rage spiked in my chest, and it spiraled into something dangerous and out of control. This wasn't going to work. I couldn't be here and watch this. I couldn't see him touch her.

If I were a calm man, the kind that didn't have fury in my veins or a darkness that was always present, urging me to hit something, I would walk away. I'd get in my truck and drive home, turn on a game, and enjoy my first kid-free evening, in I didn't even know how long.

Instead, I set the beer bottle down and moved.

My eyes stayed on her as she adjusted herself so that there was space between her and Jeffery now. But she was still smiling up at him, and his left hand was still on her hip. Her shirt had risen, so part of her stomach was showing, and it shouldn't matter. She wasn't mine.

Yet that seemed to be the only thing my brain was screaming at me as I wandered closer.

My lips.

My hips.

My ass.

My hair.

I bypassed couples dancing, cut through another until a guy yelled at my back, but I only had eyes for her.

Then I was in front of her. Her eyes were closed, so she didn't even know I was there. Like this, I could see the flecks of gold on her eyelids, and how thick her lashes were. How her pink lips were glossy and plump. All I wanted to do was kiss her. I wanted to take her out of her and tuck her into my bed. I also wanted to fuck her rough and smack her ass for coming on this date with Jeffery. She may not realize that's what it is, but Jefferey sure as fuck thought so.

"Hey, Liam! Everything good, man?" Jefferey yelled at me like we were friends.

I didn't even know the idiot. I didn't miss how his arm wrapped around Haley's stomach possessively, tugging her back into his chest. He'd fucked up, though, because as soon as she heard my name, Haley's eyes popped open, and she was clawing at Jefferey's wrist.

"Liam?"

Everything in my head went quiet.

She belonged with me, and I had never been surer of anything in my entire life.

I pulled her out of his arms, until she was flush against me, my lips at her ear.

"This isn't working."

Her eyes rounded, all large and worried. Jefferey was yelling at me, his arms wide like he wasn't sure what the fuck was going on.

"What's not working?" she yelled back, her palms going flat on my chest.

"You with him. You taking it slow, or whatever the fuck it is you think you're doing."

I tangled my fingers with hers and pulled her away from the floor, through the couples until we were outside. Jefferey was on our heels, peppering us both with questions that we ignored.

"What's going on?" he asked once we'd pushed outside, his eyes wide and shocked.

"Go back inside," I demanded, pulling Haley behind me.

She pushed at my back, trying to move me, but it wasn't going to happen.

"Haley, are you okay with this?" Jefferey tried to look past me.

I shoved him back a few feet.

"What the fuck, man?" he yelled.

"Liam, what the hell? You need to chill," Haley said at my back, pulling my arm.

I gripped her hip by twisting my arm back, holding her in place.

"We're leaving."

Jefferey muttered something under his breath. He really had no idea how much self-restraint I was showing.

"Haley, you don't have to go with him. This is exactly what I was talking about. Dude is fucking crazy!" Jefferey roared from behind me.

I had turned and was watching Haley, her green eyes narrowed on Jefferey, and after he said that, something on her face transformed. She went from fighting me to holding my hand.

"I drove here," she said quietly.

Not wanting to waste another second, I pulled her behind me. "We'll come back for it."

Jefferey could go fuck himself.

I HELPED Haley settle in the passenger seat of my truck and then we took off.

"Your place or mine?" I asked, revving the engine with more intensity than needed, but I really wanted to punch that mother fucker.

"Where are the girls?" Haley asked, watching the windshield as we drove aimlessly.

"Colson's."

She hummed, and then let out a sigh.

"My house. But Liam, we need to talk."

I drove to her house but parked a few houses down. Haley noticed and chuckled under her breath.

"Probably best, right?"

I gave a small grunt. "Colson already warned me away from you."

"Of course he did." She let out a sigh.

We walked in silence down the sidewalk, our breath clouding in front of us. Haley kept her arms tucked in tight, her hands hidden. I wanted to hold her, touch her. But walking with her to her house was enough for now.

"Here, let me go in and turn off the porch light." Haley rushed ahead of me, up the steps, shoving her key into the lock all while I stayed in the shadows. Once the porch light flicked off, I ensured Colson's house was still dark and then I ran up her steps into her house.

"Holy shit, it's freezing in here," I rasped, flipping the deadbolt.

I slid my boots off, then my jacket, and carried them in my arms as Haley blew air into her palms.

"There's no heat in this area without starting the fire. I usually just go into my room and stay there unless I need food or water."

"Lead the way."

Haley nodded and walked down the hall, taking the first right into a smaller guest room. There was a queen-sized bed inside with a dresser against the wall, and a small desk sat under the window. Thick blinds blocked the light from exiting, or any from coming inside.

"This is…smaller than I expected." I shut her bedroom door and set my things down next to it.

She laughed and tugged her coat off, setting it on the back of her desk chair. I finally noticed all the boxes she'd had in the back of her car were now all piled half inside the closet.

"I'm currently apartment hunting."

That seemed like a waste of time.

"You could just move in with us."

Haley burst out laughing and then sat down on the edge of her bed.

"It's late…are the girls spending the night at Colson's?"

I shifted, uneasy all the sudden. Why did she laugh at that offer? I was dead serious.

"Yeah."

She hummed to herself, tossing her cell behind her on the bed and letting out a loud sigh.

"So, did you want to…" She hesitated, her face flushing pink. "Did you want to stay for a bit then head home, or…?"

My brows caved, finally realizing what she was asking.

"I'm staying the night."

She stood.

"Okay, well, I need to change, so if you want to look away or whatever?"

"Since you posed it as a question, then I'm good where I am. Thanks."

She watched me, her arms a tight band across her chest. That tank she was wearing had raised and pushed her cleavage together. I tugged my shirt off to make things less awkward.

"You can stay, but we aren't doing anything. We have to talk. What you did…it sucked, Liam."

"What are you talking about?" I asked, feeling confused as I watched her shift on her feet.

She let out one of those heavy sighs as her arms crossed, her fingers digging into the bottom hem of her shirt until it was being pulled over her head, revealing a strapless bra that pushed her tits up. My mouth went dry.

"I'm talking about the fact that you only seem to want me if Jefferey is involved somehow."

Wait—that's not—

She dipped her head, then her fingers were at the waist of her jeans, tugging on the copper button and pushing them down her legs, revealing a pair of black boy short underwear.

"So you wear a thong when you come to learn self-defense, but when you go out drinking with Jefferey fucking Akers, you wear shorts?"

Her face flushed pink as she tossed her jeans over her desk chair.

"Well, I wasn't planning on getting naked with Jefferey—" She turned her back toward her closet but as soon as she said that she spun on her toes, her face pink and blotches scattered over her chest.

"Not that I was planning on getting naked with you at the gym. I just mean, I wasn't purposely trying to be sexy tonight. My gym leggings are the kind that will show underwear lines, that's why I wear my thong in our lessons. Not because I had some plan to…"

I loved her like this. Flustered and blushing, suddenly shy and toying with the ends of her hair. She did that a lot—tugged, braided, curled around her finger.

"For the record, I don't give a flying fuck about him. I wanted you before he was involved. I want you regardless of your relationship with him, but the fact that you weren't wearing fuck-me underwear, or even a matching set, tells me everything I need to know about where he stands with you."

I slid my jeans off and then my socks, until I was in my boxer briefs.

"That seems a little presumptuous, don't you think?" she joked, heading into her closet.

When Haley returned, she had a loose T-shirt on that went to her thighs. It was cute that she thought she'd be wearing that tonight.

"Your sports bra was black; it matched your black thong. There was a pink tag in the middle, where the bra zips. That tag was on the strap at your hip. You wore a matching set to the gym when we trained."

She paused mid-step, her eyes going wide, her lips parting. It was either the truth I just dropped on her, or the fact that I was in just my boxers now. I smirked and pulled the covers back and slid into her bed.

She hesitated for only a second then walked over to the door and turned off the overhead lights. Padding back to the side of her bed, she clicked on the small lamp.

"I have a whole face routine, and my teeth…"

Stretching, pulling my arms back behind my head, I said, "Skip it tonight."

Her fingers curled into the fabric of her T-shirt.

"My breath, it's bad. Let me just—"

I tugged at her shirt and pulled her into the bed.

"I don't believe you, let me smell." My nose was in her neck, my fingers brushing her hair back. She laughed, trying to pull away.

"No, gross! Liam, I am not letting you smell my breath."

I shifted until my lips were hovering over hers. "Then just let me taste you."

She relaxed into me, but still kept her face turned away.

"We shouldn't…"

Cradling her jaw, I forced her to look at me.

"Why shouldn't we?"

Her mouth was half parted, so I advanced and slowly licked along her bottom lip.

Her tiny gasp encouraged me to trace the top as well.

"Things are complicated. We should think about it. Take it slow."

"Okay."

She reared back in surprise. "Really?"

"Sure, we'll take things slow."

My mouth covered hers, sliding my tongue in between her lips, swiping inside until I felt her open up for me, and then she moved hungrily against me. Her hand went to the back of my neck, and her fingers slid up and sunk into my hair, holding me to her.

"I'll slowly kiss you…" I muttered against her lips.

My hands went to her hips, my thumbs rubbing circles into her skin as we shifted.

"Slowly touch you," I whispered, still kissing her and grabbing a handful of her ass, but as my fingers skimmed the fabric around her hips, I paused and pulled my mouth away from hers.

"You changed into a thong?"

From here, with the lamp, her green eyes were vibrant and so hungry. I wanted to disappear inside them. Have her essence take me, hold me and change me, until I was a better person.

"Hmmm, must have been an oversight," she said, smiling down at me while biting her lip.

Pressing my lips to her throat, I whispered, "I'd like to feel that oversight against my cock while I'm fucking you….slowly, of course."

She inhaled a sharp breath, and my hands moved over her ass until my fingers ran along the triangular piece near the top of her crack.

"I'm going to show you how slow I can take things, Haley. I'm going to pull right here, until it's so tight against your pussy that you beg me to rip if off your body."

Her hips rocked forward in a silent agreement. I knew her well enough to know if she didn't want this, she'd simply say as much.

Her thigh was in my hand a second later as I pulled her over me, spreading her so she straddled my waist.

My cock was hard behind my boxers, pressed against her ass as she settled on top of me.

"Take this shirt off, Haley. Let me see those beautiful tits."

She tugged the fabric over her head and tossed it behind her. I watched as she cupped her breasts and slid her thumb over the peaked nipples.

I hummed deep in my throat as my cock jumped and jerked in my boxers.

"I know we're not doing anything tonight, but if I were to hypothetically fuck you, I'd want you to know that I haven't been with anyone in over a year. I've been tested; I'm clean."

Her green eyes heated as she rocked her hips over my erection.

"Since we're taking things slow—and I agree fucking is out of the question—but if hypothetically we did, it's been about ten months for me, I'm also clean, and I'm on birth control."

I pushed the image of whoever she'd been with out of my head and focused on her writhing on top of me.

"Sit back," I ordered.

She did as I said, scooting back and helping me free my thick cock. Her small gasp was encouraging as I stroked it up and down, and then I pulled her forward until her pussy was at the root.

"Now grind against me. Get this thong soaked."

I pulled on the back of her underwear until the front was so tight on her pussy that it made her lips spill over the fabric. She hissed as her slit passed over my bare cock, grinding against my hardness.

"That's it. Keep going, you're drenching me."

One hand was on her ass, moving her against me, the other was pulling the string.

Her nails dug into my shoulders as she picked up speed, moving against my shaft in methodical strokes. She moaned above me, working herself up.

"Harder, Liam."

I did as she requested, pulling the string tighter against her pussy.

She let out a small yelp and moved faster. Her hand moved from my shoulder and wrapped around the base of my cock, then with her thumb moving over the weeping tip, she jerked me off while sliding her pussy against my length.

"Harder," she begged again.

"If I go any harder, we're going to fuck," I warned, thrusting my hips up, so my cock ran up along the slit of her soaked entrance.

She let out a strangled sound as if she was about to combust. Then she glared down at me with heated eyes, and with an edge to her tone, she begged, "Pull it harder, fuck me with this string."

This time when I pulled, it snapped. Her eyes fluttered closed as I picked her up and slammed into her heat.

She let out a cry as my cock thrust into her tightness. It was slick and wet, but it was still so goddamned tight. I slowed down as I met resistance and realized she'd stopped moving.

"You good?" I rasped, straining to control myself.

She exhaled and then tightened her fingers in the sheets next to my head.

"Um…just give me a second, okay? Maybe we can do a breathing exercise or something. You're a trainer…Talk me through this."

I pulled out and set her on my chest, rubbing up and down her thighs.

"Breathe in through your nose, out through your mouth. Okay?"

She nodded earnestly, wiggling on my chest.

"You feel so good, Haley. Do you have any idea how beautiful you are, how badly I've wanted this since the first time I met you?"

As I spoke, I ever so gently guided my pulsing cock back inside her.

"Breathe, take it as slow as you want. This is about you, so use me. Move until it feels good."

"Okay." She shuddered, her eyes were slammed close, and I pried her fingers off the sheets and intertwined them with mine.

She took me one inch at a time, slowly until I was entirely sheathed by her.

"You're such a good girl, taking my entire cock inside that tight pussy," I growled, straining to see how we connected. Her bare mound glistened as she slid out and pushed down on the base of my soaked cock. She did it again, pulling out, revealing my shaft and then she slammed home.

"Oh, shit," She whispered, looking where my eyes were trained.

I was about to lose it, so I kept my mouth shut, and turned my eyes up to the ceiling and away from her swaying tits.

Then she slowly rotated her hips in little circles.

"Okay…oh wow," she muttered softly.

Her hands were still in mine as she moved. This was better because if I touched her at all, I'd blow it, and that would be so fucking embarrassing. But shit…it'd been over a year since I'd been with anyone, and I couldn't hold out much longer.

"Liam, oh wow. Okay. My God," she moaned, tossing her head back.

"Yeah, baby. Feels good, doesn't it?"

She whimpered, picking up speed with her hips. "Yes! Oh shit. Fuck. Yes. Yes!"

"Ride me baby, fucking ride this cock."

She made a sound that resembled a hurt animal, but she began fucking me without holding anything back. Her tits bounced as she moved back and forth, claiming what she wanted from me. One hand went backward, landing on my leg and the other stayed on my stomach.

Her pussy clamped down on my cock, clenching tight as she writhed. Sensing she was close, I let go and gripped her by the hips then slammed into her as hard as I could.

"Oh my God!" she yelled.

"Fuck! Fuck! Fuck!" I thrust into her, holding her to me as she climaxed. Her moans and screams echoed in the room, and then mine joined in as I let go and released inside her.

Our heaving gasps filled the silence as we began coming down from the high, and after a few moments I was tugging her forward and turning us.

"That was…" she breathed, wetting her lips and trying to catch her breath.

"Yeah." I kissed her shoulder and pulled her into me.

She wiggled in my arms. "The mess…"

"I'll get you a washcloth in a second…just let me hold you for a little while."

She relaxed in my hold and scooted closer to my chest.

"Okay, just for a little while, then I'm doing my routine."

I smiled into her hair and pulled her closer.

CHAPTER THIRTEEN

haley

Liam's Arms
Falling Asleep against Liam's chest
Liam's Gym
Secret Kisses in the Locker Room
Chapstick that Hydrates
Sunless Tanning Lotion

LIAM'S ARMS tightened around me as his phone rang.

Or was that my phone?

Someone's phone was ringing…and it was loud.

"Liam." My voice came out raspy and a little scratchy. Shit, how loud had I yelled last night?

His grip only intensified as he let out a low groan.

"Liam, someone is calling you."

With a low curse, he let me go and turned over. Then I heard him clear his throat.

"Hello?"

"Where are you?" I could hear through the phone because the person on the other end was so loud.

Liam sat up swiftly and cleared his throat again.

"Shit, I overslept."

I couldn't hear the rest because Liam had moved away from me, but I had a feeling it was Colson on the phone.

"Yeah, I'll be there in a few."

I moved to sit up, realizing we'd fallen asleep after sex last night. My thighs were sticky, my breath was horrendous, and my hair was probably a rat's nest.

"I have to go grab the girls," Liam said, gripping the edge of the bed.

I stared at the outline of his back as light from the shades filtered in enough light to see by.

"Okay, do you still want to meet at the gym later?"

He turned, giving me a sly smile.

"You still want to meet after it opens?"

My core heated instantly, remembering how good he felt last night. How different it was than the other two times I had sex. Liam knew exactly what he was doing. He didn't fumble or ask me what I want. He told me, and it was so liberating. Sexy. I wanted that again, but I also really did want to learn self-defense.

"Yes, apparently we need accountability."

Liam scoffed and then reached for my ankle, dragging me closer to him.

"The only thing we need is more time like this, alone. I was hoping I'd be up in time for another round with you."

Me too.

With his arms around me, it was easy to fall into a sense of peace and security. Liam's arms felt like a band of steel, like the strongest force on earth that would protect me from anything.

"You know I'm not ashamed of this—of us, right?" he asked, kissing my temple.

I nodded, facing the wall, my back against his chest.

"But I think…" He hesitated, but I was already there. I knew and completely agreed with him.

"We should keep it private, get used to it."

He hummed his agreement. "Just for the girls, and your brother… might be easier."

I hated the way those words made me feel, even if I agreed with them.

"Yeah, I think so too."

He let me go, and I moved to sit up.

"But every time we're alone, you're mine."

My gut tightened, both loving and hating his words. A part of me wondered if this was how my mother had felt when she became my father's dirty little secret. If she lived for the moments he shed his family and became a different person, making her promises in the dark.

I tried to shake the feeling and pressed a soft kiss to his lips.

Liam kissed me one more time after he dressed then hurried out through the back door, watching carefully to make sure he wasn't seen as he walked down the block to get his truck.

After he left, I took my time showering and dressing.

The gym didn't open for another hour, which would give me time to get coffee and maybe some breakfast from the cute coffee shop across town. I pulled my coat and my boots, opened the front door, then stopped in my tracks.

Oh crap.

My car was still in the McGrady's parking lot.

Right as I was about to shut the door, my brother Colson walked out of his house and peered over at me.

"Missing something, sis?"

My face heated, but thankfully he couldn't see that from here.

I called over to him. "Drank a little too much last night, had someone drop me."

My brother started his truck then shut the door and rounded his hood. I shut the door behind me and walked down the porch steps.

"Well, if you're ready, I can give you a ride."

Shit. As much as I wanted to get to know Colson, and have a relationship, this morning was not one of those times I wanted to spend with him.

"Uh…I could wait for Nora if she's heading out later?"

Colson was right in front of the steps now, his eyes bouncing around my frame like he was looking for any clue of something out of place.

"She's taking the day to come up with design plans here at home. This weekend we're planning to move her completely out of her house and into mine. If you're around, maybe you could help?"

I nodded. "Yeah, of course."

Turning back toward his truck, he waved me toward it. "You look like you're ready to go, you have your keys?"

"Yeah."

He got into his truck, and I crawled in next to him.

"So, you went to McGrady's last night?" Colson asked, reversing out of his drive and heading down the street.

I tugged on the end of my ponytail and shrugged. "Yeah, for a little bit."

"Seems random for a Wednesday night." He peered over his shoulder then focused back on the road. Outside, there was an entire group of people in track suits, walking around the town square. They had on big puffy vests and thick ear warmers around their head.

"I was invited by Jefferey. We went as friends."

Colson turned his head, giving me a surprised expression. "Really? You and Akers, huh?"

I kept my gaze out on the town, noticing how much snow had melted, revealing yellow grass and asphalt. I had just assumed no one knew how to park here, but maybe it was that all the parking lots were covered by the ice.

"We're just friends." At least I thought we were. I had no idea if he even wanted to talk to me again after last night. I honestly had planned on standing my ground against Liam last night, staying with Jefferey at least until Liam left, but then he said that little thing about his warning against Liam and I snapped.

Colson didn't respond, just kept his gaze straight.

Finally, we pulled into the parking lot, where my lone car was parked, frost coated the windows.

"Maybe Jefferey could come help move this weekend," Colson suddenly said, shoving his parking gear up and letting the truck idle.

I reached for my buckle, acting nonchalant. "Maybe, but if you have me, Rae and Davis, plus Liam… Doesn't that seem like a lot?"

Colson's expression didn't change as he watched me, other than his finger tapping his knee. "Wasn't planning on asking Liam, unless you can watch the girls while he helps, but Nora asked if you wanted to be a part of the weekend since we'll do lunch and hang out. I think we were planning on not having the girls underfoot, so we didn't have to worry about them getting hurt as we moved stuff around."

"I'm good with whatever you guys decide. I haven't talked to Liam yet about whether he needs help with the girls or not, so I can just let you know."

My brother nodded, tapping away at his leg.

"You and Liam getting along?"

I nodded, giving him a smile. "Yeah, he apologized for being a bit of jerk in the start. I like being around the girls a lot."

"Yeah, they're great," he agreed, still tapping on his knee.

I wanted to tell him to come right out and say whatever was on his mind, but I had a feeling I already knew. He was making assumptions about Liam and me. He'd already warned me, and apparently warned Liam last night. If I mentioned it right now, it would just confirm his suspicions.

"You talk to dad recently?" I decided to change the conversation, even if it meant we changed it to something unpleasant.

My brother's face transformed from open and agreeable to closed off and shut down.

"No, not since all the shit went down with Nora."

I understood why. I hadn't either, but I had heard through Blaire that they'd moved out.

"The house is empty, according to Blaire."

Colson's eyes expanded. "Vacation?"

I shook my head. "Trouble with taxes. I think they're hiding."

"They didn't sell the house?"

I understood the hopeful tone he expressed, because that house meant so much to him. To his mother.

"Not that I know of. Have you talked to our brothers?"

Cole let out a sigh, shaking his head.

"Yeah, me either." I looked outside, seeing across the street the gas station bustling with people.

"Life has been crazy…I'm just trying to get this Community Center open and Nora moved over. Then I assumed we'd figure it out."

I grabbed the handle of the door and pulled it.

"Well, I'll keep you posted on anything I hear…thank you for the ride."

"No problem, and Haley?"

I waited, ass half on the seat, watching his blond hair shift as he dipped his head.

"This thing with Liam and the girls…just remember that you have your whole life in front of you. He'll get along fine without you."

I gave him a smile as a response, but his words were as effective as a butterfly knife being shoved into my chest.

Exiting his truck, I walked around with my heart barely intact. Once my car started, he finally drove off and I sagged into my seat. Liam would get along fine without me. He had before I got here, and he would after me. Me being here didn't make or break their life; they would just keep on living it once I moved on.

But me?

I already knew, Liam and the girls would be an imprint on my soul that I'd carry for my entire life. Whether they wanted me a part of their lives or not, they'd be a part of mine.

I WALKED into the gym feeling relieved. When Liam put me on the bag and gave me a few drills, it felt so nice to release the pent-up energy in my system. I was hoping he'd allow me the same opportunity today.

I wore a different pair of leggings today with a scoop-necked tank and my hair up in a high ponytail. I kept my snow boots off this time and traded my coat for an oversized, zip-up hoodie. By the time I pushed through the door, the overhead speakers were blaring Three Days Grace.

Liam wasn't at the front desk when I arrived, so I sauntered further in until I saw him working a bag near the back. His shoulders rotated and muscles bunched, pulsing with each thrust of his arm against the bag.

Holy shit.

His punch moved the bag so far back that I thought it might break.

"See, that's how you know it's too light of a bag. You don't want to use that heavy of a punch on these bags. You would be better off reserving your energy," he yelled over the music, explaining all this to some teenager.

I was standing off to the side, behind him, when the kid turned and caught sight of me. He shifted on his feet and did a double-take, his face turning red.

Liam watched the kid's reaction then glanced at me.

"Eyes here." he scolded, shoving him until he was facing the bag again.

"Haley, go start stretching, I'll be there in a second," Liam directed.

I nodded and moved over to the mats and fell into the few stretches we'd done the day before.

Within a few minutes he was walking over. He wore a dark tank top that gaped on the sides, showing his defined torso and all that ink covering him. His heated eyes fell on me, and I already knew it was a mistake to ask him to meet me when the gym opened. His gaze lit me on fire, and after last night, all I wanted was to step forward and kiss him.

Instead of saying anything to me, he started stretching with me.

A few of the guys around the room rotated, moving to speed training bags. A few others swapped partners, boxing each other in one of the elevated rings.

Within minutes, we were falling into a routine where he began to show me different techniques for evading, and where to put my hands and arms. Unfortunately, the music was so loud it was difficult to follow along with anything he was saying, not to mention the yelling and jeering from the guys sparring in the different rings. Eventually Liam realized I was getting frustrated by not being able to hear him and then someone coming by every five minutes and interrupting.

Finally, I just moved to a heavy bag and did the drills he told me to do. Once I was done, I headed into the locker room, feeling a sense of routine now. Honestly, just hitting the bag was pretty nice, and even if I couldn't do the self-defense with Liam, I wouldn't mind coming in every day to work the bag.

Once inside the locker room, I took my time undressing and wrapping a towel around me, and by the time I was headed into the shower stall, Liam was walking in behind me, locking us inside.

"You still want to start lessons when the gym is open?" He smiled, pulling me into his chest.

I let out a sigh and threw my hands around his neck. "Fine, you win. Today sucked."

His nose was in my neck a second later, his hand fisting my towel.

"I know, and that kid I was training is eighteen, which I realized is closer in age to you than I am. Do you have any idea how stupid it made me feel to be jealous of that pimply kid?"

"Jealous?" I tilted my head back, raising my brow, "I thought you didn't get jealous."

His hands came around me until he was cupping my ass.

"I said I didn't give a shit about Jeffery Akers, which I don't, but when there are guys more suitable for you to date that are closer to your age, I get insecure. Jeffery is an old fuck, just like me."

"Too bad I seem to like you, and drool over your old man strength and old man muscles, and your super old man tattoos."

His grunt told me I'd done my job and gotten to him.

"Now you're going to make me show you how young I still am."

"You showed me last night, and aren't those guys going to need you again soon? They kept bugging us every few minutes. Where did all these guys come from anyway?"

Liam exhaled, nipping at my neck. "It's the weekend crew. A few guys drive down and train here. They stay at one of the cabins at the lodge, I think. Do the whole weekend thing then go back to Portland."

"Liam, that's amazing. You're big enough of a name to draw people from a different part of the state. That's a big deal."

His eyes closed off, his head turning away like he didn't want to hear the praise.

"Yeah, it's nice. Just isn't nice enough to make a difference on my books, or to investors to take a chance on backing me."

"You're looking for investors?"

I knew the second the words left my mouth he was going to completely shut down, and like an idiot, I said them anyway.

"No." It was firm, flat, with no room for questions.

Suddenly he ripped my towel away and starkly demanded, "Sit on the bench."

For some reason I did exactly as he said, sitting naked on the small bench inside the stall. Meanwhile, he watched, lowering his shorts and boxers.

"Good girl."

His thumb swiped over my nipple, making me arch my back and then he traced my lips, shoving his thumb inside my mouth.

"For too many fucking nights, I fisted myself, just thinking about this mouth, wondering how well you'd take my cock, then I finally had you and we didn't even find out. Now all I can think about is having you again." He trailed my lips ever so softly, his eyes heating.

"Miss me, Liam?"

I opened for him, letting his fingers invade my mouth while my eyes stayed on his.

"Open up and find out."

He stepped back, fisting his erection and led it to my mouth. I unlocked my jaw and tilted my eyes.

"Spread your thighs. Touch yourself."

I did as he said. Taking his cock into my mouth, I slowly sucked, while circling my clit with two of my fingers.

He pumped forward, holding my jaw while I sucked him off.

My core heated at the idea of him fucking me again.

"Having your pussy was perfect, but this…having your mouth, that's…*fuck*."

I sucked harder, hollowing my cheeks.

"I thought of filthy, dirty things last night, Haley. Things that would make you blush…things that might even scare you."

Oh God. I wanted him to tell me. I wanted him to *show* me.

"I thought I'd last doing this, but I need you," he confessed, and then I was being pulled into his lap while he sat on the bench, his back against the wall.

"Spread for me." He touched my pussy and widened his legs, so my thighs spread further apart.

There was a nudge at my entrance, a slick pressure as he rubbed his cock along my slit and then he was hissing, pressing his head into the wall.

I held him by the root as I adjusted myself, sinking down along his length, loving the feel of him going deeper and deeper.

"Fuck, you have all of me," Liam said through clenched teeth.

My head fell back, my hair touching his thighs as I pushed my hips forward. His hand gripped my ponytail as he thrust up into me, muttering about how badly he needed me. We stayed like that, the two of us moving like a greedy wave clamoring to beat against the sand. He held my hair tighter in his fist as he growled into my neck. His lips marked me there, then his teeth, sinking into my shoulder as he sucked.

The sound of our skin slapping together filled the empty room as we fucked on the bench, my knees pressed into the wood as I rode him, taking everything I wanted, insatiably chasing another orgasm. Suddenly his thumb pulled my bottom lip down, tilting my head, and my eyes were on his. That silver burned and heated as he stared at me, his hips rocking, his arm a band around my back, then he ordered, "Come for me, Haley."

Right as he said it, he squeezed my nipple then leaned forward to lap at it. I squeezed my thighs tight and ground down on his throbbing length and fell apart.

"That's it, yes," he rasped, keeping me close to his chest as he found his release. A deep groan filled the room as he continued to pump into me, and then our heavy breathing filled the empty space, our heads tipped softly against one another, his lips were on mine.

"I know what we said about keeping this private, but I don't want to be away from you."

His confession pried my chest open, gently cradling the terrified organ inside, coaxing it to believe him. I closed my eyes and leaned into the crook of his neck, so he didn't have to see my hesitation. Handing my heart over to people always came too easy to me. I trusted blindly, believed the best…and then they'd walk away, and most of the time they didn't even offer my heart back before they left.

So I shuddered against him and whispered in return, "Me either."

"Then stay with me tonight," he said, and helped me off his lap.

I nodded then pressed a kiss against his lips.

Once he left, I thought over his refusal for help and realized it was still bugging me. I could feel Liam's stress, and his fear over losing this place…the way he said no meant he already knew about me. Probably from Cole…but was he really that prideful that he wouldn't even entertain the idea of me backing him?

It wouldn't work. I hated pride…and stubborn men.

Liam Croft just became a challenge, and if there was one thing I was professionally good at, it was accepting them.

haley

Baking
YouTube
Nature
Waterfalls
Hope
Maddy, Seraph, and Mila
Liam. Always Liam.

I WAS HEADED to pick up the girls, but I wanted to stop by the center. I told myself it was to see if there was anything I could pick up for Nora and Rae, but there was a tiny part of me that wanted to check on Jefferey. I knew he had to be pissed at me, and I wouldn't blame him if he was with how our evening ended. I didn't want to make excuses for Liam, and I had willingly accepted an invitation to go out with Jeffery and then left with someone else. Regardless of my frustration in the moment with him, it was still shitty.

I pushed open the door and found him in one of the back classrooms.

Nora wasn't in, neither was Rae…but there were a few other guys milling about the place.

Leaning against the door frame, I waited for him to acknowledge me.

His hat was backward on his head, pushing all that unruly blond hair back. Without looking up, he gruffly said. "Need something?"

His tone cut through me, and even though I didn't have romantic feelings toward him, his derision still cut.

I took a deep breath and then just decided to get into it. "Last night was shitty. I wasn't going to go with him, but—"

Brown eyes lifted, landing on me in a curious way. "But what?"

Shifting off the door, I explained. "I don't like being warned away from people. It bugs me. You tried to scare me away from Liam the first chance you got, and I don't think you even understood what that could have done to our working relationship. But Liam matters to me, just like you do. And if Liam had said that about you, I would have left him too."

Jeffery's eyes narrowed before he lowered his head again and punched a few more nails in.

"So that's it? Nothing else is going on between you two, you're just friends, like we're friends?"

My heart felt frenzied and panicked at his question. Liam and I said that we didn't want to tell anyone about us, and I wouldn't betray him that way.

"Nothing else is going on." The lie was bitter on my tongue, but I swallowed down the taste.

"He acted like—" Jefferey shook his head then run a hand through that messy hair.

I shouldn't press, but I was also trying to figure out what his perspective of all this was.

"Like what?"

He stood and walked closer to me, leaving his nail gun behind. "Like I had just stolen from him. He acted like you were his, always had been and always would be."

Well, damn.

My throat was suddenly dry, so I lowered my face and shook my head.

"I think he knows I'm not legally twenty-one and freaked, given he's my brother's best friend."

"You're not?" His tone picked up, bordering on panicked.

I laughed. "One more month."

"Oh. Then yeah, he probably did freak out."

There was a silent sigh that fluttered in my chest.

"So are we good?" I asked, and I was expecting maybe a nod or a knuckle bump, but he pulled me into a hug.

"Yeah, we're good."

I hugged him back, not like I hugged Liam, more like that time Colson hugged me.

When he let me go, I waved to him and promised I'd be back tomorrow to help him.

On my way back to the car my stomach churned so badly I worried I'd throw up. That was two people I had lied to today, and while I understood the importance of keeping details to myself, I really didn't like it. Lies always caught up with you.

That was something Blaire always said.

"Don't bother dabbling in the dark, the sun always moves, and eventually shows what's been going on in the shadows."

THERE WAS something so soothing about having three little faces smiling back at me while I drove around town. We were on our way to school, and the girls were rocking out to Taylor Swift, and the sun was shining in a bold attempt to stanch winter temperatures. We had a tradition now where every morning we picked up our "mochas"—theirs were just hot chocolates with whipped cream, and mine was a skinny vanilla latte.

I had a smile I couldn't smother because I loved this feeling and I loved how the girls seemed to transform each morning I showed up to take them to school.

Regardless of Liam asking me to stay the night each night, I only gave in if the girls asked for a sleepover at Uncle Colson's or if they were already in bed when I came over. I still arrived before breakfast each morning, whether I stayed overnight or not, to help them get ready, and Liam always managed to ravage my mouth in the pantry when I went in to grab the kids snacks. Or the garage…

One morning, he'd tucked me behind a tall tool chest, shoved my leggings down, and then with one swift movement, he'd entered me and fucked me right there in his garage.

I was still dragging my feet on all relationship-related things, feeling weird that we were hiding and sneaking around. But there was a part of me that felt so insatiable for him that I couldn't stop myself from giving in. I was so selfish that I just didn't want to give up the touches, or the secrets. After I dropped the girls, we were meeting again at the gym, and my legs clenched tightly together at the idea of what he'd do to me.

The brake lights in front of me brought me back to the present and the little slip of road where I parked the car so I could walk the girls to the front of the school. It was ten times faster than waiting bumper to bumper in the car pool line. We'd done it once and the girls said it made them late, so now I parked and walked them straight to the door.

We crossed the wet grass, each girl still wearing their heavy-duty boots and coats, then I hugged each one as they disappeared behind the front doors. Liam had said that Maddy was in fifth grade this year, and by sixth, she'd migrate to the middle school. I couldn't wrap my brain around the idea that she'd be a middle schooler next year. Even more so, I couldn't fathom my place in her life at that time. Would I still be here? Would Liam and I still be sneaking around, stealing kisses?

My hands were tucked tightly against my chest as I walked back, my eyes on the wet ground at my feet, so when I approached my car, I startled when I saw a woman resting against it.

The woman had long blonde hair that kissed the top of her heart-shaped ass, her lithe form slightly hidden under a large brown leather jacket, and those blue eyes… Those I recognized. I'd just watched three pairs of them my rearview mirror from three beautiful little girls. My throat went dry as I slowly rounded the hood, standing a few feet away.

"My sister was right, you are cute." She cocked her head to the side as she propped her arm against my car.

That confirmed my assumption that this was, in fact, Lacey, Liam's ex-wife. My stomach churned as I stared at her.

The silence stretched as the sun dipped behind a cloud, and it began drizzling.

"He fucking you yet?" Her pink lips slung to the side while her nose scrunched.

I narrowed my eyes and asked sharply, "Did you need something?"

Blue eyes turned into slits, as if her mask dropped.

"He tell you how much he likes his dick sucked? He really likes it when you swallow his jizz down too…goes wild if you let him disrespect you a bit."

I pinched the inside of my arm where she couldn't see. I absolutely would not be doing this right now. I had no idea what the fuck this woman's problem was, but I wasn't about to have a cat fight over Liam.

"Can you get the fuck away from my car please?" I asked coldly.

I moved closer to my door, but she blocked me.

"The girls have any massive meltdowns in public yet? The little one, she likes her dramatics."

My stomach knotted at her choice of words… Did she not even remember her daughter's name?

Her eyes scanned me, like she was waiting for me to respond, but I wouldn't be.

"He feels real good though, right? I've had a lot of lovers, but none have that stamina that man has."

She took a step closer, and I had to fight the urge to step back. If I did it once, she'd make sure she did it again and again.

"Get. Away. From. My. Car," I demanded sternly.

Was I about to fight a meth addict? How was this real life?

She inspected her nails then licked her lips. "I think I might still have one of our sex videos. I tried to upload it to one of them websites, but Liam had a little panic attack and threatened legal action. But maybe I could give you a few pointers."

Giving her a sharp glare, I repeated, "What do you want?"

"To remind you where they came from and ensure you understand where they'll end up. They're mine, make no mistake, honey." Her feet brought her closer then she cracked a sinister smile before turning on her heel and swaying her hips as she stalked off.

I quickly got into my car, ignoring how my hands shook.

Starting it up, I breathed through my nose a few times to clear my head, but even as I pulled away, there was something painful being pieced together in my chest. I could feel it.

I just wasn't sure Liam and I would be the same once it solidified and I understood the gravity of what formed.

I DROVE toward the edge of town and parked near a bridge that overlooked a massive waterfall. It was one of my favorite places in Macon when I first got here. I liked how quiet it was, how serene, and best of all, it offered silence when my thoughts seemed too loud. After the encounter with Lacey, I needed to calm my nerves. So, I began walking the trail, ignoring how cold the spray from the water was against my face.

The closer I got, the better I could think.

Liam was expecting me at the gym, but I couldn't face him right now. He'd know, and it wasn't that I would hide the encounter with Lacey from him, but I didn't want to seem broken when I told him about it. He didn't need to carry an unnecessary burden.

So, I climbed trail after trail until I circled the entire waterfall. Once I finally reached the top, I walked out along the bridge and stared down into the water and tried to sort out my loudest feelings.

Realizing what the girls had likely been through with Lacey weighed the heaviest on my mind. Second was the painful awareness of how unstable their lives must still feel when it came to new people, especially females. My heart seemed to unwind slowly, and with each turn, something else would hit me. The image of the girls finding Liam and I sneaking around…the fear that might come from us breaking up…the drama behind a messy argument. What would happen if they caught us before we'd told them?

What if someone else caught us and told them?

Then there was the tiny tendril of horror that I'd essentially become my mother. While not in the same way, I didn't have an affair with a married man, but I was still a secret. One that Liam wasn't ready to share with people in his world. I was hidden in plain sight from my brothers, labeled as merely the daughter of their father's secretary until I was six years old. They all liked me for the first few formative years—until the secret came to light.

This felt eerily similar.

My body seemed to fold in on itself as a cold feeling invaded. I was young, but rarely was I this naive. Liam wasn't some twenty-year-old bachelor. He'd had a life with someone, a career…he was father to three children.

Liam wouldn't carelessly introduce someone he was romantic with in his girls lives unless he was sure—I knew this deep in my core—but how long did he expect us to sneak around? My mind kept thinking back to how long my father had hidden his relationship with my mother. *Six years*.

I didn't want that. Not for me, or the girls. Not for Liam.

After meeting Lacey, I realized those girls didn't need the threat of a messy relationship. They needed stability. They needed people they could count on to be standing in their corner. They needed mature adults to be in charge of keeping them safe, and I wasn't being very mature about my relationship with Liam.

I was falling for him, too fast…too hard. In the end, it would be like an egg falling from a two-story building. If I gave us some time, maybe I'd be more like a rock so I could withstand the fall, but right now, I wouldn't…and the girls wouldn't either.

They'd been through so much.

I refused to put them through anything else.

I felt a tiny pinch to my chest as I made up my mind, and resolve settled into my core like cement. Liam would eventually understand that

I was giving us a foundation. His daughters were his entire world, and if I ever wanted to be within that orbit, I'd have to become something more substantial than a passing light that only blinked in their lives for a moment. I wanted to be something that made them better. Someone who could sacrifice and put them first, so that no matter what, they wouldn't have to deal with someone like Lacey again.

With tears falling from my lashes, I finally turned and left.

CHAPTER FIFTEEN

haley

The sun coming through the window
Kleenex
Hozier
Morgan Wallen
Sad songs
Mila's giggle
Seraph's quiet peace
Maddy's strength

I WAITED TWO DAYS, cowering away at Nora's house.

I'd texted and told Liam I wasn't feeling well. He offered to swing by and bring me food. He wanted to check on me, but I'd asked that he didn't. I assumed the only reason he listened was because of his schedule.

By day three, I couldn't put it off any longer. Liam had swung by right when Jeffery did, both wielding flowers and various forms of cold remedies. I wanted to sink into the earth when they both walked up the driveway at the same time.

Liam must have said something to Jeffery because he left his gifts on the porch as Liam advanced inside the house. He didn't stay long, but he wanted to make sure I was okay.

NOW I WAS WALKING through the gym as Liam finished instructing one of his regulars. As soon as he spotted me, he turned to me with a smile curving his lips.

"Hey…" His eyes traveled down my body. "You feeling better?"

I swallowed thickly to regain my composure.

"Can we talk?"

He gave me a small nod as worry bled into his features, and he led me to his office.

Once he shut his door, I tugged the ends of my hair over my shoulder and began to twirl the pieces into a tight coil.

"What's wrong?" Liam asked, gently pulling my hand into his.

My chest felt like it was being pried open with a rusty butter knife. Even in an effort to salvage the organ, the method to retrieve it would leave a poison in my blood stream.

"I need things to slow down between us. I don't want to sneak behind the girls' backs."

My eyes landed on Liam's jawline, sharp enough to carve marble, and a muscle jumped along the rigid plane as he processed.

Time slowed as he watched me, thinking.

Silence stretched as I heard the clock on his wall tick, until finally his mouth parted.

"Then we tell them."

My chin fell to my chest, my head shaking.

"I think they need more time. *I* need more time. They've been through more than I'll ever know, Liam, but deep down I feel like they need time before we drop this on them."

My eyes lifted, catching the sorrow in his. I pushed through the searing pain his expression left resonating in me.

"I think you need time, too. I mean, I'm not saying your relationship with Lacey ended recently or anything—"

"It's been four years, plus years before that of sheer torture. I'm more than over her," Liam cut in.

I mashed my lips together then just decided to pull it off like a Band-Aid.

"She was waiting by my car the other day after I dropped the girls."

His body tensed, like it did when I had told him about the park and the girl's aunt. His eyes went frantic as they tried to pull the rest of the story from my expression with a silent request.

"What did she do?" he asked quietly, likely trying to restrain his anger.

I wanted to touch him. To remind him it was okay, that I was still here, but that wasn't entirely true. I wanted distance. And I wasn't sure he'd still want me after I took it.

"She just reminded me how much your girls went through and put this entire thing into perspective. My feelings for you…they're not so small that they'd be over any time soon. It's not a fling to me, Liam."

"You think it is to me?" he asked taking a step back, getting defensive.

"No, that's not what I meant. I'm just saying, I want to do this right."

His hand tunneled through his dark hair, his jaw tensing, his eyes pleading.

"And the only way to do it right is to take a step back?"

I nodded.

"Fuck, is this why you've dodged me for days?" He paced around the room before turning to me again. "What does a step back mean exactly?" His tone went high, like he was getting desperate.

"It means platonic everything. I need space. I want to help with the girls, do lessons if you're up for it, but no secret relationship. No kisses. No sex."

His hands landed on his hips as he shook his head, staring at the wall. Then his gaze cut to me.

"So you'll still be everywhere, just nowhere that I can have you?"

My head screamed to stop this. I didn't want this.

I wanted his arms to come around me and erase the last five minutes.

But I loved those girls. I wasn't sure how I did so easily and so quickly, but I did, and because I loved them, I would do this right. I would wait and build a foundation here in their lives, so I'd never be shaken from it.

"I want solid footing with them, Liam. They deserve to have someone in their life that won't leave."

He nodded, his Adam's apple bobbing nearly as painful as my throat seemed to feel.

"If this is what you want, then fine. It's not like I have much of a choice. I don't agree with it. I want you, and if we need to tell everyone in order to make that happen, then we should just do it."

"I want you too, Liam. I just also want them…and I won't risk losing them."

His head turned, his eyes glossy. "No, it's just me you'd risk losing."

"Liam—"

His hand went to the door, his back to me as he began to leave.

"I'll respect your wishes, Haley, but I won't like them. And I'll never be okay with you not being mine. So, if along the way you decide that you want to be with someone else, all bets are off. I'm coming for you, that's the only warning you get. We're not dating other people. Not fucking them. Not anything, do you understand?"

My voice came out rattled as I said, "Yes."

His head lowered, then he left.

Tears soaked my lashes as fat drops fell down my nose, and over my lips. Salt touched my tongue as I inhaled a deep breath. I stayed on his desk for a bit, pulling myself together, and then I left.

BY THE TIME I picked up the girls from the bus stop, they had no idea that I was all broken porcelain pieces on the inside. I kept a smile on my face, which wasn't as hard as I first assumed. The girls made me laugh, which was always a strange balm to my frayed emotions.

I made dinner like usual, but I ate mine early while watching a few of the girl's favorite shows, so by the time Liam came home, they were ready to eat with him and I left for the evening. The first time I left without giving Liam any second glances, or having him walk me to my car, was like fighting a wave.

I wanted to look back.

I wanted him to walk me to my car, and I could tell by the way he hung back, he wanted to as well. But once that door clicked shut behind me, I knew this would be our new normal.

I asked for a divide, and Liam had no choice but to give it to me.

THAT FIRST NIGHT, I ended up at the diner and slumped down into the same booth that I had been in when the girls first came up to me. I ordered pie and hoped it would soothe the weird chasm in my chest that had opened.

I wasn't really paying attention to any of the other patrons until Tammy, the original waitress who'd waited on me, stood next to my table.

"Looks like Macon is starting to dull your shine."

I glanced up from my game of solitaire that I was playing on my phone and gave her a pathetic smile.

"Yep, guess I'm not made for Macon," I joked, adjusting into the booth. My chest hurt. Why did it already hurt this bad?

Tammy gave me a pitying look before clicking her tongue.

"None of us are, honey. This mountain was made for the bears, deer, and wild cats. We're all just a bunch of idiots up here trying to coexist with them."

Hadn't really thought of it that way before.

"Here's your pie, and can I just give you a little piece of advice?" she asked, sliding the steaming rhubarb in front of me.

My mouth watered immediately, not really processing her words, but I nodded anyway.

"In order to last in the mountains of Macon, you have to find something that makes you feel as solid as the trees that grow here—something or someone. I'm still working on that, but the people who last here, they've found the right people. It's like finding your very own mountain peak inside of someone. Isn't that a crazy thing to even think? Have you been up to the top of Mount Macon yet?"

My fork sank into the flaky crust as I tried to swallow the thick lump in my throat.

"No, not yet."

Tammy's eyes rounded as she gripped her hip. "You gotta go, there's a whole trailhead and everything. I think it's right off the main road, with a sign—"

"Tammy!" someone yelled from the back counter.

My waitress winced as Millie, the owner made her way out.

"What did I tell you about talking people's ears off?" Millie asked quietly, walking closer to the booth so she didn't embarrass Tammy any more than she already had.

The owner glanced at me, giving me a smile.

"Haley, it's nice to see you. How do you like the rhubarb?"

She knew my name? my mouth gaped for a second before I realized I had words.

"Oh. I love it."

"And how are Liam and the girls?" her gentle eyes implored kindly.

Just like that I felt like I'd taken a slap to the face.

"Uh."

She stayed put but moved to the side as Tammy left to help another customer.

"Sorry, I thought you were nannying the girls or helping Liam, weren't you?"

I nodded, trying to gain my voice again.

"Yes, sorry…just took me a second."

"Well, I'm sure glad they have you." Millie squeezed my shoulder supportively before heading back behind the counter.

I watched her go, thinking that maybe—just maybe—I was doing the right thing. Maybe in the end this would be a good thing, and even though my heart felt frail, my foundation with the girls would be solid enough to make this whole thing worth it.

16

———

LIAM

WHY DID it feel like I had lost her, yet she was here every single fucking day?

Dark hair that trapped bits of sunlight when she turned her head the right way. Her green eyes bright with laughter when she spent time with my daughters. Baking…fuck, she was baking so much. Fluffy, buttery pies, scones, cakes, and biscuits. She kept trying new recipes, and every time I caught her in my kitchen, hips pinned to the counter, all I wanted to do was wrap my arms around her and hold her to my chest.

I wanted to tell her things I had no business feeling so soon.

Day in, day out, she came into my life then drifted out like a wave that's turned to foam, kissing the shore with nothing but fragments of what was once carried within it.

The girls only fell harder for her.

I only fell harder for her.

Because while I was pissed as hell that she'd done this, I also respected her for doing it.

No one put my kids first…not even me, most of the time. My daughters just rolled with whatever I decided, whatever happened—they just took it all better than any fighter I'd ever faced in the ring. Here was this woman, pulling my girls off the ropes, sitting them down and baking them cupcakes while braiding their hair.

They loved her.

I loved her.

Even if I wasn't ready to really accept it or face it. Deep down I knew it to be true.

Which was why I needed to leave.

I couldn't do this—not when I wanted her so badly and there was no reprieve from her scent that filled my halls. Her small touches were everywhere.

I had lasted two months.

The Community Center had its grand opening, and I watched her. I examined her every move as Jeffery fucking Akers flirted. I watched as she brushed him off, hating how relieved it felt to know that in the end she was still mine. Just frozen for now, like a time capsule I could bust open when we'd finally hit the right date.

Whenever that fucking was.

Haley never told me, not that I actually thought she knew. She wanted a foundation with my kids, and since she was with them nearly every day, I assumed she had it.

But the last time I tried to kiss her, she turned me down telling me, "Not yet."

I had to get some space, and I also needed to make some money, so this was going to be the best option for all of us.

HALEY HAD JUST STEPPED into the house, and I wasn't supposed to be here.

"Hey…" I said, catching her off guard.

She spun and gasped.

I couldn't help but laugh. "Sorry."

She slapped my arm, walking past me. "You're not supposed to be here right now."

"I know." I followed her into the kitchen, where she began unloading groceries. Fuck if I knew what she ordered half the time. I didn't fight her anymore on what she spent or got for the house.

"Listen…"

Her head popped up from digging into the paper bags.

"What's up?"

"I have a gig that's paying me…it will help take care of some of my debt, until I can research a new backer."

She slid a tray of raspberries out and then another.

"Okay…what sort of gig?"

"Boxing. There's some international circuits my agent told me about that's doing a 'retired heroes' thing." I cleared my throat. "The tour's in Europe."

The box of graham crackers slipped from her hands as she stared at me, mouth slack, her dark brows high on her forehead.

"Wait…Europe?" she shook her head. "I don't understand."

She did, though—she just hadn't processed it.

So, I waited and drank in the sight of how beautiful she looked. Her hair, that small slice of skin showing near her stomach. That gloss on her lips.

"How long would you be gone?"

My chest might as well have cracked and revealed how deeply she'd embedded herself into me. Her voice was so full of worry and fear that I wanted to close the space between us and erase that line between her brows, smooth out the crinkles near her eyes.

Instead, I gripped the back of the chair and rasped, "Ten weeks."

Haley fell into the nearest seat as if her legs wouldn't hold her up anymore.

"Ten weeks?"

I clicked my molars together and nodded.

"What about the girls?" Her eyes watered but she quickly swiped at them.

I gestured toward her. "That's where you come in. I was hoping you'd be able to stay here with them."

"Of course, I can, but—"

I moved, kneeling in front of her. "They love you like you belong to them…you're the best person for it."

She shook her head, more tears falling. "Liam…why?"

I couldn't help it. I leaned forward and kissed the tip of her nose, then her jaw, until finally I claimed her lips. I moved slowly, deliberate and sensual.

Her fingers sunk into my hair, pulling me closer as she moved her head to the side, and she met the slide of my tongue against hers.

When we finally broke apart, I confessed. "Because I can't keep walking around here not having you. It's too painful. This is the best option."

I stood and grabbed her chin. "Besides, I wanted to earn some money, and it will give me an excuse to check in on my dad."

She watched me as tears gathered in her dark lashes.

"When do you leave?"

I needed more space, because I wanted to taste her again.

"Tonight."

"Liam." She pulled her chin down, and a sob cracked her voice.

I turned away and grabbed my bag.

"I'm going to pull the girls out of school early to tell them. If you want to go pack your things from Nora's then you can just plan on staying here with the girls until I get back."

She nodded sadly then whispered, "Of course."

I gave her one last look before turning to go, knowing damn well my heart would be staying here with everyone I loved.

haley

A few scattered lists:

New Notebooks
Prime Delivery
FaceTime
Google
Calendars
Post-it Notes
Jeffery Akers
Millie
Flashlights
Pottery Barn
Costco

Week One

The days passed slow at first.

Understandably the girls missed their dad the first week, so we all slept in Liam's bed, and I gave them one day where they got to be sad and not go to school. I decided we needed a little pampering, so I took them back to the spa up on the mountain and let them throw more coins into the fountain. This time all their wishes were about bringing their dad back.

Colson and Nora came over often, and I was always taking the girls over there.

It helped.

But we missed him.

I used my phone for the girls to FaceTime him, but the girls kept fighting over it. The next night they each had their own tablet after I did a run to the local Target twelve miles away.

Liam saved ten minutes at the end of each call to talk to me. We spoke about the girls, how they were doing, how school was going. His face was bruised and usually being held together someplace with medical tape in every call. I only asked if he was being safe and taking care of himself. He always assured me he was, but I still worried. Then he'd tell me he missed me, and I would cry, explaining how much I missed him in return.

By the end of week one, I felt like we could get through the other nine.

I was a fool.

HALEY

Week Two

Mila apparently *was* prone to meltdowns, but so was Seraphina. Even Maddy got sassy from time to time.

Not going to lie, those days nearly broke me.

But we made it through. I ended up in the diner, venting to Millie and occasionally Tammy. They'd quickly become a safe place for me to gain perspective and to garner advice. Millie never spoke her opinion on Liam's leaving, but Tammy did. I had to ignore how often she spoke of him being careless or unfair, leaving me in charge of the girls. I wouldn't have accepted if I didn't want to do it.

Spring in Macon meant storms. Lots of them.

I wasn't used to the strong winds, so that was also a new thing for us. The power went out, so we huddled in Liam's room with a flashlight and told fairytales until they fell asleep.

When I finally clicked the light off, I let my tears free.

There were many.

HALEY

Week Three

Nora, Rae, and Millie became my lifelines as they answered my frantic texts when the girls came down with the flu.

Colson was over a few days after that when I became ill myself.

As the weeks passed, something in me began to weave together… something solid, strong and vulnerable all at once. I felt it pull together at night when I picked up after the girls and the house fell silent as they slumbered in their beds. It solidified as I fell into the role of a mother figure to the girls, day after day. My mind slowly began to cut the distance between myself as an outsider and claimed the girls as my own. In my head, I went from referring to them as *the* girls to *my* girls, and by the time I realized I was doing it, it was too late.

I was happy.

Happy even without Liam. I missed him. I ached for him…

But Maddy, Seraphina and Mila made me feel whole.

These girls were filling in deep holes, ruts, and gaping canyons in my heart. My love for them was big, and scary—but it was vast and real too.

Then my brother proposed to Nora, and suddenly it felt like too much.

Liam was missing everything.

Week Four

Working through hurt with someone overseas is not advisable.

Liam missed me, and I missed him.

We got into an argument over how much we missed each other.

But in the end, he was under contract, and there was nothing he could do.

He apologized.

I forgave him.

Then I tried to forgive myself for doing this to us in the first place.

Week Five

Notes were something I learned I liked writing, just like my lists. I'd leave the girls little messages in their lunches. They started writing them back and leaving them on my bedside table to read at night. Slowly, over time, it became a tradition for us.

Then there was handling all the school things. There was an app each of the girls' teachers used to communicate with parents. I always felt like I was falling behind. I didn't want to risk a run-in with Lacey again, so I dealt with the carpool line in the mornings, which made me want to scream. Why did people have to get out with their kids to hug them? It was the fast drop-off line where the kids were supposed to jump out of the car.

I attended an impromptu parent teacher conference for Mila that both humbled and terrified me. Apparently, I needed to be more of a stickler for Mila practicing her letters. We used her tablet to practice every night. Seraph was a deep soul that her teachers didn't seem to understand. They didn't like that she drew on everything. Her desk, her arms, her jeans. She was an artist that was always trying new mediums. I found pencils in her bed, markers, and even chalk once. She drew on her bed post, her wall, her ceiling.

I had to figure out what to do about that.

Week Six

Chalkboard Paint.

I was down at Home Depot with Jefferey, of all people, picking out three gallons.

He helped paint Seraph's room all in one weekend.

That was a surprising twist of events. Jefferey turned out to be a pretty amazing friend. It started with him finding me at the diner one afternoon, asking about where to buy salt for the lingering ice that was covering the sidewalk and driveway every morning. He brought over a bag that afternoon to Liam's house and then stored it in the garage for me.

Maddy kept me on time with garbage days, and would always pile all the bills into a nice neat stack when she grabbed the mail for me. Liam had left behind a card to use for everything, but I never once touched it. I paid the bills from my account, I bought groceries, paid for field trips, and new school supplies.

HALEY

Week Seven

Liam:

Happy Birthday. I miss you.

My twenty-first birthday came and went, and a single text from Liam was what I had in the form of gifts from the man I had fallen in love with. Colson and Nora threw a party for me.

It was fun, but when I looked at my girls and realized Liam had missed yet another moment, my heart squeezed tight. I cried myself to sleep that night.

Week Eight

I'd started buying little things for Liam's house that made it feel like mine. A blanket ladder for the living room, pictures that added contrast and color to the living room. Flowers on his nightstand, and a new plush chair to go in front of his massive bay window that overlooked the street. I drank my coffee from it most mornings.

Other mornings, Jefferey would invite me to tag along as he picked up lumber or had to pick paint samples for a job he was working. It was a needed distraction, especially as the weather warmed and time finally seemed to catch up with me.

Reality hit like a stone wall. Liam was missing everything, and I couldn't take it anymore.

Week Nine

We were on our way to help Nora finish up the last few details of the wedding, which was taking place next week. Nora rode shotgun as I drove up the mountain, heading to Rae's house for our big girls' night. Liam was due back in a few days, so this was our last chance to really come together and do our last fittings and measure the girls for their dresses as well.

Nora filled the silence along with the girls as they all discussed the upcoming trip to California. My big brother wanted to marry his wife over the garden his mother once planted there, so we were all boarding a plane next week.

"The mountain is gorgeous today." I leaned forward, taking in the image of Mount Macon in the distance. The house looked like it was a part of the mountain, yet there were acres of tall evergreens between the summit. Snow was still in patches on the ground up here, but with the tiny tendril of smoke coming up from the chimney, I didn't even mind.

We unpacked our things, and by the time we reached the porch, Rae was standing on it with her arms spread wide. "Finally! I have been waiting for this all week!"

We all laughed and then headed inside.

Two huskies were in my space as soon as I stepped foot inside the two-story house.

"Dove, Duke…relax," Rae chided, and they lowered their heads—moving toward the fireplace.

"Okay, I thought we'd just be in here tonight." Rae dipped to move the coffee table to the side.

"Sounds good to me," Nora chimed in from the kitchen, already pulling out the Margarita mix.

Rae eyed the takeout bag in my hand. "Haley, oh my gosh! You stopped at all my favorite places!"

I lifted it. "Oh yeah, we might need to warm some of it up."

Moving into the kitchen, I placed all the containers on a big platter, Nora made the drinks, and Rae instructed Maddy and Seraph on how to set up a ton of pillows and blankets for us on the floor while she browsed for a rom-com for us to watch.

Once we were all settled and the girls all had a plate of food, we moved on to the dresses.

"These are so beautiful." I admired each dress that the girls tried on, having them all sized and tailored perfectly.

Nora smiled dreamily as she watched Maddy spin. "They are…and oh my gosh, just wait until we add the crowns."

Helping Maddy down, Nora turned toward me and Rae. "Okay, now I need to see my bridesmaids."

Rae walked toward the stairs where she'd hung the garment bags and handed one to me. I had purchased the dress, but we'd had our dresses altered and now needed to try them on one last time before we were in California.

Gripping the garment bag in my arms, I headed upstairs. Maddy, Seraph and Mila had all changed into pajamas and were snuggled on the massive, feathered bed, watching cartoons.

After checking on them, I slipped into the bathroom to change.

In the mirror I took in the subtle curve of my hips that the waistline accentuated and the low dip of the neckline that gave my cleavage a boost. The yellow fabric complimented my skin, but I was paler than usual, which was something I'd have to get used to if I was determined to live this far from the beach. I swept my hair up off my shoulder to test a few different styles until I heard Rae calling for me to come down.

When I returned downstairs, Nora and Rae were arguing over wedding details.

"We can't get a platform over the garden without it looking like a platform over a garden…" Rae said, shaking her head.

Nora scoffed. "Please do not insult me by insinuating I can't make a raised platform look like a floating cloud if I want it to."

They both began laughing as I rounded the stairs and came into view.

A few things happened at once.

Nora's jaw dropped, Rae's hands went to her chest, and then the dogs started to bark as the front door opened.

Everyone's heads turned as boisterous laughter carried in from the foyer.

I froze in place as Davis and Colson walked in, laughing and cracking huge smiles, seemingly unfazed that they'd just crashed our girls' night. Then a third member joined them, and my breath caught in a painful, frozen gasp.

Liam.

18

———

LIAM

IT FELT weird to be back.

I used to travel all the time when I was on the circuit. I'd go all over the country and even abroad from time to time. But I had never done anything as extensive as a nine weeklong rotation out of the country.

I made a decent amount of money, but half of it was already going to my lawyer because Lacey wanted to go back to court. Again. Wasn't this just the same revolving door that had been my entire fucking life for the past four years? This time, I couldn't even really be bothered by it. I had the money to pay the lawyer; I was just hoping I could have saved it and used it to pay off some of the debt on my gym.

I wasn't focusing on that right now. I hadn't really been focusing on it or the trip back. Not even arriving in Portland, having my best friend secretly grab me, and drive me back up here without telling anyone. I was still thinking about the text I had received from Haley a few weeks back. The argument and absolute hopelessness we both seemed to feel from it.

I cut my trip short by an entire week, but it was worth it. I missed my daughters so much I could barely breathe. The FaceTime sessions helped, but it wasn't the same as wrapping my arms around them and holding them.

The FaceTime sessions with Haley were harder. As hard as it was to be away from here while being physically close, it was a thousand times harder with an ocean between us.

So here I was, surprising everyone and crashing what had apparently been a planned girls' sleepover. All I knew was that all four of my girls were up at Davis Brenton's place, and I needed to see them. The second Cole picked me up, he decided crashing the night wouldn't be such a bad idea.

It was already dark when we pulled into his driveway, and my heart nearly crashed through my sternum when I saw Haley's car parked right there in front. My breathing came out as a jagged as a timber saw as I scaled the porch. Davis and Cole went in first, and then I trailed not far behind.

Nora and Rae were standing in the middle of the living room, staring off toward the stairs, and as soon as I rounded the corner, I realized why.

Haley.

She had on a yellow dress that made her look like some sort of woodland fairy princess. Nearly ten weeks with just my hand to satisfy my needs, and I was two seconds from tossing her over my shoulder and taking her upstairs. The swells of her breasts pushed against the low neckline, showing how hard she was breathing, and her dark hair was down, nearly kissing her waist with tiny curls at the bottom.

I froze, waiting for her to make a move. We were in front of everyone, so I wasn't sure what she would do. I hoped she'd run into my arms and kiss me. I hoped she'd tell me this divide we needed was over, and we could go back to what we were doing before. Realizing she wasn't moving, I finally took a step. Then another.

Cole, Davis and the others were talking to each other, seemingly unaware of this suspended moment between us. Which was weirdly nice; it offered a small slice of privacy. Her green eyes were so full of emotions, tears welling, and she blinked furiously to hold them at bay. She took a step back toward the stairs, then another, until finally she broke the silence.

"You should come surprise the girls."

She waved me over, heading upstairs and I followed, already knowing this would be the only opportunity we would get to be alone.

She was ahead of me as I slowly scaled the steps, taking my time as I watched the sway of her ass in that dress. Once I was on the top stair, Haley hung near the bathroom door, flicking her eyes toward the end of the hall. I could hear my daughters laughing, and my heart squeezed tight. I'd go to them in a minute. I just needed this one moment with Haley alone first.

I pushed her into the bathroom and quietly shut the door, flipping the lock.

"You came back early," Haley whispered, stepping away from the door and toward a black duffel bag lying on the tiled floor.

"You asked me to." It wasn't the only reason I came back early, but I wanted to remind her of what she'd said.

Letting out a small scoff, she shook her head. "That was weeks ago."

Was that an edge of annoyance I felt from her?

"I signed a contract to stay the whole ten weeks."

She gave me her back while reaching for the top button on her dress. She was fumbling, enough that I stepped up and helped her. This close, I could smell that deliciously sweet floral scent. I still had no clue what flower it belonged to, but I loved it.

"Thank you," she murmured then slid the dress down. She stepped out of the buttery material in just her lilac-colored thong and black strapless bra. *Fuck I missed her.* She must think more of me if she assumed she could strip in front of me and not be touched.

My hand went to the curve of her neck as I gently pulled her back against my chest.

Putting my mouth next to her ear, I whispered, "What I'm about to do next, you'll have to forgive me, but I won't wait another fucking second to have you."

I pressed a kiss to her spine, then unfastened my jeans.

"Liam…" she warned, but it held no weight. I tested my theory by spinning her and lifting her onto the bathroom sink.

She let out a tiny moan as I gripped her thighs and spread them apart.

Her eyes locked on mine, silently challenging me.

I raised an eyebrow, asking if she'd allow this. When her fingers drifted down her body and slung that lilac material to the side, I had my answer. Fisting my cock, I held her gaze as I thrust inside her with one go.

She released a harsh gasp, her nails digging into my shoulders.

"Liam."

I pulled out of her slick center, only to push in harder, loving the tightness and warmth that cradled my cock like a vise.

I moaned softly into her neck, moving my hands to her ass and pulling her closer.

She was too busy gripping my hair, marking my neck and murmuring how badly she needed this to notice that I was controlling her hips as she fucked me. I had so many words I needed to say, so many thoughts…but where would I even start? I felt like this was the only language we understood; forever and always, this physical connection would be our strongest form of communication.

She fucked me earnestly, lifting her hips to get the friction she needed from me. One of her arms went behind her on the counter to stabilize her as my hips thrust forward at a rapid pace, the other latched to my shoulder as my pace picked up. Her breathing was labored as the top of her cleavage bounced under the confines of the bra.

Finally, her pink lips parted as she looked down between us. "Liam," she moaned. I moved my hand to cover her mouth, but the damage was done. Whoever might be up here would have heard us. The only saving grace we had was that the girls were watching cartoons.

Still, I was enraptured by her lithe body wrapped around mine. I was drunk on her addictive sounds, how good she felt as I held her. How impossibly perfect it felt as I released inside her, breathing heavily into her neck. How much I had missed this—how much I'd missed *her.*

Pressing a kiss to her forehead, I leaned against her as I murmured, "I think Rae and Davis might hate us for fucking in their guest bathroom."

She laughed, still trying to catch her breath. "They'll never know, just be careful when you pull out."

Shit, had we really just done that?

"I haven't been with anyone…just so you know," I muttered close to her ear, pressing a kiss there. She should know that, but just in case…

She smiled up at me, making my heart feel like lava. "I trusted that you hadn't. I'm still on birth control, but yeah, I haven't been with anyone either."

The relief that hit me was so intense…and strange. I guess, deep down, a part of me worried that I'd come back and she'd have moved on, or would have realized I was too old for her, or basically just do something that would end us for good. I hadn't actually expected her to open her legs and let me fuck her within the first few minutes of seeing her. But she had…and that had to mean that she was done with this distance.

I was ready to have her with me. All the time. Every night.

"We better go out there. You go see the girls. I'll change."

I nodded, holding her hip. I was struggling to let her go. I felt like the second I did, she'd talk herself back into needing distance.

Once I fixed myself, washed my hands, and pressed a quick kiss to Haley, I exited the bathroom and went to find my kids.

I watched through the crack of the door as they laughed at something on the television, their little smiles radiating peace, and it all hit me at once: the distance. The time away.

Mila giggled loudly and I broke. Emotions clogged my throat as I pushed inside, and the girls looked up.

"Daddy!" they screamed, jumping from the covers and throwing their arms around me.

A few tears actually slid down my face as I pulled them close, hugging them to me. Their little faces were buried in my shirt as they talked about how much they missed me. Mila was crying, so was Seraph, and even my Maddy was tearing up.

"We missed you so much. I have so much to tell you," Maddy said as I settled onto the bed next to them. This would be where I stayed until they fell asleep, because there wasn't a single chance they'd be willing to let me go before then.

IT WAS about an hour before I wandered back downstairs. The girls were asleep in the guest room, and I was exhausted from traveling. I needed sleep, but I wanted to find Haley. The living room was lit only by the light from the fireplace when I found everyone else. Nora and Colson were cuddled up on one couch, Rae and Davis were on another, and Haley was on her own, covered by a huge blanket on the third sofa.

I didn't say anything as I made my way to her. Haley moved for me so that I could recline back against the cushions. I expected her to lay on top of me, but she stayed erect, ignoring me and watching whatever was on the television.

It was some wilderness survival show.

"I love this guy!" Rae said from her spot on top of Davis's chest.

Nora was next, narrowing her eyes on the screen.

"Oh my gosh, I love Ryan Prince. Did you know he did a few episodes with his step kids? It's like the sweetest thing ever, and he managed to get his wife on there once. I died."

Then Haley jumped in, joining their tandem.

"Oh wait! Was he the guy who stopped acting to be with his ex-girl-friend from like his college years?"

Nora snapped her fingers in the air, trying to remember. "Yes! He was on vacation, and she was the maid at the resort he was staying at. I swear, I devoured their story when I read it. I was following their socials like my life depended on it."

The women laughed, and I was slowly drifting off, unable to keep up with the conversation. I was leaning back, and Haley had moved enough that I got my one leg up so I could lay all the way down. She settled in again, but this time she laid the blanket over both of our feet. She put a pillow in my lap and rested against it. I idly toyed with her hair until I drifted off to sleep.

HALEY WAS on my chest when the sun filtered in through the far wall, all made of glass windows.

Eyes sill shut, my arm still around Haley, securing her to me, I tried to act like I had no idea that Nora was awake and whispering about us.

"There's something going on. I swear I heard them banging upstairs."

Cole scoffed and then whispered back, "Let it go. I'm sure they've grown close but there's nothing going on there. He was gone for almost ten weeks. Plus, hasn't Haley been hanging out with Jeffery quite a bit?"

What the hell?

She was spending time with Jeffery fucking Akers again? I thought we were past that. Why was she spending time with him, and on what scale? Must be a big enough scale that my best friend assumed his sister was dating him.

Rage made my head swim, and my hands grow tight around Haley's hips. How many times did I need to remind this girl that she was mine?

Leaving for nearly ten fucking weeks might have made her question that.

"They're not dating…at least I don't think—" Nora whispered back.

I wanted to roll my eyes. No, I wanted to open them, stare at Nora, and tell her she was right, there was nothing going on with them. There couldn't be. Haley wouldn't do that to me.

"Stop worrying about them," Colson said then launched into something about California and next week.

I dozed off, pulling Haley impossibly closer, which included having her hike her leg up against my waist. It might have been ten minutes, or an hour later, but eventually Haley woke and seemed to freeze when she realized where she was.

By then, thankfully, we had the room to ourselves.

She sat up, leaning against my chest, brushing against my hard-on with her knee, then straightening to get free of the blankets.

"Oh good, you're awake!" Rae beamed from the kitchen.

Guess we didn't have it to ourselves.

I slowly sat up, feeling every ache and creak in my neck and back as I went. Being thirty-two meant sleeping on couches with another human lying on top of you caused neck problems.

Haley gave me an indifferent expression before stretching and walking into the kitchen.

Okay, fuck. I didn't love how that felt.

She'd slept on my chest all night, and fucked before that…so why was she looking at me like I was the awkward tag-along friend that no one wanted around?

Now that I was back, I was needed at the gym as soon as possible. I had a friend of mine covering for me while I was gone, but he was retired and probably wanted to get back to that.

Once I was standing, I could see the back yard through the windows. Past Davis's massive porch, there was a hen enclosure, a goat pen, and something else there along the edge of his property for animals. I did a double-take when I realized he had three small helpers clomping behind him in their pajamas and little rain boots. It was the tail end of spring, probably a chill in the air, but Haley had made sure they wore thermal pajamas.

As if I'd summoned her into action, suddenly Haley opened the back door, while cradling her mug and yelled, "Maddy, watch out for Mila! She's going to try and climb that enclosure again, like she did last time, and she's going to fall in the mud, also like last time!"

I saw Maddy wave at Haley then turn back toward the goats.

Why did it feel like I was suddenly in the backseat of my own life?

Haley came back in, but her eyes remained on my kids, which now that I was back… I guess, that would all change now…or would it?

I folded all the blankets on the couch and found my keys, wallet and phone. Then I walked into the kitchen to find Haley. She had moved, leaning against the counter while holding her mug of coffee, talking to Rae.

"Sorry to interrupt, but I have to head back. I was going to see if you wouldn't mind driving us back?"

Haley glanced once at Rae before clearing her throat and setting her mug down.

"Actually, this girls' weekend extends to today, we're helping Nora spray and decorate all these Mason jars. I was planning to bring the girls down when we're done, if that's okay…"

Colson came up before I could respond, slapping me on the back.

"I'm headed back. I'll take you."

Haley beamed. "Perfect, we'll see you once we get back."

She turned away and started talking with Rae again, leaving me with the same sense she had before I ever left—like she wasn't ready for this. Fuck if I was going to let her do that again. I tried to steady my heart, but the blow still hit as heavy as a sledgehammer.

I gave her a fake smile and dipped my head.

"Of course…I'll just see you guys at home."

I turned on my heel and headed toward the door to get my boots, unsure why it suddenly felt like coming home early was a colossal mistake.

19
———

LIAM

There was a new picture hanging above the entryway…it was fashionable, something with barnwood and white cursive writing that boasted about being home and something else I didn't put the effort into reading. My eyes moved to the gap above the wall, where green plants now sat in large ceramic pots, at least five of them artfully draped over the ledge. It added color to my white walls, and so did the blanket ladder…and did she buy a new chair?

Above the couch were four huge canvas photos of my daughters hung in place. One of each girl individually, and the fourth was all of them sitting on an exposed river rock, giggling while the sun caught in each of their hair.

My breath caught, and my nose burned as the reality of missing so much of their lives sank in. My eyes kept jumping to every little detail the photographer had caught of my kids. Their smiles, their eyes…their little chubby cheeks. The coordinating outfits they wore. Maddy and Mila were in pale pink dresses, and Seraph was in a deep burgundy. I had never had professional photos taken of them. Lacey and I had some taken before Mila was born…but nothing on my own, nothing with all three of them.

I coughed to clear away the tightness in my throat and moved so I'd get past the emotion.

The kitchen was different too. New cutting boards, knives…I opened the cupboard, and a matching dish set was there. She'd upgraded our chairs, and added a new cushioned bench. Was the table different too? It was a pale gray, modern—fashioned to fit the newer style she'd thrown up on the walls in different pictures. She'd added a huge bulletin board near the pantry door, where each girls schedule was printed with a colored sticky note system. I read a few of her notes on the side and smiled.

Drop-off: 8:40
Pick up: 3:25

Groceries:
Little oranges…whatever those are called, just not the big ones. Pop-Tarts, strawberry—check into organic if that's such a thing, new pens and a new notebook- and fruit roll-ups.

COSTCO:

Chicken, spinach, Pasta (the kind Mila loves) toilet paper, zip lock baggies, chicken nuggets (the dinosaur kind), panda snacks (google this—she had no idea how to explain it), healthy snacks, cereal, multivitamins, tampons.

I didn't have a Costco membership, so that must be something new she'd done along with everything else in my kids lives. Part of me was glad she didn't sit around and wait for permission. She took the reins and accepted a role I thrust on her with no training or preparation. I ran my hand through my hair as guilt settled into my chest.

Going up the stairs, I nearly passed Seraph's room when I paused and walked inside. Her white walls were all replaced with black chalkboard paint. Seraph had drawn large murals on nearly every wall. She had bright curtains and a white comforter to offset the dark colors in the room, and with a few plants and soft lamp lighting, it actually looked really good.

I wandered further down the hall until I reached my room. Haley's delicious floral smell was everywhere. There was another new chair up here, facing the window. She'd added lilac sheer shades over the large window that looked over the street. It added color to the room. The bed was also covered in a light lilac feather duvet, and there were four huge pillows where my flat ones used to be, and about fifteen throw pillows. *Was this Haley's favorite color?*

At the edge of the bed sat a cushioned bench with a cozy-looking throw blanket. The dresser, where my TV used to sit, was replaced with something larger and the TV was now mounted on the wall.

Who the hell had helped her hang and move all this shit?

There were fresh flowers on the nightstand, lotion, Chapstick, plus a kindle and tablet. On the opposite side of the bed was a little notebook, with a few lines scribbled across the page.

Long talks with Millie
The end of flu season
Allergy medicine
Weddings
Vacuum lines in the carpet
The walking path behind the house
End of day baths that can be taken with wine

WHAT WAS THIS LIST?

It was odd and seemed incredibly random.

I pushed the heels of my palms into my eye sockets and threw myself back onto the bed. What the fuck had I missed?

It felt like I was a stranger looking in on my life, only I wasn't here anymore and there was no way I'd catch up.

HALEY WAS BEING ELUSIVE, which I wasn't sure if it was due to the wedding and being stressed or something else. She'd come back after the night up with Nora and Rae and went on with business as usual. The girls were out of school for the week to prepare for the trip, so they were mostly hanging with me at the gym and Haley was busy doing a million different errands for Nora and Rae.

Still, it felt like I was missing something…or if I was digging deep, like she was hiding something. Maybe I was just messed up because we hadn't really talked yet. We'd seen each other in passing, but with the kids around, we hadn't done more than that, and at night, she was over at her brother's house. When I pressed for a reason, it went back to helping Nora with last-minute wedding details that were keeping them up almost all night.

I was sure that was the case. I mean, she had called me late last night, around eleven, and talked to me until she had to go again. She was sweet, even flirtatious, but it didn't change the gnawing void in my gut that we needed to talk.

I wanted to end this distance shit officially, especially before we went to the wedding. So, I swung the girls by the diner and asked Millie to keep an eye on them for a bit while I tried to catch Haley alone.

She wasn't answering her text messages, so I tried Colson's house first. She wasn't there, so I headed home. Her car was in the garage, so I knew she was here, but when I walked in, she wasn't around.

"Haley?" I yelled, but she didn't reply.

Must be upstairs.

I was about to run up when her cell phone dinged with a new

message. I looked down, seeing that it was right next to me on the kitchen counter. I wouldn't normally ever invade her privacy, but in this case…

I tapped in her code and cradled the phone, swiping open her text messages.

Jefferey:

Did we agree to meet here, or over there?

Then another message came through.

Jefferey:

I know you're eager to get this wood up *winky face*

What. In. The. Actual. Fuck.

She ran down the stairs a moment later, all bubbly and happy.

"Hey, I didn't know you were here. Are you alone?"

I held up the phone, feeling every inch the jilted boyfriend, about to make a scene.

"Want to tell me what the fuck this is about?"

Her steps slowed as she focused on the phone in my hand. Slowly a line formed between her eyebrows as she gently took the phone from my hand.

"Oh this…it's nothing."

She set the phone down on the counter and moved around me.

"Are you packed, and did you by chance download the airline app on your phone so they can just scan your ticket?"

I already had it on my phone.

She spun on her heel and tilted her head. "And I know you think you already have the app, but this is a different airline."

"Haley, why is Jefferey Akers asking if you're meeting here and why the fuck is he referencing wood getting up?"

She let out a sigh but didn't answer me.

I didn't have the energy for this shit.

"You want to fuck him…then go. If you think you can. I warned you what I would do if you wanted someone else."

Her head snapped up, eyes wide and her mouth parted. "Wait, what?"

I threw my arms wide. "Isn't that what the fuck this is about?"

My nose was burning again, and I fucking hated the sensation. I felt like was going to lose her again. And hadn't I lost her for nine weeks while she played this stupid fucking game of building a foundation. All for what? So she could fuck Jefferey Akers on top of it?

I turned and was ready to leave but Haley grabbed my forearm, stopping me.

"Liam. Oh my gosh, that's not at all what's going on. Jeffery was going to help me pick out the right wood for an extra shelf in your office. I saw that you came back with a few new trophies, and I thought it would be nice to have a place to display them. I was trying to surprise you."

Her eyes went soft, like this would magically fix everything, but it did the opposite.

A scoff left me as I gripped the edge of the counter and tried to regain composure, but it wasn't working. There was a tornado in my chest.

"So he's the one who's helped you with all this stuff?" I lifted my eyes, and Haley looked up to the large picture frame on the wall.

The blush that followed told me I was right.

"The dresser, chairs, pictures…" I watched as she took a step back, lowering her face.

It hit me. "Seraph's room?"

Tucking a few loose strands of that silky hair away, she lifted her chin.

"We're just friends, Liam. He helped me while you were—"

"Fuck, Haley!" I snapped, throwing a magazine we'd gotten in the mail across the room.

"So while I was away, giving us distance and space for the foundation you wanted, you were here playing house with him? Replacing everything in my house like it's your own. Not asking me a single time for my input, much less my permission! We spoke every night, it's not like you couldn't get a hold of me, or like I just left you."

Her face grew determined as she stepped forward. "Liam, come on, you know me better than that. He helped me hang and move a few things, that's it. And as far as the rest—you did leave me. You left all of us. And yes, over the past nine weeks, I made this place feel like my home because that's what it became. If you have a problem with it, then change it."

With her face drawn in tight, she waited for me to respond, but I didn't even know what to say, so I stormed off and slammed the door behind me.

CHAPTER TWENTY

haley

Ocean Breezes
Summer
The sand
Malibu
The Boardwalk
Surfing
White-capped waves
New Family

I TRIED to focus on Nora, my new sister-in-law.

She was gorgeous in her white dress that hung off her shoulders, her beautiful curls hanging loosely down her back. My brother was watching her with tears in his eyes, and it made mine watery too.

Mila, Maddy, and Seraph were all standing in front of me, holding their baskets as we watched two of our favorite people make a lifetime of promises to one another.

I ignored the looks Liam continued to give me.

He was stunning in his fitted tux, freshly shaved with a new haircut that made my thighs clench together, because Liam was good-looking on his rough days, but cleaned up like this? Holy shit. I had to bat away dirty images all morning of me surprising him in some hall closet, just to feel his chest through that suit. I wanted to run my fingers over every inch of him, see him slip out of each layer, until he was in my favorite position: naked and erect.

But I was so pissed off at him it was ruining the image.

I glanced up at him for the hundredth time and just like always, his silver eyes were on me. His jaw tensing, focus solely on us and not the bride and groom.

We were assholes.

I wasn't sure what Liam wanted. He'd essentially walked out on our argument the day before yesterday and didn't seem to care that it ended any chance of us working through this argument. It was so stupid.

Cheers erupted, bringing my focus back to the wedding. Colson was kissing his beautiful bride and fresh tears coated my lashes. I wanted them to be happy with all my soul.

But, after being alone for so many weeks, I was also starting to crave my own happy ending. The foundation Liam spoke of was more than in place, and I knew we were ready for that next step, until he assumed I was sleeping with Jefferey.

The bridal line began filing back down the aisle, and I put my focus on Mila and Seraph as Maddy grabbed Liam's hand.

We converged together into the tent with the rest of the party, and right as we did, everyone seemed to freeze in place, watching us. Rae clung to Davis, her eyes on us, her mouth gaping. Nora and Colson, who should have been running off to wedded bliss, had similar positions, as did Millie and a few other people looking on.

Liam peered over his shoulder at me, I looked at him, and then Rae broke the silence.

"You guys look…" Her mouth wouldn't shut, and…was she crying?

My brother Colson narrowed his eyes on us then quickly glanced at Nora, who was smiling deviously.

She finally stepped forward, grabbing her cell phone from Rae's pocket, and snapped a picture of us.

"You look like a family."

Mila giggled and loudly proclaimed, "We *are* a family, silly."

My heart was a leaf, lost to the wind, pounding in my chest at her words.

Seraph hugged my waist, and Maddy edged closer.

Nora finally spun away, that smile in place, and then everyone else slowly did the same.

Colson begrudgingly walked away with his bride, but not without sending one last glare our way.

What in the hell was that?

And why did it feel like we'd just had all of our secrets exposed?

AFTER THE RECEPTION ended and a few lanterns lit the walkway back to the house, Liam pulled Mila up into his arms and I grabbed Seraph and Maddy, leading them into the house. We went up the stairs to my old room. It was sparse now, with three twin beds moved inside. Colson had arranged it so that the girls could have this room to themselves. Right next door was the master, which used to belong to my parents, but now that they'd left, and this house belonged to Colson, it was empty. I had assumed Colson would take it, especially for his wedding night, but he said he wanted his old room.

"Do we have to go back home tomorrow?" Maddy asked, yawning as she pulled her pajamas into her arms and headed for the closet.

"We have one more day before we have to go back," Liam said, helping Mila sort out her pajamas. I handed Seraph hers and then moved to help Mila change, carefully taking the dresses and hanging them in the closet.

Seraph pulled her covers back and let out a loud yawn. "What will we do?"

Liam handed me a backpack, and I settled it in the closet.

"Should we try surfing?" I asked, smiling at the girls as they perked up excitedly.

"You know how?"

"I do."

Liam smirked then dipped to kiss the girls' heads.

"Get some sleep. We'll figure it out tomorrow."

I shut off the light, and the room glowed as Seraph's star machine threw a million stars in varying shades of blue across the ceiling.

Mila sat up. "Wait!"

Liam and I turned toward her, still near the door.

"Where will you be in case I have a bad dream?"

I was about to open my mouth but realized I had to stop rushing to answer them. Liam was back now, and I wasn't their mother.

I waited for Liam to respond.

"Right next door."

"No, Daddy. Haley. She knows how to get me back to sleep when I'm scared."

Silver eyes found mine as a blush crept up my neck.

"I'll be right down the hall."

Mila tilted her head. "Why don't you just share a room with Daddy? You sleep in his room at home."

Liam coughed, lowering his head.

"I slept in there while your daddy was gone, honey."

She didn't seem to understand that.

"But don't you love Daddy?"

Oh gosh, where was this coming from? And why now?

"Mila, honey, it's time for bed. We'll talk tomorrow, okay?" Liam promised.

I blinked, shuffling backward out of the room.

In the dim light of the hall, I paused as Liam towered over me.

No one else was on this floor with us, and it felt like we were tucked away inside a bubble. There were no words as Liam tugged my hand, leading me into his room. The master didn't look anything like it used to. It seemed many of the rooms had been gutted and remodeled. I couldn't be more grateful as the light breeze from the ocean carried through the room. It was warm enough that the windows would stay open all night, allowing the fresh air to flow through the house.

"We need to talk," Liam muttered close to my ear, pressing a lingering kiss along my neck.

My memory served up the image of him walking away the other night, and I slipped past him.

"How convenient that you'd like to speak now."

Liam turned with me, watching as I slipped out of my shoes and pulled the pins out of my hair. My hands went to the top button at my back, quickly hoping somehow this time around I'd manage to unfasten them without his assistance.

His shiny shoes brought him closer, and my heart thundered in my chest at the sight of how perfect he looked in his suit.

"You're being stubborn."

"You're being rude, not to mention the lack of gratitude. I tried to do a nice thing for you, and you made me feel horrible about it."

His fingers lingered on my back as the dress pooled at my waist. Then he unclasped my bra, leaving my breasts bare and me with no choice but to step out of the material in just my thong.

"Black tonight?" Liam's hands skimmed my spine until he grazed the top of my underwear. "I liked the purple."

"Lilac…it's my favorite color."

His hand wrapped around my hip, pulling me flush against his chest.

"How did I not know that about you?"

My hands went to his chest, digging into the lapels of his jacket.

"There's a lot you don't know about me."

He hummed, his chin going to the side of my face then suddenly we were swaying.

"You didn't dance with me tonight." Liam remarked, close to my ear. The breeze from the ocean ruffled the curtains, forcing them to shift in the unruly wind.

Both of Liam's hands went to my hips, pulling me impossibly closer, mashing my breasts against his broad chest.

Desperate to fulfill the fantasy from earlier, I pushed the material of his jacket off his shoulders until it fell to the floor. Then I dug into his bowtie, unraveling it and pulling it free from his collar. The buttons at his throat came undone at my gentle touch, all while we swayed to a silent tune.

"I overreacted to the Jefferey thing." Liam confessed, tightening his grip on me as I slowly freed him of his shirt and vest.

It was my turn to hum, encouraging him to continue.

"I was jealous. And while it doesn't make me happy to know your new friend has been around my home, I understand the position I put you in."

"When you left me in charge of your children for almost three months?"

His Adam's apple bobbed, as his left hand moved lower, skimming my ass cheek.

"Forgive me." His posture changed as I trailed a line over his muscled chest and strong pecs. He curled in, lowering his arms almost in a hug. But then his hands closed over my ass, and he lifted me.

I let out a surprised sound as Liam carried me to the bed.

My anger began to thaw, my righteous indignation fizzling as the weight of missing him mauled my chest.

He watched me with a hunger that I wanted to keep in my heart forever, then his fingers gathered at his waist, freeing his dress pants until they fell to the floor as well.

I raised up on my elbows, watching him.

"Forgive me," Liam repeated.

I smiled deviously and had a wicked thought.

"Beg me"—I slid my thong down and parted my legs—"with your tongue."

Liam hovered over me, his lips spread in a cunning smile, and I relaxed into the pillows as his head found its way between my thighs.

CHAPTER TWENTY-ONE

haley

Macon in the summer
Officially Moving in with Liam
Disney Movies & Blankets
Secret Kisses

WE ARRIVED BACK in Macon a few days later.

Liam had allowed me the privilege to spoil his daughters rotten with shopping trips, all the ice cream they could eat, and their very own surf boards, which I stored at my old house—well, Colson's house. I would have to get used to that. Now, after checking in on Nora's garden, I was pulling into Liam's.

As I pulled into the driveway, I pressed the garage door opener, but it didn't work.

Confused, I tried again, and nothing.

I'd have to ask Liam to look at it. As soon as I thought him up, he appeared in front of the house, wearing a pair of loose basketball shorts, and nothing else.

My heart flipped over itself.

I exited the car and grabbed my purse, walking directly in front of him until the sun wasn't in my eyes.

"The garage door isn't working."

He nodded, dipping his chin to his chest. "I pulled the line, so it won't open unless you do it manually. I'll fix it, but one thing first."

His gray eyes landed on mine in a determined manner. Resolve had landed in his gaze, and it settled on me like a piece of granite.

"Before you come in, you need to be sure."

"Be sure?" My voice was more of a whisper as fear rattled in my chest.

His fingers wrapped around my wrist, pulling me until my chest was flush against his.

Then he pushed a piece of hair behind my ear.

"Be sure you're ready to stay. Once you step through that door, that's it. You're mine. I'm not playing this distance game anymore. I want you in my bed at night."

He placed my palm over his heart.

Then he continued with a voice rough and cracked.

"You belong in here, but you keep finding a way out. You keep needing to be away from me, and it's like the rest of my body just has to learn how to function without you."

My heart was a runaway train, speeding—with sparks shooting from the tracks in a clear warning that it was about to derail. I wanted to hide, turn around and leave, because the risk was too much. He could devastate me—no, *they* could. If he let me go, I'd lose them all. So far, I'd been safely dancing along the fringes of their lives. But this…this would put me in the center. It was so much, and yet I felt like if I didn't say yes it would be the greatest regret of my life.

I guess it really would be better to have loved them than to have never had them. And I knew in that moment that while neither of us would say it, he loved me. That confession meant he did, and I understood with a fathomless truth that I loved him, too. As broken and misshaped as love always looked in my life, the love I had to give wanted him.

"I'm sure."

Liam's smile was slow, sensual and… *completely mine.*

He lowered his mouth, tracing my lips and cradling my jaw. I opened for him, allowing him all the access he wanted. My hands went up around his neck as he deepened the kiss and slowly moved his hands down my body. We were in front of his house, his neighbors could all see, but I didn't care. This was our moment, and no one could take it from us.

He pulled away with a smile and was about to tow me inside when I tugged on his wrist, needing to say one last thing.

"One thing, just one." I held up one finger. "The girls deserve to adjust to this news properly. I don't want to do anything that's going to mess with them."

I loved how soft his eyes turned when he thought of his girls. He brought my hand up to kiss it, then nodded.

"Fine. No PDA in front of them, and at night we'll make them think you're staying in the guest room, but only because I just got back, and they've only had you for weeks. I don't want anything to throw them off."

That could work, at least until we worked up to that conversation where I explained that I loved them all and wanted to be a part of their family.

We went inside and found the girls all sitting in the living room, snuggled under blankets while watching a movie.

MILA SLOWLY WALKED over to me, carrying her blanket. I bent down and scooped her up into my arms and continued to the couch, where I slumped down with her in my lap.

"We're watching *Tangled*," Maddy said.

I frowned down at the five-year-old in my arms. "Again?"

Seraph laughed and snuggled closer to me. "We told her."

"Mila, he isn't even the best-looking prince."

She was madly in love with Flynn Ryder and watched *Tangled* endlessly.

"Daddy needs a special blanket like we have," Mila observed, tilting her head back to see her father.

I eyed my blanket that was folded on the back of the couch. I'd bought these for us when we went to visit Davis Brenton's new store.

Mila's expression narrowed, seemingly still stuck on the blanket draped behind me.

"Haley, you can share your special blanket with him, it's bigger than ours."

Liam looked over at me, then back at Mila. The other two were watching the movie, ignoring us.

"Sure. Liam, do you want to share my special blanket?" Liam was holding back a smirk; I could tell by the way his eyes sparkled.

Obviously, this was awkward because it was his home and his kids, but he'd been gone and the kids and I had built little traditions to cope with his absence. Our comfy blankets were one of them.

"I'd love to," he finally replied, moving toward the couch. I tossed the quilt at the end of the couch and scooted closer to Liam until I was near enough to share half the blanket with him. It put us shoulder to shoulder.

Once I relaxed into the cushions, Liam's hand found mine under the fabric and our fingers intertwined while we watched the movie. Liam traced the inside of my palm as Rapunzel went on adventure after adventure with Flynn Rider. I laughed, and swooned at the lantern part, and then Liam flipped my hand over and began drawing circles into the skin, over my knuckles. I tried to ignore it when he drew a circle around my ring finger.

My eyes stayed trained on the movie, and not how quick my pulse had begun to thrum under my skin.

My hand was in his lap, directly over his dick, so every so often when my hand would graze him, he'd jolt or thicken. Regaining use of my hand, I brushed over the outline of his semi deliberately, loving how heavy it was getting under my touch. I was blissfully watching the colors on the screen, zoning out and thinking about where I was touching when suddenly Liam stretched, pushing his hips up and his swollen cock into my palm.

"Girls, Haley is going to help me set up the guest room, since she'll be sleeping in there now. So, you guys finish, and we'll be right back."

The girls didn't really respond so much as nodded then focused back on the screen. Liam stood, gathering the blanket in his arms with strategic draping over his hips, and then gave me a look that said I needed to follow him. I stood up and scurried up the stairs after him.

Once we reached the end of the hall and stepped into a modest guest room with a full-sized bed, he dumped his blanket and then gripped the back of my neck, walking me to the nearest wall.

"You can't touch me and think I can take not being inside you, Haley."

I tilted my head back, parting my lips, but he was already moving, viciously sealing his mouth to mine. He had me against the part of the wall that was blocked by the door, so if someone came in, we could break apart without being seen, but it was still a risk. I was finding with Liam that I was willing to take them—as long as they led back to him.

We kissed as if we could orgasm simply with our tongues. His lips parted, his tongue wrestled against mine, devouring me in sloppy, wet strokes that somehow soaked my inner thighs.

I made a sound of surrender, which was like a weak, feeble animal begging to be set free from a trap. Liam's hand moved, sliding down the front of my jeans, his strong fingers, quickly spread me.

It was his turn to groan into my neck as he tore his mouth away and caught his breath.

"Liam." I whispered, begging him to give me more than just his fingers.

He leaned back, giving me a villainous smile.

"You made me suffer, Haley. I've gone months with blue balls."

I was still trying to catch my breath, so my voice came out rushed as I said, "We fucked in California."

He shook his head and pressed a quick kiss to my lips.

"I have wanted you in *my* bed. Getting to spread you out on my sheets, see your hair fanned out behind you as I fuck your cunt so hard that you have to bury your face into my pillows to muffle your screams."

I writhed against his fingers for friction; hearing him speak was only making it worse.

"So, you're making me wait?"

Another quick kiss landed on my nose. "Yes, until I've punished you for making *me* wait."

He pulled his hand out of my pants, licked his fingers clean, and then we heard the ending credits begin on the movie downstairs.

Liam was going to fuck me tonight, and he was going to punish me while he did it.

Why did a tendril of giddy excitement swim through me in anticipation?

22

LIAM

SHE INSISTED on doing her face routine first.

I sat on the edge of my bed watching as she rinsed, applied a spray, used a little scrubber on her face and then a rag. Then there was more lotion, and a serum of some kind. I knew because I asked. All the while, I watched as she stood at my bathroom counter, in just her bra and underwear.

I was so hard and so ready to fuck that my boxers were soaked from precum.

Finally, when she was about to brush her teeth, I clicked my tongue.

"Seems awfully premature considering how dirty I plan on getting that mouth."

The buzzing from her toothbrush stopped, and she turned toward me with a raised brow.

"You can bring that attitude over here and wrap those pretty pink lips around my cock if you want to keep raising your eyebrow at me like that."

She set the toothbrush down and stepped closer, her bare toes pressing into the tile of the floor.

Flicking the bathroom light off, her hips swayed as she walked until she was so close, I could touch her. Instead of pulling her into me, I waited to see what she would do.

When she lowered herself in between my open legs, I exhaled a shaky breath.

"You said you wanted to punish me." Her voice was soft but held an edge of excitement that was like a jolt of adrenaline straight to my dick.

Staring down at her, I pushed her hair behind her ears.

"Do you want to be punished?"

She nodded. "Only by you…"

I leaned forward and whispered in her ear, "You want me to treat you like a dirty slut, Haley?"

Her only response was to moan and rub her hands up and down my thighs.

Fuck, she was beautiful on her knees like this. My cock strained against my boxers, so I stood and slid them down enough to release my aching length.

Then I gripped the back of Haley's head and pulled her forward using more force than I ever had with her before.

"Open up for me," I demanded, guiding my cock to her lips. "Wider. I'm not stopping until I hit the back of your throat."

She took me, every fucking inch.

Jesus.

Her hands came up to rest on my thighs, since there was no way for her to grip my shaft, and she pushed her nails into the back of my legs.

I hissed and gathered her hair into my hand, making sure it was off her face.

My hips rocked as she sucked, choking on my length.

"Good, baby—fuck, you're so good," I said roughly as she moaned around my length, bringing her mouth up so she could lick the tip of my dick and grip the base with her other hand. Her tongue swirled slowly over the head then she stroked down my length and back up. It was nearly too much, and I still had so many things I wanted to do to her.

So I pulled away and lifted her chin.

"Remember when I said I was going to make your mouth dirty?"

She watched as I held her hand, pulling her up then pushing her panties down her legs while she unclasped her bra.

I ordered. "Get on the bed."

She slowly crawled on, displaying that ass as she went. My hand was on her in seconds, touching smooth skin, as if I couldn't get enough. She was perfect, and it was weird feeling her in my hands, almost like she'd disappear any second.

Instead of slapping her ass, because I couldn't bring myself to mar any part of that perfect skin, even for the sake of a red handprint, I gripped her hips. Once she was on her back, staring up at me, I shoved her thigh to the side and slid my cock inside of her.

It was still such a shock; how tight she was. I pulled out slowly, then gently pushed back inside, lubricating my shaft with her slickness.

"Open that mouth again, Haley. You're going to taste yourself."

I pulled out, gripped my cock, and moved on my knees up the bed until I was hovering over her. The veins on my cock glistened from her arousal, but her lips parted just the same, ready for me.

"That's right, my dirty slut, open wide and taste yourself. Lick up every drop of your juices off my cock."

She did as I said, sucking and licking, rocking her hips to get the pressure she needed to get off, but I wouldn't give it to her just yet. I pulled out, letting go with a pop, and then I lowered my mouth to her peaked nipples, sucking on them as my fingers plunged into her soaked pussy.

She moaned and began riding my hand.

I rubbed her clit then fucked her with my digits, rolling my tongue over her pink nipples. Pulling my hand out of her and pushing those fingers into her mouth, I said, "Suck."

I marveled as she gripped my wrist and closed her eyes, taking three of my fingers into her wet mouth, sucking on them as if it were my cock she was tasting.

"Fuck that's hot," I groaned, needing to be inside her again.

I moved, flipping her over until her face was pressed against the bed, her hair tossed over her shoulder, and I stroked down her smooth ass again.

"Lift." I put my hand under her stomach until she was up on all fours.

"You're so fucking perfect."

She scoffed, finally breaking her silence, "Well I'm twenty-one, Liam…give me a few years and then tell me I'm perfect."

The idea of giving her a few years had that place in my chest thrumming again. Images of her in my house, a ring on her finger, a baby in that belly.

Fuck.

My throat grew tight, and to mask the emotion, I slid inside her, trying to lose myself to the ecstasy of fucking her.

Being with her was like walking in the sun after being chilled in the shade for years. She was the heat from the fire when the snow was falling outside. She was peace and perfection. She was *home*.

I picked up the pace, rocking harder into her. The sound of our skin slapping echoed in the room, but I was too far gone to worry about the noise. Haley's face was shoved into the mattress, masking her moans, and I bit back my own, only allowing a few grunts out. As much as I wanted tonight to be about punishment, there was too much contentment over having her in my bed, like a blessing I didn't deserve.

So, as I found my rhythm, and rubbed slow circles into Haley's clit so she found her release, I slammed my hips forward, plunging my cock so deep inside of her that I exploded in pleasure. A groan that had been tethered in my core unleashed, filling the room in a sudden burst, and Haley's muffled scream rose, tangling with my own. It was pleasure so intense I swear my heart missed a couple of beats.

My breathing was ragged as I slowly pulled out of her and stepped to the carpet. I walked to the bathroom, cleaned up and then grabbed a washcloth, rinsing it with warm water before bringing it back to Haley. I lifted her leg and gently swiped between her legs, wiping up the mess we'd created. Her dark lashes fanned her face with her eyes still closed, but as I pulled away, her eyes opened, and she gave me a warm smile.

"Thank you."

If I could freeze this moment in time, I would. The way she looked tangled in my sheets, the way her hair looked against my pillows. The gentle glow of her skin under the lamp light, and the way her green eyes seemed to heat.

She was perfect.

I tossed the rag to the floor, caring about nothing else other than holding her.

"Come here."

She moved, slowly at first, and I helped guide her under the blankets, until her head was on the pillow next to mine, and I was holding her to my chest.

"I forgot to hit the switch," I whispered through a yawn.

"Alexa, turn off the lights," she said loudly, and I jumped.

The robotic voice came back with, "Okay." Then the room plunged into darkness.

"You bought an Alexa while I was gone?"

Haley laughed, burrowing under the covers. "It sort of became my room as you left, so yeah. There's only one in here, and the kitchen…"

I hummed in response.

The room was quiet as I held her, and as exhausted as I was, I couldn't find it in me to fall asleep.

"What are we going to do when we wake up?" My lips skimmed hers in a quick kiss, but I was already getting worked up again.

"Do you have to go into the gym?" she asked curiously.

I moved to her jaw and trailed kisses along her skin. "No, I'm still technically off."

"Then pancakes. We make them every Sunday, and each girl takes a turn learning how to flip. Then we can maybe go somewhere all together."

I was hard again as she trailed touches down my stomach and over my cock. Gripping the shaft, she stroked once, twice and that's all it took. I was on her, spreading her legs, sliding my erect cock deep inside her. In the dark, I couldn't see her, but I heard her intake of breath as her nails came down hard against my back.

I pulled out then slid back home with a hiss leaving my mouth.

"We're not going to get any sleep tonight, are we?" I joked, feeling my balls tighten as she wrapped her heels around my ass and fucked me back.

"I don't think I want to sleep, not when I can feel like this instead."

I lowered my mouth to hers and continued to fuck her slowly, letting myself get lost in the sensation of holding her in my arms. She smiled against my lips when she finally found her release, and I found myself trying to get lost in that too.

I was realizing that when it came to Haley, being lost was the only way I'd ever feel found.

THE SOUND of my door handle jiggling woke me.

"Daddy, Haley is gone!"

Oh shit. That was Mila.

"Daddy, open up! It's an emergggenswee." Mila's mouth sounded like it was mashed against the door, blurring the last word with extra syllables.

Haley stirred next to me, and we both realized we'd fucked up. How was I going to get her out of here? Not only that, but we'd also finally fell asleep after our third round of sex, so the room was a mess. There were blankets on the floor, pillows scattered everywhere, and Haley was tucked into my chest, but we were facing the wrong direction on the bed.

"Daddy!" Mila called again.

"I'm getting dressed!" I called back, which caused Haley's eyes to pop open and jerk up in the bed.

"Oh my gosh," she whispered, holding the sheet to her chest.

Her head turned, eyeing the door where the handle kept jiggling back and forth. The lock was holding for now, but Mila was creative and had a weird ability to break through locks.

"Here, I have a screwdriver." That was Seraphina.

Haley moved at the same time as me. Sheets were flung to the side, and I caught just a glimpse of Haley's naked body as she briskly walked to the bathroom.

"I'm getting dressed, girls!" I yelled again, but it didn't seem to make a difference on how ardently they were working to break in.

Haley emerged from the bathroom, dressed while throwing her hair up in a ponytail.

"Can I sneak out?"

I was already pulling on a pair of sweats, moving closer to the door just in case the girls found a way to actually break in.

"Just stay in here; I'll lead them downstairs and then you can slip out, I whispered."

Haley bit her thumb nail, watching the door.

"Tell them I went to get mochas; they'll know what that means. Then I'll sneak out through the garage and go to my car."

I loved that she wasn't bailing. I guess after being with them for so many weeks, she wouldn't bail. My chest tightened like my heart was growing bigger, and I leaned over to kiss her.

"Don't take too long, okay?"

Her arms wrapped around my neck, and my hands went to her hips.

"You missing me already? Some might call that an addiction."

The tightening in my chest got worse. She *was* an addiction; she was everything, and she didn't even fucking realize it.

It was odd that a term that had brought so much brokenness to my life was now something I was using to describe my utter dependence on someone I was in love with.

"You are my addiction, Haley Hanes." I kissed her again, then whispered, "My obsession, my salvation, and my demise. Every second you're near me, I'm one step closer to relapsing."

She laughed then pushed my shoulder. "You're cheesy in the morning. I kind of like it."

Heat hit my face because I wasn't even joking with her…that cheesy shit was real, and I'd never wanted to be that much of a sap. With anyone.

"Okay, they're getting impatient, go out there." Haley pushed on my arm, but I glanced over my shoulder one more time just to save the memory of her standing in my room, early morning hair, knowing I'd fucked her all through the night. I'd tuck it away and hold it for whenever she finally realized she could do so much fucking better than me.

CHAPTER TWENTY-THREE

haley

"REMEMBER if you slide your spatula under the batter just like this and flip…" I watched as Maddy did exactly as I said and smiled. We were standing next to the stove, our heads hovering over the flat pan, while the smell of butter and doughy goodness filled the air.

"Exactly like that!" I hugged her to my side and then told Seraphina to come up next. She moved her hair out of her face and pressed her knees into the chair, sitting tall so she could see the pan.

I poured a small circle of batter, and we watched together as it began bubbling. I waited to see if she'd remember when to flip it.

She was watching the bubbles form, and not moving. I waited.

I couldn't take it any longer.

"See, once they pop like that?" I pointed, watching as her blue eyes narrowed on the circle, "That's how you know the bottom is ready."

"Can I try and flip it?" She held her hand out for the spatula, and I guided her to show her how to turn it over.

We both smiled when the golden brown surface showed.

Seraph hugged me at the waist and then ran to the table to take a seat. Liam had Mila in his lap as they worked on sounding out certain words that popped up on his phone. She had a Micky Mouse pancake in front of her, as did Liam.

"What are you guys doing?"

Liam's eyes bounced up; Mila's remained on the screen.

"It's this learning app… it's supposed to make education fun. I let her practice whenever we have free time like this."

Mila's little fingers kept poking at his cell phone screen.

"Wouldn't that be easier on the tablet?"

Liam's gaze went back to his phone, where he gently corrected Mila on something.

"We had one, but it broke. It's fine, this works."

Uh-oh. Did he not realize I had bought each of the girls one?

Maddy looked up at me, and I read her expression. She was about to grab Mila's tablet for them, but I shook my head. Liam was being sweet, and I didn't want to ruin that.

WE RELAXED A LITTLE LONGER, while Mila showed us the new words.

Then I excused myself to shower and get ready for the day.

It felt weird, almost like I was living with Liam and the girls. He'd told me to just use his bathroom, but I felt like that would be a strange thing to do now that Liam was back. The other two might dismiss it, but Maddy was old enough to understand that using her dad's shower would be weird unless he and I were involved.

So, I used the kids' bathroom, and then quickly dressed and got ready. I had looked up a few places to go on Google and had an idea of what to do with the kids today, but I wasn't sure I could convince Liam. This was so different, having to worry about his permission since they were his kids and not mine.

He was working in his office while the girls were upstairs, so I sauntered in and perched on his lap.

"Hi." His hands came around me, securing me in place.

My arm went up around his neck, my fingers digging into his hair.

"Could I convince you to let me take the kids to that big pizza place that's outside of Portland?"

I read up on it. The whole place was massive, including a kids play area that went up five stories, with multicolored tunnels and slides. There was laser tag, bumper cars, bowling…it looked so fun.

"Pizza Palace?" Liam tipped his head back, which made the office chair lean.

I listened to ensure no one was coming down the stairs as I traced the space near his eyebrow with my finger.

"Yeah, that's the one. I want to go."

Liam's grip tightened around me, and under me he was getting hard.

He stared thoughtfully as I continued to trace his face. His lips, his nose, his forehead.

"I suppose this is like the snow boots and everything else you've paid for on your own?" The brow my finger was on raised.

I nodded and I appreciated him not making me say the words, knowing he certainly didn't want to give voice to that scenario either. He was a prideful man, and it wasn't like I hadn't noticed his overdue notices for the gym…or the bills coming in from his lawyers. Liam was struggling financially, and while I assumed his earnings from the overseas fighting would help some, I had no idea how much debt he was in to begin with.

"If you don't want me to then I understand and I won't push it, but I was never invited to any parties held at places like that, so I've never been before. I think it would be fun."

My face suddenly flushed, realizing how young that sentence just made me sound.

Liam pulled my chin down and pressed a kiss to my lips.

"Fine, but if we go, I get to hold your hand in front of the girls, and if one of them asks then I'm telling them."

"Liam." I pressed my forehead to his. "We just agreed last night that we would make sure we did it at the right time."

His hand came up, gripping my neck.

"Yeah, well, I didn't know what it would be like to have you in my kitchen and my bed and then not get to touch you."

He'd pulled my chin up again and stared into my eyes when he delivered that last part, and a piece of my tattered heart seemed to knit together. Old wounds of being discarded, healing over, leaving a feeling of hope hanging there in my chest instead of an ache.

Releasing a shuddery breath, I whispered, "Deal."

THE GIRLS WERE beyond thrilled when they realized where we were headed. We took my car because I didn't want to argue with Liam over gas, but I let him drive. I also cut a path to the food line before Liam could say anything, and I ordered two massive pizzas, something called potato skins—which ended up being the best thing I ever tasted—then soda. Stuff the kids never had. They loved it. After being the one alone with the girls everywhere I went, it was a world of difference having him with us.

I felt less worried all the time, and less stressed out.

First, they played in the massive play place, then did two rounds on the bumper cars, and finally were playing arcade games while Liam and I walked behind them. His hand was laced with mine, our fingers hanging together, and every time I thought Maddy or Seraph would notice, my heart squeezed tight, but somehow, they never seemed to look down where we were joined.

I felt like we owed the girl's a conversation, but what did I know? I wasn't a mom, nor had I had any kind of decent parenting to use as an example. I had no idea what the proper way was to do this; I just knew it felt good to be touched by Liam. It felt good to have him and to have him hold me in a possessive way. He would stand between me and the crowd if there was a guy dominating the space. Or he'd move me behind him if he caught someone staring at me too long.

I'd never been super confident in my looks. As I got older, it became easier, but seeing the way Liam acted when another man looked at me was doing something to me…undoing all my broken pieces I'd been trying to hold together all these years. His large hands had come over, taken them, and showed me I didn't have to carry them anymore. His feelings for me shone through every place on my body that he touched, and every single hidden kiss he snuck.

During laser tag, he'd managed to steal several.

"Daddy, I won!" Seraph yelled excitedly, looking over at us.

She didn't act like she'd noticed our hand holding, and we didn't think on it too long as Liam knelt down to help her with all the tickets shooting out from the machine. I held on to Mila and Maddy so the crowds moving around didn't take them away.

"We're the biggest winners in the whole universe," Mila squealed excitedly, tugging on my hand. I dipped to pick her up, and while my hand was free, Maddy took it.

Liam's gaze swung over, noticing us then his eyes homed in on Maddy's hand in mine.

He'd missed so much.

He had missed the first time Maddy reached for me on her own, and how that made me feel like my heart had flipped off the edge of a tall canyon.

He had missed when I read the girls bedtime stories and held them during storms.

This new dynamic was going to be so different when he really registered how implanted in their lives I was.

By the time Liam walked over with a massive bear that Seraphina had used her tickets on, we were ready to leave.

It was an all-day event, and since it took over an hour to get there, the girls were all fast asleep in the car when we pulled into the garage.

He leaned over and kissed me, chaste and quick, but it was like he wasn't really paying attention and it was just something he did auto-matically.

My heart burst in my chest with so much love and affection that I nearly cried. I was in love with him, desperately so, and I had no idea what to do with that.

I swallowed the thick lump in my throat and exited the car, pushing all my love down.

Liam carried Seraph in his arms, I carried Mila, and then he went back for Maddy last. Once the girls were tucked into their beds, Liam pulled me into ours.

"On my face. Now," he ordered roughly.

I stripped, as desperate for him as he seemed to be for me.

Crawling naked on the bed, I hesitated at his chest, realizing I maybe hadn't heard him correctly due to the butterflies that had shot off in my chest like they'd been locked inside bottle rockets.

"What do you mean…your face?"

Liam lifted up on his elbow, stroking his erect cock, while staring at me.

In the low cadence of light, he looked like an exhausted god, all lazy and perfect.

"You see the headboard?" He gestured to the blue fabric behind him.

I nodded.

"Grip the top, straddle my face."

Oh.

"So like…" My face flushed, inexperience clearly showing.

His lips twisted into a smirk. "You've never sat on anyone's face before?"

No.

I faltered, my face getting redder by the second. "Not exactly."

He hummed deep in his throat, watching me like a predator with its prey.

"I can't tell you how fucking happy that makes me, baby. On the other hand, it's a shame because your pussy deserves to be feasted on *frequently*. This is your pass to sit on my face whenever you need to get off. I can be reading, for all I care. Come over, spread those pretty thighs and take a seat."

I grew slick between my thighs as I crawled closer to him and marveled as he stopped me, putting a hand on my inner thigh.

"First"—his eyes darkened as my glistening center showed—"I want to see how wet you are for me."

There was no hiding it. He seemed to agree because he made some sort of groaning sound as his thumb lightly grazed my clit. He hissed, moving his thumb over the sensitive nub again and again.

"Yeah, you're going to taste so fucking good, baby. Get up here."

He laid flat, while I did as he instructed, gripping the top of the headboard with my fingers and then bracing each knee on either side of his face. His eyes were on mine as I looked down, and he gripped my hips.

"Ride my face. That's your job, and when you come, you do it on my tongue."

I nodded and let him pull me down until I covered his mouth and felt his tongue.

Sweet Jesus.

The first swipe was hot against my aching center, but it was also thick and firm as he licked along my slit.

My fingers dug into the headboard as I went with the natural rhythm he set with his tongue. I clung to the instructions he'd given me; to ride him. So, I closed my eyes tight and got lost in the sensation.

My knees pushed into the bed beside his head, but my core moved over his mouth in a fevered, desperate way.

He let out muffled groans while kneading my ass in his massive palms. He pulled me down against his mouth in harsh strokes, until he finally seemed to lose it.

He pushed me up to my knees and then he lifted me.

"You ever sixty-nine?" he rasped, flipping me around until my hands braced his chest, my eyes flying open, landing on the door of his bedroom and television mounted on the wall next to it.

"No." It was a breath, a single ounce of air I gathered before he was pushing my head.

"Open up those pretty lips for me and wrap them around my cock.

I'm going to keep licking this pretty pussy until you come on my tongue, and you're going to suck my cock until you taste me."

My hands moved to the bed, bracketing his hips while I lowered my mouth onto his erection. The thick head of his cock glistened with precum, and my tongue lapped that up first before I slid down his length and took him fully into my mouth.

I moaned as his tongue resumed its work around my clit, his finger joining the party by sliding into my core. I decided I'd do the same and cup his balls, lightly squeezing while I hollowed my cheeks and sucked.

"Fuckkkk," Liam groaned behind me while pushing down on my head. Our bodies curved as he moved to reach the back of my head, but my hips stayed secured to his chest, his face buried in my cunt as he licked and sucked my pussy.

I groaned around his length until the slow build up in my core burst like a billion pieces of stardust and I heard Liam muttering something around the sucking and licking of my release, and then his hips were thrusting up in quick bursts until I felt him freeze and groan. His hand was on the back of my head, pushing it until his cock pressed against the back of my throat. I nearly choked. This was different from quickly bobbing down and then getting relief.

"Swallow, Haley, take all of me."

My thighs clenched at his order, and pleasure coated my sex as I relaxed my throat and took him deeper.

"Fuck, that's it. Shitttttttttttt…" he moaned.

Salty liquid filled my mouth a second later, and I swallowed quickly to keep his release down. Once the pulsing stopped, I lifted my head and gently licked the root of him all the way to the tip of his length. Feeling like part of my soul had been yanked out, I rested my head against his thigh and tried to regulate my breathing.

My hips were gently moved until I was resting fully on the bed, and Liam was moving so that he could gather me into his arms.

"You did so good, perfect actually." He kissed my shoulder. "Did you like that?"

I didn't even have words, so I smiled and tried to lift my hand so that I could play with his hair. I loved his hair.

"Very much so."

He hummed his pleasure, stroking my skin.

After a few minutes of us just lying there, his hands moved over my body in soothing strokes, and it must have been because of the orgasm— or the fact that I now knew I loved him— but my mouth parted with a question.

"Will you let me financially back your gym?"

Liam paused his ministrations against my skin, his closed eyes popped open, landing on mine. My heart felt like it was slowly crystalizing.

He didn't respond. Instead he sat up with a sigh and rubbed his forehead.

I slowly sat up, too, following him into the bathroom. He turned the shower on and stepped under the spray while I crossed my arms over my chest and watched.

"You coming?" He held out his hand, and I gently took it, feeling some of my frayed nerves settle.

Steam filled the shower, and I watched as the water ran down along the gray stonework that reminded me of his eyes. He must have noticed that the spray was hitting me but not warming me, because suddenly he pulled my arm until I was standing in front of him, taking up the bulk of the shower.

The heat hit my back in a delicious way, which made me relax enough to throw my arms around Liam's neck.

We stood like that for a while, until he used soap on his hair and scrubbed mine with the same product. I didn't mind. It would mean that I smelled like him.

"What made you think of the gym?" he finally asked, those gray eyes speared me with fear.

I had no idea what he was afraid of. I'd never hurt him—not intentionally, at least.

"I think…" I paused, looking up while the water hit my eyes and I tried to see through the drops coating my lashes. "It's been in the back of my mind since you left for Europe. I mean, I know part of why you did it was to give us time, but you mentioned that you needed the money. I want to help. You're important to me, Liam. The gym is your dream, and I just want to help protect it."

His forehead lowered to mine, and we let more steam fill the space until he finally reached behind me and turned the shower off.

"Haley, I appreciate your efforts and that you care. I know you bailed Cole out of some hard times, but this is my thing. I have to be the one to protect it. Okay?"

He exited the shower and pulled a towel around him, handing me one too.

"Is my money going to be an issue?"

"Not if you don't assume we *need* your money."

Ouch. That sucked.

I wrapped the towel around me and tucked it in, walking to the counter to start my skin care routine.

"It's not about you needing it; it's just me wanting to spend it on the people I love."

I bent over and wet my face, pumping a bit of face wash into my hands then rubbed it into my skin, closing my eyes.

It wasn't until I rinsed, wondering why Liam hadn't responded, that I realized what I had confessed.

I met his gaze in the mirror.

His arms were crossed over his chest, all the ink and those sculpted muscles on display. I wanted to trace each vein with my tongue and then end with the one that ran along his shaft.

"Do you mean that?" he asked, lowering his voice until it was almost a whisper.

My face felt blotchy as the realization hit me square in the chest. I'd walked right into an opportunity for him to reject me.

Likely sensing my discomfort, he stepped closer and pulled my towel until it came off. Then he hit the lights and pulled me to bed.

"Did you mean it?" he asked again. This time he sat on the bed and I was standing in between his legs. His Adam's apple bobbed.

I ran my fingers through his wet hair and nodded.

"Yes, I—" Words died on my tongue as I tried to explain it. I knew he thought I was too young and too naive, but I felt what I felt.

"I love you…and the girls. I love all of you, so when you say you want to take care of it, you don't understand that I also want to take care of all of you."

My palm was lifted to his lips where he pressed a quick kiss then he pulled me again until I was landing next to him, my head on the pillow, his too.

"Alexa, turn off the lights." His voice echoed through the room all while his eyes stayed on mine, until that last bit of light was blocked out.

"I need you to know…" he started, his voice raspy and low, like a dark cloud stuck inside of a cavern bobbing around for a way out, "I wouldn't have left you with the girls, or waited, if I didn't feel the same way. I'm just as scared as you, and I have just as much to lose."

I shook my head, tracing a muscle in his arm. "I could lose all four of you. You would only lose me."

"Only lose you?" he scoffed, his hand moving to my hip. "How long will it take for you to see that you're not replaceable? You're not just anyone. If we lost you, we'd be devastated. In a world full of unremarkable people, you've carved yourself onto my heart. Whether we work out or not, you'll be there forever."

Exhaustion tugged at my senses, especially as my mind played with his words like a crossword puzzle, wondering if Lacey had left her mark too. I couldn't keep my eyes open, and I decided to just accept it for what it was. Liam's complicated confession of love was still more than any I've ever been offered before. I'd take it a thousand times over.

"Set an alarm for me to slip back into my room." I said, groggy and tired.

He hummed something before pulling me to his chest, and then I fell asleep.

24

———

LIAM

Haley:

Do we need sour cream from the store?

THE TEXT HAD me smiling down at my phone, which apparently all the guys had noticed.

"There he goes again!" Rex yelled, while a few other guys joined in laughing.

I ignored them.

> I think we still have some…but I know we're
> out of whipped cream.

Haley:

Why would we need whipped cream? I'm cutting back on the pie, I already told you and Millie that.

I bit back a laugh.

Because I want to see what it tastes like when I
lick it off of you.

"Hey, Liam. We gonna spar, or not?" Rex slammed his gloves together, bouncing in place.

"All right, all right," I said, leaving my cell behind. Haley loved trying new things in bed, so I had no doubt she'd pick up a ridiculous amount of whipped cream now.

"You ready?" I asked, sliding my gloves on, hearing the front door buzzer go off. From the way everyone seemed to fall quiet, I had a feeling it wasn't Jay coming in to train.

I turned around and saw Colson walking toward me, wearing his workout gear.

Aw, shit. This was not going to be good.

"In the middle of a session, man." I tipped my head to him, trying to be respectful, but my best friend just dropped his gym bag, letting it fall to the floor with a loud slap.

"Rearrange it. I want in the ring with you."

Shit.

If Haley knew her brother was about to get his ass kicked, she'd be pissed at me.

"It's all good, man. You took too long texting your woman, anyway." Rex gently hit his glove against mine then exited the ring.

Colson's jaw tensed while he slipped his gloves on, and then he was climbing into the ring.

"You good?" I asked, trying to gauge where he was at with things. He had texted me after the wedding and it was not a thank you for being his best man.

He jumped in place then huffed. "I'm good. Clean fight."

Right. Clean, my fucking ass. This asshole wanted to kill me.

"Fine." I began mirroring his movements until we'd both warmed up enough. I watched as he began looking for an opening.

"We gonna talk?"

"About what?" I played it like I didn't get his text messages, but they were seared in my brain. The morning after his wedding, he had come up to our floor and knocked on our bedroom door. Haley never woke, but I slipped out and quickly shut the door behind me.

We didn't say a single word to one another as his gaze flicked to the door at my back. I could almost hear the wheels turning as he processed what he saw the evening prior, along with how quickly I'd shut the door. We only stared at one another for thirty seconds before Nora walked up and interrupted, calling Colson away.

Then his messages started coming in.

> Colson:
>
> MY FUCKING SISTER, LIAM?
>
> You better explain yourself.
>
> Never mind, there is no explaining THIS. She's too young, Liam. I warned you about this. I fucking warned you not to go after her.
> Why her?
>
> Does this have anything to do with you leaving for 9 weeks?
>
> Fuck, man. I'm so pissed off at you, but for now I am going to enjoy my honeymoon, but the second I'm back, we will discuss this.

THAT WOULD BE NOW.

"How was your honeymoon?" I asked as if nothing at all was amiss.

He came at me with a hook, going for my jaw, and since I didn't even have my mouth guard in yet, it would have fucking hurt, but I blocked.

He lunged again, all anger and rage, zero patience or thought.

I went for an uppercut but realized he didn't have his mouthpiece in either and ended up hitting his arm.

"You want to fight without properly protecting yourself? Do it somewhere else."

I lowered my fists, and Colson chose that moment to hit me in the nose, making my head snap back.

"Fuck!" I groaned, holding my glove up to my nose.

My eyes burned as the sting spread around my face. Blood gushed from my nostrils, but I knew it hadn't been broken.

Cole rushed forward, ripping his gloves off. "Shit. I didn't mean to make you bleed."

"What the fuck did you think was going to happen when you punched me in the nose?"

My gloves were off, my fingers gripping the bridge of my nose and my head tilted back.

Colson stood there, his face grim as he watched. Someone tossed us a rag from below and I held it to my face.

"She is my sister, Liam," Colson said after blowing out a heavy sigh.

My eyes were still watering but I watched as his face took on a million different expressions. Sadness, shame, fear...all of that played out as he stood there, rubbing the back of his neck.

"I am aware."

It was a low blow, but so was that punch.

He let out another gust of air, "You get women fawning over you all the time, Liam. Why did you have to go after her? She's just starting her life; she's been through so much shit from her parents...from me. She needs someone who will be good to her."

"And I won't be?" That fucking hurt.

Colson bowed his head, shaking it before asking, "Why her? Is it just that she was around?"

I pulled the rag away from my nose, finally feeling the flow clot. There was going to be a bruise and zero chance I could hide this from Haley.

"Why did you wait for Nora?"

Cole's head snapped up, his eyes latching on to mine in challenge.

I shifted forward, needing to grab some ice.

"You couldn't have her, yet you didn't date anyone else. You said you did, but we both know that was bullshit. You waited for her. Why?"

My friend ducked under the rope and held it for me so I could exit the ring. Once we were on the mats, I moved toward the locker room with him on my heels.

"I waited because I knew that no one else would ever fit with me the way she did."

Finding the mirror, I saw my nose. It was red and puffy, and there was swelling around my eyes too.

"That's why it's Haley and none of those other women. No one has ever fit with us the way she does. I love her, Cole."

My friend watched me, as if he was sure I'd add something else to the end of that statement. Or take it back. When I dipped my face to rinse off the blood, I heard him clear his throat.

"Love…that's… I thought—didn't it just start at the wedding?"

I grabbed a paper towel and blotted my face. "No, man. It's been going on for months. Shortly after she got here. And yes, it is why I left. She wanted more of a foundation, and I couldn't handle being around her if I couldn't have her."

His face remained impassive as he watched me in the mirror, until he finally asked, "Does she know?"

Turning away from the mirror, I sat down on the bench and stared at the floor, thinking over how I wanted to word this.

"She knows I feel strongly for her, but I haven't explicitly told her that I love her."

Finally settling next to me, Cole leaned forward placing his elbows on top of his knees.

We sat there in silence, just watching nothing as the sounds from the gym lightly reverberated through the locker room door.

"Have you told her anything about Lacey?"

This was not something I wanted to discuss, but for the sake of transparency and getting back in a good place with my best friend, I answered.

"She knows some things. Lacey confronted her before I left. It's what made her want space."

Cole turned and lowered his head so that when he spoke it was quiet.

"Does she know what Lacey did to Maddy?"

Fuck. No. At least I didn't think she did. I assumed Haley would have mentioned something if she heard that story from Maddy.

My best friend knew all this shit about me because for the first time in my life, I actually had someone to share the burden with, but I wasn't eager to share my greatest failure as a father with Haley. She would be sweet about it, but there's no doubt she'd look at me differently if she knew what I had allowed to happen, all because I was in love and wanted the mother of my children to be okay.

I let out a sigh and decided we'd done enough sharing. I had people to train and investors to reach out to.

"Are you going to be okay with us? I'd like to know so we can come visit. The girls will miss you."

Cole stood, tucking his hands into his pockets. His jaw clenched and then his eyes lowered. That was answer enough for me.

I began to walk away when he stopped me.

"Just promise that you're going to be good to her...that if Lacey comes back into the picture, suddenly sober and looking like the world's greatest mom, that you won't drop Haley for her."

What—why would he ever even assume that?

"Why the fuck would that even be in your head?"

With a lift of his left shoulder, he simply said, "Because she's the mother of your children."

"My girls are the greatest gift I've ever been given, but surely you don't honestly think I would ever take Lacey back," I looked around, outraged by the notion that my best friend honestly thought I was that much of an idiot.

The way his eyes fell told me he was ashamed he did.

Seething, I paced away from him, bringing my hand to my nose, only to remember too late that it was busted.

"For the record, I am not pining for my ex-wife. She's been playing the sober, perfect mother card for over a year. After what she did to Maddy, there's no fucking way I would take her back." I sighed, feeling defeated.

"We have to get past this. For the sake of our friendship, the girls, and definitely Haley. All of it."

He nodded, and finally gave me his full attention.

"I'll support you both. It might just take me a while to get used to it."

I searched his face, needing to make sure. "You won't freak out if I kiss her in front of you?"

Cole's eyebrows shot up. "You already told the girls?"

My chest squeezed at the thought of sitting them down and telling them. There hadn't been anyone permanent in our lives since their mother. This was a big deal.

"I will be telling them tonight."

"Shit. Okay, yeah, we'll get on board. I haven't said anything to Nora yet. I won't until you give me the green light that you've told the girls, okay?"

I nodded and then we stood and clapped each other on the back.

Now I just had to figure out how to convince Haley that it was time to tell the girls.

I REVIEWED the email from another potential investor and tried not to feel discouraged. Honestly, I thought at least one of them would take me on, simply because of my name in the boxing world, especially after my recent tour in Europe. It wasn't like I headlined or anything, but my name still circulated. I guess you could say I was a little cocky about it… but fuck, how that humility burned now. I just needed one person to take me on…just one who saw me as having something worth betting on.

I checked the books, and there wasn't a single new membership sign up in the past two weeks.

Worry frayed my nerves, coiling in my gut.

What was I going to do?

Right as I closed my laptop, I heard my phone ring. Deciding I was done at the gym for the day, I grabbed my stuff and pulled the phone up to my ear.

"Hello."

There was a pause, and then a breathy voice. "Liam?"

I froze in place.

Pulling the phone away from my face, I checked the number. It wasn't familiar.

"Lacey?"

"Hey…" she said softly, and man if this wasn't just the worst fucking day.

I focused on locking the gym doors before veering for my truck.

"Where's the mediator?" We only ever spoke with a third-party between us.

"I figured we could chat, just the two of us."

Opening my truck door, I set the phone down on the console, slammed the door shut, and while I started it, buckled.

Once I was situated, I pulled it back up to my ear, "—and anyway I thought it was time for me to see them."

"Have you been talking this entire time?"

She paused, and then launched into it again.

"Liam, I want to see the girls…and you. I miss you."

Rolling my eyes, I waited for the phone to connect with my Bluetooth.

"Lacey, our parenting plan says you can't contact me unless you have a mediator."

Someone spoke in the background, and the chatter and laughter got louder.

"No, it says third party…"

"Hi, Liam." Fucking Julie.

Lacey spoke up. "See, now we have a third party."

Fuck this.

"No, we're not doing this."

"Just half an hour at the park where your pretty little nanny took the girls that one time. Please, Liam." It grated my nerves like no other when her tone dipped into mockery around the words, "pretty little nanny."

"Lacey…No. Follow the parenting plan. It's that simple."

Julie made some comment about being right, and telling her so, but I ignored it.

"So you want me to have to be supervised like a criminal while I see my own children? How will the girls even look at me if there's a stranger in the room with us? No, my girls need their mother without all that shit."

"How about Maddy? Does she still need you after what you did?"

Silence met me for only a second before Julie started in.

"Fuck you, Liam. You know Lacey was in a rough place back then. She never would have left her—"

"That's enough. Julie, get off," Lacey commanded, and I heard some shuffling then it was a bit quieter.

"Look, Liam. Fine. I can't see the girls. But what about me and you seeing each other? I miss you, and I know you're missing me. Maybe we could meet somewhere, just for a while. I'll suck you off real good, let you treat me like a dirty slut. I remember how much you used to like that."

I barked out a laugh.

"Lacey, I will not ever be touching you again. I'd become a monk before I let that happen. I will, however, be touched tonight by that pretty little nanny of mine, who sucks my cock a thousand times better than you ever did. Don't call me again unless you have our court-mandated mediator on the line."

I hung up, realizing I was strangling the steering wheel and still parked in the gym parking lot.

I hated that she'd done this, that she reduced our relationship to this. I hated that her daughters didn't have her. I hated that she was so selfish.

It was the icing on today's shit cake.

All I wanted was to go home and curl up with Haley on the couch, and tonight, that's exactly what I planned to do.

PULLING into my driveway made some of the tightness in my chest release. Even more so when I opened the garage and found Haley's SUV secured inside, safe and sound. There was just something to her being safe, and knowing she was going to be behind that door as soon as I opened it that did something to me.

Once I entered the house, I could hear the sound of the television and singing. I dropped my gym bag in the laundry room, hung my truck keys, and slowly padded down the hall. The lights from the lamps in the living room illuminated the floor and the huge blanket spread out on it. All four of my girls sat on it, wearing ribbons in their hair with little foam inserts between their toes.

"Daddy!" Mila jumped up and ran to me and then the other two made their way a little slower. Once they were all in my arms, my eyes landed on Haley's green ones, and my entire day just seemed to disappear. All the shit, all the pain—

Her eyes narrowed, her brows furrowing into a hard line.

Oh shit. The conversation with Lacey totally made me forget my fucked-up face.

"What happened?" She uncrossed her legs and stood quickly, walking over in a rush. Her tanned thighs led to a pretty purple *lilac* color painted across her toes, and I nearly laughed because she still had the foam piece in between each one as she stalked over.

I was on my knees, hugging the girls, when she made her way through our little throng and cupped my jaw in her hands. Gentle strokes from her thumbs brushed against my cheeks, and her eyes were so full of worry and concern that she must have completely forgotten about the kids.

"Who hit you?" She searched my eyes, still unaware of how she was touching me. I stared up at her feeling completely undone.

I loved her.

It beat like an anthem in my chest, reminding me she had no idea because I hadn't said the words.

"Cole got in a lucky shot," I finally answered, because I did notice that Maddy was inspecting the way Haley held my face, her eyes wide, like she was trying to piece together a puzzle.

Haley finally dropped my jaw and stepped back.

Mila's little nose scrunched, her face twisting as if she tasted something sour. "Why did Uncle Cole hit you, Daddy?"

Oh shit. Right. This would make no sense whatsoever to them.

Haley's eyes darted down to Mila, widening as she realized what I had.

"Daddy and Uncle Cole always hit each other in the gym," Seraphina said dismissively, turning back to their blanket setup on the floor.

"Ohhhhh, that's what you mean, with boxing gloves?"

I rubbed her back. "Of course, honey…"

"You didn't have your hands up? You always tell us to keep our hands up."

I had to bite back a smile and I saw Haley was too, then keeping my eyes on Haley, I said, "Daddy was distracted."

Mila shook her head, clomping back to the blanket like her sister had.

"Last time Uncle Cole was distracted, it was because of loooove." Mila drew out the word like she was trying to make it sound dreamy.

I knew what they were referencing. Back before Cole got with Nora, he'd come in to train, and the girls watched me clock him good. I told them it was because he was distracted. They also had overheard little bits of conversation through the year about his growing crush on his boss's daughter. So they assumed his distraction was because of Nora.

Haley's hair fell forward as her chin dropped to her chest, likely fighting another smile or a laugh. "Can I take my boots off before you start interrogating me?"

I grabbed Mila in my arms and tossed her on the couch. She let out a loud squeal of laughter.

I headed to the front to put my things away, and then I ran upstairs to shower.

By the time I had returned, the girls had all resumed their spots on the blanket, and Haley was pulling out the little rollers that each one of them had in their hair.

Once they were done, we'd lost a good amount of the evening. So, instead of the girls cuddling on the couch to watch a movie, I told them to go get their pajamas on.

Haley walked with me to the kitchen while the girls ran upstairs. I pulled out the dinner she had made earlier and popped it into the microwave.

Her arms were crossed as she leaned against the counter.

"Why did he hit you?"

I pulled her into my chest and kissed her neck.

"Uh…well, he knows about us…"

"What? How?" she leaned back to catch my eye.

"He knocked on the door the morning after the wedding."

Her mouth dropped open in shock. "And you opened it?"

"I didn't realize it would be him. I thought it was one of the girls."

Her fingers found their way around my neck as she pressed a kiss to my chest.

"So he pieced it together?"

I nodded, kissing her nose.

"What else happened today?" She gathered my hair into her fingers and gently tugged.

This was the part of being in a relationship that I wasn't used to… talking, being vulnerable. My immediate instinct was to say that nothing else had happened and brush the conversation with Lacey under the rug, right along with the fact that I was likely going to lose my gym.

But that was a shit way to start something I wanted so fucking badly.

"Got turned down by another investor…then Lacey called me."

Even saying it left a bad taste in my mouth, a souring feeling in my stomach.

Haley stepped back and tilted my jaw until I was making eye contact with her.

"What did she want?"

Swallowing thickly, I launched into it.

"Being an addict wasn't what broke up my marriage," I said in a rush, no clue at all why that's what left my mouth. But Haley's eyes had me continuing. "I've seen families work through addiction."

Haley watched patiently, stroking my jaw.

"There was always something deeper with Lacey…a selfishness that I turned a blind eye to. She was never content. There was a part of her that was harsh and mean, something I always justified as exhaustion or stress. But—"

I paused, listening for the girls. Even after everything they had been through, I was always careful not to speak badly about Lacey in front of them.

"The addiction seemed to amplify all those traits. Tonight she called because she wanted to see the girls. When I told her she could by following the parenting plan, she changed tactics and asked if she could meet me somewhere alone."

Haley dropped her hands and stared at my chest.

"To talk?"

Gently, I gripped her elbow and pulled her closer.

"To do other things."

"Oh." Her voice was soft and quiet, like a gentle hurt that she wanted to hide or tuck away into herself.

"What's going through your mind?"

Her nails curled through my belt loops; her eyes stayed on my chest. I wanted her eyes on me, but I knew this whole scenario would take some getting used to, and she might need a second.

"Do you—I mean have you… She's very beautiful."

Stroking her hair, I finally tipped her chin up so she was watching me.

"No, I haven't touched her in several years. And she doesn't look like how she used to—there's a darkness there now that dulls how I used to view her. It's hard to find someone attractive after all the terrible things they've done. They tear the lining of your heart and it just can't be put back together."

"What did—"

Mila's raised voice came filtering down, breaking into our conversation. She was standing with her older sister at the top of the stairs, making both Haley and my head turn to the side.

When the screaming and yelling hit a level we didn't think they'd work through, we left the kitchen, and I broke into their argument.

"Hey, what if I rocket ship you up the stairs?" I perched with my arms on either side of the wall, looking up at the top of the steps. Both girls immediately stopped arguing and turned their heads.

"Can we do Spaceship night?" Mila asked, rubbing at her eye.

Seraphina perked up excitedly. "Yes, Spaceship night!"

Haley stepped up from behind me, curious.

"What is Spaceship night?"

"Daddy rocket ships us up the stairs, all the way to his bed. Then we turn on a space movie and we pretend we're in a spaceship. Daddy always pretends to be the captain and makes his voice sound like he's talking into a radio, and if he sees an asteroid, he shakes the bed."

I rubbed my neck, slightly blushing. My kids loved Spaceship, and after Lacey left it was one of the only ways to calm them down and keep them distracted. Some nights, I'd let them eat dinner in my bed, just to keep them from crying.

"Haley has to be in our spaceship too! She could be a navigator!" Mila yelled, pointing at Haley.

"Okay, all right. We'll do it. Who's up first?" I stretched my arms across my chest. I was getting too old for this, but so were they, and we wouldn't be able to do this much longer. I'd risk a strained muscle if it meant I could see them smile.

Mila ran down the stairs, wearing a brand-new pair of *Frozen* pajamas I had never seen. Either Cole or Haley must have bought them for her.

"Me first!" Mila jumped into my arms.

I secured her to my back, and then made rocket sounds and ran up the stairs as fast as I could, smiling as Mila laughed and squealed. Then I ran down the hall, still sounding like I was a spaceship and tossed her on my bed. It was freshly made with clean sheets, thanks to Haley.

Once I jogged back down the stairs, Seraph and Maddy were waiting for me. I repeated the process with each of them, and finally they were on my bed, safe and secured. I was about to shut down all the lights and head up myself when all three girls appeared at the top of the stairs.

"You have to rocket ship Haley, too."

My head snapped back, and Haley's tilted up, watching the kids.

"Oh no, that's—" Haley started but Maddy interrupted.

"If you're going to be on our crew, the only way up is the rocket ship."

Haley's mouth parted like she was about to argue then she turned her head in my direction.

"I'm not the same size as you guys. I think that would hurt your dad."

I coughed to cover my laugh because just last night I had held her while we fucked against the wall. In most positions, I used her like a rag doll, lifting and grabbing her in any way that I wanted to fuck her. And there were a lot of ways that I enjoyed fucking Haley. She was standing near the dresser yesterday afternoon while the kids were in school, so I lifted her until her ass was perched on the edge, ripped her shorts off and licked that pink pussy until she screamed my name.

Kneeling down in front of Haley, I smirked and said, "Get on my back."

"Yay! Rocket ship up here, Haley and we'll show you how to travel through space!" Seraph yelled, and all three of them ran back to my bedroom.

"Liam, you don't have to—"

"Wrap your arms around my neck, baby, and get those legs around me."

"This should not be turning me on," she whispered.

I laughed and hooked my hands behind her knees. Her hands connected around me, and once I knew she was secured, I shot off, running up the stairs. She let out the cutest little giggle that hit me in the chest harder than any punch ever had. I held her to me as I passed each step, and instead of throwing her on the bed, I jumped in the middle, making the girls squeal with laughter.

"Do you have the control panel, Maddy?" I asked, moving around the bed to get settled. Haley had nestled in next to Seraph and pulled Mila into her lap while she scooted back against the headboard.

Maddy ran to her closet and grabbed the massive piece of cardboard that we'd drawn buttons onto, pretending it was our control panel. It was long enough that it reached across the length of my king-sized bed. She drug it over, and I set up against the footboard of the bed, and then grabbed the remote and selected a science video that was about space discovery.

Once the lights were lowered and the movie started, I looked back at my girls and smiled. Haley was tucked in between my kids like she'd always belonged there. This was a tradition we'd never had with Lacey, and now it was something that we had with Haley. This was ours. *She was ours.*

I just had to confess that I was in love with her.

Oh, and tell my daughters…

CHAPTER TWENTY-FIVE

haley

Wine
New Recipes
Sex Toys
Groveling
Eavesdropping
Feeling Wanted

"DO you think the pie is even done all the way?"

Liam gripped the steering wheel and glanced over at me with that same expression on his face he'd had the last time. It was like I had disrupted him from a dream, or a trance.

"What?"

I shifted in the seat, adjusting the hot pie in my lap.

"It only baked for forty-five minutes…I just don't know if the bottom is cooked through."

I knew Liam wouldn't know if this pie was baked or not; I was just rambling because I was nervous.

My brother Colson had reached out and asked if we wanted to come over for dinner. I initially thought that meant Liam and the girls would go and I would arrive separately, but no. Liam said we'd be arriving together. Which meant he was going to tell the girls, or just kiss me in front of everyone and let the kids play catch up.

I wish he'd talk to me about it, but after the past few nights it's been hard to bring up.

After the rocket ship, I had passed out on Liam's bed, along with the girls and Liam. We were all a big pile of bodies, snuggling each other under blankets. When I woke up, Maddy was between Liam and me, but his eyes were on me and the sweet smile he gave me was still melting my heart days later. His expression spoke a thousand words.

Words I may have wanted to hear, but knew I likely wouldn't. That's just how people were. I understood. Actions spoke louder than words.

"I'm sure it's fine," he said distractedly and focused on the road.

Liam parked along the curb outside of Colson's house, and my nerves felt raw. If the girls weren't in the back, I'd just ask him what he was planning tonight. I knew he'd had a conversation with Colson about us, one that seemed to settle this entire dispute over whether or not I should be dating Liam. The thing was, I still hadn't ever kissed or done anything with Liam in public. Behind doors we were insatiable for one another, but the furthest we'd gone in front of anyone else was holding hands at the fun center with the girls.

Once we exited the car and piled up on Cole's porch, Liam knocked and then the door swung open.

"Hi guys!" Nora said, welcoming us in. She wore an off-the-shoulder shirt that managed to match her eyes. Eyes which bounced from me to Liam, with a small smile curving her lips. I knew what she was thinking, and she was right, but I had no idea if I was allowed to tell her.

"Hey, thank you for having us over," I said, stepping inside once Nora moved aside.

My brother was in a pair of dark denim and a heather gray shirt. His eyes went soft the second he took me in.

"Hey…"

I smiled. "Hey."

I tried not to act awkward now that he knew about me and Liam, but it wasn't easy. Colson had just recently accepted being my older brother, and while I appreciated that he cared, it didn't automatically give him the right to have an opinion on my dating life. Not that he'd said anything to me about it—and I wasn't sure he would. But I didn't love that he had given Liam a hard time about it.

"Can I take that pie for you?" he offered, stepping forward.

The others filed in, and the girls ran to their toy room. Nora headed for the kitchen, busying herself behind Cole.

"Sure." I handed it over with the potholders still attached.

"That smells so good, Haley," Nora groaned from over her shoulder.

Taking a seat on the stool, and ignoring wherever Liam slipped off to, I decided to focus on the conversation in front of me.

"Thanks. I've never made marionberry pie before, so I have no idea how it will taste."

Cole waved me off, moving to dice up a few carrots. "You make great food, it'll taste great."

I smiled and then there was an awkward stretch of silence. Thankfully Liam rejoined us, and when I assumed he'd pull up the stool next to me, he chose one further down, putting an empty stool in between us.

Trying not to let my confusion show, I leaned forward and snagged a carrot from Colson's cutting board. My brother and Liam began to talk about the gym, and work.

Bored by their exchange, I walked over and decided to help Nora.

"What can I do?"

She pointed at wine glasses, "Would you mind pouring?"

I found the opened bottle and lined up four glasses. As soon as I finished pouring the three, Liam piped up from behind me.

"You're not old enough for that."

I spun on my sock, totally shocked that he'd just said that. Out loud, no less.

Cole's eyes burned, bouncing from Liam to me, that same confused expression dulling his face with crowded brows and a downturned smile.

"I'm twenty-one." My voice became frosty as I added, "Did you forget?"

Liam's eyes widened the smallest bit before a smidge of red colored his cheeks.

"Shit. I'm so sorry…" he muttered, hanging his head.

"It was just a few weeks ago, Haley…give the man a break," My brother joked, keeping any emotion out of his voice.

I turned back to the glasses to hide my reddening face. Why was it okay for him to fuck me in every position he could imagine, degrade me when it fit his sexual needs, then suddenly have an opinion on my drinking age?

Fuck that.

Not to mention he forgot I even had a birthday! *Jerk.*

I realized I was still staring at the glasses with a blazing glare and gripping the wine bottle when Nora gently pulled it from my fingers.

She poured my glass and I smiled, giving her thanks.

Nora and Colson moved to the table, setting up all the plates and dishes there as Liam helped the girls wash their hands. I stood by the mantle looking at Colson's photos, sipping my wine feeling totally unsure of what the fuck was going on with the man I'd fallen in love with.

Finally, once we were all seated, conversation began to flow easily about projects, plans, and the future. Mila stole the show a few times, choosing to sing her debut music that Seraphina had written for her. She couldn't read all the words, so I leaned over to help her. It was hilarious and worked long enough to shake my mood.

But it returned after dinner as the four of us sat around the living room to have our pie and coffee.

The girls had theirs and were cleaned up, playing in the room and Nora perched on Colson's lap in an oversized chair which left the entire couch open for Liam and myself.

Liam picked a spot on the floor after I sat on the middle cushion.

I scowled at him, long enough that I caught my brother watching us. His jaw clenched tight as he watched Liam, but he changed the subject quick enough that no one even noticed the awkwardness in the room. But as Nora and Colson came up with new conversation topics and Liam joined in, my chest filled with ugly thoughts and even uglier emotions. It felt like Liam was embarrassed by me. Like he was upset with me about something, but I hadn't done anything.

Every time my thoughts began to churn and I'd ask what I did wrong, I had to correct myself.

I would not be that girl. I wouldn't sit here and wonder what I did wrong. I didn't do anything wrong, and he was just being a dick. Plain and simple. Finally, by the time we had to leave, I was fuming. I had my empty pie plate in my hands, gripping it for dear life, when I looked over at Nora's house.

Maybe I should stay somewhere else tonight.

My head was turned when I felt a tug on my arm, and Liam's silver eyes were on mine.

Worry.

Fear.

There was so much in his gaze as he looked at the house behind me and then clenched his jaw. We didn't say anything as he opened my door for me, and stood there waiting until I got in. I knew he could feel the animosity between us. I knew he could feel the frustration brewing in me, but he didn't want me to be apart from him.

That little thought made my rage simmer down the slightest bit.

We drove home in mostly silence, save for the questions Mila kept asking about whether birds had warm houses to stay in at night. Once we got home, I went to soak the pie dish in the sink then headed upstairs to help Liam get the girls ready for bed. This was our routine now. I would help Mila take a bath, by washing her hair and singing my favorite songs with her while we did it. We'd even convinced Liam to put in a little Alexa device in the bathroom so we could tell her to play our favorite music. Mila loved Taylor Swift, just like me.

Then Seraph and Maddy would brush their teeth if they didn't have to shower, and before bed, I'd brush everyone's hair out. Liam would come in and say goodnight. I was trying to give back his space, and not stay stuck in the routines we'd created while he was gone. So the girls weren't seeing us both in there at the same time, making it seem like we were a couple. If Liam picked up on it, he never told me. I usually cleaned the bathroom while he said his prayers with the girls, and then I would go in.

Once they were asleep, Liam and I usually went to his office, where we knew the girls couldn't peek over the railing and see us. His office had a couch, so we'd usually cuddle while decompressing about our days, or we'd watch something on his laptop until we knew the girls were asleep. Then we'd go to his bedroom.

Tonight, once the girls were asleep, and I realized Liam was already down in the office, I went in the opposite direction to the guest room and went to bed.

I HAD no idea what time it was when I felt someone touching me. I passed out the second my head hit the pillow. I even skipped my face routine and everything. But now, in the darkness of my room, there was someone perched on the edge of the bed and a hand stroking my calf.

"I know you're awake." Liam's deep voice rumbled softly in the empty room.

I shifted, pulling my leg away from him.

"Haley, stop it…come on." He moved with me, gathering me into his arms. The street light from outside filtered through my sheer pink curtains, making it light enough to see. The door was closed, and he was now in bed with me, which gave me anxiety because if the girls needed him, he'd be missing from his bed and that would probably scare them.

"Just go to bed, Liam." I groused, my voice muffled by the blanket.

He held me tighter. "I can't. You're not in it."

I rolled my eyes, even if his words did melt me just a little.

"You didn't need me earlier at dinner, when I was too young to drink. Or when you couldn't even sit on the same couch as me. I have no idea why you think you need me now."

His arms loosened around me, and he let out a heavy sigh.

Minutes passed as we lay there, and I wasn't sure what he was waiting for. Finally he gathered me again, this time turning me so that I was facing him.

"I'm sorry. I was trying to show that I cared and was responsible to Cole…that I wouldn't be careless with you."

My forehead creased as I watched his lips move, confusion spinning my thoughts.

"Why? That makes no sense."

"Well, love doesn't make sense, does it? It fucks up your brain, has you doing weird shit, like sitting on the fucking floor so that you don't mess up the best thing that's ever happened to you. Love has me wanting to impress the only family member I've ever heard you say mattered. Love is me not able to sleep in my bed unless you're in it, because my sheets smell like you, and my arms are empty without you."

He stopped…and the silence seemed so loud as my heart hammered in my chest.

He loved me?

With actual words, he did?

My tongue was stuck to the roof of my mouth as he continued.

"I just felt like if I said it out loud, if I told the girls and showed it in front of Cole, then somehow I'd lose it. It would slip through my fingers, and it'd be gone."

My hand went up to his jaw, stroking his chin and his bottom lip.

"I did it anyway though because I'm an idiot. I love you, and I don't want to hide you in this room anymore. I don't want you to think you have other options for where you might stay if you're mad at me. If you're mad, you're still here, with me. I want you in my bed every night."

I didn't allow my skeptical self to overthink it or doubt it. I leaned forward and kissed him. I pressed my lips to his and allowed him to hold me to his chest and deepen our kiss. His hands moved under my sleep pants, cupping my ass and squeezing. His other hand tangled in my hair, moving us until he was hovering over me.

"You want to punish me tonight? I fucked up, make me earn this pussy."

I pulled away, smiling up at him.

"Why that is an excellent idea, Mr. Croft."

He groaned, leaning down to kiss my nipple. "It does things to me when you call me that. Okay, what do you want me to do?"

I sat up against the headboard as an idea hit. This would be so kinky, and maybe pushing things too far, but I loved exploring with Liam, and at least it would be something that would always make us remember the night he confessed loving me.

"Go into that drawer next to the bed and pull out the box inside."

He raised his dark brow but did as I said. I leaned over on the other side and grabbed the key I had taped under the desk. I wasn't ashamed of my toys, but I didn't want the girls to go snooping and get traumatized.

He held the box in front of him, and I handed him the key. While he worked the lock, I stripped out of my clothes and got comfortable against the headboard.

Once he opened it, he began to pull out the items inside.

"Okay, wow…I did not realize you had all these." He gripped a very lifelike dildo that was about nine inches long and girthy. I loved that toy.

"Vibrators too…and wow, what the fuck does this do?" He held up my dual simulating thrust sex toy.

"Why don't you find out?" I asked, spreading my legs open.

"So I have to pleasure you only using your toys?" Liam's eyes sparked.

I nodded, biting my lip.

He put a few toys away except for the dildo and then slowly stood and stripped out of his pajamas and boxers.

Crawling near me, he whispered, "Then I get to choose which one I use."

Heat spread through my center, loving the devious look his face as he got closer. Right as he reached my feet, he grabbed my ankles and pulled.

"I'm going to fuck you with your toy, but you'll be begging for my cock by the end of it because none of these toys can make you feel as good as I do."

My hands went to my breasts, kneading and touching as his eyes watched.

Then he lifted the toy to my lips and said, "Open."

I did as he instructed, and he inserted the phallus into my mouth. He pushed it in, then slowly drug it out, repeating the process a few times.

"Get it nice and wet, baby. We need it ready to fuck your tight pussy," he grated roughly, pushing the dildo further into my mouth, until it hit the back of my throat. "Look at you, so fucking beautiful."

My thighs desperately wanted to clench, but he was in between my legs, and when he looked down, I knew he realized what I wanted. Instead of touching me like I craved, he used his free hand and pried my pussy lips open.

Then he spit.

A slow drop landed on my clit and then another, and then he pulled the dildo from my mouth and plunged it into my core.

"Oh shit!" I rasped as he pushed the toy inside with a rough stroke.

Liam watched, his hand resting close to my slit as he pulled the cock out and shoved it back in.

"You want me to fuck you hard with this toy?"

He was really working it now, in and out at the right speed.

I nodded.

"Tell me you do. Tell me you want me to fuck you with this cock."

"Fuck me hard with that cock."

He hissed as his free hand went to his own shaft and he began stroking. I rocked my hips and moved against the pressure in my core, needing more, desperate, when he suddenly pulled it out and brought it back up to my lips.

"Taste yourself, slowly." He rotated the tip over my lips and then gradually immersed it as I stuck out my tongue. I tasted myself, and while it should have embarrassed me or made me feel self-conscious, it didn't. I tasted like I was desperate for Liam to fuck me.

I groaned as I lapped at the toy, now imagining that it was his length in my mouth, his weeping tip spreading that salty taste over my lips. I envisioned his cock inside me, fucking me hard and raw, making my tits bounce.

I pulled out the toy and begged him, "I need you…please."

Liam muttered a few curses before pulling on my legs and fixing his shoulders between them.

His tongue slowly swirled my clit as he gently pushed the silicone toy back inside my pussy. Once it was fully sheathed, he left it there and began sucking my clit into his mouth. The swirling of his tongue mixed with the pressure of the toy had me on the precipice of coming.

I pulled him closer by gripping his hair as I tipped over.

He removed the toy and swore. "I get to taste every fucking drop of this."

Then his lips sealed around my pussy, and he sucked my release into his mouth. Even after I was spent and my limbs were weak, he lapped up my release like it was the best thing he ever tasted.

The next thing I knew, Liam was over me, pushing my leg to the side and sliding in to the hilt, hissing as he went.

My eyes opened as he stared down at me. His hands went to my tits, as he squeezed my nipple and then began to slowly fuck me.

"We're going to have a lot of fun with these toys, Haley, but one of the things we're going to do is get you nice and relaxed and slowly open up that tight spot for my cock. You're going to beg for me to ruin that ass once you feel me there."

"Fuck. Liam!" I cried as I met him thrust for thrust.

The bed squeaked, and the headboard kept hitting the wall, but he didn't seem to care. He couldn't seem to stop.

"You didn't make these sounds with that little toy, does my cock make you feel better?"

"Yes." I gasped, clinging to his arms.

He rocked harder, pushing my leg further to the side so he could go deeper.

"Tell me you won't fuck yourself with that unless I'm there." He slid deeper, hitting that G-spot over and over again and the sound of the headboard hitting the wall had gotten so loud I was worried the kids would come in.

"Tell me, Haley. Unless you need me to finish in that mouth and come so hard down your throat that you choke."

"I promise. I won't fuck myself unless you're there."

"Good girl. Now come for me again."

I did, releasing a cry that he had to cover with his hand as his strokes slowed and the sound of the slapping headboard diminished. Once he was finished, he pulled out of me, but placed his hand over my sore center that was leaking his release.

"This right here is the best fucking feeling. Knowing you have me in there, and it's dripping down your thighs." He stared and then pushed the tip of his cock back in ever so gently.

"So fucking beautiful when you've got my cum dripping out of you."

I needed a shower, but I was too exhausted to move.

I could hear Liam rustling around, then the drawer opened, and my box of toys disappeared. I'd have to clean the one later. Then Liam tossed a sheet over me and carried me to his room. The hallway was quiet and dark as we walked to his room. Once we were inside, he gently placed me on his bed and tucked me under the covers.

"Your place is here, beside me." He kissed my forehead then whispered, "I love you."

I fell asleep immediately afterward.

THE NEXT MORNING, I woke up alone in our bed.

I hadn't grabbed my clothes before being carried into his room last night, so I had to wear one of Liam's. As I opened the door and was about to turn toward my room at the end of the hall, I heard voices coming from below.

It was the girls, and Liam from what I could tell. I wasn't trying to be nosey but I heard my name mentioned a few times…so I got closer, and sunk onto one of the steps so I could hear.

Liam was talking to the girls about us.

"I know Haley's been around a lot…do you guys like having her here?"

My heart took off like a rocket in my chest. Leaving fire, and smoke behind that clogged my eyes and throat as I continued to listen.

"Yes." They all chimed in accord.

Liam spoke up again. "Well…I was thinking about asking her to move in permanently, what would you guys think of that?"

Mila's cute little voice carried up next, "I thought she already did."

"Yeah, I thought she did live here." The other two chimed in.

Liam seemed to hesitate and then continued. "Well, what if I ask her to move out of the guest room…and move into my room, how would that make you guys feel?"

There was silence that stretched for way too long, until finally Maddy asked.

"Are you guys in love?"

Mila gasped, and Seraph made a noise too.

Liam laughed and must have nodded his head because all three girls started yelling and giggling uncontrollably.

"I knew it! I had a feeling you guys were." Maddy said, but she sounded happy. That was good.

"That's why you were distracted!" Mila said, connecting the dots.

My eyes watered as I listened and processed.

"We love her too, Dad. I thought she knew that." That was Seraph.

"Of course she knows, but I wanted to talk to you guys alone to make sure it was all all right with you."

Maddy asked. "So you guys might kiss in front of us?"

Liam laughed. "We probably will at some point."

"Can we start calling her mommy?" Mila asked and everyone seemed to go quiet.

Even my heart seemed to go quiet, waiting to ensure Liam said the right thing, because I did love these girls, but I knew they weren't ready for that… Heck, I wasn't ready for that.

"I think we should wait a little on that…that's a very big title." Liam said cautiously.

Mila's little voice took on a confused tone. "But she is like our mommy. She picks us up from school, takes us shopping, she put a Band-Aid on my scraped knee. She helps with homework. She took care of us while you were gone."

"Yeah," Seraph added.

Maddy, who had been really quiet, added, "I already call her mom in my head."

Still, my heart seemed to thrash around at the idea of them one day saying it to me.

"Well you guys better get ready for your big day. I heard there's a big summer celebration in the town square and Haley wants to take you guys."

That was enough of a reminder to get me moving. It had nothing to do with the fact that tears trailed down my face.

CHAPTER TWENTY-SIX

haley

New milestones
Dating Liam
The smell of Liam's T-shirts
Summer
Flip Flops
Kids' Sunglasses
Milkshakes

"THERE'S MUSIC!" Maddy gushed, taking my hand.

I held Mila's hand on my other side and Seraph held hers.

"And a bounce house!"

There were so many people, I wasn't even sure where to look. There was a small stage with a few people playing guitar and singing. Four massive bounce houses in yellow, red, and blue were set up on the grass, and there were tables scattered around the grass with red and white checkered tablecloths wrapped around each one.

"Haley!" someone called, and I turned to find Nora walking our way.

Her hair was in tight spiral curls today, and she wore a cute Mount Macon tank top and jeans. She must have gotten that from Davis's shop. They had anticipated it being a tourist stop, but from what I gathered the locals were enjoying it, too.

"Hey!" I said, appreciating it when she bent down to hug each girl.

"Let's go find Rae and get some food."

"This is crazy," I mused as Nora took Seraph's hand in hers and we walked through the throng of people. My anxiety flared the smallest bit. I didn't like being so unfamiliar with everyone, especially with being with the girls without Liam. I had gotten used to him being back and didn't like reverting to how it felt when he was gone.

Nora weaved through the masses seamlessly.

I continued to follow her until she found a mostly empty picnic table where Rae was sitting, tapping away on her cell phone.

She had her dark hair swept up into a high ponytail with a cute blue ribbon tied around it. Her eyes snapped up when we approached, and a huge smile speared her lips up.

"Haley! Yay, you have the girls."

"We are here to party," I said feeling awkward the second the words left my lips.

The girls settled in on the benches, and since it was lunch time, I knew I needed to go and grab them some food, but there were so many people around I didn't to drag them through the line with me.

"Can we go jump for a while?" Maddy asked.

I looked over and realized all three girls were eyeing the bounce houses.

"How about I take them?" Colson appeared behind Nora from some-where in the crowd. He wore a pair of designer glasses that made him look like a movie star.

"Uncle Cole!" Mila jumped up and she was in his arms within minutes, the other two holding on to him while they headed to the bounce house. I watched them go, strangely feeling like a part of me had exited my body.

"Okay, so you have to tell me why Jefferey Akers has asked about you like three times since we got here." Nora leaned in close, pushing an iced drink in front of me.

Rae angled closer as well, whispering, "He keeps asking random people too. He awkwardly asked Colson like a billion times."

Oh, Jeffery.

We'd essentially stopped texting after I had told him we weren't going to hang out anymore. It wasn't that Liam bossed me into it, it's just that deep down I knew Jefferey had feelings for me, and I didn't want to lead him on. We had been friends in my head, but there were things I had ignored that he'd done while we were together. Like small brushes of his hand, or the way he touched the small of my back when we were in the store. The way he always had coffee for me. I put a stop to it, but he still occasionally texted. In fact, this event was one of the things he had texted me about, asking if I was attending.

Oh shit.

"You guys, I think I should go talk to him. I feel bad." My eyes began searching the area for him, and I found him standing with a small group of guys that had worked at the Center. They were a part of Cole's construction crew, if I remembered correctly.

"If the girls come back, will you have them stay here, and one of you stay with them until I'm back?"

They both smiled up at me and sipped their drink. "Of course we will."

They were absolutely going to watch my interaction with Jefferey. I hadn't even really had the chance to come out to them about my relationship with Liam. So I was sure they were confused and incredibly suspicious.

I held my drink, picking my through the crowd, until I was closing in on his group. Jefferey looked handsome today, wearing a nice blue button-down with fresh denim and boots. His hair was obviously styled, and his face was clean shaven. My gut sank, thinking he'd done that for me.

His eyes found me, and a smile lit up his face.

"Haley!" He stepped away from his group. "I've been looking every-where for you."

"Hey Jefferey." I lifted my cup in acknowledgment.

He led me away by my elbow, until we were alone away from the crowd.

"I'm glad you came; I didn't think you would…I mean, you've kind of been ghosting me since Liam came back."

Aw, crap. That made me feel like shit.

"I had the girls with me…" I started, already considering chickening out.

I hated how his eyes searched mine for something, anything that said I felt what he did.

"Well, that's okay. I figured now that the center is done, and I won't be seeing you as much, that maybe I could ask you out…see if I could take you to dinner?"

Funnily enough, the idea of dating someone like that—in a regular way where we just went to dinner and he called me the next day—sounded so far from anything that I would ever want again. I wanted secret kisses in the pantry. Stolen moments in the office before little eyes caught us.

"Actually, Jeffery, I can't. I—"

He stepped forward before I could finish, and his hands were on my face, pulling my mouth to his in a scorching kiss.

I pushed against him hard, forcing his lips to tear away from mine.

My eyes were wide in shock, and so were his, but they were focused behind me.

"You better fucking hope someone stops me from breaking your jaw!" Liam roared, storming up behind us.

I turned and moved to the side. He took my spot immediately, and he was already throwing a punch.

"Liam, I didn't tell him we were together yet. I was about to when he—"

Liam's eyes were huge and round—*crazy*. "When he fucking kissed you?"

Jefferey was holding his jaw, dagger eyes on both of us.

"You're with him?" Jeffery asked, sounding outraged.

I nodded. "I was trying to tell you…"

"Fuck." Jefferey wiped the blood away from the corner of his lip.

Liam pointed at him. "Lose her number. You're not her friend or her buddy. Do not come near her again."

"Fuck you, man. You don't tell me what to do!" Jeffery snapped, gaining a second wind.

My face flushed a deep red as a crowd began to form around us. Where were the girls?

They didn't need to see this.

"Liam's fucking that piece of high school trash?" someone jeered from the edge of the crowd. There was laughter and titters around that part of the horde. I scanned the group and saw Julie, Lacey's sister. My gut clenched tight as she locked eyes with me and then whispered to the woman next to her.

Lacey.

I hated life. Why did she have to look the way she did today? Long blonde hair touched her waist, her eyes a crystal blue that contrasted with her pouty pink lips. Her shorts showed half her ass cheeks, and her top dipped nearly to her navel.

"No, Liam and I were at the hotel just the other night fucking; there's no chance he left me for that," Lacey mocked.

Obviously she was lying, especially because Liam had shared with me what she had offered, but it still stung to even hear it. To know there would be gossip about him doing that with her because she simply said it was true.

Liam must have heard, because he turned and gently pulled me to his side.

"Stop talking, Lacey. You need to leave; we have a restraining order."

My face swung to the left, taking in Liam's profile.

Oh shit. I did not know that.

Why wouldn't he mention that to me?

Lacey straightened her shoulders, pushing her boobs out which were concealed just barely by her tank top. "I'll leave as soon as you let me see my babies."

Suddenly I wanted to step forward, tell her exactly where she could shove that thought. My girls weren't going anywhere near her.

Jefferey took the opportunity to laugh. "You're choosing this train wreck with a fucking addict for a wife over me? He's broke…fucking losing his gym. Everyone knows it. What, his dick that good that you're willing to settle for that? You're not that type of girl, Haley."

Record. Scratch.

What the actual—?

My hands shook as his words wound through me like one of those big twisty straws the girls liked to use in their smoothies. I had never really been an angry person. If I grew upset, I'd cry or tuck it away for later, but this—this rage—it felt like I could breathe fire and burn down everything around me.

"Fuck you, Jefferey," I spat, taking a step closer to him. He flinched at my words, probably reading my face too.

I wanted to slap him.

I wanted him to feel what his words just felt like on the inside of me where each and every letter landed with a painful pop.

"Liam is ten times the man you are, and their private affairs aren't any of your business."

Despite seeing my reaction, he laughed again, tipping his head toward Lacey. "Funny you say affairs, considering she had one on him with nearly every guy in Macon."

Tears burned my eyes, especially as Liam pushed away from the crowd. Thankfully he pulled me by the hand, taking me with him, until he stopped in his tracks, nearly making me run into his back. Right there at the edge of the crowd were all three girls. Colson held Mila in his arms, Nora had Seraphina in hers, and Maddy was clinging to Colson's side with tears in her eyes.

I kept my head down and bit my lip to hold in the sob.

"You can't keep my kids from me forever!" Lacey yelled from a distance away.

Maddy's eyes rounded when she looked behind me and saw Lacey. Then all at once, she rushed me, shoving her face into my shirt as she burst into tears.

"Please don't let her take me again. Don't let her take me. Haley, help me! Get me out of here!"

I couldn't breathe around the lump in my throat. What the fuck was Liam keeping from me?

I scooped her up and walked off with her in my arms. Colson, Nora, and Liam followed as I led the way to my car. I didn't know about anyone else, but I needed to figure out what the hell this girl had gone through and why she asked me, of all people, not to let her mother take her again.

Opening my door, I set her inside and shut it.

Liam was at the door, his arms crossed. His fist was red but that was the extent of the damage. Over his shoulder I watched as Colson set Mila and Seraph in Liam's truck.

"I want to talk to her," I said angrily.

I loved Liam, but I didn't like that he hadn't told me there was a restraining order against Lacey, or that his daughter would have a full-blown panic attack at the sight of her mother. Why the fuck was there a parenting plan in place if this was the situation?

Liam's chin hit his chest as he agreed. Then he leaned forward and pressed a light kiss to my lips.

"I'm sorry for not telling you."

"You need to stop keeping things from me."

He nodded, looking somber. I wish I could remove the words Jefferey had said that likely dug under his armor and nicked his pride. With him it was the type of wound that would fester, and it would take weeks to help fix that damage—if it was repairable at all.

I walked around the front of the car and got in, leaving everyone else behind.

"IS it okay that we're here?" Maddy asked, pushing her drink around in front of her.

I smiled and sipped from my milkshake. We had left Macon city limits and were nestled up in that same mountain spa that we'd gone to last time. Upon arriving, we had our toes painted and our faces massaged, and now we were at the restaurant, drinking milkshakes, something they didn't actually serve here at the restaurant, but the cook took pity when he found out there was a ten-year-old asking.

"We're okay. Your dad knows where we are. I texted him."

She seemed to immediately relax when I said that.

"So…today was sort of crazy," I started, trying to coax her to talk. But I had already decided if she didn't, it would be fine.

Her hair was braided today into two symmetrical lines, her blue eyes full of sorrow and an old sadness that if I had looked more carefully, I would have realized was there long before this.

"What happened, Maddy?"

She let out a little sigh and played with the condensation on her cup.

"My mom wasn't always this bad…actually, I don't know, maybe she was." She shrugged her little shoulder, looking off to the side.

"I remember when I was Mila's age, she told Aunt Julie she hoped her next kid would have blonde hair because it would be prettier. She talked about Seraph and me like we were ugly or something because we had dark hair. She would talk about dying our hair when we were young…see if she could get us in any beauty pageants. That was way before she started doing the drugs, too."

She took a break to sip her milkshake, but my heart was in my throat as she watched the table and continued.

"I tried to find the good in her…I tried to love her…that's why I went with her that day. Why after all the bad stuff, I agreed to go. She begged my dad to allow her to take me to my cousin's birthday party. It was supposed to be this girls' night thing…and Lacey wanted to take me."

I didn't comment on her changing her mother to Lacey in her story, but I did start to pick at my nail and kick my leg under the table as she kept talking and my nerves were running raw.

"Dad didn't want to let me go, but eventually she wore him down. She was doing really good, whatever that meant…he just kept saying it. So she took me. No one else, and we were driving fast. She kept talking to me about the different ways we could do my hair or change my clothes to make me look prettier. I wasn't really paying attention until she stopped for gas. The guy took a long time to come out and pump it for us, so she ended up getting out of the car to go get him. She told me to stay put. But I watched her through the window, the whole time. She was on the phone with someone outside the store. The gas guy came and started pumping gas but she didn't come back. She just kept talking and yelling at that person on the phone. Finally, she came back, and told me to get out and go with her into the store. I thought it was to go to the bathroom or something."

Maddy's eyes started to water as her cheeks turned red. I reached over and rubbed her hand.

"Hey. If this is too hard, you don't have to talk about it."

Her little face lifted, as tears fell from her dark lashes.

"I want you to know. I feel safe with you."

My heart melted, but my gut still twisted as I waited to hear how Lacey had hurt my girl. I didn't want to hear it, but I wanted to help carry this burden of hers. Sharing something painful that made us vulnerable was like extending a piece of yourself to someone and them saying they would be willing to help heal it.

Maddy wet her lips, swiping at her face with her sleeve as she went on.

"She took me in the bathroom and then told me to stay there—that she had to go somewhere for a little bit. I asked her not to, but she said *he* wouldn't let her bring me, so she went anyway. She left me there, in the bathroom that had toilet paper all over the floor and smelled like pee. I ran after her as soon as she left, but she was already running to her car. I stood in the parking lot, crying, watching her drive away. I didn't know who *he* was, but he didn't sound nice."

Oh my God.

"Maddy," my voice broke as I reached forward to hold onto her hand, I had to ground myself and remind myself she was okay, "How did you get home?"

"The gas station worker ran outside after me and took me back in. He gave me a bag of Chex Mix to eat while he called the police, and when I asked if I could call my daddy, he told me yes. I had memorized his number after being left at school a few times. I called him; he got to me before the police did."

I smiled as a few tears slipped free. "Of course he did, he would move the whole world for you."

Maddy sniffed, swiping at her face with her sleeve again.

"I used to think she wanted me—like really wanted me—but now I know she only wants herself, and I don't ever want to be around her again."

I shook my head. "You won't. I promise you."

I was going to make it my personal mission to talk to the few attorneys I had on retainer to see what could be done about blowing this parenting plan to hell. I had no idea if Liam would let me, but I was about to majorly stick my nose into his business. These girls were my business now. I loved them and would do everything within my power to protect them.

"I'm sorry you went through that, sweetie. I don't know Lacey, or why she chose to do that, but I know you're worth more than how she chose to reflect your value in her life. I know from my own mom that sometimes there are some parents who just don't know how to do it right. It really just takes love, and if you don't have that, then you get ugliness. And you, sweet girl, have had to endure too much of that."

"You had an ugly-hearted mom too?" Her blue eyes glistened under the lights.

I nodded, taking her hands in mine. "I did, but the key is to find someone in your life that helps you focus on the good. I make lists every day; they help me remember what's good in my life, and what I'm thankful for."

Maddy considered me for a moment, finishing off her milkshake.

"Can I try making them?"

"Of course you can. When we get back, I'll show you mine."

She smiled and nodded, seeming happier and lighter than when we walked in.

"You ready to go home?" I asked, taking a generous sip of my shake.

Maddy did the same and nodded.

We took our time going home, stopping to a local farm to grab some honey, lavender, and berries. Maddy loved it so much she asked if we could go back in October to get pumpkins. The thought of being with them around Halloween was something I hadn't even processed, but suddenly images of dressing all three girls up in the cutest outfits swam through my mind and my heart flip flopped in my chest.

Once we entered Macon and pulled into the garage to park, Maddy rounded the car and wrapped her arms around my waist in a tight hug.

Then she whispered something that changed my insides around.

"I love you, Haley."

My heart swelled until my chest was tight, and I could barely breathe. It was heavier, something you knew you'd have to work harder to keep intact; something you'd have to care for differently from this day forward because it wasn't just you who mattered. There were other lives that counted on whether that thing inside your chest kept beating.

I bent over and hugged her back, choking back a sob. "I love you too, Maddy."

We stood there for a few long moments, but they'd live in my mind and stretch further, into a thousand brilliant sparks that held all the good in this world.

Mila cracked open the door to the laundry room, stepping into the garage with a white bag in her arms.

"Haley, you got mail! Can I open it?"

Maddy and I broke apart, and I swiped at my face before taking the parcel from Mila's hands.

"Let's open it together inside."

Once we cleared the laundry room, and took off our shoes and coats, we found Liam nursing a bottle of beer in his office. The second he saw me, he jumped up and rounded the desk.

"Hey."

I smiled at him and let Mila begin to tear into the package.

He walked over and sat with us as Mila pulled out a thin shoe box.

"You got shoes!" Mila yelled excitedly.

Maddy narrowed her gaze, turning the lid to see the words on the front. "Hush Shoes. What are those?"

"Oh, these are actually for your dad. I had Daniel send them over."

Liam opened the box and pulled out the black shoes, turning them over in his hand.

"They're light."

Tossing them from one hand to the other, he inspected the material as I slid closer.

"These were designed to be lighter, but I was thinking… Would you be willing to try them while you train in the ring? If you love them, then maybe we can do a little tiny snippet of you on social media using them?" I put my hands together like I was praying.

I hadn't warned him in the least that this was coming, but I found with Liam, sneak attacks were the most effective.

His eyes flicked up, assessing me for a moment before returning to the shoes in his hands. He set them back in the box and then scratched his temple.

"Uh…I don't know."

My gut coiled the smallest bit.

"You would get paid. I mean, I'm not talking about an ongoing thing. We're just trying to find celebrities and influencers before the launch—it would mean a lot if you—"

Sliding the box back in the bag, Liam stood and kissed the top of my head.

"Let's talk about it later, okay?"

I sat there as he moved past me and got the girls excited over helping with dinner in the kitchen. Meanwhile, I carefully tucked my emotions away and tried not to let it show how disappointed I was.

I honestly didn't care about the shoe; it wasn't my brainchild or my baby. I was just a financial backer, but if he agreed to show them, he'd get paid a couple thousand dollars for the promotion. It would be easy money…and the exposure would be great for the gym.

Why wasn't he willing to let me help him?

Why was he so fucking prideful?

Grabbing the rest of my mail and my purse, I headed upstairs to collect myself.

I could hear the girls giggling with Liam in the kitchen, and all I wanted was for that sound to last. I wanted him to keep all the things that made him happy.

Clinging to that sound, had my fingers clutching my phone.

Desperation and reckless love had me dialing the man who mentored me and helped me field new business acquisitions.

Each ring had my heart hammering in my chest as I shut the guest bedroom door and sat on the bed, pulling the ends of my hair into my fist.

"Hello?"

"Gunther?"

He let out his signature laugh, and it instantly calmed me.

"Haley, sweetheart, how are you?"

"I'm doing good, but listen, I need a favor…"

27

———

LIAM

I'D BEEN in the shower for almost ten minutes, just letting the hot water hit my back. I knew Haley was likely waiting in the room, ready to talk about this entire fucking day, but I just wasn't ready to face her yet. I felt raw and exposed after what happened at the town celebration earlier today. The same images kept running through my mind, tormenting me.

It would start when I caught sight of Haley talking to Jeffery and how close he stood to her, watching her with hearts in his eyes. Then it would flip to him grabbing her face and kissing her.

Obviously, as a fighter, I dealt with a certain amount of rage, but it had always been reserved for the ring. For the sake of my kids, I was always in control, constantly reserved, and even if a quiet anger would slip through, I'd wait until I was in front of a heavy bag or an opponent. But when I saw him touch her, I lost it.

I'd never cracked like that before. The only other time was when he was with Haley in the club. Funny enough, that fucker was right about my ex-wife. Lacey had cheated on me, multiple times, which all came out toward the end of my marriage, but that didn't anger me. I'd never had this type of visceral reaction to someone touching someone that belonged to me.

Haley was mine, and there wasn't a soul on earth that I'd share her with. Not in friendship, or any other bullshit excuse anyone used to spend time with her. Aside from punching him, which wasn't even a regret, those images spilled out like a busted jug of spoiled milk, souring the air and creating a goddamn mess.

All those words about how I was broke, losing my gym, *pathetic*… They echoed through my head, making my fists curl and my temper ready to test how it would feel to punch the tile in my shower. It would hurt, but maybe I needed to hurt for a minute. Maybe I needed a fucking wake-up call, because things felt like they were spiraling.

Haley knew about what Lacey had done to Maddy…about how I had failed my little girl. How I had let her go with someone who *abandoned* her. That shame still suffocated me late at night when I would think about what could have happened. When I let my mind wander to darker places, like if that gas station attendant wasn't a good human being, or if he saw an opportunity and chose to take it.

Fuck.

I shifted under the spray, turning it hotter.

The girls had long since gone to bed, so I let the spray burn my skin and soak my eyes so that any trace of emotion would be erased. I needed to hit something. I needed—

The glass door to the shower opened, and I didn't have to turn to know Haley was inside. Her hands ran up my chest from behind, her face resting against my back.

Then her sweet voice filled the space where all my rotten thoughts had been.

"You've been in here for a while."

The water poured over my head, forcing my hair to the side as I peered over my shoulder. Holding her hands to my chest, I replied, "Just thinking."

We stayed like that for a second, and then she tugged my arm until I faced her. The water made the varying hues in her hair stand out, and as rivets of water trailed down her breasts, all I could do was watch in awe. She was so perfect, but the sort of perfection that was bone deep, transcending her looks. I'd know her anywhere, because of that kind heart of hers.

"Talk to me," she said softly, letting the water ricochet from my back to her face. It made her blink, flashing those dark lashes.

Trailing her lips with my finger, and watching as her green eyes drifted shut, it felt like a thousand bricks fell into place at once, barricading these emotions and making it impossible for any of them to get out. I didn't want to talk. I couldn't hear all the damaging words leave my chest, hit the air, tainting this moment. I couldn't admit all the defeat that hung around my neck like a millstone. Just another reminder that I had fucked up once, and if I wasn't careful, it could happen again.

I loved Haley.

But even love had some limits on how much misery the other person could withstand before they just wanted to move on. She was so young; she could have anyone…the whole world was at her feet. I finally understood why Colson was so adamant about her not dating me. He loved her, and he wanted her to have a future. One with fresh starts. The chance to have her own family, someone the same age as her.

When I turned fifty, she'd still be in her thirties… She'd have friends with husbands in their thirties, and what if she didn't want a husband that had hair that was turning gray, or shit— what if I had wrinkles and back pain and erectile dysfunction by then? What if she wanted to have a kid, or kids… Was I ready to start over? Did I want that?

"Liam…" She grabbed my wrist and kissed my palm.

I should do it.

I could push her away and make her leave. She could have all that.

No doubt, she'd find someone, and she could be happy.

Haley lifted on her toes and pressed her mouth to mine, wrapping her arms around my neck. Then once she broke the kiss, she whispered, "Come back to me. I can feel you drifting."

The memories of us that night playing Spaceship slammed into me. Her making new memories with us. Her fitting with us.

I wrapped my arm around her back and held her to me as tight as I could, kissing her shoulder. Emotions tangled in my sternum like rough rope, burning and chafing all my vulnerabilities and making my voice hoarse.

"I'm here," I said in her ear, clinging tighter to her, knowing this was forever. I was too fucking selfish for any alternative. "I'm not going anywhere."

I stroked her back as she played with my hair, and we stayed like that until the water ran cold.

I TOOK Sunday off to be with Haley and the girls.

After the shower that night, there was no talking. We fell into bed and then got lost in each other over and over, until the tangled sheets held our silence. The next morning, Haley was downstairs making scrambled eggs with the girls.

We relaxed, built a massive fort in the living room, and then we played a few board games. It was peaceful, like we were in our own little bubble. Haley hadn't brought up the shoes again, and while I understood what she was doing and was appreciative of her efforts, the gym had to be something I did on my own. I couldn't explain it except that like her own business ventures, when she followed her gut to buy a company, I had to do the same with my own business. Even if it was failing, and it made no sense at all to turn down her help.

I had to, otherwise in the back of my mind I'd always know that I couldn't have done it on my own, I had her to step in and rescue me. And after all the shit that happened with Lacey, I needed to have something in my life that I resurrected myself. A financial backer was fine, as long as it was someone who genuinely thought I was a good investment, not out of pity or some other misplaced notion.

Today, I was heading back into work, dragging my feet. I already knew what the books would show, and I knew it was going to be hot today, and the fans only did so much and that was if they worked today. I knew that Rex would be the first in, droning on about the shit he'd heard around town through the grapevine. The dude wouldn't think twice about raving about something that would be a sore subject for me.

Flicking on the lights to the gym, I tossed my bag down and keys, booted up the computers, and flicked on the first fan near the desk. I'd have to open the back bay doors to let the cooler air in with the fans blowing.

Right as I was about to leave the front desk, the door swung open and a man in a business suit and shiny loafers walked in.

"Can I help you?"

He looked like all the other investors that had turned me down, but I had yet to reach out to anyone new after the last rejection.

The man fixed his cufflink, dragging his gaze over the gym, until he finally stepped toward me. He was tall, and had thinning hair, aging him past sixty-five at least.

"Hello, yes, are you Liam Croft?"

Placing both my hands on the counter, I nodded. "I am."

His hand shot out. "I'm Gunther Ross. I received your name and address from a colleague of mine that had passed on financially backing your gym. I'm an old fan…and when I heard him use your name, well, I hope you don't mind me taking it upon myself to drive down and see for myself the gym in question and make you a proposition."

What?

I tried not to get my hopes up because this could be a scam. I mean, he literally walked right in off the street. Maybe this was a joke.

I cleared my throat. "Do you have any credentials I could see, or could we go into my office so we can talk?"

Rex walked in right as I said that and stopped midstep when he saw Gunther.

"Sorry, you in a meeting?"

I tossed a key ring over to Rex and rounded the counter.

"Yeah, can you finish opening up and watch the counter? Also see if you can get the fans working."

He eyed the key ring. "Sure thing, boss man."

I showed Gunther to my office and sat across from him, hoping he didn't mind the Barbies Mila had left behind, or all the stickers and drawing utensils Seraphina had scattered around the desk.

"Can I get you water, or coffee?" I didn't have either, but I'd figure it out even if I had to go find a cup of instant brew and use the locker room to get hot water.

Gunther waved me off. "No, thank you, though. I found a charming little diner down the way and had breakfast. I'm still full."

Okay, it was right to business then.

"Sorry to be so forward, but can you give me a business card or…"

"Of course, here you go…and my license, just to put you at ease."

He slid over a glossy card that said R&H Industries. I typed the web address into my computer browser so I could ensure it was legitimate.

"Industries…so you're apart of multiple companies then, that's usually what that type of affiliation means, right?"

Gunther placed his left leg over his right knee. "Yes, we're currently made up of at least ten different owners, thirteen shareholders, and five CFOs. Each partner works to find businesses that need a backer or financial help. We acquire them, support them, and get them on their feet."

That sounded similar to what did Haley did…

"Right." I held his license in front of me next. "California?"

He nodded. "Flew up to Portland yesterday and drove the rest of the way up. Nice drive."

Handing his ID back to him, I relaxed into my chair.

"Well, I appreciate you coming all this way. What did you have in mind for my gym?"

Gunther leaned forward and handed me a portfolio.

"You'll find the offer inside, and I think you'll be pleased."

I flipped the folder open and scanned the page.

My eyes snapped up.

"Wait…you're willing to cover the debt, pour in an additional thirty grand, and you're only asking for franchise rights?"

"The franchise name or names would have your approval, and you have the final say on any location."

I shook my head, leaning over the desk.

"I don't understand. Why aren't you asking for equity, or partial ownership?"

Gunther steepled his hands and smiled, gesturing toward the papers on the desk.

"I told you I was a big fan. I think it would be wonderful for you to keep your gym, and all the rights. But all franchises would funnel money back to us, and you'd keep thirty percent of whatever they make."

This was…holy shit.

"This…I—" I couldn't form words.

"I can give you some time to think it over if you'd like, but I am really hoping you choose to partner with us."

I still didn't understand. "But…this is so much more than I asked any investor for. Franchises would allow future income, and I wouldn't even know how to—"

He waved his hand, like that wasn't a big deal. "We would take care of that, and the timing can be up to your discretion as well."

"What's the catch?" Because there had to be one; there was no reason that someone just stepped off a plane and decided to give me the opportunity of a lifetime.

Gunther shrugged, giving me a wide smile. "I mean, what you see is what you get. It's straightforward. No catch."

Well then. Fuck.

I stood and held out my hand. "Okay, then yes. My answer is yes, let's do this."

I didn't know how this was possible, but I wasn't going to second guess it. Maybe my mom was looking out for me from up in heaven, or all the bad shit my dad put me through as a kid allowed me some good fortune. Either way, I wasn't letting this slip through my fingers.

CHAPTER TWENTY-EIGHT

haley

Friends
Celebrations
Smiles
Cupcakes
Passing on Traditions

DIRT CLUMPED under my fingers as I dug into the soil.

"Nora, I swear if I touch a worm, I am going to make you pay," Rae whined, shoving both her hands into her area of dirt.

I laughed, but part of my hair fell in my face, which I then used my arm and elbow to try to move, which made dirt smear my cheek.

Nora focused on digging through the dirt, her gaze steady on the clumps.

"This is a form of therapy ladies; you need to embrace it."

Rae snorted then shrieked when a crow dipped down from the sky, landing on the outskirts of Nora's yard.

We all started laughing as Rae fell to her ass, taking a handful of dirt with her.

"That shit is not funny!" Rae kept her eyes on the bird until it flew off. "Crows are from hell, there's a scientific study on it."

I couldn't stop laughing as she tried to get herself back into position on the grass.

Nora was in the process of selling her house, but she wanted her original garden to be attached to Colson's yard, so we were helping her move the boundary line. I tried to explain to her that legally, if she sold, the new owners had every right to challenge her. She replied saying she'd have it written into the deal of the sale.

What we assumed would be done with shovels turned into us kneeling around a garden bed, moving over dirt with our hands. Nora said she was worried about disrupting the balance of the garden's energy. I withheld an eye roll and both Rae and I had started shoveling the dirt with actual shovels when Nora went in to use the bathroom.

"I get to call our next group activity," Rae said, swiping at her forehead.

I laughed again because the notion that this was just a hangout session was hilarious. I was getting sunburned and frostbite at the same time. Oregon was weird. I guess the dirt cooled so much overnight that it was cold enough to make your fingers numb if you went digging in it.

"What are we going to do, draw on posters with markers for three hours?" Nora mocked, shifting her position by moving on her knees around the perimeter of her yard.

Rae gave Nora a glare and pointed a dirt-stained finger at her.

"You loved my posters when you were getting married."

"Okay, before we get into another discussion about posters or weddings, I have to hear what her group activity would be," Nora said, lifting her head until she was watching me.

Shoot, what would I do? I didn't really *do* anything but watch the stock market, cyber stalk up and coming startups, and plug numbers into my excel sheet. I also liked to spend time with the girls. I liked to shop, and Liam was still working with me on self-defense—I loved training on the heavy bag.

It finally hit me. "Baking! We would bake, have an entire competition and everything."

Rae watched me with a smile. "Do the girls love baking with you?"

"They do, I've been teaching them. I was actually kicked out of the house today because Liam is baking me a surprise with them."

I thought about how he had come home a few days ago smiling and that burden I had seen him carry for the past few months seemed to disappear. Gunther had texted me a thumbs up after he'd visited Macon, which told me he'd pitched the offer to Liam and Liam had accepted. I was so relieved that a few happy tears trailed down my face that night when Liam sank into me and whispered how much he loved me.

He, of course, had no idea I was the one behind the offer, but it didn't matter. He was going to be okay, and his dream was safe. I was going to take this win and tuck it away in my heart, and maybe one day far from now, when Liam's gym had been franchised a hundred times and he was sitting on more money than he ever imagined, I would tell him what I did.

Until then, I would be taking it to the grave. Liam was too proud to accept that it was me who pitched the deal. It wouldn't matter that Gunther had initially agreed with me that Croft Gym would be a smart choice, or that Gunther himself used to be a huge fan of Liam's and would have made the offer himself. All Liam would see was my involvement.

Nora sat back on her heels and let out a sigh. "Well, I'd be down for a baking competition, especially if we got to eat what we bake."

"Haley, you never told us what happened with Jeffery Asshole Akers," Rae said, flicking her gaze to me briefly before focusing on the soil.

I shrugged, digging into the dirt harder than necessary. "Not much to tell. He was an asshole, and I won't be speaking to him again."

"Agreed. My mom refuses to serve him at the diner now, after what he said about Liam," Rae said with a malicious snicker.

"Colson would fire him if he could, but he doesn't technically have grounds. He did give him a crappy rotation on one of the new projects, though. He also sat him down and warned him that if Haley ever set foot on another build site, that Jeffery was not to go near her."

Both women paused their movements, their eyes set on me as a refreshing wind blew dead leaves around the yard.

Rae asked curiously, "So were you ever going to tell us you were seeing Liam?"

I stopped digging as well and sat back on my heels, staring between the two of them.

"I wanted to, but Liam wanted to wait until we told the girls. Then Cole found out, and I think he wasn't very happy about it."

Nora winced just the slightest bit. "Yeah, crazy thing about that…he didn't even tell me you guys were a thing until *after* the fight with Jeffery."

Honestly, I was shocked too. Rae's mouth gaped as she stared at her friend.

"Seriously?"

Nora bobbed her head. "Dead serious. He grumbled about them up on the very start of our honeymoon, but he never said a thing to me."

Rae pointed her finger, narrowing her eyes. "I knew they were together; I told you I had a feeling."

Letting out a sigh, I dusted my hands and started getting up. I was done digging in the dirt for the day.

"I wanted to tell you guys so bad."

"When did it start?" Rae asked, mirroring my movements, dusting the dirt from her palms. Nora joined us too.

"Uh… that first self-defense class I took…we sort of had a moment while the gym was closed."

"A moment?" they asked in unison.

I blushed, making my way inside.

"Well, he pinned our bodies together in one of his lessons, and well, one of his body parts wasn't being professional, and my lady parts really liked that he wasn't being professional."

Nora and Rae broke into laughter as we each stepped inside the house and walked to the kitchen sink. Colson was gone somewhere, thankfully, so he wouldn't hear me talking about Liam's body or mine.

"Oh my gosh, poor, grumpy Liam—falling for his best friend's little sister," Nora mused, scrubbing her skin with a nail brush.

Rae seemed to realize something because she grabbed my shoulders and gasped.

"Holy shit. Isn't there like ten years between you guys?"

Nora turned, sopping wet hands, dripping all over the floor, her eyes laser focused on me.

"Twelve actually." I said meekly.

Nora clapped her hands together and water went everywhere. "Shit, that's right, I totally forgot about the age gap!"

Rae let me go and couldn't stop smiling.

"I love it. Oh my gosh, Colson must have died when he found out."

Rae pushed Nora's shoulder jokingly. "How did you not know?"

Nora finally dried her hands and then reached into the cupboard for three glasses.

"That man is so hard to read sometimes, and we've been so busy with wedding stuff, and —just being real, sorry Haley—but we fuck like rabbits then we're so exhausted all we talk about is food."

Ew. I closed my eyes and plugged my ears. "I don't want to hear this."

Rae pulled my hands down, laughing while she did it. "Okay, Nora won't talk anymore about being a rabbit. I want to know how serious things are with Daddy Liam."

Nora began pouring our glasses full of the sangria she had made earlier.

"Daddy Liam sounds deliciously wrong but oh so right."

I was blushing so intensely my face felt like it was on fire.

"Oh my God, you guys stahhhhp!" I held my face, trying to cool it down.

They laughed, now sipping their drinks while we stood around the kitchen.

"For the record, things are serious. I mean, I live with him," I said, looking at Nora.

She pointed her glass at me. "See, I knew it. Colson said you were staying in the guest room, but I knew you were sneaking into Liam's room at night, getting dicked."

I took a generous sip, so they'd hopefully move on from me, but both their gazes fixed on me, encouraging me to continue.

"Okay, yes. I've been sleeping with him at night ever since he came back…and a little bit before he left. But we've still been taking it slow. He just recently told the girls, and that's huge. He said he loved me."

Now their gazes softened as they both stared at me.

"Do you love him?" Rae asked, lifting her eyebrows.

I nodded, smiling into my drink. "So much."

"If we play our cards right, ladies, and make them wrap that shit up at the appropriate time, we can potentially plan our pregnancies."

"That's assuming we can get pregnant. Neither one of us have siblings, and Haley's mom only had her." Nora lifted her eyes to me then looked down at the floor.

"I don't even know if I want kids," I said off handedly but then it slid into place, making the most sense of anything I had ever wanted.

Both women stared at me with curious expressions.

"I mean, Liam's girls are enough for me. I already love them like my own…I never really wanted to be a mom, but if I get to be theirs, it would be enough."

They both gave me a big hug while cooing and laughing.

I smiled into their shoulders, ready to go home and see my family.

LIAM TOLD me that he needed another hour, so I decided to drive over to the local coffee shop and work for a little while. If I was going to be helping Liam with his gym anonymously, I would have to start prepping things now. Pulling out my laptop, I got to work creating an excel sheet for the gym that would include my to-do lists. I wanted to talk to Rae about marketing ideas as well, see if she had any experience with sports marketing. I knew we would need to get Liam's gym on social media. It would be even better if he'd be a part of it, but I already knew that wouldn't be likely.

Maybe there would be a way to pull old footage of his fights and trim them to fit within the videos we'd need for social media. I was so focused on my laptop I didn't even notice when someone pulled out a chair from across from me and took a seat. It was when they cleared their throat that I looked up.

And then immediately slammed my laptop shut.

"Lacey."

She sat there in a thin leather jacket with a V-neck tank top that hugged her body like a glove. Her leg, clad in pleather, was crossed, her back relaxed into the chair and a devious smile tugged her pink lips up just the smallest bit.

"I can see why he likes you."

My fingers wrapped around the edge of my thin laptop, the metal cold against my skin. I didn't reply, but I didn't stop her from talking either. Was there some sick part of me that wanted this conversation to happen?

"What can I help you with, Lacey?" I asked, dipping to grab my laptop bag. I secured my mouse, charger and phone.

She bounced her leg a few times then clicked her tongue.

"You're going to be in my daughter's life…from the way he pulled you away from that crowd and how Maddy hugged you, you're already in deep. I want you to promise you'll help me get a way back in."

I laughed, feeling it bubble in my chest like she'd genuinely said something funny.

"Why would I do that?"

Quick as lightning she leaned forward and jammed her pointer nail into the table.

"Because they're my goddamn kids, and you're a teenager who thinks she can take my family."

"I'm twenty-one."

She rolled her eyes and then sneered. "Doesn't make a fucking difference. You're too young for Liam."

I didn't want to get petty, but this woman had the other day, so I felt like maybe it was deserved.

Smiling sweetly at her I sat back and said, "He doesn't seem to think

I'm too young when he's fucking me."

Her brown eyebrows dipped as her eyes flashed and then her venom came, and I wished I hadn't even bothered.

"You think he loves you? You think he'll change for you? He won't. Liam doesn't change for people, and he doesn't have patience either. You mess up once and that's all it will take. He'll never forgive you, and he'll never let you back in."

I hovered over the table, getting in her face like she was trying to with me.

"I would never do anything to hurt those girls, that's where you and I differ."

Letting out a howl of laughter, she threw her head back.

"You think that's when he decided he was finished with me? No honey, it wasn't the drugs or the hurting the kids that ended it for us."

This wasn't real; it wasn't true. She was a liar. Why was I even here listening to her?

"He was finally done with me the first time I fucked with his business. Stole from him to score drugs. That big lie was what reframed our relationship…one that had nothing to do with our kids…one that shouldn't have made such a big difference in our relationship but did. He's so self-righteous he thinks the entire downfall of our marriage was on me. Maybe if he'd extended a little grace that first time, we'd still be together."

Why was my heart hammering against my ribs so hard? It was clearly the last straw for Liam—not that he hadn't had grace. And I knew Liam. There was no way he kept letting her back into the girls' lives if she was dangerous; she must have been showing some sort of improvement…but still. Her words were like string, tying my hands to the boards of a marionette.

Why had I stopped trying to play defense and now felt entirely overwhelmed, like she was standing over me with a big white sign that read VICTORY across it?

I watched as she stood and stared down at me with a tiny smirk.

"Mark my words, little girl, Liam Croft has a one strike policy… You mess up once and you're out of his life forever."

Lacey turned with her ominous words hanging in the air and exited the café.

Meanwhile I sat there with my thoughts churning over what I had done…and what it would do to us when Liam found out.

AN HOUR HAD COME and gone, but Liam never texted me, so I decided to drive back and ruin the surprise. I couldn't handle the guilt any longer, either. I had to come clean, tell Liam about the offer, and how it was my idea…he could get mad, but at least it would be on my terms with how he found out.

Pulling into the garage, I quickly exited and rushed into the house.

The smell of baked goods permeated the air, making my mouth water.

"Did you make cupcakes?" I asked with a smile, rounding the corner into the kitchen. There were a dozen cupcakes, all iced with pink frosting. There were words on them, but I couldn't make much of it out; it looked like maybe the frosting had melted off.

I lifted my gaze to ask what they had said, but Liam was sitting at the kitchen table with his head down. He hadn't registered that I had come in. My stomach tightened as I waited for him to look up.

"Where are the girls?" I asked, looking around. Originally, he had said this was a surprise from all of them, so I figured they'd be here.

Liam finally gave me his attention, and his silver eyes were dull, his lips thin, and his face blanched red. With a curt tone, he said, "Colson came and got them."

That didn't make any sense…unless he wanted me to himself for some reason.

I took a seat across from him and peeked at what was on the table in between his elbows.

"What is that?"

Liam's strong fingers gripped the letter, and he roughly tossed it in front of me.

I couldn't make sense of his emotions. He was like a blank piece of paper that had eraser marks all over it. There was something there, I just couldn't make it out.

That is until I realized what he had been looking at.

It was a piece of mail with my name on it, and the initials for the company that had just made him a business proposal a few days prior.

My head snapped up. "I can explain this…"

Liam's eyes narrowed; his jaw clenched so that the muscle jumped along his face.

"Explain what, Haley?"

He stood and shoved his hands into his hair. "That you went behind my back and did the very thing I specifically asked you not to?"

"Liam—"

"No!" he yelled over me, and it startled me so much, my mouth snapped shut.

"I asked you not to interfere. I told you I had to be the one who did it. I told you!"

He trailed off and tugged at the ends of his hair.

But when his voice broke, a piece of my heart did too.

"Do you have any idea what it's like to think you finally did something right? To think you finally made it, that all your hard work paid off because this amazing opportunity landed in front of you…only to find out it wasn't real at all. It was just your rich, pretentious girlfriend posing as someone else, tricking you into doing business with her."

Tears clouded my vision as ripples of pain hummed through me. I had fucked up so bad…

I stood, reaching out for him.

"Liam, please! I'm sorry, it wasn't like that, I didn't want—"

He snatched his arm away from me, his eyes wide with rage.

"You need to leave. I won't have liars living in my home."

What?

No.

I shook my head as tears freely fell. "Liam, let's talk about this."

"There is no fixing this, Haley! Don't you get it? My gym is ruined…

I'm fucked, and the only hope I actually allowed myself to hold on to wasn't even real!"

He barged into the living room where all my stuff was already waiting.

No. No. No. This wasn't happening. Why was my stuff already packed?

"Liam, stop. This—just think this through."

He gripped my suitcase and bag and stormed into the garage to where my car was.

"They'll eventually be better off. They already had one woman lie to them, they won't survive another."

Holy shit, that one hit hard. I didn't lie to hurt them.

"I lied to protect them, because you're too fucking prideful to accept help!" I yelled at his back, my face red with rage and hurt. All of it twisted in my chest and swirled into a massive mess.

"It's my life, and my kids to raise how I see fit. This was something I needed to do on my own, and if you can't respect something as fundamental as that then you have no right being here."

"Liam, stop. You're being irrational. Just take the night, or the week, but we're not over… I mean, you don't just stop loving someone because they messed up."

He paused, and turned on his heel, glaring down at me. After a few seconds of just staring, he laughed.

"I forgot that you haven't had a single ounce of life experience. You're twenty fucking years old and have no clue what or how grownups handle things like this. Protecting their kids, managing their work life, businesses started with nothing and kept alive with sweat, blood, and tears. Everything in your life that you have was handed to you on a silver platter, Haley. You're going to pretend that you have a frame of reference for my life?

"I had a fucking wife, Haley. I was married. I know what it's like to still love someone even though they messed up. I know what it feels like to still want your wife even though she's gone. What I felt for her, you'd never understand, because you're not my wife, and as of right now, you're not anything to me. I want you to leave."

He turned, about to toss my suitcase in the back seat of my car, but his arm dropped the second he saw Mila's car seat. I had bought one specifically for my SUV. The girls' tablets were in their little tote bag, along with headrests and blankets. The girls were spoiled as hell, but I wasn't about to apologize for that. Not when he left me in charge of them for almost three months.

His face twisted as he stared, and maybe he was considering all he'd said. Maybe he was regretting the words that had left him in a fleeting moment of anger, but the damage had been done.

My heart raged as violently as if I'd tossed it into the middle of a storm on the Pacific.

He'd just torn through all that we'd built…all that he'd done to get me, to have this…he'd just thrown it all away. He'd had his fun, but now that the hard stuff came in, he was out.

And fuck him for generalizing my life, and my experiences…and for getting my age wrong *again*. He had no right to speak to what I knew of life—and fuck his silver platter. I created the platter and served myself. I may not have kids, and maybe I hadn't ever been married, but I knew my worth, and he clearly didn't.

Lifting my chin, I turned on my heel and went back for the rest of what I could carry.

"Haley…" His voice broke, but I paid it no mind.

I gathered what I could, the most important things, and kept my gaze down. I saw his socks…they were ones I had bought for him. There was extra cushion in the toes.

His hand went to my waist, trying to stop me, and my determined gaze met his.

His silver eyes watered and had a red tinge around the skin, but they begged me to stop and listen. The problem was, I already had, and his words had branded my heart and assaulted my confidence.

His mouth parted, his grip firm on my hip.

"Just…wait, I—fuck, but I—"

"I'll have Colson get the rest of my things," I interrupted. "Please leave it in the garage so I don't have to go back in *your* house."

Then, without a single look back, I moved past him, and he let me go.

CHAPTER TWENTY-NINE

haley

My big brother
Beautiful Views
Perspective
Truth
Rebellion
My kids
The Guest Bedroom

LIAM WAS AN IDIOT.

At least in whatever he assumed was going to happen or not happen with me getting to see the girls. I knew they were his, but they were also mine.

He'd kicked me out, but the first place I went was my brothers.

Cole didn't know what was going on yet, at least he didn't act like he did, so when I walked in and gathered the girls around me, he didn't seem to catch on to anything being different.

"Haley! Did you see our cupcakes? We made them with Daddy just for you!" Mila yelled, wrapping her tiny arms around my neck as I knelt down. Seraph gently hugged me next while Maddy stood there smirking.

"I saw them! They were the most beautiful cupcakes in the whole world."

"Dad messed up on the first batch," Maddy said with a giggle.

I stood, carrying Mila with me.

"What was written on them?"

The girls all blushed, looking down…then Seraph spoke up.

"We talked to Dad about it, and he thought it would be a good idea."

My heart squeezed tight at the mention of Liam, and the memory of those cupcakes. I wanted to sit with the girls at home talking about this. I wanted them to point to what they had done, so I could tell them how proud I was that they'd done it at all.

"But they were too hot when we put the words on," Mila added, her little face dropping in disappointment.

"Well, don't keep me in suspense, what did it say?"

Maddy looked at her sisters, and they looked up at her.

"It said, 'Will you be our mom?'"

Oh shit. I wasn't prepared.

I'd come over here with a plan. I came with my pride slightly still intact because this wasn't my first verbal spat.

It wasn't the first time I had to hear someone's unfiltered and unchecked thoughts about me, spoke, to my face in a fit of rage. I survived then, I'd survived again.

But this…hearing this. *Fuck.*

"She's crying. We made her sad," Mila whispered to her sisters.

I couldn't see their faces through the tears.

"She's crying worser than usual… We broke her. Uncle Cole!" Mila yelled, hopping off my lap.

I tried to swipe at my eyes, but it just got worse and then the sobs started. It all hit me at once: The realization that Liam didn't want me. The fact that he'd asked me to go. The bone- deep loneliness that had trailed me my entire life. The rejection. And stealing the biggest moment in my entire life—the girls asking me to be their mom.

How would I cope with losing them, not when something so

wonderful and amazing had finally happened to me? I couldn't lose them. I couldn't leave them.

The couch dipped next to me, and Colson started rubbing my back.

"Sis, you okay?"

I sniffed, swiping at my face.

"Yes, sorry." I needed the girls—where were they?

I got up and went to where they were standing over by the fireplace and knelt in front of them. Opening my arms, I tried to control myself as I gave them a wobbly smile.

"I love you girls so much. With my whole entire heart. That was the sweetest thing anyone has ever done for me."

Maddy hugged me first, a few tears slipping free, and then the other two crowded around me.

Once I was sitting back on my heels, I gave them all a resolute look.

"I have to go on a little trip back home to tie a few things up, but I'll be back...." I pulled their little hands and herded them back to the couch.

"We don't want you to go," Seraph said.

"It's just for a while. I'll be back. But until then, we can talk on the tablets."

The girls didn't move.

They all sat, silently staring at one another. Mila sniffed. Maddy's eyes watered, and Seraph's face turned a deep shade of red as she crossed her arms.

"Here, let's check out the new filters." I held the tablet in my hand but Seraph suddenly grabbed it from me, stood, and threw the device on the floor as hard as she could in a shocking display of rebellion.

"No!" Seraph yelled at the top of her lungs.

Liam burst through the front door, his eyes searching the scene before him. Seraph didn't even blink or look at him. She didn't see Nora's gaping mouth, or Colson's worried expression.

She focused solely on me. "We had to talk to dad for months on that stupid thing. I won't do it again." Tears poured down her face as red blotches sprouted along her cheeks. "We aren't losing you now, too. We asked you to be our mom. You can't just tell us you love us and then leave. You have to be our mom now!"

She was shrieking, and I was silently sobbing.

Liam's voice broke as he stepped forward, saying her name.

Seraph moved out of the way.

"Are you our mom or not?" Seraph cried, swiping at her face.

Mila was crying, hiccuping as she looked between me and Seraph.

I moved swiftly. I pulled Seraph into my arms and tried to breathe through my tears.

"Yes, I am. I'm your mom, and I'm not leaving."

My eyes found Liam's; they were red, watery…but relieved.

Maddy and Mila came over, joining our hug. My arms wrapped around them.

"Can we go home?" Mila asked, turning her head into my neck. I stood with Seraph in my arms, holding onto Maddy as Liam grabbed Mila. He said something to Cole and Nora, but I didn't wait around to hear. I put the girls in my car, and when Liam buckled in Mila I locked eyes with him.

"I'm going home."

He swallowed, his Adam's apple bobbing as he nodded.

THE KIDS WERE FINALLY ASLEEP.

It took a lot of snuggling, pizza for dinner, and another viewing of *Tangled,* but they were finally out.

I walked out of Maddy's room, clicking her door shut, and then turned toward the guest room. I planned to figure out what my life was going to look like now that Liam wanted to break up with me, but the girls had adopted me. It was some weird backward bullshit that I had no idea how to manage.

Surely there were ways I could still be their mom but not live here. I could get a cute house with four bedrooms, and Liam and I would just split the kids…and the girls would have two moms that were on the outskirts of their lives.

Fuck. That wasn't going to work.

I was crossing the threshold of the room when Liam stopped me.

"Haley—"

"Don't, Liam." I pulled my hand away, "I'll figure this out. I know you don't want me here."

He pushed us inside and shut the door, and I crossed the room in a flash, my arms folded over my chest as I stood on the opposite side of the room.

"I was wrong. Please let me explain—"

I shook my head. "No. You need to go to bed."

"I am—in here, with you."

I was so angry at him. So hurt, and he didn't get to stand there and make jokes.

"Fine, sleep in here."

I pushed past him and stormed down the hall. He was right behind me, but not fast enough. I walked into his room, shut the door, and flipped the lock.

He wouldn't risk waking the girls by knocking or yelling for me.

I was doing perfectly fine until I saw that Liam not only brought in my suitcases, but he unloaded them. All my skin care products were back on the counter, my pillows back on the bed. My Kindle was in its usual spot, my paperback too. He'd put it all back.

I wasn't sure what to make of that, but I was so frustrated that I decided to just get into bed and turn off the lights and hope sleep would claim me fast.

"HALEY, THIS IS RIDICULOUS." Gunther slammed my resignation notice down on his desk—at least it looked like he did from our Face-Time view.

I was using Liam's office while he was at the gym. The kids were at Colson's for the day, hanging with Nora. Days after our fallout, I was still trying to piece together my life. Liam had finally stopped trying to "talk" to me. All he was saying was that he didn't mean what he said, but I believed a part of him did mean it. Why else would the words have been on his tongue in the first place?

"Gunther, I know what I'm doing."

Abandoning his desk chair, he paced in front of his window, which only made our connection fuzzy and his form blurry.

"You can't leave the company just so your boyfriend will accept the deal of a lifetime. This doesn't make any sense."

He paused long enough for me to catch his brown eyes flashing, and I understood it. I'd be mad if he were doing the same thing, but I couldn't help feeling more resolve on this decision than any other in my life.

"Gunther, it's more than that. I'm moving permanently to Oregon. And besides, Liam and I broke up. This isn't about him…not exactly. I just want to tie things up here."

He shook his head, letting out a sigh. "You've managed working from Oregon this entire time. Why remove your name from the company now?"

I didn't want to explain it. I just wanted Liam not to have a reason to turn down this offer. If my name wasn't attached, then there would be no reason at all for him to turn it down.

"I'm paying out my shares, so financially you won't even take a hit. Why are you so upset?"

Honestly, this was just business, and associates came and went all the time. I mean, I realized Hanes was the H in R& H Enterprises, but still, it shouldn't make that much of a difference if I decided to leave.

Gunther's face softened as he stood and tucked his hands into his pockets.

"I have watched you go from an unsure teenager, wearing big, black glasses too large for your face, taking notes so quickly on legal pads that your hands were stained black. I watched as you quietly grew into this confident young woman who had a mind sharper than half the men I work with. Your goodness and kindheartedness were always as much of a tool in this business as your negotiating skills. I have been honored to mentor you, my dear. A privilege you likely don't understand, but you've always meant more to me. You're like a daughter to me, Haley. A daughter I watched my business partner squander away for years as he hid you then neglected you. The life you deserve to live is vast—it's bigger than this company, bigger than Oregon. Bigger than a boxing legend who let you slip through his fingers."

He stepped closer as quiet tears trailed down my face, each word like thread, winding through my lacerated past.

"But if this is the journey you've chosen then I wish you all the best. But if this man loves you the way I think he does, he wouldn't want you to leave something you worked so hard to build. You don't share with many people how endless the nights were that you stayed up and studied, the courses you took while sitting in meetings with me, learning. You were a sponge for four years of your life, squeezed and wrung out. Could you blame me for wanting the very best for you?"

My lashes felt heavy as I shook my head. I sniffed and worked to hold off on crying. I sat back in my chair, taking in the room. Which helped, because this room was a testament to why I needed to ensure Liam kept his gym.

"I just want him to be okay."

"Being okay is objective, isn't it? He may financially be all right, but what if his heart never recovers from you?" Gunther took a seat and leaned forward, pushing his face closer to the screen.

"Do you not understand that you find your way into hearts like a dandelion seed? No way to fight it—you land and love grows. You are not easy to recover from, my darling. I doubt very much that man will be okay without you."

I heard him but doubt still wiggled its way into my mind. Liam was so hurt by what I had done. This was the right choice; it was the least I could do. Give him this one thing to have, and he would be fine without me. He made it clear the gym was his first priority. Otherwise, he wouldn't have let me go.

30

LIAM

THE GIRLS ASSUMED I was sick.

It was the only conclusion they could come to without me telling them what was wrong.

And really, it was so ridiculous, because it wasn't like Haley had left. She was around every morning at breakfast, every afternoon and night. She was here… She just wouldn't speak to me unless it was to be cordial in front of the girls. For the past three days, I tried to get her to speak to me, to listen…to hear that I messed up.

I had this festering void that had grown talons and pierced my heart. So much so that I spewed all of that toxic bullshit onto Haley, desperate to protect myself. Protect my kids. When I had made the connection to R&H Enterprises on that letter, addressed to Haley, all my assumptions clicked into one ringing phrase.

She'd lied to me.

Pitied me so intensely she went behind my back and faked an investor. Even now the shame of it tugged on my soul, reminding me what an ironic twist of fate this was. I had someone I refused to live without, and she did the one thing my pride would never survive.

But that moment I wanted her gone—the second I opened her door and saw that car seat— the venom was gone in an instant. It was like watching myself in a dream. I'd gone too far, said too much…and I wanted to go back, rewind time. My children loved her, and this argument of ours, it wasn't so immense that we couldn't get past it. It wasn't something to end a relationship over; we could work through it. We *would* work through it.

I had backtracked immediately, only to have her close herself off and seal her heart shut.

I was ashamed of my behavior, but more than anything I just wanted a chance to make it right. But each night, she would go on little errands, filling her time until bedtime then she'd come home, do the girls' routine, and once they were in bed, she was behind our bedroom door with the lock clicked in place.

I had been sleeping in the guest room, which if the girls knew, they hadn't let on.

I received the investment money for my gym, but I hadn't touched it.

Anger over the situation was still there, just slightly skewed. I was angry at myself, not her. It was an embarrassment that we were even in this fight, and maybe if I weren't so fucking pathetic, this never would have been an issue for us. But how did I take a handout from the woman I loved, who I wanted to see me as a provider?

How could she see my strength if she was the one covering everything that made me weak?

It didn't seem possible to fix, so we lingered in the painful in between. I loved her. I wanted her. But I refused to be saved by her.

That refusal would ultimately be our end.

COLSON MET me at the gym early.

He'd been doing that for the past few days. We hadn't really talked through what happened. I think he knew I was already down and didn't need another kick in the gut by being told that I was an idiot.

He let me spar with him, expelling the extra energy.

Then we'd sit quietly while we listened to the music blaring from the speakers, and the other guys working out around the room.

"I have regrets," Colson suddenly said, packing up his gloves.

I tilted on the bench, trying to recline against the back of the wall. "About what?"

My best friend turned and I couldn't quite read the look on his face. "What I did while I waited for Nora to come back to me."

That made me laugh. "No shit. All you did was drink."

His wince wore off after he shifted and then touched his wedding ring. The small gesture hit me in the chest. Jokes aside, at least she came back to him.

"Haley tried to make me better. She wasn't forcing us to talk about our past, or our issues. She was here helping me become a better person. Swapping my chips for carrots, bringing by plants which reminded me of Nora, opening the shades. Getting me to go on walks, taking my beer away."

I had a lump in my throat because that did sound like my girl. My beautiful, strong, selfless girl.

"You're saying you don't know what to do to get her back, but I think you do."

I let his words slowly sink in instead of snapping back. Because I didn't. If I knew then I would have her.

"What would you have done differently while you waited for Nora to come back?"

Colson stood and stretched while looking off into the distance. "I would have fixed her garden. I would have pulled it into my yard, made a statement that she was going to be with me. I would have torn down our fence. Anything to show her that we were going to be together. Instead, I just fucking waited. Some things require action."

I looked down at my feet and tried to sort through what sort of action he meant but realized it didn't really matter. Colson walked away, leaving to go meet Nora. I stayed put, knowing I needed to move but terrified that I was about to make the wrong one.

IT WAS SHORTLY after I dropped the girls off at day camp when I pulled into the parking lot and saw another car already parked.

Once I opened my truck door, Gunther Ross stepped out of his vehicle. He wore another suit, looking every inch the distinguished businessman.

"Nice weather today, isn't it?"

In my miserable state, I had barely noticed that summer had started, bringing higher temperatures and fewer clouds. The girls only had a few days left of the outdoor camp they were at. Shit, I needed to figure out what we were going to do this summer. Was Haley sticking around? Was she leaving?

"What can I help you with, Mr. Ross?" I asked, squinting through my glasses. I needed a darker prescription.

Gunther fixed his suit jacket and cleared his throat. "Can we talk inside?"

Fine by me. I didn't give a fuck. I was still dragging my feet on getting a lawyer to help me undo the signature I gave him for the deal we'd made.

Once we cleared the door, Gunther rested his hands on the counter as I rounded it and began opening procedures.

"She gave up the company."

My eyes flicked up, but the sun had caught me off guard, so I hissed and lowered my gaze.

"What?"

Gunther placed a new document in front of me that said *Ross Industries* across it.

"She left, gave it up so there would be no tie from your investment deal to her."

She did what?

"Why would she do this?" I asked, barely above a whisper. My eyes stayed glued to the paper, as if it could explain her decisions.

Gunther made some sort of sound in the back of his throat which gave me the impression he didn't like me very much.

"Love, I think. Which reminds me, you should probably hear this."

He pulled his cell phone out and pressed play.

"Haley?"

"Gunther, hey…I need a favor."

"What's going on?"

Haley broke into an explanation, and it wasn't what I had conjured up in my head about this entire situation.

"I have a business that I want to financially take on. I'm sending over the numbers to you right now, but there's a few things you should know. The owner is super close to me, and there's a conflict of interest, so I'd like the offer to stem from your side of the business, not mine. You'd need to be the face entirely. Whatever offer you come up with is fine by me."

Gunther was quiet on the line for a few moments.

"These numbers over all aren't bad…why does he need the backing? He already seems well established."

"He's in debt…something personal, I think, with his ex-wife and legal fees."

Gunther was quiet again.

"I see. Well, who is the owner?"

"Liam Croft."

"The Liam Croft?" Gunther sounded like a teenager who just found out his hero was in front of him.

"Haley…do you realize who that man is? He won two heavy weight titles in the span of five years…that's…I can't even."

Haley laughed and it was so sweet it made my chest ache.

"Gunther, I need you to be professional here. Come up with an offer you feel is fair. I don't want anything to do with it. I'll send you the address so you can deliver it, and I would be so appreciative if it could be soon."

He lowered his phone.

"My assistant records business calls for me when I'm in the office…

it helps us both remember what needs to be done afterward," Gunther explained, sliding his phone back into his pocket.

"So it wasn't really her. I mean, the suggestion was, but it was all you?" I tilted my face to catch his glare.

He gave me a firm nod. "That girl has been tossing me businesses to financially back for years, and she's never wrong. I trust her gut. And while she may have been trying to help you, she knew I'd ask for numbers. I didn't just say yes because of her. I did my own research."

Well, fucking shit. That made me feel a thousand percent worse for what I said.

"Why are you telling me all this?"

Gunther put his hand on my shoulder and leveled me with a scowl. "Because you're an idiot. Pay off your debt and work with me. *I* wanted to invest in your gym. And maybe you can talk Haley out of leaving something she helped build."

Fuck, if I could do that, she'd be with me right now. Because she had helped us to rebuild our home…our entire lives.

But she wasn't going to forgive me for this.

CHAPTER THIRTY-ONE

haley

Surprises
'Goodnight, Mommy'
All variations of mom
Chalkboards
Lists
Family Photos
Lilac

IT FINALLY HAPPENED.

I heard it.

Maddy did it first, and I thought I'd be ready because the girls had warned me. They had flat-out asked me if they could call me mom, but since that day, there wasn't a reason for them to directly call me or ask me anything, and if they did, they reverted back to Haley.

It was fine, I wasn't going to sweat it either way, but I was anxious about it. Particularly knowing that Liam was watching and listening too.

I kept trying to dodge him, but Liam was a force of nature. He was mine, and while I was hurt and angry with him, my possession of him didn't change. He was buried under my skin, deep in my heart. Fatally so.

There was no dodging him.

He was ever-present and always on my mind, even as I slept alone and woke with an ache between my legs and a stinging in my heart. He was everywhere and nowhere, and it was maddening.

So when Maddy walked into the kitchen, holding her backpack, and sweetly said, "Mom, can you help get my zipper unstuck?" I dropped a glass.

It shattered on the floor, which probably gave Maddy trauma, but I swooped in and hugged her to my chest so tight, I didn't think it would stay. My tears wouldn't stop, even as I did, in fact, unstick the zipper.

Mila said it next at bedtime.

"Goodnight, Mommy."

I wrote that down on my list.

Then Seraph got me by drawing it on her wall. She had started a gratitude list, just like Maddy had. Hers she wrote on her wall every day.

I walked in there to grab laundry and saw it.

Today's List:

New Markers
Clean Sheets
Cats
Whiskers
Mom
Mom's baking
Mom's hugs
Mom's heart

I CRIED FOR AN HOUR. I also took a picture on my phone, then Google searched the local rescue shelter to see if they had any adoptable cats.

Our lives were slowly blending into an intricate braid that, while fraying in some places, was still holding. It was that reminder that kept me sane when my heart just wanted to break.

It was Saturday morning, and the sun was bleeding into the room, proving my sheer curtains were a joke. I'd have to go back to the wooden slats Liam had before. Which meant he'd have to help…unless I went back to asking Jeffery for help.

That thought almost made me laugh. How ridiculous would that be? It was like inviting a bunny rabbit into a wolf den…a wolf that had already gotten a taste for blood.

No, that wouldn't work.

Fuck, I missed Liam.

His arms, his scruff against my thighs when he woke me up on Saturdays. The way he held me at night. The gaping hole in my chest seemed to widen as I realized we were likely never going to get past this. It wasn't what he said. I could understand being in the moment and saying something you regret.

But we wouldn't get past his pride.

It was a wall of stone. I had no tools to move it, nor any desire to.

A few tears gathered in the corners of my eyes as I stared up at the ceiling, watching the shadows swirl and spin as the sun caught pieces of the tree outside and cast it along the walls. I couldn't seem to get the dream out of my head from last night. It was the moment on my thirteenth birthday when Blaire told me those haunting words, all those years ago while sitting in my brother's garden. *The most powerful asset you will ever have is the power to forgive.*

I needed to forgive him. I wanted to. Part of me already had, but—

I heard something being slid under the bedroom door.

Curious, I crawled out from under the massive feather duvet and tiptoed over to the door and bent down.

It was a note.

Gripping it in between my fingers I scanned the text with a furrowed brow…

Today's List:
Sunshine
Air Conditioning
Lilac perfume
Pancakes
Saturdays
Family
Haley

SO LIAM WAS DOING the lists now too.

Okay, that was cute, I supposed but I wasn't sure why he was sharing them with me.

Still, I found myself pressing his note into my own notebook and starting my morning.

By the time I got downstairs, Maddy was already making pancakes, Seraph was focusing on air frying bacon with her dad, and Mila was pouring everyone's orange juice. That must have been a task Liam gave her, because I knew better.

"Mila, watch your cup, baby," I warned, garnering the attention from Liam and Seraph.

Right as he looked at me, Mila's hand moved forward too far and the cup spilled over.

"Momma, it spilled!"

Liam jumped over and began wiping things up, and I tried to hide how attracted to him I was when he helped the girls. Maybe it was because I had been on my own with them, or because I was still just in love with him, but I was legitimately ready to jump him sexually whenever he was helpful.

A text vibrated in my pocket, pulling my attention away.

Jeffery:

Hey…I know things between us are awkward,
but I left a few tools over at Liam's. Can I swing
by to grab them?

HUH. Speak of the devil and he'll text about tools.

As irritated as I was with him over what he'd said to Liam, it wasn't like I'd keep a contractor from his tools.

"Jeffery is going to swing by to get his tools," I said plainly over toward Liam. The girls ignored us, focusing on their tasks. Liam looked shocked that I spoke directly to him. He blinked, gripped the rag a little tighter than needed then dipped his chin.

"Okay…thanks for letting me know."

I knew that was a sore spot for him on more than a few levels, but I didn't have the energy to coddle Liam's feelings. Not anymore.

The rest of the morning unwound peacefully, and when Jeffery drove up, I made my way outside. Liam had been doing yard work most of the morning, so I hadn't really had a chance to tell him that Jeffery was on his way. I exited through the garage from the house, seeing that the large bay door was open, but stopped when I overheard Liam talking.

"Hey…I know I didn't handle everything right at the town thing. I shouldn't have hit you. I never thanked you for stepping in to help Haley and the girls while I was gone."

Jefferey was slow to respond, and since I couldn't see him, I wasn't sure if he was nodding or making a hand gesture of some kind.

Then he finally spoke up. "It was no trouble…I enjoyed helping her. Not just because I was slowly trying to steal her from you. It was because I liked being helpful. Sorry I said all that shit about you."

"Don't worry about it," Liam said, like he was waving it away.

I knew those words Jefferey had spoken had gotten under his armor, so him forgiving Jeffery made my heart wilt a little.

"You know the whole town sees you as this larger-than-life celebrity, right? The gym failing wasn't a thing. I mean, the whole town was failing just last year. I shouldn't have said it. I was just jealous. I really wanted Haley to pick me."

Liam waited to respond, and when he did my eyes burned.

"Honestly, she may still choose you. She's not technically with me right now, but you should know if she does choose you that she will always be mine. I love her. I'm in love with her. She's our missing piece. So, if she chooses you, or anyone else…I'll fight it. With everything I've got I'll fight it, but in the end I'll respect her choice. Just know, she comes with three little girls."

How could Liam honestly think that I would ever move on from him? I was angry, but I loved him. He was mine too.

I wasn't moving on. The notion that he'd accept it, and still be willing to allow me to have the girls, made something inside of me turn to mush. It was unrecognizable, as if all the reasons that had seemed so substantial and insurmountable just looked like mashed-up nothingness that was keeping us apart as effectively as a puddle on the ground.

Why weren't we just stepping over it?

I didn't hear the way their conversation ended, and it wasn't until Jeffery drove off that I realized Liam was moving back toward the garage. I hustled inside, not ready for him to see me crying again. I had a little pride I was clinging to, too.

It wasn't until later that evening when the sky looked like a bottle of merlot had been spilled across it, that I wandered out front to see what had kept Liam so busy all day.

The scent hit me first.

I inhaled deeply as the tart and sweet fragrance rolled over my taste buds, taking me back to the first time I had smelled my favorite scent.

Then I saw the color.

There was a burst of purple to my left, as fresh lilac bushes converged all along the base of the house and around the corner to the fence that bordered the back yard.

Damn him.

I was going to cry again. I needed to see it from the street. I walked to the curb of the sidewalk and choked on a tiny sob. Lilac crawled up the stone wall, nearly touching our bedroom window and then crossed over the arch, and back down. Our home was *encased* in lilac.

It had to have cost him a fortune to buy, and how did he find a plant this mature? Did that mean he was keeping the investment money? My heart skipped a tiny beat as I wandered inside, needing to see him.

I FOUND Liam out on the back patio, under the pergola. He already had a beautiful set of patio furniture out here, but I added a string of outdoor lights and a table that had a space for a gas fire. Liam nursed a bottle of ginger beer in front of the flames.

I wrapped the thin blanket I'd grabbed around me and curled into one of the loungers, facing him. The night was breezy, but warm. The gas fireplace flickered as the scent of lilac hung in the air. He'd planted a lilac tree in the back, too. He was sunburned and looked like he was about to fall asleep.

"You've been busy today," I said, gesturing behind me toward the tree.

His slow smile was felt down in my toes.

"It's my favorite scent."

I tipped my head back and caught sight of the stars through the glowing lights.

"That's it?"

His gray eyes caught on mine with that smirk in place.

"No, that's not it. I love you. That's it."

Keep it together, heart.

I had to change topics.

"You kept the investment?"

He nodded, clenching his jaw. "Yeah, but I added a requirement with my lawyer."

He did what?

"I thought you liked the offer."

He looked hesitant as he set his bottle down and leaned forward.

"The condition is that you stay on with R&H."

I let my blanket fall free. "Liam…no. I want you to take it and be free of me."

"I don't want to be free of you."

My head fell a bit as I searched for the right words.

"Not like that, I just mean in business."

His lips thinned as he stared at me, openly showing so much emotion it was unnerving.

"You have a stubborn heart," I remarked, tucking the blanket back around me.

He laughed, shaking his head. "Still belongs to you."

My stomach flipped.

So I pressed again. "You have a prideful heart, too."

His smile grew as he watched me walk past him, and when I was near the sliding glass door, he muttered again, "Still belongs to you."

I left our bedroom door unlocked that night.

ANOTHER NOTE WAS LEFT by my bed the next morning, this time with a piece of lilac resting on top of it.

Today's List:

Haley's eyes when she saw her lilac bushes

Hearing Maddy call Haley Mom for the first time

Hope

Haley's hair under the lights last night

The way Haley looks at me when she thinks I'm not looking

Family Photos

.   .   .

I CRINKLED my brows in confusion at the last one.

Before I could think any longer on it, Mila ran into the room and jumped on the bed.

"Daddy wants to be in the pictures that are on the wall, and he wants you in them too, Mama."

I hugged her to my chest and tried to work out what she was saying. Thankfully Seraph came in next and curled under the blankets with us.

"Dad woke us up and said he wants us to get ready in our nice clothes. He wants new pictures taken so you and him are in them."

Okay, that's what Mila had said…but why? I mean, I guess I understood it.

I had purchased photos from a local photographer a few months back…who had Liam found? I hadn't wanted him to feel left out of the pictures, but he wanted me in them too, so I suppose it made sense.

"Okay, well, let's go get ready then. If your dad wants some photos, we'll get ourselves dressed."

Seraph tipped her head back and stared up at me. "Can I wear black this time?"

I knew last time I was pushing it with the burgundy color.

"Of course you can, but I reserve the right to keep the picture that's down there now depending on which shots she gets."

Seraph crinkled her nose and laughed. "Fine."

AN HOUR LATER, we were all dressed. Liam wore a nice blue button-down shirt that hid all of his ink and somehow made him look like he was headed to Easter Sunday. I wore a cream-colored dress this time with navy flowers randomly placed all over them, and my hair down. The girls wore whatever made them feel the most comfortable, while still being stylish enough for professional photos.

Liam drove us in his truck out to a gorgeous spot on Mount Macon that overlooked the river. The girls hopped out, and I realized our original photographer, Lindsey, was here.

"Hey, you booked Lindsey?"

Liam looked over and gave me a warm smile then stroked my knee through my dress.

"I looked her up, found her info."

Okay, that was sweet. I liked Lindsey's work. Suddenly a swarm of butterflies erupted in my stomach as I realized I was about to be included in family pictures. *My* family pictures, with *my* family.

We exited the truck and began walking to the small opening in the field where Lindsey wanted to get our photos. She took a few of the girls, then some of all five of us together. Liam was holding my hand in each of them, and I noticed Lindsey continued to push us together every time I tried to put the girls between us.

And then Lindsey asked for just Liam and me to be in the shot.

I felt a little anxious but decided this would be for the girls—a photo they could have of both of us.

Lindsey got into position and told us to face each other, and I did as she said.

"Okay, Haley, can you look up at Liam?"

I did.

"Now can you wrap your arms around his neck?"

Taking a deep breath, I did as she said, keeping my eyes on his.

"Liam, grab her waist."

Oh God, this was the most physical contact we'd had in two weeks.

His eyes searched mine frantically as he followed her directions.

"Now, both of you close your eyes, and Liam—go ahead."

My eyes were closed when I realized what she said, then Liam's lips were on my forehead, and he was slightly tilting us back.

My breath hitched as the air caught under me, and then within a second, he was straightening us with a smile.

That was…

"Okay, one more pose," Lindsey called.

I brushed down my dress, trying to calm my nerves, but there was something about how he'd just held me so possessively that was slowly knitting my broken heart back together. It was done without my permission, and it irked me.

"Haley, you stand, and I'm going to have Liam kneel next to you."

I tried to focus on what she was saying, and Liam seemed to as well. But he was kneeling weird, not in the right place.

"Haley," he rasped, from his spot next to me.

I looked down, and my breath hitched.

"What are you doing?" A tear was already welling in my eye.

He held his hand out, where a small velvet box sat open, revealing a diamond ring.

"I need to ask you something."

I wanted to look over—see the girls, see Lindsey—but my eyes were glued to him.

Kneeling in front of me was a broken knight, on his knees, asking for a second chance.

"Yes." I breathed it before he'd even asked the question.

Because regardless of his speech or what he was going to say, the answer was always going to be yes.

He smiled, lighting up his silver eyes, which were brimming with tears.

"I haven't asked it yet."

A tear slipped free. "Yes you have, but if you need to say the words then say them."

He slipped the ring free of the box and cleared his throat.

"I told you that you have my heart. Prideful, stubborn, jealous…it's always you at the center. I can't be away from you, but if you tell me to go, then I will. We'll coparent and it will be okay. I just want you to be happy. But if you think you can forgive me, then I was hoping you'd marry me and save me from a life of loneliness, because you're it for me."

I heard Lindsey clicking her camera as the girls were sniffing.

Mila yelled something, but Maddy tried to smother it.

Liam laughed.

"Our girls are waiting."

"I already told you yes, you idiot. Now put that on my finger."

He finally stood, slid it on, and kissed me.

Lindsey kept clicking, and I realized as Liam's arms held me and the wedge between us slowly fell away, that he'd planned our engagement photo shoot, and I hadn't even had a clue.

I thought I would save this man, but his love—this life he offered me—ended up rescuing me. I'd spend the rest of it loving him and raising our girls.

Together, as a family.

EPILOGUE
10 MONTHS LATER

Haley

LACEY LOOKED TERRIBLE IN ORANGE.

To be fair, her hair was flat and frizzed, her skin pale and eyes gaunt, but still the color washed her out almost completely. It brought me a small measure of satisfaction to see her looking so miserable. We hadn't seen her face since that awful day in the Town Square, but I had made it my mission to keep tabs on her and ensure I was well informed of any and all missteps she might take.

Which was why I was so charmed by the news that she'd been arrested for possession, theft and a myriad of other wrong doings that had landed her with a five-year prison sentence.

That was nearly six months ago.

"You have ten minutes." The guard rambled while he connected Lacey's handcuffs to the table.

I kept my face unreadable as Lacey took in my appearance. I did nothing to hide the wedding ring on my finger, and when her eyes widened taking it in, I withheld a smirk.

Liam and I tied the knot three months after he proposed, and this was on my agenda ever since.

"You arranged this meeting?" Lacey folded her hands and leaned back.

I nodded and pulled the folder I had in my lap up, and on to the table.

"Twice you've inserted yourself into my life, demanding to meet with me. Both times you ruined a piece of my happiness, no doubt hoping it would ruin my relationship with Liam…but it didn't work."

Lacey lifted her wrists, making the cuffs jingle. "You want an apology, or something?"

A scoff scraped up my throat. "No. I wouldn't dream of it."

I continued, opening the folder.

"I came to offer you a deal."

A line formed between her brows as her eyes narrowed on the folder in front of me.

"You're not a lawyer…you can't offer me shit."

Aw, if she only knew what strings I pulled behind the scenes.

"I had them draft this, but for legal reasons they're waiting outside the room. Would you like your present?"

Lacey bristled, twisting her lips to the side.

"Ah that's right. You have a public defender, and they don't drop whatever they're doing just to show up when you want them to."

She didn't reply, but it was true. She'd have to run this offer through her lawyer eventually anyway, but for right now I wanted her all to myself.

"What's the deal?" she asked, lifting her wrists once more.

I slid the paper towards her, giving her the opportunity to read it.

"Adoption papers…?"

Her eyes grew, her brows jumping to her hairline.

"Sign them, and you're out in six months."

She let out a laugh, tossing her paper toward me. "Bullshit."

"You don't know much about me, but I have unlimited resources at my disposal, at least ten different lawyers on retainer, and three little girls who call me mommy. To say that I am motivated would be an understatement."

Rage slithered into her features, making her lip peel back and the confinements around her wrists clank.

"You fucking bitch. Those are my kids!"

I slapped the table between us, which garnered the attention from the guard at the door.

"You had your chance…more than one. You didn't account for them to find me. But they have, and I love them. They're mine now, and I protect those who are mine. This is a good deal, Lacey. Sign them over and you're out in six months. If you really want to fight for them, and try your hand at being their mother again, then change. Take these next few years and become the best version of yourself. Prison will help you to get clean if you want to be. If you don't think you're capable of this, then free them."

Her face fell as her eyes flicked back down to the paper in front of her. For the smallest moment, it looked as though she was considering it. I was honestly grateful for it.

I loved my girls, but if they had the chance to have their mother in their lives one day…if she became someone they could rely on, then that would be a gift to them. As painful as it would be for me to accept, I would…for them.

I'd do anything for them.

I was about to scoot back, allow her to think it over when she opened her palm.

"Pen."

A tiny cut opened in my heart as I registered what she'd said.

Swallowing around the lump in my throat, I cleared the blockage.

"Take a few days, think it over."

How had this boiled down to me hoping she'd chose her kids…*my kids*.

Her palm slapped against the table, the metal making the sound.

"Don't need to…I'll sign it if you can promise me, it'll reduce my sentence."

"I already had it cleared with the judge…but you should still—"

"Then let me sign."

With a heavy heart, I glanced back at the guard by the door.

"Your lawyer has to be present…"

She shook her head and opened her palm again.

"Just have the guard come in and I'll tell them you're my lawyer."

Fuck, this wasn't how I thought it would go. Liam told me she would sign, not to get my hopes up that she would choose the girls. He told me she never would.

Still, this hurt on a level I wasn't expecting.

The guard came in, and they handed the pen over to Lacey.

She signed the papers, releasing her rights for Maddy, Seraphina and Mila, once she was done, she handed the pen back to the guard.

"Nice doing business with ya." She said happily before telling the guard she was ready to go.

I hung back in my chair and rubbed my hand over my tiny bump. We found out four months ago that I was pregnant…and at first, it was terrifying but seeing Liam's response was something that would live inside me forever. Then the way we'd told the girls.

We went to a make-your-own pizza place in downtown Portland, then let each girl make their own pizzas. When we grabbed a small to-go box, we had it where when they opened the lid they found the ultrasound image inside. The comment bubble above the baby's head said, "Hi big sisters."

They are already discussing whose room the baby will live in. I smiled at the memory but came back to the moment.

I could never imagine in a thousand lifetimes what sort of person could just walk away from their kids, but I also understood there was a different world that Lacey had grown up in. A different world she existed in and that might make a difference in my perspective.

Perhaps.

But maybe she was just a selfish bitch, and it was as simple as that.

Regardless, we'd never have to worry about her trying to take us to court again. At least not with any levity. All legal recourse she had to her kids were now void.

I DROVE HOME, trying to shed the strange sensation clouding my heart over Lacey's decision. I wasn't really paying attention as I pulled into the garage. I grabbed the folder and headed inside mostly in a fog but as soon as I cleared the laundry room, a group of people jumped out from the kitchen, screaming, "Surprise!"

A gasp caught in my throat as I finally registered all the glitter.

Oh my gosh.

"Mommy! Look what we did for you, we gave you a glitter party." Mila yelled, tossing a handful of glitter in the air.

This was never going to come up. Did Liam realize this? Where was my husband?

I hoisted Mila into my arms as I scanned the faces around the room.

Rae and Davis were there, she was pregnant just like Nora.

All of my brothers were present, but Colson was the one who pulled me in and hugged me close. Millie and Tammy were there…Jeffery and his new girlfriend, Stacey. Rex from the gym and a few others were hovering near the back patio, which led out to the yard. Everywhere I looked there were people who smiled and waved at me. Gunther stood stoic and tall by the barbeque being manned by Millie's husband, Roger.

He pulled me into a tight side hug as my eyes watered, registering that all the people in my life were here, celebrating me.

I still couldn't seem to find Liam or my other two girls.

Finally, I made my way upstairs, away from the party, still holding Mila in my arms as I went. There in the master bedroom, all three of my missing family members were hovering over a gift, murmuring as they tried various ways to wrap it.

"What are you doing?" I asked, slowly making my way up behind them.

Liam quickly turned, pushing the gift behind him.

Seraph and Maddy had cute little smirks on their faces as Mila slid her tiny hands over my eyes.

"You can't see yet, Mommy!"

I laughed, tugging on them when finally, I felt Liam take Mila.

It was quiet in the room, save for the rustling sound on the bed as Seraph moved to stand. She was getting taller now, she was eight and she was letting her hair grow out. It made her look so much older, and Maddy was in middle school now, completely stealing my heart every single day as she started puberty and developed crushes.

Liam held my hips as he came up behind me and laid his chin on my shoulder.

"We were trying to wrap it for you—"

"But it's too big!" Seraph interjected, lifting a piece of wrapping paper.

Finally, they all parted, allowing me to see my gift. I walked until my thighs hit the mattress and stared with my mouth parted and a few tears lining my lashes.

"Are these?" I couldn't finish as my eyes scoured the massive photo, that took up a huge portion of the bed, the barnwood edges, the glass... and underneath.

I breathed with a shuddery gasp, "Our lists..."

"All of ours, from the past year...all the happy in our lives that led up to this moment," Liam whispered, solemnly. I traced my finger over the glass, seeing the notes I had written when I had started dating him, and all the ones after. The ones I had created while he was away those ten months, the ones the girls started...the ones he created.

Liam's lips pressed into the side of my forehead as he whispered, "I love you."

I still couldn't believe he'd done this.

"We're going to hang it on the big wall, so we will always be able to see it," Mila yelled excitedly while the other two laughed.

"I can't believe you did this." I turned into Liam's chest, letting happy tears fall free. The realization of what my life had become, of who I had become...it was so massive, so perfect.

Liam's lips pressed against my head then his mouth was at my ear.

"I had a lot to make up for, but I hope this proves that every birthday from here on out will be celebrated properly..."

The girls' arms came around me then, as they all said.

"Happy Birthday, Mommy."

Mentally I went back to being thirteen, to the rejection I had felt…the utter sadness that had overwhelmed me and stayed with me for so many years. I took that memory and held it next to this one, and smiled. Somehow in saving this single dad, he rescued me from all the loneliness that took up residence in my heart. He filled me with more happiness and love than I ever imagined possible, and now I'd always have this.

Forever.

ALSO BY ASHLEY MUÑOZ

<u>Small Town</u>

Mount Macon Series

Resisting the Grump

Tempting the Neighbor

Saving the Single Dad

Standalone

Only Once

The Rest of Me

Tennessee Truths

<u>New Adult College</u>

Wild Card

King of Hearts

The Joker

<u>Romantic Suspense</u>

Glimmer

Fade

<u>Anthology & Co Writes</u>

What Are the Chances

The Wrong Boy

Vicious Vet

ACKNOWLEDGMENTS

I relived a very dark moment in my life when I wrote that prologue…and if anyone else related, then if we ever meet in real life, let's hug. I know Haley sort of came out of nowhere and took the town by surprise, but I fell in love with her character when I wrote Tempting the Neighbor and just couldn't let it go. So, I hope you loved it as much as I did.

This book is the end of the Mount Macon series, I guess for now. I might do a next gen series or something later, but for now, it's the end and that really took me by surprise because I feel like we just started… and I'm so invested in this town!

But it's time.

So to everyone who fell in love with this series, and my writing because of it, thank you.

Thank you for the Tik Tok shares, the tags, the Instagram love, the messages, all the uplifting things that have completely swarmed my heart and made me fall in love with my own writing again. Thank you, a million times, over.

Readers are the reason I keep going, and your love and appreciation for my work is what keeps my fingers tapping away and my heart dreaming. I honestly can't thank you enough for reading this and walking through the completion of this series with me.

You should know there's a whole list of people that have helped me get this book into your hands, and I'm going to take a second to thank every single one.

Melissa and Casey.

I just wanted to thank you for finding me and loving my words. Your support and eagerness to read this book and provide feedback was so amazing and encouraging. Melissa, our late-night talks in that first initial phase of creepy Jeffery and his stalking YOU vibes he gave off will live in my mind forever. I seriously wish we had wine and table to sit at as we dug through the plot possibilities. I love having you on my team, and in my corner. Casey, you never fail to provide me with a well-timed and always needed Vampire Diaries GIF, and you always hold my words to the line and ensure I don't get taken away with just making two people fall in love. Thank you for always ensuring there's a why and that it makes sense. I'm so grateful to have you and look forward to one day squeezing you.

Amy, my ride or die. You've been with me forever and I'll never stop being grateful for your early eyes on my work or your endless help with each book.

Amanda Anderson, you are gold. Pure treasure I was honestly lucky enough to find, and seriously haven't stopped being grateful for every single day. Your feedback while I was writing, your love for Haley and Liam…your notes and messages. Honestly just melted me and having you in my corner has been a game changer. After writing in this industry for over four years, I finally feel like I have my head above water. Thank you for being so amazing and helping me find my groove and accepting that you're now in charge.

Tiffany, you keep my entire world rotating and you pivoted flaw-lessly with each new change I threw at you this year, and especially with this series. I can't thank you enough for always being in my corner, no matter how many times I think I need to change things up.

Rebecca, my sister and best friend- thank you for reading through the first few chapters and telling me to change the flow. You always help me make these books better even when you're wrangling a toddler, packing and pregnant. I love you and can't wait to move next to you. Do it Jesus.

Kiezha, thank you so much for fitting me in and doing such an incredible job on my manuscript. Brittni, I can't thank you enough for all the love and dedication you poured into each word, knowing there were so many of them.

To my agent, Savanah- Thank you for pushing my books into the hands of international publishers, and hopefully one day the hands of someone in film. I'm crossing my fingers, just like I know you are.

To Sara Massery and Brittany Taylor, thank you for being my friends and always being willing to hear me vent, and cry about the most ridiculous things. You are my people and I'm so honored and grateful to call you friends.

To my street/arc team, thank you isn't enough. I appreciate you all so much for all the shares and the love you give to my books. I wish I could squeeze each and every one of you.

To my Book Beauties, thank you for all the love you give me and the grace you extend when I use the @everyone button.

To Amanda Simpson, and LK Farlow thank you so much for creating these beautiful covers. I am so honored to get to work with you both and appreciate the love you've given to my books.

Gel, thank you so much for all the gorgeous graphics you continue to provide me especially considering I'm still nailing down my brand and everything is sort of everywhere.

To my KU TT chat, you ladies are so amazing and honestly help me so much when ever I just need someone to message wild and crazy things that happen in this industry. I can't wait to see you all and have all the mimosas. Did someone say writing retreat? Because I am so down.

Lastly, but certainly not least.

My family.

With each book, I thank you and lay out all the ways I appreciate you. Sometimes we make this author thing work, other times its hard. But even when it's hard, you all rally around me and help me finish well. You always ensure I have what I need especially when what I need is your love. Thank you for being my sun, moon and stars and for always making me feel like I have the galaxy inside me. You make me feel loved, worthy and seen. I thank God for you all every day. Mom, you're a part of this too, so is Eric. Your support means so much to me and while I know you don't love that I'm writing smut, your arms hug me tightly regardless. You're always there for me and I just want you to know how honored I am to be your daughter.

To anyone I might have missed, I appreciate you. I see you. I love you.

ABOUT THE AUTHOR

Ashley is an Amazon Top 50 bestselling romance author who is best known for her small-town, romances. She resides in the Pacific Northwest, where she lives with her four children and her husband. She loves coffee, reading fantasy, and writing about people who kiss and cuss.
Follow her at www.ashleymunozbooks.com